Just
Another
Girl
On The
Road

Just
Another
Girl
On The
Road

S. Kensington

Matador
9 Priory Business Park,
Wistow Road, Kibworth Beauchamp,
Leicestershire. LE8 0RX
Tel: 0116 279 2299
Email: books@troubador.co.uk
Web: www.troubador.co.uk/matador
Twitter: @matadorbooks

ISBN 978 1789018 622

British Library Cataloguing in Publication Data.
A catalogue record for this book is available from the British Library.

Printed and bound in the UK by T J International, Padstow, Cornwall
Typeset in 11pt Adobe Casion Pro by Troubador Publishing Ltd, Leicester, UK

Matador is an imprint of Troubador Publishing Ltd

For V

and for restless women, and the men who love them.

"The journey itself is my home."
– Matsuo Basho

Contents

I

France, 1944

S CREAMS SHATTERED THE LATE AFTERNOON AIR, causing Sergeant Farr and Corporal Valentine to dive for cover at the base of a small rise. Topping the rise was a derelict farmhouse, its roof and walls half covered with creeping ivy. A door slammed back as a German soldier and girl hurtled down the steps and into the bramble-covered yard.

The man was bare-chested except for an empty shoulder holster; his uniform trousers hung beltless and unbuttoned around his waist. He grabbed the girl's hair, yanking her toward him. Something silver glinted in her hand. She slashed at his leg and the man cried out.

Farr and Valentine crouched behind the cover of a short wall. The two men were checking the area for a possible drop zone. They were out of uniform, dressed in farm-laborer clothing. Farr tensed as another soldier appeared in the doorway. He was smiling. Christ, what was going on? He didn't want to be watching this.

The man grabbed again. Dragging the girl up the steps, he threw her against the wall of the house. The girl's head hit wood with a loud crack and her legs crumpled. He shoved her upright, knocking the knife away. Pushing himself onto her and fumbling with his trousers, he lifted her shapeless dress with one free hand. The girl kneed him hard in the groin, and the man jolted back on his injured leg, cursing. She wrenched free and tumbled down the steps, falling off-balance into the dirt. The man swore again and plunged down the steps after her.

Valentine pulled out his gun and hissed, "We ought to teach those bastards something."

Farr grimaced. They'd been ordered not to engage.

Val persisted, "We ought to teach them something."

The girl was having trouble getting back up.

Farr nodded curtly. "Right, let's go."

The men broke cover, firing their pistols. Too late, the surprised Germans scrambled for their weapons. The men worked their way up the hill, covering the building in a hail of bullets as their opponents fell. It was over in a matter of seconds.

Sprinting to the barn, Valentine dodged a tethered horse that reared back in fear. The girl was now half-sitting, one hand pressed against her shoulder, the other groping in the dust.

Farr ran up the steps to the house, gripping his pistol with both hands. He inspected the dead soldier sprawled behind the railing, then kicked open the door, stepping over the other dead body. Walking cautiously into the adjoining room, he froze in the doorway. A tumbled bed with blood-soaked sheets occupied one corner, severed ropes dangled from its bedposts. The body of a half-naked German soldier lay dead on the covers. His uniform tunic was drenched in blood, and his groin mutilated. Strewn across the floor were a few tubes holding small tablets. Farr picked one up. The word 'Pervitin' was printed across its red-and-blue label. "What the hell?" he muttered.

A shout brought him running back outside. Valentine grappled with the girl on the steps as she twisted frantically to get away.

Farr gripped the man's shoulder. "Let her go."

"She *cut* me." His hand was bleeding.

Valentine dropped the girl's arm; the retrieved knife was clenched in her fist. She stumbled into the yard staring at them, and the men stared back. Her shoulder trickled blood, and there were rope burns on her wrists and lower legs. Splotches of bruising marked her body. A knife sheath protruded from her partly laced, high-top shoes.

She was silent now, trembling violently. Dark hair rumpled past her shoulders, half covering her face. She wore a summer frock, but the sash was torn and the dress hung from her, sack-like. Farr judged her to be between sixteen and eighteen years of age.

Valentine started forward, and she fell back a few steps, raising her knife.

"Let her be," Farr said quietly, not taking his eyes off the girl. "Stand back."

The girl looked up at him, and their eyes locked briefly. Something flickered in those dead eyes, giving Farr an unexpected flush of warmth. The horse's high whinny broke the stillness, and in a moment the girl whirled, darting away.

Farr leaped forward. "Get her!"

The terrified horse reared, its forelegs chopping air. Throwing a glance at the approaching men, the girl grabbed the horse's mane, managed to swing a leg over his back, and slashed down on its tether. The men scattered as she guided the skittish animal, snorting and prancing in a nervous semicircle, out into the yard. Leaning low and clinging to its mane, she dug her heels into its sides. Barely under control the horse lunged, taking a shortcut across the fields, and headed hell-bent for the fence. The main road lay just beyond.

Farr clenched his teeth. "She won't make it."

The horse rushed the fence at a full gallop. Gathering himself, he sailed over, with the girl clinging to his back. The sound of hooves faded as they cantered down the road and disappeared.

Farr realized he'd been holding his breath, and let out a harsh sigh.

From the opposite end of the road, two men on a battered Norton motorcycle sped toward them, swerving suddenly into the cover of thick brush. Farr watched his team officers, Major Nye and Lieutenant Raphael, scramble from the bike.

Nye scanned the area, then approached. "All clear, Sergeant?"

"Yes, sir. There was a—"

The major cut him short, striding up the hill toward the house.

Raphael squinted, his gaze raking over the surrounding fields and farmhouse. "This will work well for the drop. Is everything in readiness?"

"It's ready, sir, and clear. We found a few Germans up there, probably deserters. They were acting very erratic. They had a civilian."

The lieutenant spun around. "These Germans, where are they now?"

"Dead."

"And the civilian?"

"A girl."

"A girl? Where is she?"

"Gone."

"And the soldiers. You shot them?"

"Yes, sir," he paused awkwardly. "One was already dead."

"You were instructed not to engage. Had they not been deserters, we would all be in trouble, and this drop zone unusable."

Farr's jaw tightened. "I judged it necessary, sir."

Raphael dragged shaking fingers through his hair. Spotting Valentine, he motioned him over. "Corporal, there is a first aid kit in the Norton's satchel. Tend to that hand."

He turned back to Farr. "Everything is in order for tonight's drop. We will remain until then and distribute supplies. God willing, the plastique as well."

Farr knew the evening's plans hinged not only on a successful supply drop, but the arrival of an agent from the coast, bringing with him enough plastique to blow Pont du Namandie Bridge. This would stop, or at least delay, a large group of German forces bringing fresh tanks and troops north to the Normandy battlefields. These same soldiers had wiped out a village a few weeks earlier, in retaliation for Resistance attacks. The entire village.

Raphael continued, "After this drop, my liaison will find us a new camp. Already we have stayed too long."

"Yes, sir." Farr hesitated, recalling the girl. Her battered face looking up into his. He'd seen enough battered faces to last a lifetime.

"Sergeant? Is there something else?"

"The girl is hurt, Lieutenant. I think she's in trouble."

"That is not our concern; she will go back to her village. Help Corporal Valentine with his hand."

"Yes, sir."

* * *

Valentine was repacking the first aid kit when Farr noticed Major Nye emerge from the farmhouse, heading full tilt down the hill. Nye was British and had seen combat in North Africa before training with the undercover Jedburghs. He was an older man, quick to laugh, and known for his ingenuity, intelligence, and in times of crisis, an almost cruel ruthlessness.

Nye reached the road and pulled Raphael aside. "Lieutenant, a word with you, please."

Farr strolled across the road, fiddling with the strap on his watch as he listened.

"What the bloody hell happened up there?" demanded Nye.

The lieutenant filled him in, including the wounded girl.

"A *girl?*"

"Yes, sir. Sergeant Farr said she was hurt. She has run away."

"How long ago? Where did she go?"

"I am not sure; he did not elaborate."

"Very good. Go up to the farmhouse and inspect the dead men for any documents. We'll have to get those damn bodies out of here before the drop."

Raphael started for the farmhouse, and Major Nye waved Farr and Valentine over. He glanced at Valentine's bandaged hand, frowning. "Corporal, check the fuel tank on the Norton."

"Checked it this morning, sir; it's running on fumes."

"Then we'll use fumes." He nodded to Farr. "Talk with me, Sergeant."

Both men turned away from the bike and walked into a small group of trees.

"Brief me on what's happened here," Nye requested.

Farr studied the man's face. So, he had seen it.

"I understand you had contact with a civilian: a young woman."

"Yes, sir."

Nye's voice was clipped and tight. "Tell me about it, if you please."

Farr briefly related the afternoon's incident.

"What did she look like? How long has she been gone?"

Farr described the girl and was startled to see a flash of excitement cross the major's face.

"Where was she headed?"

"She took off on the horse down the main road, toward Ange de Feu. She left about a half hour ago, sir, right before you pulled up."

Nye swore under his breath. He paced in front of a tree for a few moments, then stopped and turned to Farr. "Yes. Now I want you to go and find her."

"Sir?"

"Go and get her. Take Valentine with you on the Norton. Avoid checkpoints and stay hidden. If you're stopped, you do the talking. Don't let Valentine open his damn mouth. Show them your working papers, and you should be all right. Let us know *immediately* you find her."

"Yes, sir."

"And take Jack. Raphael's bloody pigeon knows this area better than the Germans. He's in the small carrier under the gas tank. Valentine can handle him. Raphael and I will take care of the bodies, then head back to camp through the woods."

"Yes, sir." Farr turned away, a grim smile set on his face. Whatever plans were being hatched, it now involved the girl.

* * *

Crossing the road, Nye slumped onto a tree stump, trying to absorb the last few minutes. Was it her? Could she still be alive? Wiping the sweat from his brow, he took out his map.

His Jedburgh team had been dropped just after D-Day into this Deux-Sèvres area of France. The heavily wooded area was about eighty kilometers southwest of Poitiers, and less than that distance to the coast. The trees gave his small Jed team and the local French Resistance, or Maquis, as they were known in the countryside, ample cover in German-held territory.

It could be done. The drop was not until midnight. The Maquis had found them a new campsite where they would hide the supplies and wait for the plastique. Nye knew what the others did not. Their agent, Degare, hadn't made it to the ship, and the plastique was still there. Had they been betrayed? Was there an informant among the villagers? Or the Maquis? They *needed* that plastique.

He thought again of the girl. Did she have papers? If not, he needed documentation and proper clothing. They had to have ID. Raphael's liaison, Pascal, handled false documents.

Pascal would have to move on it this evening. Stay up all night if needed. The drop must be organized. Too much needed, too quickly. He blocked these worries out. The main thing was to find her; Farr would track her down.

In the few short months they'd worked together, Nye had grown to rely on this steady American who had come to him from the Office of Strategic Services. Farr had been assigned as a wireless radio operator for Nye's Jedburgh Team EDMOND, when theirs had been killed in the parachute drop. Like other men who came from the OSS, Farr was freewheeling, independent, and unorthodox. Nye liked the man and trusted his instincts. He guessed Farr to be in his mid-twenties. Of medium height, he possessed an unremarkable face, except for his eyes. Nye would not care to see those eyes staring at him from down the barrel of a gun.

He stood up as Raphael approached, stuffing the map back into his pocket.

"Excuse me, sir, but what in God's name has occurred up there?"

"Just as you see, Lieutenant. The Germans were holding the girl. It appears she either had, or acquired a knife." He paused. "Did you see the tablets?"

Raphael nodded.

"The Germans call it *Panzerschokolade*: tank chocolate. Gives them the ability to stay awake long hours, but beats the hell out of a man's nervous system." He glanced at a small knapsack in Raphael's trembling hands. "What is that?"

"I found it in one of the soldier's kits. I think it must belong to the girl."

The major seized the bag, riffling through its various identification papers. On the front of one small card, the picture of a young woman gazed up at him. He stared. It was her.

* * *

Nye and Raphael were still sifting through papers when Valentine appeared, pushing the Norton. Farr began stowing supplies into a rucksack. Raphael winced as Valentine stuffed Jack's small wire carrier inside his jacket. "Easy with that, Corporal."

Nye pulled Farr aside. "Find her, Sergeant, we need her. And handle this with care, she might be a bit difficult."

Farr glanced at Val's bandaged hand. "Will do, sir."

"Use any bit of persuasion, Farr. Whatever it takes."

Farr straightened up and looked at him. Nye returned his look with steady eyes.

"Ready to go, sir," Valentine said.

"Very good. Report back on your status; use code names only."

"Yes, sir."

The major jerked his head, catching a disturbance out of the corner of his eye. But it was only the filtered sunlight, scattering leaf shadows across the road. He released his grip on the hidden pistol, letting out a long breath. "Right. Good luck then."

Val climbed on the Norton, and Farr settled on the back with the rucksack. Pulling a tight circle in the road, Val shot off with a lurch.

Raphael turned to Nye with a frown. "Sir, what is this all about?"

Nye shook his head. Leaf shadows or not, he was feeling uneasy. "We need to take care of those bodies, then get the

10

hell out of here. I want you to contact Pascal for some false documents. They have to be done tonight."

Raphael raised his eyebrows. "That may be impossible."

"Contact the man. I'll explain everything when we get back to camp."

* * *

She had only gotten a few kilometers down the road. They saw the horse first, its head down, and grazing in a field. Val skidded to a halt, and the horse bolted. The girl lay sprawled in tall grass, just off the roadway. Hearing the bike she pushed herself upright, rising unsteadily to her feet. Farr dismounted, handing his pistol to Val. He noticed the torn sash was now wrapped tightly around her waist, the knife sheath jammed into it. She had been crying. He approached cautiously, with arms spread. Val remained on the bike, watching intently.

Farr spoke in passable French, "Do not be afraid. We are allies. We only want to—"

She turned and fled.

"Shit." Cursing, Farr took off after her.

The girl ran away from the road and into a wooded area. She slid down an embankment and raced along a stream bed. Farr stumbled after her, just managing to keep her in view. Tripping over a log she fell, then scrambled to her feet, pulling herself up the bank and back into the trees. Farr closed the distance, and when she stumbled again, he surged forward and grabbed her by the waist. They both fell, rolling down a short slope to the bottom, where he landed on top of her.

Crying with worn rage, she pulled her knife from its sheath. He gripped her flailing arms and held her still with the weight of his body.

She was coughing in short spasms, no longer fighting. He rolled off, wrenched the knife from her hand, and thrust it behind his belt. Then he hunched over her, taking in deep gulps of air. After a moment he straightened, and pulled out a tin flask from inside his jacket. She watched, still gasping for breath. He unscrewed the top, crouching over her once more.

"Drink this."

She twisted her head away.

"Drink it."

She turned to face him, and it was there again, that long assessing look from the farmyard. He felt the same warm rush of response.

Reaching up to steady the flask, she took deep gulps, paused, and then took several more. She sank back to the ground, struggling to keep her eyes open, still looking at him. He remained kneeling beside her.

She touched his sleeve, and he jumped.

"Boche?" she whispered.

"No Boche. *Morte.* They are dead." The fierceness of his reply startled him.

Her eyes closed. In a moment she was out of it, her fingers still gripping his sleeve.

Farr gave a drawn-out sigh and sat up, gently removing her hand. He glanced around. They'd run a fair distance, but were not far from the road. Pulling out a handkerchief, he doused it with water. The gash on her shoulder needed tending.

He wiped back the tangle of hair and got a good look at her. She was older than she'd first appeared; her bruised face was fragile and small-boned. He couldn't judge her exact age, but this was no child. He remembered the shock, feeling her fully formed body beneath his weight.

At the sound of the Norton's engine, Farr gave a loud whistle and stood, raising his arm.

A few minutes later, Val appeared. Slipping the rucksack to the ground, he crouched next to Farr.

"Finally run out of steam? How is she?"

"Wiped out. Drank most of the flask. There's a slash on her shoulder. Rope burns, bruises and cuts."

Val nodded. "Well, the way she was running, I doubt there's any broken bones."

"Where's the Norton?"

"Hid it in some brush."

Farr pulled a medical kit from the rucksack. "Did the major tell you what this is all about? Who she is?"

Val shook his head. "Just that the drop is on for tonight and the plastique will be delayed, but coming. Evidently, Degare made it to the boat. We'll be changing camp after the drop. About time too."

Farr nodded. The recent Gestapo attack on a safe house had everyone jumpy. They'd interrogated the farmer for information. When he hadn't talked, they'd tied his body to a tree and looped a rope around his neck. Then using the man's tractor, they'd ripped his head off.

Val watched Farr sort the bandages and begin cleansing the girl's shoulder. "Your radio parts coming in with the drop?"

"That's what I've been told. We're dead in the water out here without a working wireless. The mobile Special Air

Service team is out past Ange de Feu, hidden in the woods. The SAS team leader sent out a coded message on their set telling HQ what we needed." He paused. "The lieutenant's pissed about the attack this afternoon. My fault."

"Well he wasn't there, was he."

Farr glanced at the young corporal's face. Valentine, or 'Val' as he preferred to be called, had come to the Jedburghs from the Special Operations Executive, or SOE, as a radio operator and mechanic. Born and raised in France until he was eight, he was sent to live with his paternal grandmother in England when both parents died in an automobile accident. Powerfully built and broad-shouldered, he'd lied about his age, and joined the army at sixteen, just after the US invasion of North Africa. They'd only worked together for a short time, but the younger man had developed an intense bond with him. Farr wanted to believe Val regarded him as an older brother, but he knew it was more than that.

Farr shook his head. "He was right. If they'd been regular troops, we'd be in a shitload of trouble right now. And the drop zone, blown." Farr poured sulfa powder onto the girl's shoulder and affixed a bandage. "What I want to know is how this girl got mixed up with the deserters. Is she French? A Maquis?" He gave Val a sideways glance, "Did you go inside the house?"

"No."

Farr briefly related what he'd seen.

Val whistled. "Then I'm fortunate to have escaped with just a cut." His tone became somber. "Do you think she was…?"

"Yes."

Val shifted uncomfortably. "This little one has had a bad time of it."

"Yes."

Val hauled himself to his feet. "Jack's with the bike. I'll send him off with a brief message and map, to tell them we have her. Guess I'll be on watch tonight."

Farr frowned. "All night? I can do half—"

Val interrupted. "The major made rather a point of it. Said if we found her, I was to come back on the bike early tomorrow. He gave me directions to their new camp. You're to stay and wait for contact."

Farr watched him disappear into the bushes, then stood up and stretched. He looked down at the girl's flushed face. There was a large stream close by and plenty of cover, if they could move a bit further into the trees. He didn't like being out in the open. It was safer in the trees.

She did not wake, but flopped her head against his shoulder as he maneuvered up a small incline to a sheltered clearing. Placing her on the ground, he went back for the rucksack and supplies, putting them next to a tree. He pulled out a blanket, carefully wrapping it around her. Then he sat down against the tree and lit a cigarette.

Farr watched and smoked, listening to her quick breathing. The evening sunlight cast long shadows over the grasses, and the rasping of cicadas disturbed the air. A faint smell of smoke drifted on the wind. He knew the French were making charcoal, burning piles of twigs. Distant memories of a camping weekend with his father came back to him. The old man had been sober that time. It was a good trip.

A while later Val returned, and Farr signaled from their new position. After unpacking the rest of the supplies, Val pulled out a small parcel of food. They ate the dark bread and cheese in silence.

"Did the major tell you anything more?" Val asked.

"Not much. Someone wants her. Badly."

Val stood up, stretching. "Get some sleep. I'll be close by, on watch. I'll come and wake you before leaving."

* * *

Farr woke to the girl's screams. He lunged forward covering her mouth, holding her to his chest.

"Quiet," he hissed.

She reacted violently to his grip.

He eased up, whispering, "Please. There could be danger. Please."

Val came running, pale-faced in the moonlight, his pistol drawn.

Farr shook his head, his voice taut, "Nightmare."

The corporal slipped back into the darkness. Farr held the girl until she stopped shaking, her heart pounding under the thin dress. Gradually he released her and she slid back down to the blanket, closing her eyes. He remained sitting close. Her screams had scattered his own dark dreams, and he reached for a cigarette with unsteady hands.

A few minutes later she stirred restlessly and sat up, flinging back the covering. "There is water near? I hear it."

Farr froze, cigarette halfway to his lips. His mind registered her perfect English, but spoken with a slight accent he did not recognize.

"Are you thirsty? Do you want more water?" He reached for the tin flask.

"I want to bathe. I need to bathe." Her voice carried a hint of rising hysteria.

"That's impossible; it's not safe."

She ignored him and stood up, heading for the stream. Farr hesitated, then scrambled to his feet. He followed at a distance, his nerves raw. She wanted to bathe. Jesus, all he needed was some late-night patrol finding them out after curfew. There was no cover story in hell that would hold up in this scenario.

Picking her way between tree roots and brush, the girl paused a few times, listening. Stopping at the bank, she gave a final long look around before reaching over her shoulders to remove her dress.

Farr stumbled back, averting his gaze. A few moments later, he heard the thud of her boots, followed by a soft splash. Edging down to the stream, he glimpsed her body rolling and knifing through the water, a pale column beneath the dark stillness. He backed uphill for some paces until he came up against a tree, all the while keeping her in his line of vision. He waited under the tree.

* * *

In the stream, Katrinka gasped. The coldness was shocking, but she welcomed it, as if waking from a stupor. The sensual feel of water gliding over her skin felt like home, and as she moved, a few invisible scars the men had made on her body washed away, leaving only outward marks. She rolled onto her back and saw a waning crescent moon suspended far above her in the starlit sky. She could smell the crisp, clean scent of pine. The water entered her most private parts, soothing and cleansing. It was very quiet.

The terror of the last few days had torn her body, and she felt unable to piece it back together. The Germans' attack had been brutally swift, as they swarmed from the bushes and onto her parents' horse cart. They'd killed her stepfather Emerson, with the quick thrust of a bayonet. Too stunned to move, she'd watched the lifeblood ooze between Emerson's fingers as he clutched his stomach. For a moment he'd stared at her with bewildered eyes, then he slipped to the floor of the cart.

Her mother's sharp cry snapped Katrinka into movement, and she'd grabbed for her knife just as her mother stood and threw her own knife with deadly aim. She caught Emerson's killer in the neck, but a red-haired soldier raised his rifle and cut her mother down. The woman recoiled as the bullets struck her body and she'd tumbled over the side of the cart. Screaming, Katrinka had jumped to the ground, gathering her mother's limp body into her arms. She'd leaned in as the dying woman struggled to speak.

The red-haired soldier heaved Emerson's body onto the road, then strode back to where she crouched over her mother. Shouting with fury, Katrinka had lunged to her feet, slashing with her knife. But he'd grabbed the blade from her hand, and thrown her into the rear of the cart.

As they jolted forward, she'd clung to its swaying sides, watching as her mother crawled across the dusty road to wrap herself around Emerson's lifeless body. She'd called out and attempted to scramble from the vehicle, but an arm had swung back, striking her with a force that knocked her unconscious. She remembered nothing else until the farmhouse.

No. She would not think of that now. She must remember; she was free again. She shut her eyes and drifted.

It seemed to Farr a long while before she made her way back to shore. This time, he stared. Bruised though she was, he was shaken by the loveliness of her body. In the moonlight, water droplets sprinkled like a spangle of stars across her pale, golden skin.

She dried herself with the torn dress, then shook it out and put it on. She had no underthings. After slipping on her shoes she walked up the bank, bending to one side, wringing and shaking out her hair. He pivoted, making his way up to their makeshift camp. When she reappeared he was sitting, leaning against the tree.

He got to his feet. Clearing his throat, he noted, "Your hair is wet."

"It will dry."

She looked drained and her teeth were chattering, but her features had a more relaxed look. The wrapping on her shoulder had come loose.

"Let me rebandage that for you."

Wincing, she peeled the old one off. He dragged the rucksack over, pulling out the medical kit. After he finished, she looked up from her arm.

"You've given me your blanket."

"I don't need it."

"Please take it."

"Lie down and go to sleep. I have my jacket."

Her next remark was sharp and unexpected. "Why are you bothering with me?"

"What?"

"Why did you come after me? What is it you want?"

19

Farr said nothing.

She studied his face. "So," she said softly, "you would recruit a corpse. She is dead. She is *dead*. Shall I show you where she died? Shall I tell you how?"

Farr was taken aback by the savagery in her voice.

She turned to the blanket.

"Wait." He touched her elbow and she flinched. "Please. What is your name?"

She pulled away from him and lay down, closing her eyes.

Farr sighed. Tugging his jacket more tightly around himself he slid to the ground, close beside her. In case there were more nightmares.

She spoke then, her voice partly muffled by the covering, "It is Katrinka."

* * *

The German was standing in the bedroom doorway, staring down at her. She twisted her arms, but the ropes dug into her wrists. He began unbuttoning his trousers. Katrinka turned in her sleep with a jerk, colliding with the body of the man lying next to her.

He woke with a hoarse shout surging to his feet, a knife clenched in his fist. His eyes were wild.

Katrinka cried out, scrabbling away from him on her hands and knees. Stumbling upright, she took off running. She heard him swear as he lunged after her, his feet pounding close behind. The pebbles and twigs were sharp, cutting into her bare feet. Grabbing up a sharp rock from the ground, she stopped and spun around, her arm raised.

"Don't take another step! I'll crush your face in. I will! I'll do it!"

The man stopped dead in his tracks. They stared at each other in the moonlight, both breathing hard.

He said quietly. "You surprised me. I didn't know, I thought it was…" His voice trailed off. "I'm sorry I frightened you."

A wave of nausea washed over her. This last panicked burst of energy had left her with no reserves, and she felt faint with hunger and exhaustion. She bent over, clutching her knees.

"Are you OK?" he asked. He took a step closer, but his voice seemed far away. The rock fell from her grasp, and she slipped to the ground.

* * *

Katrinka woke to a comforting warmth. She was back on the blanket with the man lying close, his arms wrapped around her. How incredibly good it felt to be held the way he was holding her now. Frightening images prowled through her mind. Her stepfather's eyes, darkened with pain. The look on her mother's face as she whispered her last words. The farmhouse bedroom. These images flickered then faded away, slinking into the shadows of the forest.

Carefully, she eased closer and curled into his side. The rough whiskers of his jaw scraped against her skin. She breathed in his scent of sweat, cigarettes, and wet grasses. She could let go now. Give in, and sink into the mindless comfort of sleep. As her eyelids closed, she realized she didn't even know his name.

* * *

21

Farr woke later with a painful erection. He got up to relieve himself; he could not sleep this way. Returning in the darkness moments later, he paused to get his bearings. The wind had died down, and a moist stillness settled over the trees and fields, dampening his clothes. He shivered and stared down at the sleeping girl curled in a ball at his feet. One look into those terrified eyes had told him she was in deep trouble. She was hurt, alone, and in dangerous country.

Growing up, he had seen the same look in his father's eyes. Nights had been spent lying awake in bed, with his mother pacing the floor above him, knowing the man had not come home. So he'd grab a jacket and slip out into the cold to search. He always found him. Fallen down along the roadside or shivering in some doorway, a bottle at his side. Neighbors said his father was never quite right, after the war.

Farr lay down again, curving his arms around her warm body. It was too late for his father, but he was going to make it right for her.

"Who are you?" he whispered. "Why are you here?"

He closed his eyes, but it was a long time before he could sleep.

2

B ACK AT CAMP, NYE AND RAPHAEL WAITED FOR THE
drop. The previous week, a Resistance member had
taken them to this place in the woods, close to the village
of Ange de Feu. They were grateful, but a German patrol
had been spotted recently, surveying the area. They had
stayed too long; it was time to move on. Battles still raged
along the northern coast, but the Germans serving here in
towns' administrative posts had time to track down the Jeds
and SAS teams. It was dangerous to stay in one spot. Their
survival depended on constant mobility.

The two men had fashioned a shelter with a few large
pieces of camouflaged canvas strung over low branches. It was
dirty, cramped, and uncomfortable, but offered protection.
After Farr's radio broke down, a small SAS patrol had hidden
nearby so Nye's team could use their equipment to keep in
contact with London. They'd made the major uneasy with
their brash and brazen daylight attacks on German convoys,
always fleeing back into the forest to disappear. Their luck
would run out, but still he could not help but admire their
foolhardy bravery.

Both men had eaten rations and were drinking coffee
made from chicory and toasted barley. Earlier in the evening,

Raphael had met with Pascal, and the documents were being made. Nye knew the hurried job would be poor and would bear up under only the briefest scrutiny, but it could not be helped. He sat smoking his pipe, wondering just how much to explain. He needed this man on his side, but Raphael was skittish with anything new. And rightly so. Nye watched him roll a cigarette with shaking fingers, some tobacco spilling to the ground.

Glancing at the lieutenant's face, Nye wondered, and not for the first time, how Raphael was holding up. It was said his hair had gone from deep brown to gray after the death of his wife and son during the fall of France. They'd been strafed by enemy fire amid the evacuation of his village. Although just a few meters away, Raphael had not been struck by a single bullet.

Like hundreds of other Frenchmen fleeing the forced labor of the Service du Travail when the French government collapsed, Raphael joined the French Resistance. He later volunteered and trained with the Jedburghs, a multinational undercover operation made up of agents from the British SOE, French Resistance, and American OSS. The major was aware that Raphael carried a picture of his wife and son with him, always.

Nye sighed, knocking the tobacco from his pipe, and began abruptly, "Degare's been arrested. He never made it to the ship."

Startled, Raphael looked up. "I am sorry to hear it."

Without the explosives, the bridge would stay intact. The Germans would sweep across with their supplies and tanks, heading north to where the Allies were still being held back in Normandy. Reports put them at the bridge in less than two days.

Raphael's voice was bitter, "So. No plastique."

"Exactly. The damn ship is still sitting somewhere off the coast with our supplies."

"Can it be reached in time?"

The major shrugged. "Possibly."

"You want to use the girl? The one found with the deserters?"

"Possibly."

Raphael frowned, his voice rising. "My men are seeing shadows of shadows. They will not stand for this. Why have I not been told?"

Nye's voice was calm. "I am telling you now. Two days ago, a man and woman were attacked and killed by German deserters on the road to Benet. This couple and the girl, Katrinka, had been passengers on Captain Remi Amparo's ship, *Le Flâneur*. After dropping them off, Amparo was to go further up the coast, retrieve the plastique, and return to await Degare. There is a chance he is still waiting."

Raphael poured himself another cup of coffee, still frowning. "I have heard his name mentioned, this Captain Amparo. Tell me about him. Why should he be trusted? And who were the others, the couple and the girl?"

Nye nodded. "You have valid questions, and they deserve valid answers."

"I would like to hear them."

"It is rather a long story, but an interesting one."

Raphael's lips curled into a rare smile. "I have no pressing engagements."

Nye snorted, glancing at his watch. Then he settled back and relit his pipe. "Amparo has been working with the SOE for a few years, and now with the Jeds. Doing some unofficial shipping, shuttling munitions and men from England to France. Hell, we were so desperate for supplies, at one point the government was raiding the Imperial War Museum for artillery pieces."

"This Amparo, he is a civilian?"

"Yes, French-Portuguese. Came to California in the early 1900s and obtained a visa to work the tuna fleet near San Diego. Purchased his own small ship, fell in love, and got married. He served in the Great War and came back to San Diego to settle, but he and the wife... well, it all went wrong somehow."

Raphael lit his cigarette and sat back. "There is always a woman," he observed.

"Eh? Quite right. So, Amparo outfitted his vessel into a tramp ship of sorts. Paid a large sum of money to install equipment that runs on oil. He could go long distances without refueling, and his services were in high demand. Handpicked a small crew, mostly Portuguese like him. The small ship was easy to navigate in tight spots and rough water. He left San Diego and went back to Portugal. Did operations between Europe and the Far East, shipping cargo of questionable freight. Flying under whatever flag was most convenient."

"How did you become acquainted with this man?"

"We met in Falmouth in '21, and I signed on as a cabin boy. I was just thirteen, didn't want schooling."

"My son was also just thirteen."

Nye shot him a quick look, but Raphael's eyes were blank as he studied the cigarette in his fingers.

Raphael continued, "And the couple who were killed?"

"The man and woman were Katrinka's parents. Her mother, Yujana Prasong, was the illegitimate daughter of a British missionary and Burmese sea gypsy. She'd lived with her extended family on fishing boats in and around the Andaman Sea. At age fifteen, she ran away from a prearranged marriage and wound up in Burma. Worked at a bar down in Rangoon harbor for a few years, and met Amparo there, back in '24."

"A *prostituée*?"

"No."

Raphael glanced up, and Nye flushed.

Nye went on, "She worked as singer. When it came time for the ship to leave, Yujana found out and stowed away. Cook found her one morning, and all hell broke loose. Amparo threatened to throw her overboard. She put up a fight, and he changed his mind. They became lovers.

"For the next year, Amparo took Yujana with him on our runs throughout the Far East and Ceylon. On our second return to Ceylon, we dropped off the cargo and picked up a passenger, one Emerson Badeau."

"The man who was killed with Yujana?"

"Yes. Emerson was an American archeologist, on sabbatical from some university in Switzerland. He'd been studying cave art in India, and wanted passage to Marseilles, from where he would travel overland into Spain. A few weeks after he boarded, Yujana and Amparo had a huge row over some letters she found from his previous marriage. She was furious and sought comfort in Emerson's arms."

The lieutenant was now giving him his full attention, his eyes narrowed and intent.

"One night, there was… an altercation between the three of them. Amparo backed off and let them alone. About a month later we got to Marseilles, and Yujana left with

Emerson. Soon after leaving ship, Yujana discovered she was pregnant. She left Emerson in Spain and ended up back with her family in the Andaman Sea. She gave birth to Katrinka there, in '26."

"Did you continue to work for Amparo?"

"I left the ship soon after, but kept in touch over the years and did more voyages with him in the '30s. Yujana was back with him then, and Katrinka as well. A few years after that, Emerson reconnected with us. I think Yujana and Emerson were married at that point. We all began working together, with Amparo running supplies for Emerson's expeditions until right before the war.

"After the Nazis invaded Poland, Yujana followed Emerson back to Switzerland and put her daughter into a school. Katrinka was in her teens then, and quite wild. Amparo returned to his old job, running supplies and troops from England to France. Those years in the Great War had served him well. He knows this coast intimately and has many French contacts. As you know, the SOE gets little support from the British Navy. They consider our tactics a bit unorthodox and irritating. Don't like us mucking about."

Raphael was about to reply, but at that moment Sébastien, the team's French courier, showed up on his bicycle.

Sébastien nodded to Raphael, "*Monsieur*, the bird has returned to his cage." He handed a message to Nye, who scanned it quickly, reading it aloud.

"Item found. Hurt, but mending. Will follow prearranged orders."

A rough map of their location was scrawled on the back of the message.

The major stood. "Excellent Sébastien." He nodded to the lieutenant. "They've found her." He looked at his watch. "Get the directional fires started and Maquis assembled. As soon as the supplies are dropped and distributed, we'll be moving."

"Yes, sir." Raphael hesitated, "Just one thing more."

"Yes?"

"This girl Katrinka. What has she got to do with it all?"

"I'm sorry, didn't I say? She's to retrieve the plastique from the ship and return it to us."

"Why should Captain Amparo give her the plastique? Why should he trust her?"

"He'll trust her all right. He's her father. Now, let's prepare for the drop."

* * *

Val was shaking his shoulder. Propping himself up on one elbow, Farr rubbed his eyes.

"What time is it?" he asked.

"Almost dawn." Val looked at the girl curled into the curve of the man's side. "What was she doing last night? I heard noises and saw her down in the water."

"Oh. Bathing in the stream."

"Bathing in the… who the hell *is* she?"

"I don't know."

"You made love to her, and don't know who she is."

"We didn't. She was frightened. I held her."

"Farr, this girl—you don't know what she's doing here or where she's from. A broken heart could be the least of your worries, buddy."

Farr glanced up and shook his head. "It's too late, Val."

Val looked away, nodding, then stood up abruptly. "Right. I'm off to the new camp and hopefully grab a meal, and get some sleep. Someone's supposed to be coming here early, to give you orders." He looked down at the sergeant with a tenderness that Farr chose not to see. Made it a hell of a lot easier that way.

"Good luck to you, Farr."

"And you." He sat up to say more, but Val had already vanished into the shadows. A few minutes later he heard the roar of a motor, and then silence.

Farr glanced down at the girl. He wished whoever was coming would get here. It was unsafe to be out, and it would be daylight soon. He wanted to get back to the protection of the camp.

* * *

The man had made them breakfast out of his leftover dinner. Katrinka ate continually and thoroughly, everything he offered. He'd given back her knife, and she'd replaced it in its sheath, tucked into her sash. Her hair had dried and fluffed around her face, and the food revived her. She would need to leave, very soon.

At the sound of an engine both leaped to their feet, Katrinka grabbing her knife. The man pulled her into the cover of the bushes with him, reaching for his gun at the same moment. The noise of the motor cut off suddenly, and a few seconds later Katrinka watched as a tall man appeared from a copse of trees below them. She gave a startled exclamation, staring as the man rapidly advanced up the hill.

"Wills?" Standing up, Katrinka ran to him, flinging her arms around his barrel-chested figure. "Oh *Wills!*" she cried.

Nye held her close for a moment, kissing the top of her head. Then he stood back, disentangling himself from her embrace. "So. It is you. My God, when I heard—" He broke off and nodded to Farr, who had risen. "Sergeant."

"Sir."

There was a long pause before Farr spoke. "We were just eating. Would you…?"

Nye shook his head. "Sébastien is waiting on the Norton, down below. He'll take you back to our new camp. Your radio parts came in last night, you need to get busy. And Farr? Good work. Thank you."

Farr's voice was stiff, "Yes, sir." He turned and strode away.

Nye looked down at her battered face, his eyes narrowing. "Those filthy-minded bastards."

She touched her cheek self-consciously. "Wills, what is this all about? Does Papa know you are here? Have you… do you know about my mother and Emerson?"

He nodded. "I am so sorry."

"I know that you loved her too."

"Yes."

They sat down.

After some moments he spoke again, his voice sharp. "What in God's name are you doing over here? Emerson must have known the situation. What was he thinking?"

"It was the cave."

"Cave."

"The cave at Lascaux. You remember it. He'd thought of nothing else since its discovery a few years ago. After he heard the Resistance was using it to store weapons, he became crazed with worry."

"But I cannot imagine—"

"He begged a commission from his university to meet with other archeologists already there. He knew my father was working the coast and convinced him to provide transport on his next run. He had a letter of introduction and papers guaranteeing our passage through France. My mother wanted to come as well."

"Of course."

"I had started summer break in Switzerland and knew Papa was in Porto for Grandpa's funeral. A-mah and I traveled to Porto, and Emerson met us there."

"And then this."

"Yes."

Nye passed a hand across his eyes. "I thought you were dead, you see. When I heard the report."

She squeezed his arm. "What is it all about, Wills?"

Nye regained his composure, taking her hand. "Katrinka, please listen to me. It is imperative you understand how things are."

"Yes?"

"All of France is under German occupation and the Vichy government in the south. We Jedburghs work alone and undercover, sometimes in the civilian clothing of farm laborers. That will get us shot, as we are considered to be spies, and so are not covered by the Geneva Convention."

"You're not with the army? You do not fight in the battles?"

Nye shook his head. "No. The fighting is up in Normandy. Our Jed teams work with the French Resistance, or the Maquis as they're called here."

"What do you do?"

"We send London details of German troop size and positions, by coded wireless radio messages. We also organize supply drops for the Maquis, giving them arms, money, and equipment to carry out their guerrilla attacks. Our job is to make as much mess as we can. There are many teams scattered throughout France with the same mission.

"With the help of our liaison, we blew some railway lines a few weeks ago. A large formation of German troops and supplies had to divert and are coming this way. By tomorrow night they'll be crossing the Pont du Namandie with men and tanks, all headed north. If these troops are allowed to arrive in Normandy, it could go poorly for the Allies."

"What does this have to do with me?" asked Katrinka.

"Your father has the plastique we need to blow the bridge. We sent an agent to retrieve it, but he never got there. We've not been able to contact your father."

Katrinka nodded. "After dropping us off near Martin Pecheur, he was going further up the coast, but he was returning there a few days later. That's where I was headed on horseback, when your sergeant found me."

"Katrinka, listen to me, this is important— how long was your father staying in the area on his return?"

"He told me he would stay until the morning of…" She stopped suddenly. "That would be tomorrow."

Nye's face hardened. "I need you to come back with us, Katrinka."

"What—"

"Don't you see," he interjected, "we *need* that plastique. You've got to go back to your father's ship, get it, and bring it to us."

"But—"

"Please. Just listen, then you can make up your mind."

He pulled out his map and placed it on the ground. "When you leave our camp, you will go to the market in Ange de Feu to purchase vegetables and other items. You will have a map. Your cover will be that you are bringing a food packet, a *colis familiaux*, to your aunt, who lives near Martin Pecheur. A safe house is there, and a man will be waiting. When it is dark, he will take you to your father's ship. Contact your father and get the plastique. You will leave Martin Pecheur early tomorrow morning and head back here.

"Coming back, it will be almost the same story. You are bringing items of food from your aunt's farm to a man, Bouchard, in the village. The plastique will be hidden under the false bottom of your market basket. It isn't heavy. You'll deliver the food basket to Bouchard at his farmhouse, and return to us immediately. Bouchard will take care of the rest."

Katrinka frowned, "How will I find all of these places? How will I find my way back to you?"

"I'll give you a map and make sure you're set with it. There should be no problems. Your cover is dead easy. There are hundreds of women and young girls about, searching for food and getting supplies. A man would arouse suspicion, as most men under forty have been sent away to the German factories or labor camps under the Service du Travail. The few left are farm laborers, who are helping to grow crops for the German troops. It is dangerous for us to be seen, whereas you will be just another girl on the road, with her bicycle."

Rolling up the map, he continued, "Our courier, Sébastien, will go with you. He will pose as your brother—"

"No." Katrinka stood, shaking the dust from her dress.

The major blinked, "Sorry?"

"I would very much like your sergeant to go with me."

Nye leaned back, giving her a long look. "So. That's the way it goes. You and Sergeant Farr? Rather quick, I should think."

"I trust him."

"Yes, he is a good man, and I knew he would find you."

There was a long silence before Nye spoke again. "Trinka, you don't have to do this. I've made it sound simple, but there is also risk. We're in German occupied territory, and there are frequent patrols. There will be roadblocks and checkpoints. You could be stopped and searched. If they find the plastique, things could go terribly wrong for you."

She nodded. "But I will do it. When I escaped, I wanted nothing more than to get back to Papa and *Le Flâneur*. I am involved now and I must finish it. You are Papa's dear friend. You were my mother's." She placed her hand on top of his. "And you are mine as well."

Nye blushed and looked at the ground, suddenly uncomfortable.

Katrinka studied him with affection. Of course she would do this for him. She would do anything the man asked her to do. She would love him, if only he would let her.

Since the age of four, she'd spent her life being shuttled between both fathers. Her mother was restless, leaving one man to join the other and then going back again. When she was nine years old her mother had run away once more, leaving Emerson at his site near Malaga. They'd boarded a ferry to Algiers and on arrival, Katrinka was surprised to find her papa and a young man waiting for them. He was very big, with sad-looking eyes. He was holding a leash, with a

35

dilapidated sack of fur and bones at the end of it. He already knew her parents and had worked with Papa before. His name was Willoughby Nye, but everyone called him Wills.

With a schoolgirl crush, she had quite simply fallen in love with him from the very beginning. Her young-girl adoration had embarrassed him terribly, and he'd wanted nothing to do with her. She had learned to hide her feelings for him.

Nye suddenly looked up as if reading her thoughts, and she dropped her gaze.

He cleared his throat and continued, "Nonetheless, I need Farr here. We've received his radio parts, and he's back in business. It was just a fluke he was there on patrol yesterday. And I was only able to spare him to go and look for you because his radio was broken."

"A good fluke for me."

"A damn good fluke, Katrinka."

They stared at each other for some moments.

Nye broke the silence. "Sébastien will go with you. He has had quite a bit of experience with these things."

"I think if I cannot have Farr, I would prefer to go alone. You said yourself I would be under no suspicion. I would not want to worry about another."

He hesitated, then nodded. "There is truth in what you say."

"When shall I leave?"

Nye stood and stuffed the map into his jacket. "We're walking back now. You should go as soon as we can get you ready."

"Wills?"

"Yes?"

"Has my father heard? Does he know?"

The major shook his head. "No, Katrinka."

She gave a sharp sigh. "I do not know how these things are managed here, but you will locate Emerson's body in the village near where he was killed, and A-mah's. I want them to be cremated. I will return to collect their ashes. You must do this for me."

"Of course. I've already made inquiries. The village's burial detail has taken the bodies back to town. They found papers in Emerson's jacket. I'll give these to you when you return." His voice shook. "I would not have left her in this godforsaken place."

* * *

Pascal had found them a new place to camp after the drop. They were now situated behind the farm belonging to a postmaster and his wife. The team moved into a few wooden structures used for the animals. Farr had already set up his radio and aerial a few hundred meters from the camp. With Farr's radio working, the SAS team left the area that morning. Nye sent Katrinka with the young wife. She had a pretty face and smiled at the girl.

"Go along with her now. She has the correct clothing, papers, and money. We will kit you up properly. I'm afraid she'll have to cut your hair to the local style," said Nye.

The major saw her out, and called for Valentine and Sébastien. They'd been working on the Norton's engine and were covered in grease. Nye gave them a short briefing, dismissed them, and then called for Farr, who showed up so quickly that the major realized he must have been waiting.

He turned to Farr, his features composed. The sergeant's own face was unreadable.

The major began, "I am sure you are curious as to what this is about."

"Yes, sir."

The men sat across a small folding table from each other as Nye quickly summarized everything concerning the ship, the plastique, and the missing agent. He included a brief connection between Amparo, Katrinka, and himself. "I'll need you working the radio. Contacts must be notified, plans modified, and the safe house on the coast alerted. Sébastien will help you with your message deliveries."

Farr nodded, but when told of the major's plans, his face hardened. "You're using her as a *floater*?"

Nye shifted uncomfortably in his chair. The SOE had always used floaters—a person used one time, occasionally, or even unknowingly, for an intelligence operation. Usually they were successful. Sometimes they were not. "You could call it that."

"You can't do that, sir. She's had no training. It will be suicide to send her out not knowing how to defend herself, or what to do."

"That's a chance we have to take. She appears to know how to use a knife adequately, and she managed to escape from you. The SOE has been using women agents for years. They're smart, fearless, and extremely capable."

"But she's not conscripted and has no proper identification. If she's caught, she'll be tortured or executed." He paused. "Have you forgotten the female agent they arrested just last month?"

Nye flinched. He had not forgotten. "She won't be caught if she's careful. She has papers."

"Have you even told her, or is she going in blind?"

"I've told her, and she's agreed."

Farr looked away.

The major continued, his voice rising, "Don't be an ass, Farr. There's no one else. She's young, female, and fluent in French. She could easily pass for a schoolgirl. Her disguise is perfect. She has no knowledge of other agents or operations, and could tell them nothing if caught."

Farr stared.

Nye flushed. "Yes, I'm telling you the facts. Bloody hell, man, you know how much we need this."

Farr's voice was tight. "Don't send her out on this without protection; let me go with her. I know how to blend in. My French is—"

The major roared, "Sergeant, I'm not asking your permission on the matter. This is an order, and I expect you to follow it."

The men locked eyes, and Nye experienced a stab of doubt. If his own conscience was torturing him, how could he convince Farr? *Damn* these American agents. They were all loose cannons as far as he was concerned.

"Yes, sir, of course," Farr said. "How will she communicate? We need to know when she's got the plastique."

Nye's shoulders relaxed. "Amparo's radio has been out for two days, but it doesn't matter. His agent on the coast will let us know when she's returning. She must not be caught with any equipment."

Farr's eyes narrowed.

The major amended, "She must not be caught at all."

"When will she leave? The schedule's pretty tight."

Nye stood and pulled his map out, explaining the plans. "After retrieving the plastique she'll return, and go to Bouchard's farmhouse—"

"Bouchard? Why Bouchard?"

"Degare was apprehended and arrested two days ago."

Farr sat back, looking stunned. "There've been too damn many arrests lately. We've heard rumors of an informant."

"Yes. All the more important we do this thing and leave. Bouchard's been working with the local Maquis for some time. He'll deliver the plastique to the demolition team. Now I'll let you get back to your radio. Report to me when you are finished." He sat down, returning to his papers.

"Sir."

The major glanced up.

"You know she was hurt."

"Yes, she seems to be mending properly. Nothing broken."

Farr stood, embarrassed. "I think... that is, Val and I think she was—"

"You think she was raped."

"It's pretty obvious, isn't it?" Farr's voice flicked in anger. "She should see a doctor in the village. Make up some story. She could be hurt, sir."

Nye had already considered the possibility and had put it out of his mind. She seemed steady, she hadn't requested anything. He clung to that slim fact. "Let me talk to her before she leaves. I'll sound her out on it."

Snapping a quick salute Farr exited the enclosure, swearing under his breath.

* * *

In less than an hour Katrinka had been given proper clothing, a haircut, and various documents, including some papers from her knapsack. A copy of her photo had been superimposed onto a new ID. Nye watched as she pirouetted in front of him in her new clothes.

"What do you think?" she asked.

She was wearing a dark-brown farm skirt with a tucked-in blouse, jumper, and a beret. She looked like a schoolgirl. Makeup covered most of her bruising, and the clothing did the rest. He knew her knife, the one Emerson had given her long ago, was sheathed and hidden in the waistband of her skirt.

Worry gnawed at the man's gut. There was so much more she needed. Agents trained for months in the art of field work. The slightest mistake would give her away. He counted on her going unnoticed. And deep in his heart, he knew this young woman standing before him. Had watched her grow up on the decks of *Le Flâneur*, and its rough-and-tumble sort of life. Her schooling had been an assortment of tutors and teachers, old deck hands, her French grandmother, and both fathers. Her morals and values had been formed by close observations, and her heart. And the thread running through it all had been her fierce, unequivocal need for independence. Although not formally trained, she had an instinct for survival, naïve bravery, and a rather wild, almost savage unpredictability that was perfectly suited for the job.

He smiled at her. "You'll do fine, Katrinka."

She picked up her bag.

"Wait."

She looked at him.

"I just want to make sure you're set for this."

"I'm fine, Wills."

"You've had a rough couple of days."

She paled.

He took a deep breath. "I think you should see a doctor or a clinic in the village. It can be arranged when you return."

"I'd rather not."

"I really must insist. There are… the men might have given you something. A simple test could clear it all up."

She was sweating. "I don't like doctors."

Nye knew of her deep-seated, almost irrational fear, but this could not be ignored, and she knew it.

"So, you would put Farr at risk?"

She colored to the top of her hairline and her face clenched with anger. Swinging her arm, she swept the papers from his table. They fluttered in the air like disturbed birds, scattering to the ground. "So, it is not over. It was not enough—now I must worry about disease as well. Or how about pregnancy? Have you thought of that one?"

Nye was silent.

"Make the appointment! Let the doctor prod and poke, to see what he may find. I've never—" She stopped suddenly, catching sight of his expression.

God knows what she saw there, the misery he was feeling must have shown.

When she spoke again her voice was quiet, her anger gone. "I'm sorry, Wills. I am being stupid. And you are right. I'll go. If you could tell me where…?"

"Sweetheart, don't worry about it. Raphael will arrange the appointment for you when you return. I'll go with you if you like."

"And who would save France while you were holding my hand?" She shook her head, giving him the ghost of a smile. "Thank you, Wills, but I'll be all right."

He felt a great sense of relief. "Well then, that's settled. Now I think you'd best be on your way."

They walked outside, to where Farr stood waiting beside the bicycle. Nye handed her a piece of silk with a map and various directions written on it.

"Conceal this in the handlebars of your bike. They unscrew easily. Remember, all you need to do is contact your father, get the plastique, and bring it to Bouchard's farm. He's been told to expect a delivery by an agent sometime tomorrow evening. He'll take the plastique from there."

"I'll give Papa your love."

"Do that." Nye pulled her close for a moment. "Katrinka, I have no right to ask you this, but if you should be stopped, if you can manage to hold out even for a day, it would give us time to move the team. It would give them a chance."

She replied, her eyes somber. "I would hope they would get nothing from me. I know so very little as it is."

He turned her around, her back to Farr. He did not want the man to see what he was about to do.

"In case you are detained, if it gets bad, I want you to have this." He slipped a miniature vial into her hand, containing a small tablet.

"What is it?"

"It gets you out of it all."

She stared at the vial, and then him.

He whispered softly, "If it gets too bad."

She nodded wordlessly, tucking it deep into her pocket.

43

Farr stood beside the bike, arms crossed, staring pointedly into the distance, trying not to watch the major with Katrinka. How closely they stood together. How he looked down at her, and how she gazed up at him. He half-turned his head as she approached. Almost angrily, he hooked out an arm and pulled her to him, placing his mouth just next to her ear.

"You come back safely, you understand? Don't let yourself be caught."

He had to let her go then. He did not want to let her go. He watched as she mounted the bike, adjusted her beret, and with a wave, pedaled off down the road.

The major turned back to the shed, and Farr returned to his radio. There was nothing to do now but wait.

3

A FTER THE MARKET, KATRINKA WHEELED ALONG, pacing herself for the long ride ahead, reflecting on her conversation with Wills. Another examination. She'd not been to a doctor since the one at Emerson's dig in Spain. It was just after the incident. She was nine years old, and nothing had prepared her for the experience.

The doctor had touched her like she was unclean. Prodding and intruding with his cold instruments while she lay back on the hard metal table, the garish overhead light blinding her, increasing her sense of helplessness. She'd cried and struggled to get away, but the nurse's cold hands held her down. They'd made her mother leave the room. No. It was useless to think of that.

Her thoughts turned to the previous night with the man Farr, and she experienced a frisson of sexual electricity. She did not want him mixed up in her rage. He was a good man. He was not to blame for what others had done, that was something else. It belonged in a box, locked up tight inside her heart.

Katrinka pedaled along the village lanes, crossing over creeks and through pasturelands smelling of freshly cut grasses. The air felt soft and slightly damp, its moisture beading like tears on her cheek. The houses were shrouded in a fine yellow mist, giving everything a faraway look, as if she were traveling through the illustrations of an old storybook.

She passed a few German soldiers on the road and occasionally, farm laborers, dressed in the same type of clothing Farr and his team wore. But everyone seemed too occupied to notice a young woman on her bicycle. There were so many of them out: daughters and mothers without their men, scavenging what they could.

She came to a large town with an abandoned playground at the edge of it. One of the swings was broken and hung by its rusted chain. Its clanging made a discordant sound that carried on the wind. Where were all the children? Shouldn't they be out in the streets, playing their games and chasing one another? Maybe they were in school. But she had not seen any school buildings.

Wills had warned her that the Wehrmacht carried out sporadic checks at the entrances to villages and towns, and she was stopped more than once. But the soldiers just glanced at her papers, sometimes not even checking her basket. One young soldier gave her a wink and a smile as she rode away.

Her hands grew tired of gripping the handlebars and she raised them, one at a time, flexing. A branch lay across the road and she swerved, almost falling from her bike. She passed another checkpoint and entered a small village. Few shops were open, and a line of women waiting with numbed patience, snaked around one entrance. She guided her bike carefully, weaving between young children and mangy-looking dogs playing in the dusty street. Sometimes German soldiers appeared in automobiles, or motorcycles with sidecars. Their engines disturbed the quiet air, and the clean-looking uniforms were a sharp contrast to the shabby clothing of the French.

Tired and needing to eat, she found shelter under a tree on the outskirts of town. She opened the small packet of food. It contained hard cheese and a harder piece of black bread, but it was better than the food Farr had shared with her this morning. She frowned as she chewed. Hunger was becoming a constant problem.

The sun was setting when Katrinka stopped for another rest. Rubbing her sore muscles, she studied the map. She was very close to her destination. She must remember what to say and use the properly coded phrases. She wondered what would happen if they refused to help her. What if they called the Gestapo?

The air was cooler and soon it would be dark. Putting the packet and canteen back in the basket, she continued pedaling and soon arrived in a small coastal village. There was just one main road going through the town, lined with an assortment of stone houses and shops, all shouldered together with their shutters drawn tight. The streets were empty.

She pedaled through the silent town until she reached her destination, a run-down farmhouse just on the outskirts, at the end of a narrow bramble-bordered road. An evening mist was settling, and Katrinka shivered despite her sweater. The tangy smell of salt and seaweed rose up from a nearby beach, mingled with wood smoke. A thin cow stood in the pasture, staring at her with round eyes. She parked her bike and approached the house.

* * *

Amparo was uneasy. He should be gone, but a flurry of last-minute, urgent reports held him in this secluded bay. *Damn* Emerson and his quests. Anchoring in the same area twice was foolhardy. The German lookouts were stretched thin, but there was only a brief window of time when this small bit of coastline had minimal guard. He and his crew had to get out before dawn.

He peered at his watch in the darkness. If the agent did not show soon, he would find another way to deliver the plastique. But, in his heart, he knew it would be too late to stop the Germans.

There was a splash, and Amparo grabbed for his gun. Nicolas, his second mate, appeared from the shadows.

"Steady, Captain; Santos has arrived, and the agent has as well."

Both men leaned into the darkness. Amparo heard soft voices, and a ladder was thrown over the side. In a few minutes, two figures appeared on deck. Amparo approached silently, his pistol ready.

"Papai?" queried a voice.

The man lowered his gun. "*Katrinka?*"

"Papai!" She ran to his arms.

He turned to Santos and nodded, and the old man and second mate faded back into the shadows. Amparo held her close, hushing her.

"Yes, I see you are upset. Calm yourself. What has happened? Why are you here?" He cupped her head in his hands, peering into her face. Seeing the blotches of bruised skin, he pulled back, his voice deadly quiet. "Trinka, what has happened? Who has done this?"

Katrinka's teeth were chattering. "Papai, please, there is terrible news. I must speak to you."

They went through an open hatch that led down a passageway into his small office. He guided her to the old sofa. "Sit here. I will get you something warm to drink."

He returned a few minutes later, holding a steaming cup. "Drink this, then we will talk."

He waited until she had finished the tea, then took the cup and sat down beside her, his heart already heavy with foreboding.

"Now, Trinka, what has happened? What have you to tell me?"

"It was after you dropped us off," she began.

As she related the events of the past few days, Amparo stared at his daughter.

"She's dead, Papai. They killed her, and Emerson too. They left them on the road."

Amparo thrust himself from the sofa, the world tilting around him. It seemed he'd forgotten how to breathe. Yujana. And Emerson. He spared a moment of compassion for a man he'd once thought his enemy, but over the years had proved a steady friend. Looking down at his daughter's stricken face, he again saw the bruises, like dark smudges on her skin. She was crying now. That was good. He let her cry. His own eyes felt scorched.

Later he handed her a handkerchief from his coat pocket, and she dried her face.

"Find what you need in your cabin, Trinka, and then come to the galley. We will eat."

Amparo stood as he watched her go, and the fury came rushing back, choking his brain. He would return with her. He would find out who did this. He would track them down, and with his bare hands, kill each one. He would make sure they knew the reason why.

He was grinding his teeth and the pain roused him. He must move. Do something. She would be hungry. He passed through a narrow corridor and into the small galley to prepare a meal. A skillet dropped from his hands and he grabbed it up, slamming it onto a pile of dishes again and again, shattering them to pieces. He threw the skillet into the wall. Exhaling in sharp gasps, he stood with hands clenched, his nails scoring his skin.

* * *

A short time later, Katrinka entered the galley. Her father had drawn the blackout curtains and was cooking tinned stew in a large pot. Seeing the shattered remains of dishes, she pulled a broom from the corner and swept up the debris. Then she perched on an anchored stool and wrapped herself in an old blanket. Her face felt puffy and tear-streaked, but her hair was neatly brushed back. She watched her father by the stove.

"It smells good in here, Papa."

After the meal was prepared and the dishes laid, they sat across from each other at the table. Amparo poured wine from a bottle. They ate quietly, talking of other things.

Katrinka waited until the meal was finished. Then carefully, she explained to him her mission. About the German deserters, and Farr, and Wills. The captured agent, and their desperate need for the plastique. Nye's plans to retrieve Yujana and Emerson's ashes.

He listened with a forced calmness. "These men took you. Where? For what purpose?"

"Papa, I do not want to talk about it now. They are dead. Sergeant Farr was patrolling the area. He found me. He killed the men—"

"All of them? *Did he kill them all?*"

Katrinka replied, her voice as hard as his. "The one who murdered A-mah I killed myself, with my knife."

A shocked look passed over her father's face, followed by something else. Was it pride? Gratification?

She continued, "I escaped. I wanted only to return to you and *Le Flâneur*. Later, we could go back for their bodies. But Wills heard about them from radio reports. When Sergeant Farr told him what had happened, he thought the girl must be me."

"So, our good friend Nye has put you in this mess."

"Papa, the men need this plastique. There is a large formation of German troops, coming up from the south. These are the same men who attacked the village of La Sansoune. They killed every man, women and child. The babies too. They cannot be allowed to cross this bridge."

She pulled out her silken map. "Here is where they will come, to the Pont du Namandie. The Maquis will plant the plastique I bring back, and destroy the bridge."

Her father studied the map, his face grave. "Yes," he said with a heaviness. "It must be done."

After drying the dishes, Katrinka found her father on the lower deck, leaning against the gunwales and staring out at the water. His face was haggard in the moonlight, and his eyes bloodshot, but he managed a smile. They stood together enveloped in light mist, the stars dim lights in the sky.

"Papa?"

"Yes, *filhinha*?"

"Why did you and A-mah never marry? Before she died… she told me she loved you, she had always loved you."

"She said that?"

"Yes."

Amparo nodded, turning back again, to stare at the sea.

Katrinka waited for him to go on, but he was silent. With a quick embrace and a kiss, she slipped away.

* * *

Later, after making a final security check, Amparo snuffed his pipe and walked out along the bridge. *Le Flâneur* was shrouded in a thick blanket of silence. The light mist had grown heavy, blocking out the stars and making the moon a pale shadow in the sky. Now he had time to think, his heart coated in a protective numbness.

Yujana dead. He remembered the first time he'd seen her, on stage in a smoke-filled bar in Rangoon, singing to drunken men. Then later, she was dragged before him on his ship. Always so defiant, always so sure of herself and her charms. The discovery of his private letters, and later, her affair with Emerson. That crazy, passionate night in the cabin when she'd shared herself with both men. He'd stayed away from her after that, and in Marseilles she'd departed with Emerson.

A letter arrived from Emerson months later. She had left him after finding out she was with child, and had gone back to her family in the Andaman Sea.

He'd continued to stay away as months turned into years, his pride not letting him look for her. Until one summer when Emerson tracked him down, arriving from the desert in Alexandria Port. And throughout the rambling drunken night, the two men talked, swore, and reminisced.

Then Emerson made a remark that seemed to have no relevance. "Got the mumps when I was in college. Everyone gets it, but they have sense to do it while young. Damnedest thing. Caused a lot of problems, and the upshot was that my family took me to a specialist. It turned out my tool was damaged; couldn't produce what's needed to get the job done. It looks like you're it, old man."

Amparo stared.

Emerson continued, "It's you she loves. Always has. I'm excitement for her, an adventure. But she's always loved you. I could never compete with that, and I never tried. And if you had an ounce of sense in that fat head of yours, you'd go and get her."

After Emerson had left, Amparo turned the facts over. She'd had his child. He felt no surprise. Deep down at some biological level, hadn't he always known?

So he'd hauled anchor from Alexandria Port, setting his crew and compass for the Andaman Sea. Many weeks later, *Le Flâneur* pulled into the port of Myeik, the capital of Mergui, and its main trading center. In the past, Amparo had done profitable business in pearls and had many acquaintances in the main town. It was only a matter of time before he tracked her down.

He first saw her squatting on the deck of her family *kabang*, chopping seaweed. Her fair hair was caught up in a scarf, and a longyi was knotted tightly around her waist. She glanced up, shocked at seeing him clamber over the side, surrounded by her chattering family members. A flash of undisguised joy crossed her face. Wiping her hands on the longyi, she walked up to him, cupping his face in her hands.

"Remi, you've been so long away," was all she said.

That afternoon, they swam out to board *Le Flâneur* and made love in the afternoon heat of his cabin. When it became too hot, they plunged over the side and made love again, in the ship's cool green shade. In the evening, they swam back to the *kabang*.

Later, as the stars were coming out, a small girl came splashing up to the *kabang*, and hoisted herself onto its deck, laughing and shaking water from her dark curls. She stopped when she saw him, and he got a clear view of her face. It was as if he were gazing into a mirror, with his own large, blue eyes looking back at him, and the last doubt vanished. Yujana always claimed that the minute they had placed Katrinka in her arms, she had known the child was his.

She'd followed Emerson on that last expedition, soon after Amparo had explained to her about his wife, Maria, the woman who had written the letters. Was that why she'd left? Surely, she had known the risks. But Emerson could ignite anyone's imagination with his stories. He had an aura of excitement and intrigue about him that many found irresistible, including Yujana. She'd lived most of her youth without a home or roots. She had the ability to float about the world, happily experiencing life events and the men that came with them. A half-wild, passionate woman, moody and intense. She'd found something in him worth loving, returning to him again and again. But ultimately, unholdable. He'd never been able to hold her.

* * *

Early next morning, they assembled a packet of food from the remains of dinner, and placed the bars of plastique under the false bottom of the basket. Nestled next to it incongruously, was a small bottle of Porto wine, a favorite of Katrinka's. Spying it, she smiled. She placed the food from the safe house atop the false bottom.

"You will need money. I've written the contact information of my solicitor in Switzerland. He will know where to find me, and will give you whatever you need. In the meantime, take this." Amparo handed her a small packet of French francs. "It is not much, but it may be useful."

She tucked the bills into her skirt.

"This man, Sergeant Farr. I would like to meet him someday and thank him."

"I would like that as well," she replied.

They slipped over the side into a small dinghy, and Santos rowed them ashore. The water was silent; it was still very dark. Katrinka found the place where she'd hidden the bicycle. Settling the basket on the handlebars, she turned to face her father.

"Papa, you know I want to bring A-mah's ashes back."

"Back?"

"To Coronado. She wanted to be scattered among the roses."

"Trinka, that may not be possible."

"I promised her, Papa."

He sighed. "Then we will do it. What of Emerson?"

Her voice tightened, "I would like to take him to Lascaux. I think he would be happy there."

He nodded and embraced her one last time before standing back, watching as she pushed her bike up to the road.

Turning back, she called to him softly, "I love you, Papa."

Amparo stared into the blackness, long after her small figure had faded into the distance.

* * *

Katrinka made good time on her return, pulling into the woods whenever vehicles approached and avoiding roadblocks. The long night's sleep and hot food had rejuvenated her, and the terrible burden of having to tell her father was over. There had been no problems. The plastique would arrive on time.

She stopped around noon, eating a hurried lunch. Later, needing to relieve herself, she found a secluded area of trees away from the road. When finished, she separated the lips of her vulva and probed inside with an exploratory finger. Although the pills had put them in a constant state of sexual arousal, the soldiers at the farmhouse had experienced problems maintaining their erections. Except for one soldier. Well. She had taken care of him.

Gently she moved her finger around, searching for anything amiss. It was still sore, but much better than yesterday. Katrinka felt the anger building inside her. Would she ever have pleasure again? Would it stay numb and deadened as it had been these past few days? Was she broken? A glance around satisfied her that she was alone, sheltered by the leafy greenery. She could find out for herself. She didn't need a doctor for that. A doctor wouldn't care about that.

She lay in the soft grasses, feeling the sun's warmth on her face. Lifting her skirt, she cupped her fingers around herself. She rubbed with a languid motion for several

56

minutes, enjoying the buildup, probing softly with her finger. As the pleasure intensified, she rubbed faster, arching her body and grunting tightly from the back of her throat until her muscles contracted in a clenched spasm. Then it was over, and she flopped back, panting.

Gradually removing her hand, she gave herself one last affectionate squeeze. She felt immense relief. Everything appeared to be in working order. The poor thing had just wanted a friendly touch.

A tear trickled down her cheek. She wiped it away, overcome with an intense desire to sleep. The droning of bees made a peaceful sound in the stillness. Couldn't she just stay here? She would curl up into an invisible ball, hidden by the tall grasses, and let herself heal.

But Wills was depending on her. She stood and adjusted her skirt. Then mounting the bicycle, she continued on her way with a sleepy but much lighter heart. The sun sprinkled its dappled rays through the tree leaves, and the air hovering above the road seemed freckled with golden dust. She drowsed along, with half-closed eyes.

Too late, Katrinka spotted a pair of soldiers ahead and a small German jeep parked across the road. A checkpoint? There was no time to hide. They were signaling her forward.

With stomach lurching, she coasted up to one soldier who stood a little away from the other. He looked young, and not quite at ease with his gangly, broad-shouldered body.

Smiling, she spoke in halting, schoolgirl German. "Hallo, may I pass by here?"

The youth broke into a grin. "Your *Deutsch* is admirable, *mademoiselle*, but there is no need. I know a bit of French, as you can see. I would ask you where you are going and to view your papers." His green eyes gave her an appraising look. Seeing the bruises, he was suddenly alert, his face hard-edged.

Katrinka noticed and switched tactics. Placing a trembling hand on his sleeve, her eyes filled with easy tears. "Oh, *monsieur*, as you see, I have had a bad time. My grandfather... he is difficult when he is drinking. I have ridden this bike to my aunt's, near Les Sabit, where there is more food. I bring back some good cheese, potatoes, and beans. Yes, a few eggs as well and some apples. It will please him."

He glanced at her papers, then handed them back. He seemed more interested in the basket of food. The other soldier had come over, and looked—if possible—even younger than the first. They had a quick conference, giving her glances, which she returned with a warm smile. She waited.

The tall one, called Josef, spoke again. "Yes, *mademoiselle*, all is in order. You may go."

She began to wheel away.

"But first..." Josef reached out and took hold of her arm.

She winced but turned with a smile. "Yes?"

"It is warm today, and you are fatigued. Perhaps you would like to share with us an apple? We are hot and tired as well."

Relief made her weak, and she smiled again.

"Of course, that is a good idea. They come from my aunt's trees." She pulled the basket over. "Please take one."

Both boys crowded around her basket. Katrinka held her breath, trying not to think of the bars of plastique nestled just inches away, under the flimsy false bottom.

58

They finally selected a sweet-smelling red one with yellowish freckles. Josef laughed. "Yes, this one, I think. It looks like your face, Horst!"

They offered her a seat on the hood of their jeep, and Josef gave her the first bite. He watched as she broke into the flesh, a bit of juicy sweetness dribbling down her chin. Reaching over, he gently wiped away the juice, licking his fingers.

She flushed. It was as if he'd left a trail of flame upon her face. He took the apple and handed it to Horst, who took a bite and handed it back to Josef.

There was a scrabbling sound, and a small dog with a bent ear and freckled muzzle bounded from the back of the jeep, skittering onto the hood with them.

Josef burst out laughing, "Of course, when there is something to eat... *mademoiselle*, I present Monsieur Rolf. A connoisseur of good food, lately living in the gutters, and rescued by me. He has rough manners, as you can see."

Rolf wiggled between Katrinka and Josef, begging for a bite.

Katrinka laughed, breaking off a small bit from the apple.

"No, you must make him ask politely for it." He took her hand in his, holding it above the dog's head. Rolf immediately sat up on his haunches, his front paws curved into his chest, sliding a bit on the slanted hood of the jeep.

Katrinka laughed again at the dog's eagerness and gave him the bite. They sat in the sunshine eating, Josef sitting close, his shoulder pressed lightly against hers. The scent of his body was palpable, both tangy and sexual.

"This is good," he began, "They remind me of my parents' house."

Katrinka stopped chewing, giving him a long look. His face had lost its earlier hardness. She guessed him to be about her age. And homesick.

"We live in a town called Schönwerthbach, have you heard of it?" asked Josef.

She shook her head.

"It is very far from here, in Bavaria. You must first go to the city of Nürnberg, and then take the bus or train to my village." He took a large bite of the fruit. "And in the autumn, all the apple trees are full. My mother makes many jars of marmalade and cider for the *Christkindlesmarkt.* There is a very large one in Nürnberg. Then the air is scented with *Wurst*, spiced wine, and *Lebkuchen*."

"What is that?"

"A kind of gingerbread, with many spices."

"You talk quite a lot about food."

"I am always hungry."

"So am I." She smiled. It felt good to be talking to him, someone her own age, sitting in the warm sun, sharing the fruit.

They finished the apple, and both boys hopped to the ground, Josef offering his hand to her.

"I must go, my grandfather is waiting."

"I wish you well, *mademoiselle*, and a good meal tonight with your grandfather."

Josef continued holding her hand. Again, she could feel his heat. Her own body was feeling quite warm.

She was startled to see Horst hunch into a spasm, his face ashen. He made a quick dash across the road and into the brush. Josef watched him go with troubled eyes.

"He has been ill; the sensitive stomach. We get so little fresh fruit."

He followed her to the bicycle, helping to adjust the basket to the handlebars.

Tightening the beret around her hair, she turned to smile a farewell. But again he took her arm, this time pulling her close.

"One moment, please," he requested.

He was so near, she could smell the apple on his breath.

"Yes?"

"You have shared your food with us. Now I would like to give you something as well."

"There is no need—"

Without warning he grasped her waist, kissing her fully on the lips.

She pulled back laughing, and Josef laughed as well. They stood in the road, regarding one another. He was breathing fast, and his cheeks were flushed. Katrinka could see his very visible excitement. She was shocked at her own arousal, and even more, at her sense of elation. She was free again. They were both young, and it was a warm summer day. He had given her a kiss, and it felt good. She was not broken. The whole world stretched out before her. Although possibly painful, there would be pleasure in this encounter. She would have many more, and soon the taint of the others would wash away. She would be clean.

"*Mademoiselle…*"

"Kiss me again."

He moved quickly, his lips crushing hers as his tongue probed inside her mouth. Katrinka pressed into him, feeling his hardness against her stomach. She reached for his fly and began loosening the buttons. She wanted him so badly. Would it hurt?

Josef swung her off the ground and stumbled with her into the shelter of the trees. He fell on top of her, frantic with his trousers. She helped pull his penis out, just as it discharged in their hands.

The boy was truly stricken, "It cannot be so!" He looked as if he would weep.

Katrinka sat up, dismayed. She could smell the mustiness of his sperm where it had spattered. Was this his first time?

"No! Do not leave. I can be ready in a moment; just one moment more."

His tone was so earnest, so eager, that Katrinka hesitated. Would a few minutes matter? She would pedal very fast and not stop to eat. Everyone's first time should be good. Hers had not.

She smiled. "Then we will wait."

They waited.

She heard a rustling. Was that Horst? A sharp twig dug into her bottom. The absurdity of their situation caught at her throat, and she stifled a giggle. To laugh now would be disastrous. She looked at him. He was staring at the limp organ clenched in his hand, as if willing it to move. His cheeks were flushed, and dark hair tumbled onto either side of his sunburned forehead.

"Shall I whisper to you?" she asked. "Shall I tell you what I want you to do with me?"

He looked up, nodding with relief.

She pried away his fingers and took the flaccid penis into her hand, bending down to kiss it. She whispered some words into his ear. He seemed dazed.

She drew back, studying his face. "Shall I be more explicit?" Some men loved the talk, but it could so quickly cross their line of arousal to disgust. You could never tell.

62

"*Explicit?*"

"Would you like me to be more clear? To be frank with my desires?"

Again, the boy nodded.

She leaned forward, licking the inner part of his ear, and whispered once more. She was very frank.

In a few minutes Josef was hard, and Katrinka sopping wet. She spread her legs as he tugged down her panties with excitement, positioning himself to thrust.

"Stop." She placed her hand on his arm. "Do you have a *presérvatif?* A *Kondom?*"

He paused with a look of frustration. He was breathing hard. Quickly he sat back and unsnapped a pouch attached to his belt.

Katrinka waited. She lay amid twigs and leaves, watching the trees sway above them. The spicy odor of the boy's sweat mingled with the afternoon's weedy scent of wildflowers. The wind made a clean, rushing sound through the trees, like the sound a tide makes along the shoreline.

Josef was fumbling with the small packet, so she reached up and helped him open it. He slid it over his penis. It was short and thick, slightly bent to one side.

She smiled up at him. "Now you must enter me slowly. Slide it into me gently."

He slipped into her with a delicious rush. She cried out once, but the pain was replaced by dizzying pleasure. She lay back, sucking dry air between her teeth, feeling his quickening rhythm between her legs. She wanted it to go on and on, but he was huffing in exuberant breaths, already reaching orgasm. It was over much too soon. When he pulled out, the condom slid off, and his sticky wetness dribbled between her legs.

Raising up on his elbows, he held her head between both his hands and gave her a lingering kiss. "You cannot leave. We will make love again. Horst will watch the road. I will last longer this time, and I promise it will be good for you." He reached into his snap pouch, pulling out the small packets. "You see. There are two more."

Katrinka laughed and pulled him back down onto her. "There is a road to watch, and I have a grandfather to feed. We cannot spend the day making love." But she had to fight down her own desire to remain. To make love over and over with this young boy, and his hard cock wanting her. It had been much too quick.

She caressed the mop of dark hair away from his sweating face. "Am I your first?"

"Yes. Now if I die, it will not matter so much."

She smiled at his melodrama. "Are you so sure of dying?"

Josef sobered, his hard edges reappearing. "*Mademoiselle*, there are many ways the soul can die."

Katrinka stared. It seemed incongruous on this faded, sunlit afternoon, with the tall trees shimmering green above their heads, that men should be shooting and killing one another. With a shiver of apprehension, she wondered where he would be this evening, when the bridge blew up.

Josef rose, adjusting his uniform. He held out his hand to help her up, removing a twig from her hair, and kissed her gently on the nose. They walked back to her bicycle. Horst had not returned.

Mounting her bike, she smiled at him. The hard edges were gone now, and his eyes vulnerable. Again, she brushed back his mop of dark hair, giving him a quick kiss.

As she pedaled away, he called after her, "*Mademoiselle*, when the war is over, you must come to my village. We will share another apple!"

Katrinka laughed and waved. The sun's rays continued to be warm, and the scent of late summer flowers filled the air. For a long time after, Katrinka could feel his wetness between her legs, and taste the lingering sweet juice of apple on her lips. Or perhaps it was the young boy's warm kiss.

* * *

Farr finished his last radio transmission. He'd set up his position a few kilometers from their new camp, in case he was traced. A dry-cell battery was used to receive messages on the Jed set, but another person was needed to crank the generator when transmitting. Usually, Raphael or Sébastien helped him by turning it, watching the meter and keeping the pace at a steady 200 volts. But earlier that morning, Pascal had helped him rig up a small transformer for the set. Now he would be able to transmit solo, from anywhere that had an electrical source.

Farr packed up the radio into its small suitcase and pedaled back to their camp on neglected farm roads. The farm had burned down, and only the abandoned bull pen with its cement shed remained, half-hidden in the overgrowth of the forest. It was barely tall enough for the men to stand in, but offered protection when it rained and was far from any main roads.

He had nothing to do but wait. The major was inside the cement structure, working on reports. Raphael had gone out after the transmissions to meet with a group of Maquis and set up an incoming drop. Farr was worried about him. Raphael was soft-spoken and rarely given to conversation, but he'd seemed especially withdrawn this past week. Farr had never seen a man with such dead-looking eyes.

To ease tension, Farr settled under a tree to read his tattered book, an Armed Services Edition of *A Tree Grows in Brooklyn*. ASEs were hard to locate, and he'd waited a long time for this particular book, but he could not keep his mind on the words. He recalled his conversation with Nye the day before, concerning the British SOE agent who'd been arrested and later executed. The whole Jed network in this area of France had heard about it.

"Just bad luck," they'd said. "You have to be careful."

Her death had been a bit more personal to Farr. Code named Sylvia, and fresh from her training in England, she had just celebrated her nineteenth birthday. She was spunky and sassy, and filled with an intense desire to be a credit to the job. He'd trained with her back at the SOE school in England. She worked as hard as any man, learning weaponry, unarmed combat, and sabotage techniques. She had endured grueling, mountainous training treks, in extreme conditions.

On that night back in June, she and her wireless operator had been on the same parachute drop as his. Every move had been timed down to the second, with the high-winged Lysander circling over the drop zone, and small directional fires lit by the Maquis, in the field below. Her radio operator, Ratner, froze in the doorway. It happened. Men saw the darkness looming below them, and they choked. The plane's crewmember quickly shoved Sylvia to the fore, rightly suspecting that no man wanted to be shown up by a young girl.

She'd spun around right before jumping, her eyes wide and laughing, and given Ratner a kiss on the lips. "For good luck," she said. Then she'd turned and plummeted out into the moonlit field below.

Two weeks later, she was dead. She was observed looking the wrong way before crossing a street—a habit that immediately identified her as British. An alert German soldier had seen it, and she'd been arrested, interrogated, and executed. When her body was retrieved, they found she'd been badly kicked and beaten, and her ribs broken. There was a bullet hole in the base of her skull. Undercover agents in the nearby area scrambled for new hiding places, but she had not talked. And the carefully constructed network that she'd helped form, remained safe and intact.

Farr closed his eyes, gripping the book. It was just bad luck. These things happened, and you couldn't let yourself think about it, or you'd go crazy.

Telephone relay reports had come in from the coast that morning. The plastique was retrieved and on its way. Farr wondered for the hundredth time that day where Katrinka was, and how she was doing.

* * *

Katrinka stopped at a crossroads and squinted down at her map. The sunlight was fading, and she shivered at the slight chill in the air, pulling her sweater tighter. The road to the left led to the next village, and to the right lay the way to the farmhouse and her rendezvous. There was not much further to go. She got back on and pedaled faster.

* * *

Farr was still reading, when he heard the rushing approach of Sébastien on his bicycle. The boy dismounted in a tearing hurry and entered the small structure. A few moments later, Farr heard the major's explosion.

"Bloody hell!"

Tossing the book, Farr sprinted inside, where Sébastien stood, stiff and waiting. Nye was leaning against the table, his face pale. He turned as the sergeant entered.

"Sweet Jesus, Farr. We've just gotten a message from Degare—"

"But—" interjected Farr.

"He's managed to escape. Bouchard's an informer."

Farr froze.

"Find Valentine. Get out to the farm before Katrinka does and take care of this mess. We've been compromised. We're getting the hell out of this area right now."

Nye stood upright, shuffling through the files on his desk. He handed Farr a slip of paper. "Here are the coordinates of our new camp. Memorize it, then eat it."

"Yes, sir."

"German troops and tanks have been sighted. They're heading this way. ETA, two hours maximum. Bouchard is going to screw this entire thing. For God's sake Farr, get her back. Get the plastique and get her back. SAS men will be near the bridge to collect the plastique."

"Yes, sir." Farr spun around, his stomach churning.

"Wait! Take Jack. We'll be clearing out of here on foot and can't be seen with his cage. Brief Valentine while I try to locate the damn Citroën."

Nye and Sébastien began stuffing papers into a rucksack as Farr pounded over the ground. What had they done?

* * *

Katrinka paused at the end of the road, staring at the farmhouse. It sat in the evening twilight, a soft light glowing from behind a partially curtained window. It was very quiet. But there was something wrong, and she could feel hairs rising along the back of her neck. As a child swimming through coral reef, she'd always sensed the sharks. She sensed something now, hiding in the shadows of this peaceful scene.

Reaching down to the basket of food, she lifted its false bottom and stared at the bars of plastique nestled against the bottle of port. Fingering her knife, she looked again at the house.

4

"GㅤOT YOUR GUN OUT?"

ㅤFarr nodded, studying the map as they sped down the road, hitting ruts hard and skidding around tight corners. Valentine handled the vehicle like a weapon. They wouldn't be stopping for any roadblocks. Jack squawked with alarm from his carrier in the backseat.

Farr glanced over his shoulder. "You kill that bird, we might as well not come back."

Val grinned, "He loves it. Mother's milk."

Farr returned his gaze to the map, concentrating on their plans. If she had not arrived, they would wait. Take up a post outside the house, and get her and the plastique away, to the designated spot near the bridge. If she was already there, they'd attack the house, recover Katrinka and the plastique, and make the delivery. It was a simple plan, but he knew how badly it could go if Katrinka was caught in the crossfire. He wondered if the Gestapo had her already and what they were doing. His sweating hand slipped on the butt of his pistol. He stole a glance at Val, but the man's profile told him nothing.

Just before they reached the farmhouse, Val swung off the road and killed the engine. The men got out of the car and crept toward the building, weapons in hand. Without any warning, Katrinka emerged from the trees, holding a basket. She stepped up to the door of the house and knocked. Farr lunged forward, but Val grabbed his arm. Farr turned in anger as the younger man stared him down.

"Too late," Val hissed. "Wait. We need to see who's in there. How many of them."

Farr shook him off, nodding, his entire body rigid.

There was commotion from the small house and a voice called out an order. The door swung open, and Katrinka was facing down the barrel of a rifle. A man in German uniform reached out, dragging her over the threshold. The door closed and reopened a moment later, as another German soldier emerged to stand guard. Angry voices sounded from within. Stepping from the porch, the guard began an alert pacing in front of the house.

Jerking his knife from its sheath, Farr signaled Val and crept forward. As the soldier turned, Farr raced the last few paces, grabbed the man from behind, and quickly slit his throat. The soldier sank noiselessly into the dust. With Valentine's help, Farr dragged the body into the bushes.

As they crept back to the window, the voices grew louder. Peering in, Farr spotted Katrinka immediately. There were two other soldiers in the room: an officer and an enlisted man. And Bouchard. There was no one else. The officer was frowning as he scanned Katrinka's documents; the other soldier still grasping her arm. The men were conversing in French, and Farr leaned closer, in an effort to hear more clearly.

Turning on Bouchard, the officer hurled the papers at him. "*Idiot*. You said it was to be an agent—the one who escaped. Who is she?"

"Hauptmann Fleischer, I don't—"

"Bah. Jürgen, search her," commanded the officer.

Jürgen spun the girl around to face him and patted her roughly up and down. Holding both wrists behind her back, he lifted her skirt, moved his hand up between her legs, and gave a sudden, vicious thrust. Katrinka cried out, and Jürgen's lips curled upward.

Farr watched, his hand moving spasmodically on the gun.

Val steadied his arm, whispering, "Wait."

Jürgen finished his search, shaking his head. "*Nichts.*"

Twisting away, Katrinka asked, her voice strained. "Hauptmann Fleischer, is there a problem? I was told to bring these items to this gentleman, Monsieur Bouchard. You see—"

"Silence!" barked Fleischer.

Seizing Katrinka's basket, he spilled its contents onto the table. His hand paused at the bottom, feeling around the edges. He gave a tight smile. "It appears, *mademoiselle*, that there is another bottom to this basket." Jerking Katrinka's hair, he tilted her face up to his. "After my interrogation, you will be hung for this, you stupid girl."

He thrust her toward Jürgen. "Hold her."

All eyes were on Fleischer as he tore open the bottom of the basket. Outside, the men shifted imperceptibly, hands on their weapons. Fleischer tossed the false bottom away and stood back, staring at the contents. Reaching in, he carefully lifted out the small bottle of port.

Silence followed.

Katrinka pulled away from Jürgen, who also stared at the bottle. She rubbed her wrists. "Hauptmann Fleischer.

If I may please explain? I was told to bring these items to Monsieur Bouchard. He pays very well. I know it is wrong, but times are hard, and my aunt does what she can. She has prepared this—"

Again, Fleischer roared, "Silence!" He swung to Bouchard.

The Frenchman was sweating.

"Well, Bouchard?" Fleischer inquired softly. "Have you double-crossed us, perhaps? Do we need to remind you of the consequences?"

"*Non*. She is lying. I do not know who she is. She has been sent here. She must have the plastique."

Katrinka turned to Fleischer, pleading. "Hauptmann Fleischer, he has requested items of food, and we have supplied them. I do not know what this is about, but if I do not return with the money, my grandfather will be very angry." Touching her bruised cheek, she added, "He has been out of sorts lately." Her lip quivered.

The officer waved the bottle in her face. "Why have you hidden this drink at the bottom of your basket?"

Katrinka offered a small smile. "You see, I must pass soldiers at checkpoints. Sometimes they find no wrong in taking my food. When I return without it, my grandfather is very angry. He shouts that I have eaten the food. My cousin helped me to construct this basket. They seldom look closely, and if they take the food, there are still the best bits left."

The room became so quiet that Farr could hear the mantel clock ticking. Both Germans looked to the Frenchman. Jürgen's hand moved to his gun.

"It is a lie," Bouchard cried. "She is lying."

Discreetly, Katrinka backed away, glancing at the door. Spotting Farr in the window, her face flooded with intense relief. He signaled for her to move away, just as Fleischer looked up.

There was an explosion of movement. Grabbing his gun, Fleischer ducked for cover and fired at the same time Farr and Val burst into the room, shooting. Both Fleischer and Val fell; Fleisher's second bullet struck Farr's gun with a loud crack. Fleischer lay still, but Valentine rolled across the floor for his weapon. Farr leaped onto Jürgen, his knife drawn. In a moment, Bouchard jerked a knife from its sheath beneath his jacket. Seizing Katrinka and twisting her in front of him, he shoved it against her side.

"*Arrêtez,*" he shouted hoarsely.

The men froze.

Bouchard leaned on the table, pressing down on Katrinka. "Jürgen, get their weapons."

Jürgen grabbed Farr's knife and turned, giving Val a vicious kick in his wounded arm as he reached for the man's gun. Doubled up in pain, Val lunged for the table legs, wrenching them violently, and tripping Jürgen. Bouchard pitched back, as Katrinka fell. Farr rammed the Frenchman, and they wrestled to the ground. Jürgen surged to his feet and grabbed the bottle of port, shattering it on Farr's head, while Bouchard struggled to get his knife into position on Farr's throat. Still on the floor, Val found his gun, just as Jürgen tackled him. Screaming with fear, Katrinka seized a knife from Fleischer's belt and plunged it deep into Bouchard's back. The Frenchman shrieked as his body convulsed, then lay still.

Farr lurched upright, hauling Jürgen off Valentine, and kneed him brutally in the balls. Jürgen's legs crumpled, and he kneed him again, before spinning him around, holding the man's head in the crook of his elbow. "This is for your search methods, you son of a bitch." With a sharp crack he snapped Jürgen's neck, and the limp body slipped to the floor.

Katrinka ripped the knife from Bouchard's back and fell to her knees next to Jürgen, slashing at the man's hand and hacking each of his fingers to pieces. Farr leaned down, resting his palms on her shoulders until she quieted. Then taking the knife, he pulled her up.

Val retrieved his pistol from the floor, and the two men limped outside, Farr's arm wrapped tightly around Katrinka's trembling body.

* * *

That night, a series of explosions destroyed the Pont du Namandie Bridge. Word came back of several German casualties, as well as a few Maquis. The German troops were forced to wait for supplies and to find another route. Farr guessed London HQ would be jubilant once he sent them the message. In turn, HQ would contact the appropriate field officers in Normandy.

Their new shelter was situated between Ange de Feu and the larger town of Trois Cloches. A local farmer working with the Resistance had offered them a portion of the stable and a few outlying storage structures.

Exhausted, Farr took the radio and antenna to a distant outbuilding, and hooked into its electrical mains. Katrinka bedded down for the night in a feed storage shelter behind the stable. Both she and Farr had been given castoff clothing to replace their bloodstained ones.

A trusted medic was sent for to repair Val's arm where the bullet had grazed. Farr returned to camp after his transmissions, limping and bleeding, so the medic wrapped his ankle and applied salve to the cut on his neck. He continued to work, hobbling into the stable to clean his weapons and replace his gun. When finished, he glanced at Valentine's pallet in the corner. He was sleeping, with his arm wrapped in a large bandage and a smaller one still around his cut hand. He looked much younger than his eighteen years.

Farr realized he was hungry. He limped outside to see if the farmer's wife, Aimee, had made her promised food delivery, when Katrinka's panicked cries ripped through the stillness.

Struggling to the storage shelter, he found her sitting on a rumpled blanket in the major's arms. He was stroking her hair, and she was clinging to him.

"Katrinka."

Both turned at his voice. Releasing her, the major heaved himself up, his face gaunt.

"Can you sleep now? Do you need a tablet from the medic? It might help."

She shook her head.

Nye turned to Farr, who had not moved. "Sergeant, if you're done with the radio, I need your briefing on this evening's activities."

Still Farr did not move, grappling with his emotions and the fact that the man standing before him was his commanding officer.

Katrinka looked up, "I'm all right now. So stupid of me. Wills heard me scream."

Farr forced his muscles to relax. Avoiding the major's eyes, he followed him out. The two men walked in silence to the stable, where Nye wheeled on him.

"Bloody hell, man. I was close by and reacted. I know how it is between you two."

Farr nodded, abashed. "It's been a rough night, sir."

On entering the stable, Farr noted that Nye had fashioned a tiny office in one of the cleared-out stalls. There was a folding table and a few chairs. Both men sat.

Nye nodded to the stacks of reports. "Nicely done, don't you think? The cozy smell of horse and dung."

Before he could continue, Aimee appeared through a small doorway, carrying a basket of food. She was an older woman whose heavy makeup did not succeed in covering a large facial scar. Placing the basket on top a wooden crate, she stood back, hands on her hips. "The young lady, she is all right?"

Nye spoke reassuringly, his French fluent. "*Oui, madam.* All is well now. Thank you for the food."

"It has been a trying evening. There were bad dreams?"

"She is sleeping well now. There is no concern, *madam*."

"It is a concern to both my man and me when one screams as loudly as that one. And she will have many more before this is over. She is no good for this job. Let her go back to where she is from."

Before Nye could answer, Aimee was called away by her husband's voice.

There was an extended silence. The major cleared his throat, "It seems Bouchard was the only leak."

"He caused enough grief," replied Farr.

"Yes. And, of course he assumed it was another agent bringing the plastique. Must have been a complete shock to the man. What happened at Bouchard's? I take it she was not found with the plastique? Or her knife?"

"No. She hid them in the bushes before going in. Said she had a premonition. They grabbed her right away." He finished relating the events.

"Well, whatever it was, intuition or damned good luck, it saved her life and our hides. What was she doing with a bottle of port?"

"Her father gave it to her." He hesitated.

"Yes?"

"It was her reaction when it was over, sir. It has me worried, especially with her nightmares." He told Nye about Jürgen.

Nye winced. Refusing to meet Farr's eyes, he became very busy with loading his pipe. "So. The plastique was retrieved and delivered. The bridge has been destroyed." He paused, frowning. "I need to tell you. There was—"

Farr interrupted, "I want her out of this, sir."

"Eh? What's that?"

"She needs to stand down."

Nye stopped what he was doing and glanced at the sergeant's troubled face. "Don't reproach yourself, man. She's tougher that you give her credit for. And has a cool head, it seems."

"She needs to stand down. She's lost both a mother and a stepfather. And… the trouble with the deserters. This isn't her first nightmare."

"No, she's had them before."

Farr started.

"Always has. Used to wake up the entire ship with them. Look, you and I both know she's not the only person in this war to have disturbed dreams. God only knows how Raphael gets to sleep at night. No man will share the same room with him. I've had them. I daresay you've had a few yourself. Besides, we're going to need her." Nye sighed wearily. "There was a skirmish near the bridge tonight. Some Germans were killed, along with a few Maquis."

"Who?"

"Sébastien."

Farr jerked back. "What's that?"

"He'd gone back after the explosions, taking a message to one of the SAS members. He was caught out in the crossfire."

"He's dead?"

"Yes. The village priest will see to his mother. There will be a service in Ange de Feu in a few days' time."

Farr gave no reply. He was remembering a young boy streaking along the road dressed in racing stripes, practicing for the day he would compete in the Tour de France. Well, the race was over for him now. Christ, he was sick of this war.

"He was in the wrong place at the wrong time, Farr. There are going to be a lot more patrols roaming about in the coming days, and a lot more retaliations after this incident with Bouchard. I want Katrinka to replace Sébastien as our courier—your courier, really. It will be safer for everyone if you're moving."

Farr's mind snapped back to the conversation. Katrinka as their courier? Immediately, he grasped the unexpected consequences of this tragedy. Being fluent in French, she could rendezvous with the Maquis, coordinate drop zones, and deliver messages. She could work as a liaison between the team and safe houses. Maybe even do a bit of sabotage. She would be perfect for the job.

Farr stopped, filled with sudden remorse at his selfishness. Was he willing to put her life in jeopardy? Was he thinking of the team or himself? He sat sweating in the little horse stall, considering the risks. The image of Sylvia's battered face came back to him, and he shuddered.

Nye seemed to be reading his thoughts. "She's perfect, Farr; we both know it. As a female, she can keep a low profile and blend in, which none of us are able to do. She can move openly, where we cannot. She's smart and has strong nerves."

Farr protested. His voice sounded half-hearted even to his own ears. "Sir, I don't need to remind you that she's had no training for this."

Nye shook his head. "Look, you don't have to make up your mind immediately. We're all dead tired. I'll talk to her about it tomorrow. Let's see how it goes; I think she'll be agreeable. Your transmissions are done for the night?"

Farr nodded.

"Good." He hesitated. "Just one more bit. I've... that is, Raphael has scheduled an appointment for Katrinka."

"You mean for the—"

"Nothing to be concerned about, just to be safe."

"It's a damn good idea."

"As for the nightmare, she'll be all right."

"Yes, sir."

* * *

A short time later, Nye finished his work and put out the lamp. He stared into the darkness for a long time, troubled by Farr's story. He *did* know Katrinka. But something was off now; different and disturbing. He wondered, not for the first time, what had happened to her in that farmhouse.

He gave himself a mental shake. Whatever it was, she would come out all right. People witnessed horrible things during war, went through unspeakable, unimaginable trauma, and they came out all right in the end. She would be all right as well. He thought again of Farr. Bloody lucky man. But God help him.

* * *

After the men left, Katrinka tried to sleep, but images of the evening haunted her. Taking her blanket, she climbed up a small hill to a clearing just beyond the hut. Sitting with her knees drawn up, she wrapped the blanket around her. It was worn thin, and very soft. She stared into the star-strewn sky, willing her heart to quiet.

Her talk with Josef had stirred memories. He had been homesick, just as she was homesick. But for what home? *Le Flâneur* was her home. Ever since that bright summer morning when she and her mother had boarded it, and never looked back.

Katrinka had spent her early childhood among the sea gypsies of Burma. The Chao Le conducted their entire lives aboard small covered boats called *kabangs*. They came on land only during monsoons, when they constructed temporary housing on stilts.

She had called this limitless expanse of turquoise water her home, and knew how to gauge the soft, moist winds that trailed through the islands like gentle fingers, ruffling her hair. The swells of the sea were forever entwined and in harmony with the fluids of her body.

When she was four years old, a tall, thin-faced man with straight, dark hair and mustache had arrived in a ship. He seemed to know her mother. He was Captain Amparo of *Le Flâneur,* and when he left a few days later, they went with him.

Katrinka was entranced with the size of her new home. In warm seas she slept on deck, watching stars fall from the sky, and feeling the steady rocking of waves and thrum of engine, until this new rhythm became part of her. Sometimes at night, she heard strange moans and laughter coming from behind the cabin door, after her mother and the dark-haired captain went to bed. She was told to call him Papa, and he gave her the name Katrinka. She'd never had a name. Her mother had called her *Thamee*, the Burmese word for daughter.

The next summer, Amparo took them far across the ocean to America, and a town close to the Mexican border. It was a place of sunshine and tumbling blue seas. Papa gave her a pale-green bicycle and she learned to ride it, speeding along the sea wall past large lawns of flowers and graceful houses. At the end of town was a dazzling white hotel sprawled graciously on the shore, and just beyond that, an entire small city of gaily striped tents.

During the year when her father worked with the fleet of commercial fisherman, she and A-mah took a room in a boarding house surrounded by fragrant smelling roses. But when summer came, they would rent one of those tents for the season. Tent City had its own main street, shops, restaurants, and cafés. Katrinka would watch trained seal

82

and monkey shows with other groups of children. They would swim in Tent City's large swimming pool and ride the merry-go-round. Tent City even had an ostrich farm. But her favorite show was a horse called Paycheck. Three times a week, Paycheck would mount the steep ladder to the top of a tiny platform. Three times a week, he would plunge head first into a pool of water, popping to the surface like a cork. It thrilled Katrinka every time.

Often in the early mornings, Papa took them horseback riding out along the beach at low tide. In the evenings, there were long walks along the seawall and rowboats with colorful lanterns to take out into the calm waters of the bay. There was a large dance pavilion with an orchestra. Her mother worked there sometimes, as a singer.

Amparo obtained certain documents, and in the fall, enrolled her in a public school. When she entered the third grade, Papa gave her a book. He said the author had lived in this very town and often read to children in the park.

All of this came to an end in the winter she was eight years old. News came that Amparo's father was ill. So Katrinka packed up her book in a small knapsack, and they moved out of their room at the Cherokee Roses Boarding House. Papa set a southern course along the Mexican coast, passing through the Panama Canal, then crossing the stormy Atlantic to Porto. And somehow, they never made it back to that sun-spattered seaside town of brightly colored tents.

* * *

Farr limped to Katrinka's hut, but it was empty. Going outside, he spied her sitting cross-legged on a small rise.

"You OK now?" He sat down next to her. Exhaustion lined her face, but she gave him a shy smile.

"I came out here where I could breathe and look up at the stars."

"So, they're still up there? All's right with the world?" He hadn't felt this tongue-tied since high school.

"Isn't it beautiful."

He looked up, catching his breath. Thick clusters of brilliant, tiny lights prickled the blackness, all the way down to the horizon. It gave him a dizzying sensation.

"I used to sit on deck of *Le Flâneur*, feeling the sea surging beneath me, with the full moon coming up over black water. Straight onto me and my rice mat."

He moved a bit closer, inhaling the faint scent of her hair. It reminded him of faded roses in his mother's garden. He was so damned tired. "That sounds nice."

"I felt part of it all. I felt safe. On *Le Flâneur*, and under those stars, I felt it was OK, even if there is nothing else."

There was a sadness in her voice, and he let his arm fall around her shoulders. When she turned, he kissed her.

She drew away. "You never told me your name."

He hesitated at the breach in security, but what the hell. He knew her name. She knew Nye's name; soon they'd be one big cozy family. "It's Wolfe."

"Wolf?"

He spelled it. "My mom loved Mozart. My full name is Wolfgangus, but you will never, never call me that."

"Is she…?"

"She's dead."

"I'm sorry."

He shrugged. "It was a long time ago."

"So, your father raised you?"

"I guess he did his best. He drank."

Why was he telling her all this? It was better to forget. The old man was dead now, his last act of violence self-inflicted. They'd buried him next to Farr's mother in the town churchyard. Their graves just far enough apart so that if his father's raging arms should thrust from the earth, he would be unable to harm the gentle woman slumbering next to him.

He kissed her again, with sudden urgency.

She shook her head. "I am so tired."

He pulled back, feeling incredibly stupid. "I can hold you."

"Yes, Wolfe, please hold me. Hold me tight."

He held her tight, tucking her body into the curve of his side and wrapping his arms around her. They were both asleep in moments. He was too tired to even be hard.

* * *

The next day, Nye called Katrinka into his cramped office. She'd slept late. He stood up when she entered, motioning for her to take a seat.

"I have something here for you." He pulled an object from a basket on the floor and grinned as her face lit up. "It's your knapsack. Raphael found it, and your necklace too."

She took the knapsack, quickly undoing the buckle, and pulled out a tattered book. She placed this on her lap as he handed her the necklace, draping the delicate chain over her fingers. A miniature silver vial and a medallion of a running boy were suspended from it.

"My jasmine!" She turned away from him, lifting her hair. "Can you help me?"

Leaning across the table, Nye fumbled awkwardly with the clasp, very aware of the vulnerability of that small neck. He managed to fasten the hook, just above the tattoo of a tiny swallow, etched in the curve of her shoulder. He had an identical but larger one on his upper arm.

"And my book, remember? You used to read this to me on the ship." She held up the worn copy.

"You made everyone read that to you. It was a real blessing when you could finally do it yourself. I can still recite parts of that story by heart."

She laughed and rose from her seat. "Thank you, Wills."

Nye stood as well, speaking quickly. "Trinka, are you all right now?"

"Yes. Quite all right."

"Good. Excellent." He hesitated. "I want to tell you… that is, I need to let you know. Raphael made an appointment for you early tomorrow, for what we'd talked about. He can take you. He has the morning clear."

It had been one hell of a job to find those few hours free.

Her smile faded. "Yes, of course."

"Right, that's settled then. Come back this afternoon, and we can go over things."

She nodded and walked out of the door into the sunlight.

* * *

Farr had spent the morning decoding in one of the distant outbuildings and then sending out coded messages to London with details for the upcoming drop. The camp was expecting a large amount of ammo with the delivery, and HQ needed the specific coordinates. The supplies would be distributed evenly among the small bands of Maquis.

He'd just finished when Katrinka showed up, standing in his doorway. They both stood, grinning at one another.

Jesus, if he was going to get hard just looking at her...

He spied the small pack. "What have you got there?"

"Oh, my knapsack. Wills remembered and has given it to me." She sat down on a small stool, and Farr dragged his chair over, sitting close.

"He also gave me my necklace. My mother had one just like this." She lifted the silver chain from where it nestled between her breasts. Carefully releasing the vial's diminutive plug, she waved the opening under her nose and let out an appreciative sigh. "Smell it."

He took a whiff. The aroma wafted into his nostrils; dazzlingly intense and sensual. "It's wonderful," he admitted. "What is it?"

"Egyptian jasmine. My Papa Emerson was in Cairo once and came across a peddler selling small vials of oil. He told us these oils kept their fragrance for thousands of years. He selected jasmine because of my mother's name. Yujana means 'jasmine' in Burmese. She was given the name because of her fair hair."

"How'd your mother come to have fair hair?"

"Her mother had a British lover. A missionary."

"What happened to them?"

"They died." She did not elaborate.

Taking another whiff, she stoppered the vial. "I have to be careful not to waste any vapors, so I don't open it often."

He grinned, but saw she was serious. "And this?"

Hanging on the same chain as the vial was the wafer-thin silver medallion of a boy, running on tiptoe. He hooked it with his index finger, examining the details.

Instead of answering, Katrinka pulled out the book, waving it in front of him with glee. The cover was smudged and worn, and Farr could not make out its title.

"Papa gave me this when we lived in Coronado, near San Diego. Have you heard of it?"

"San Diego? Yeah. There's a naval training base out there. So why the book?"

"In this place, Coronado, a man once lived there who was a famous author. He loved children, and he wrote this book for them. He gave a copy to Papa's friend. But when she left, she also left the book. Later, Papa gave it to me."

Farr took the book, flipping its pages.

"I learned to speak English listening to Papa read it to me every evening. Do you know it? There is a young girl and her dog. She gets lost from her home and everyone she loves. So she begins a long journey, to find her way back again."

Farr looked at the cover, squinting at the title, *The Wonderful Wizard of Oz*. "Son of a gun. I read this when I was a kid."

"*Did* you?"

"Yeah. It was a favorite for a long time, till I discovered Tarzan." Farr was embarrassed.

To regain composure, he again lifted the small medallion from its chain around her neck. "And this?" he asked.

"Oh, that one. It's—" but their conversation was interrupted. Raphael's rusted Citroën turned into the camp, carrying supplies, and they went out to help unload. Farr hoped for Katrinka's sake, there would be food.

* * *

Later that evening, the major again called Katrinka into his office. Farr watched her go, and when she came out, he could tell she'd been crying. Nye had not wasted any time about it.

"Are you OK? What was that about?"

She tried to brush past him, but he stopped her. She turned to him in anger. "How can you stand this all? How can you bear it?"

He dropped her arm. "What are you talking about?"

"Did you know about Sébastien?"

"He told me last night."

"Did he also tell you what he wants me to do?"

Farr nodded.

"What did you say?"

"I told him I wanted you out of it."

She walked to the stable door and gazed out to the pasture. "You know I can't do that." She looked back at him. "And you know why."

"Yes. I know why."

He hated the part of himself that rejoiced. It seemed so callous. So cruel. They were in it together now, her entire trusting soul rested in his hands. It would be up to him to keep her safe.

She smiled up at him. "So, where do I begin?"

5

NYE SAT HER DOWN THE NEXT DAY AFTER SHE returned from the clinic, explaining her job as their courier. He gave her a pistol, showed her how to use it, and took her outside for some practice shots. After watching her first few efforts, he told her he hoped to God she'd never have to use it.

Katrinka received a new set of identification papers. Her cover would be that of a tutor, servicing scattered farms in the area. The school had been closed for quite a while, and the community wanted an instructor for their children.

Nye told her of a safe house several kilometers away. The farm was owned by a woman; code name Lucienne, who lived there with her child, Alain, and her grandmother, Jeanne. Katrinka would deliver messages and supplies under the guise of tutoring her son.

* * *

She began a few days later with her new identification, along with a map of the area. The team had moved to a roughly structured farm storage building, far off the main roads, and surrounded by thick trees and bushes.

After a meager breakfast, she set off to Lucienne's on her bicycle. In her basket she carried a box of grenades, packed tightly inside a large sack of potatoes. Lucienne would distribute them. She passed other women on the road, some on bicycles, some walking, and some riding in horse carts. There were no checkpoints, and the few soldiers she saw didn't stop to bother her. She wondered if any of the women she passed carried similar packages.

Katrinka arrived at the small farm mid-morning. Pedaling into the yard, she found Lucienne hanging up a load of washing on the clothesline. Lucienne's son, Alain, was playing near the smokehouse, swinging from a knotted rope attached to a tree. He would lean back and swoop to the ground, then gather speed and sail up again, his sturdy little legs pointed skyward. She was struck by the serenity of the scene. It was perfect cover.

As Lucienne approached, Katrinka noticed a hard look in the woman's dark eyes. She had a masculine face, deeply angled with heavy brows. Her hands were graceful, but chapped and red from the rough farm work. She wore a faded checked dress covered with a stained apron.

They exchanged certain coded phrases, and the hardness disappeared from the woman's face. Lucienne took the large sack from the basket. "Please, come inside. I have just made a broth."

With a small whoop, Alain hurtled himself from the rope, mid-swing, and scrambled after his mother.

Katrinka followed them into the farmhouse through a cool, flagged passageway that led to a sunlit kitchen. The heavy aroma of sweet onions and garlic filled the air, and her mouth watered. Lucienne's grandmother Jeanne sat in a shaft of sunlight at a large wooden table, peeling eggs. As Lucienne made the introductions, the old woman looked up and nodded to Katrinka.

Alain seized a book from a small basket on the floor and tugged at Jeanne's hand. "Read me a book, Mémé," he demanded.

The grandmother smiled and rose from the table, leading Alain into the front room.

Katrinka helped Lucienne serve the soup into two large bowls, and the women sat down to chat. The soup was very hot, and Katrinka waited for the liquid to cool.

Lucienne's husband had been sent off to work in the German labor camps, and she had no idea if he was still alive. She spent her time working as a liaison between the Jed teams and the Maquis, coordinating drop zones, delivering supplies, and sometimes housing downed pilots. It was a dangerous job, but the woman carried an aura of calmness that Katrinka found incredibly soothing. If only she could have such peace. She felt herself relaxing for the first time since entering the country.

The kitchen felt light and airy, with large, open windows. Blue-and-red-painted china rested in rough-sided cabinets. There was a pump at the sink, and various gleaming pots and pans hung from the wall. A scattering of wooden toys lay in a patch of sunlight on the floor. In the corner was a small table, with schoolbooks for Alain. He was just seven years old, and Lucienne said he much preferred to be outside swinging from the tree rope than inside the house studying.

Katrinka marveled at the normalcy of it all, and wondered what it would be like to have her whole life upended violently and under the occupation of an enemy.

She admired Lucienne's ability to keep her home life as ordinary as possible for Alain and Jeanne.

Katrinka drained the last bit of soup from her bowl. After making a quick trip to the outdoor bathroom, she requested a few items from Lucienne, who nodded in sympathy. Before leaving, she gave Katrinka three messages that needed delivering to another team, several kilometers away.

* * *

Katrinka did not arrive back at camp until after dark, and then had to find Wills. She knew there would be no proper sanitary supplies needed for her menstruation. The most she could hope for would be a few surgical bandages to help absorb the flow. She would ask Wills.

She found him seated in a corner of the dimly lit shed, studying papers. He looked up and smiled as she entered. When she made her request he reached out for her hand, and his grip hurt.

"Trinka, sweetheart. Thank God." Recovering himself he dropped her hand. His face turned a deep red.

"Absolutely. I'll check with Raphael in the morning to see—"

"If there is nothing available, Wills, it's not a problem. Lucienne told me what she uses, but I thought I would check with you as well."

Nye seemed relieved. "Of course. In the meantime, are you…"

"Yes, I'm fine. I borrowed some handmade ones from Lucienne."

She could tell this kind of talk embarrassed him. After wishing him a goodnight, she turned and went outside. Wills had offered her a place in a corner of the small building, partitioned by a blanket, but she preferred to sleep out in the open. It was dry, and the air mingling with the trees had a clean smell to it.

She had not seen Wolfe at all. She knew messages from London came at night, and these messages had to be decoded, which could take hours.

She found a spot that was well cushioned with grass and lay down, wrapping the bedroll around her. As her eyes adjusted to the darkness, she stared up at the constellations, reflecting on Wills' reaction to her news. She also felt immense relief. It had been a dreaded fear that had always been in the back of her mind since the attack.

She'd tried telling herself that she would love the baby, no matter what. A child had no control over its parentage. But could she have held it? Nurtured and suckled it? Could she have looked into its eyes, knowing what she had done to its father? She wondered if she could have borne it.

* * *

The following week, Katrinka set out on her bicycle to Lucienne's with information about a midnight supply drop. The team had moved several times since the debacle at Bouchard's farm. German checkpoints and retaliatory raids were escalating, and she sensed an edginess to their camp despite its remote location. Farr was away working the radio, and Nye had gone with Raphael to organize the evening's drop with the local Maquis. A brief cloudburst that morning had turned everything into a pit of puddled mud.

On the way to Lucienne's, she met Jeanne coming back from the market, and the two women pedaled to the farmhouse together. As they neared the house, Katrinka noted the darkened windows. Lucienne should be expecting her, but there was no sign of anyone. From the corner of her eye, she saw lights flickering inside the old smokehouse.

Hairs rose along the back of her neck, as if by static electricity. Quickly dismounting, she hid her bike in the bushes and motioned for Jeanne to do the same. The two women crouched in the darkness. A disturbing emptiness surrounded the place, so the scream that followed was all the more shocking.

Pulling out her pistol, Katrinka flew silently over the ground to the smokehouse, with Jeanne following close behind. A small figure hung from the rope swing. It was Alain. He was dead, with the rope still wrapped tightly around his neck. Stifling a sob, Jeanne pushed past her and together they lowered the little body to the ground. Jeanne knelt, covering him quickly with her sweater.

A loud moan jerked Katrinka to her feet, trembling in fear. She raised a finger to her lips and indicated for Jeanne to stay with the body. Creeping to the side of the smokehouse, she leaned against the wall and peered inside.

There were a few lit lamps, and in the flickering light she saw Lucienne; her body was suspended from the floor, dangling from protruding meat hooks. She moaned again; it was a horrible sound. A wave of dizziness swept over Katrinka, and she fought it down. Lucienne was staring at her from across the floor.

They'd made a mess of the woman, and she was bleeding heavily. Katrinka ran over, dragging a small stool. She dropped her pistol and attempted to lift Lucienne from the metal hooks, but could not support her weight. She was tearing flesh. A black sickness swarmed up through her, and she began to shake.

"Stop. Please. Where is my son? He ran when they came."

Katrinka hesitated. She knew the woman was dying, and there was nothing to be done about it. "He was hiding in the trees. He is safe. He is well."

Lucienne's eyes were luminous in the dim light. "He is dead. The soldier ran after him, and I heard his cry. Tell me."

When Katrinka replied, her voice was gentle. "Yes, he is dead."

Lucienne's body seemed to shrink into itself, turning a grayish hue. "I told them nothing. Nothing."

Katrinka roused herself. "I'm getting you down from here."

Lucienne shook her head. "Take your gun. Please. Take it and…"

Realizing what she was asking, Katrinka jerked back, tripping over the stool. "No."

"Please."

"*No.*"

"Please. Alain will be needing me. He will be waiting for me."

The two women stared at one another. Finally, Katrinka picked up the gun. She checked the chamber, then looked at Lucienne. The woman's eyes were calm and steady. Katrinka raised the pistol, her hands trembling. Then with a sharp cry, she flung it to the ground.

"I can't do it. I *can't.*"

There was a sound next to her, and she swung around, choking on a scream. It was the grandmother. She watched as Jeanne picked up the pistol and walked over to Lucienne, speaking to her in a soft voice. Katrinka covered her ears and turned her face away. She heard the crack of gunshot, and her legs gave way. She hunched over, pressing her palms against her eyes.

She did not rise when the grandmother left, nor later when she returned with two young men. Somehow, the men got the body down from those terrible hooks. She heard their feet as they shuffled across the floor and out the doorway, taking the body away. A few minutes later, she heard them again, just outside the door. They were taking Alain now.

The grandmother returned and sat down beside her. She could hear the woman's breathing. It seemed to Katrinka that there were long, struggling pauses between each breath.

She sat up then, putting her arms around the old woman's frail shoulders, and they clung to one another.

She asked Katrinka over and over again, in a monotonous voice that held no inflection whatsoever, "*Qu'est-il arrivé aux hommes de ce monde.*" What has happened to the men of this world.

* * *

The news spread fast. Farr had just returned to the camp after sending a hasty message to abort the drop. He paced up and down the soggy ground. What the hell had he been thinking to drag Katrinka into this? He continued to pace, his boots making squelching sounds in the mud.

He finally saw her, a dark shadow on the path, moving slowly. He ran up and put his arm around her shoulders, but she flung him away.

"Get your hands off me," she hissed.

Farr drew back, shocked. He waited for her to say something else, but she stumbled on, leaving him alone in the dark, staring after her.

Katrinka made her way out and away from the makeshift camp. She crawled into her sleeping bag and lay on her back, staring up at the black sky. But the stars seemed too far away tonight. They were just a smattering of bright, cold dots, suspended in a void. Why had she ever thought this was a beautiful world. That a basic goodness ruled the universe.

She had been wrong. The universe did not care at all. Life was a string of unexplainable events, lumped together until you died. You were slammed from one episode to the next, trying to keep afloat, until a wave came that was just too big. And it would sweep over you, and you would go under for good.

She could see that wave far out to sea. It was coming for her.

* * *

Life went on. Jeanne fled from the farm and went south to live with her sister. The team scrambled to find a new camp. Katrinka missed Lucienne with a dull, heavy ache. She missed the peace of the farm, the warmth of the kitchen, and a child's scattered toys lying upon its sunlit floorboards.

Katrinka took the events of Lucienne and Alain and locked them up tightly in another box inside her heart. She wondered how much longer her boxes would stay locked.

A few days after the incident, Raphael dropped a message off with the major. The test for venereal disease had come back clear. Nye thanked God that whatever else had happened to her in the farmhouse, she'd not have to deal with that. He went out to tell her the news. She was not back from a delivery, and after running into Farr, Nye told him instead. He pretended not to see the man's face light up.

Farr worked late that night, and when finished, he hurried to Katrinka's hut. He was not quite sure of his welcome. On the few times they'd spoken since Lucienne's death, she'd been moody and distant.

The structure was dark and smelled of pig. He found her outside, with her bedroll spread across the ground. She was standing on a rise, with her back to him and her arms crossed over her breasts. The wind sifted through the tree leaves, giving them a low, restless sound. Thunder rumbled in the distance. He hesitated, then sat down on the bedroll. Pulling a cigarette from his shirt pocket, he lit it, watching her.

She glanced back at him, then looked away. Her eyes were dark, and the shadows under them heavy.

After a few minutes, he spoke. "Trink?"

She turned.

"Do you remember the day we met? At the farmhouse?"

Her body tensed.

"You never talked about it. What happened, I mean."

"No."

"I went in after the shooting, when you were outside. I saw the man. The one on the bed. Did you...? I don't blame you. Did he—"

Her eyes seemed blank, but something was moving behind them. "What are you trying to say, Wolfe?"

Doggedly, he pressed on. "What happened?"

She returned to the bedroll and lay down next to him, closing her eyes. "I don't want to talk about it."

He smoked for a while, studying the sky, every nerve in his body on red alert at her closeness. After a few minutes, he flung the stub away and settled on the blanket next to her.

She was shaking.

He was furious with himself. Furious with what had been done to her, and furious that he could not find the right words.

"Trink."

"Shhh." She turned and rolled on top of him, brushing the hair back from his face. Her breasts were soft and pressed against his chest, inflaming him with their warmth.

He wrapped his arms around her, his voice rough. "Never mind. I was just trying to make sense of it all, but there is no reason. It doesn't matter why. I don't care anymore. I would've cut the bastard up myself. I would've…"

Moonlight turned her tears to bits of glass. She shook her head, tracing a finger around his lips. "Kiss me, Wolfe."

He gripped her head between his hands, kissing her hard. She tasted salty but sweet. It made him a little crazy. Then he remembered and pulled back. "The test result came in."

She pushed up on her elbows, studying him. Finally, she asked, "Am I good?"

"*We're* good."

She was silent a few moments. "I was so angry."

"I know."

"I *hated* them. I hated what they did to me." She was crying.

"It's over now."

She drew a hand across her eyes, trying to see his expression in the darkness. "Do you want—"

"Do you?"

"More than anything, Wolfe."

He held her face in his hands again, kissing her. Kissing her hair, her eyes, and her throat. She was fumbling with his buttons. He raised his hips as she slipped his trousers down, releasing his erection. He lifted her skirt. He did not take time to consider a condom. He did not take time to pull down her panties, but pushed aside the thin material. Then with a headlong rush he was inside her, where it was wet and hot.

* * *

Later Katrinka woke, with Wolfe nuzzling her. He'd taken off the rest of her clothing, as well as his own. His muscled body gleamed in the moonlight

She pushed him over and sat up, straddling him, still half asleep. He cupped her breasts as she placed her hands on his shoulders. With eyes closed, she slowly rotated her hips, feeling him harden beneath her, wanting her. She raised herself up and slid him into her, squeezing and contracting her muscles around his shaft. She would keep him there forever. Her body would drink him in, and his fluids would flush out everything that had gone before. She kept her eyes closed as tears slid down her cheeks, falling onto their bodies like soft rain.

It was early morning when they finally drifted off to sleep, still clinging to one another, Wolfe still inside her. And for Katrinka, a few more of the invisible scars slipped away.

* * *

Several mornings later, Katrinka woke to gunshots in the distance. Raphael and Valentine were out scouting for a drop zone, so the girl jammed equipment into rucksacks while Farr and Nye stripped the camp in seconds. Throwing everything into the Citroën, Farr jumped behind the wheel, and they tore down the road toward the gunfire.

In less than a minute, they came upon an ambush between several Maquis and a group of five German soldiers. It was over very quickly, with the Germans lying dead or dying on the ground. The Maquis sprinted into the road, inspecting the bodies for weapons and papers.

A small dog with a bent ear bounded from the bushes, barking at the men. It ran up to one of the bodies and pawed it frantically. With horror, Katrinka recognized the dog and Josef, the boy from the roadblock. He lay stretched out in the dust, his eyes wide with pain and fear.

Katrinka ran over to him and knelt down, cradling him in her lap. His chest was bleeding profusely.

Josef whispered, and she leaned over to hear.

"*Mein liebling*, we meet again."

"Don't try to talk, we'll send for a medic. You'll be—"

"Rolf. Will you…?"

"Yes. Yes, of course. Please don't talk." She looked up to Farr. "*Help* him."

"Thank you again for the apple and—"

"Please…"

With a small, almost inaudible hiss of breath, the boy died.

"*Josef?*" Katrinka's voice cracked as she bent over him, her tears mingling in his warm blood.

102

The major strode over, his rifle leveled.

Casting a wary eye to the Maquis, Farr placed a hand on her shoulder.

"Trink, we need to—"

She flung him off. Emptying the pockets of the boy's tunic, she found a single white glove. It was small with soiled fingertips, smelling faintly of scent. She took this, as well as a torn and mud-spattered letter. Reaching in again, her fingers brushed against a rough-edged object. Pulling it out, she stared at the dried apple core in her palm for a moment, fingering the browning teeth marks still visible in the pulp. She returned it to his tunic with great care.

Stuffing the glove and letter into her skirt pocket, she placed his head gently on the earth and stood up. Her clothing was streaked with blood, and her face pale.

Farr stepped around her and pulled the boy's jacket over his face.

A young Maquis had been watching, and he now sprang forward.

"*Collaborateur!*" he spat. "*Putain!*" He struck her full in the face and knocked her down.

In an instant, she swirled to her feet, knife in her hand, but Farr swatted the boy with a blow that sent him sprawling in the dust. The remaining Maquis turned from their grisly inspection, shouting angrily and weapons drawn.

"Get that girl out of here! We do not take kindly to *collaborateurs*." This was echoed by the others, "A *collaborateur*. A traitor. She needs to be shot." There was menace in the air.

"Steady, Farr." Nye put a hand on the sergeant's arm.

"*Arrêtez!*" An older Maquis held up his hands. He walked across the road to pull the young man up, grasping him by the shoulder. "You want to be a man, but you act without thought. Go back to camp." He turned his attention to the others. "We must leave at once, there will be retaliation for this act. Take their weapons and go. We have done enough today."

The men slowly lowered their knives and rifles. Although angered, they were aware that the Jed team supplied their guns and ammunition. They did not want trouble. Within moments, they disappeared into the trees.

The boy pulled away from the old man's grasp, wiping his cheek where the blow had cut. Avoiding their eyes, he strode across the road, following the others.

The old man turned to Nye. "He is young. He was not supposed to have come. It is a terrible thing when children are involved." After nodding to the men, he paused and gave Katrinka a cool, calculating stare. Then he too, disappeared into the trees.

* * *

Farr let out a deep sigh. The dog had returned and was quietly licking the dead boy's hand, nuzzling him with small, distressed sounds. Katrinka sheathed her knife and stumbled across the road, gathering the animal into her arms. She turned, facing both men.

Nye pointed to the body. "Did you know this soldier?"

Katrinka nodded. "We met at a roadblock. This is his dog. I am taking him with me." She did not ask permission.

With astonishment, Farr noticed Nye move to block her way, his eyes hard.

"Katrinka, put the dog down."

"No. He is coming with me."

"Get into the goddamn car. You're not bringing that animal."

"I am! I will!"

"Major—"

"Keep the hell out of this, Sergeant."

Farr stared.

"I'm taking him with me. You stood by and let the boy… you let him *die*."

Something in Nye snapped. He lunged, jerking the animal from her arms, and threw it into the road. The dog yelped in pain, and Katrinka cried out.

"The dog stays. Get into the bloody car. Now." He grabbed her arm.

Farr sprang forward, his face contorting in anger, but Katrinka jerked away.

"How *dare* you." Raising her hand, she slapped the major with all her might.

There was a stunned silence. Nye stepped back, bringing a hand to his cheek. Except for the red imprint, his face was white.

"To *hell* with you," she hissed. Spinning on her heel, she gathered up the dog and ran away from them, down the road.

Farr turned on the major, his eyes blazing. "Sir, you were—"

"Shut the fuck up, Farr. Get in and drive."

"Fuck you. I'm going after her."

"You do and you'll find yourself court-martialed, Sergeant."

Farr turned in the road.

"We've been compromised. We need to move, *now*. I'll send a messenger out to notify the SAS men. They'll bring her back."

Farr felt an overwhelming and helpless anger. He knew that men's lives depended on what he did or did not do.

The major's voice was curt. "She may not be safe. They need to get her quickly."

"I'll use the field telephone. It'll be faster."

It was illegal use of communications, and they both knew it, but Nye nodded.

"Right. Let's go."

* * *

Their new camp was further from Ange de Feu, on the site of a partially bombed-out schoolhouse. Farr moved into one small room with his bedroll and set up his antennae, plugging it into the electrical mains. He stayed up the rest of the night waiting, but she did not come back.

The next day was quiet. Valentine and Raphael were expected, and the major stayed downstairs, working on reports. Upstairs, Farr concentrated on coding messages and sending them out, keeping the transmission time short so they could not be traced. He slept for a few hours in the afternoon, and woke up groggy and disorientated. More reports were waiting to be coded and transmitted. He got to work.

Downstairs, Nye had finished his reports and was sitting at a small folding table, head in his hands. What had happened? Everything occurred so quickly. Her words reverberated in his brain, "*You let him die!*" Then it was a mother's tormented voice, and a mother's anguished face. *"You let her die!"*

He sprang to his feet and began to pace. It seemed to him that the entire room was flooded in brackish light. Long-buried memories rose up, floating through the air with their phantasmal cries and reproachful glances.

The hair on his skin rose, as if caused by a cold wind. What time was it? Midnight. Jesus, hadn't they found her? Farr would have told him. There were no messages. Had the Maquis waited in the woods, then grabbed her? He'd behaved like a lunatic. The look in her eyes when she struck him. Where was she?

It was late when Farr completed his transmissions. Pulling off the headphones, he grabbed his jacket and weapon, and ran downstairs. He was going out to find her. He'd found her once and, by God, he'd do it again. Noticing a light at the end of the hall, he wondered if Nye was still awake.

Slipping outside, he almost stumbled over a small figure sitting on the steps in the darkness. He gave a sharp grunt as Katrinka emerged from the shadows, holding the dog. She stood regarding him in the dim light, but she did not speak.

Farr stared at her. When he spoke, his voice was rough. "I didn't know if they would find you. I didn't know if you were safe."

"I had nowhere to go. One of your SAS patrols found me. I spent the night at their camp. They were afraid the Maquis might be looking for me, so we waited. They contacted Pascal, who located your new camp and brought me here."

"I was coming after you, Katrinka. I had to do my job, but then I was coming after you."

She quavered, "I am so cold."

He moved fast, putting his arm around her shoulders, and guided her into the building. He led her up the stairs and into a small room. Her knapsack was there, and he'd found an old mattress to put under her bedroll. Placed beside it on the floor was a cracked vase filled with wildflowers. She sank onto the mattress and Rolf jumped from her arms, burrowing next to her.

"Is Wills here?"

"Yes, he's doing reports. It's pretty busy right now."

She nodded.

"Trink, what happened?"

"With Wills?"

"Yes, that too."

"Lie down with me, and we can get warm."

"In a minute. I need to let the major know you're back."

"Why should he care?"

"He was worried about you Trink, I need to let him know. I'll be back in a few minutes. Get into bed."

Katrinka had undressed down to her slip when Wolfe returned. She watched as he took off his boots, and threw his jacket and trousers onto the floor, leaving his shorts on. She knew he had a fear of being caught by surprise. He hardly ever took them off, even when they were in bed together.

He slipped onto the mattress beside her, and she wrapped an arm and leg around him, resting her head on his shoulder. With a sneeze, Rolf curled into a ball at their feet.

Farr commented, "I've never seen the major angry with you."

"I think it must have been what I said."

"What was that?"

She sighed. "Before I met him, Wills had a dog. He'd found it in the marketplace in Bristol. It was a straggly, gray thing with a broken tail. He named him Billie. He brought Billie with him when he came back to the ship to work for Papa again.

"One summer, right before the war, he invited his fiancée and her mother to join us on the ship. Billie was old then, and having a hard time."

"Wills—I mean the major—was engaged?"

"Yes, Sofia was a Spanish archeologist, an intern really. They met on one of Emerson's supply runs into Spain. Wills brought Sofia and her mother onboard *Le Flâneur* that summer. They were going to Marseilles to be married.

"One night, there was a bad storm. Sofia was on deck looking for Billie. A big wave hit *Le Flâneur*, and Billie was washed over the side. Sofia ran to the railing, screaming, and we all came running. Another wave washed onto the deck and pulled her in as well. Wills vaulted over the side before anyone could stop him. You could hear him calling above the wind and waves. Calling and calling her name. My father and Santos finally got him back in the raft, hours later. He was half-drowned.

"They never found Sofia. Or Billie. Grief destroyed her mother. She accused Wills of letting her daughter die."

Wolfe was silent.

"That night, there was no noise from his cabin. I was worried he would... I tried to comfort him, but he sent me away. He stayed in his cabin for two days. When he came out, he told my father to drop him off at the nearest port. He said he was through with the sea."

"That must have been tough."

"I don't believe he has ever quite gotten over it."

Wolfe was quiet for so long, she thought he must have gone to sleep. Then he asked, "Trink?"

"Yes?"

"Who was this Josef? How did he know you?"

She turned away from him then, facing the wall.

"Katrinka?"

"He was a soldier I met on the road. We shared an apple."

He was silent, waiting, but she said nothing more. He moved closer, sliding one arm under her and wrapping the other around her breasts, pulling her into the curve of his body.

After a minute, she snuggled her backside into him, his hardness pressing against her in a way that was comforting. She felt herself growing moist in response.

She murmured, "Do you want to have sex?"

"Yes."

"I'm too sleepy, but you can do it if you like."

"You sure?"

There was a smile in her reply. "If you do all the work."

Wolfe didn't respond. Leaning away from her, he reached across the floor to his pack. She heard a rustling of foil, and then he was fumbling with the fly on his shorts, rolling the rubber down his penis. He pulled her close again, slipping one hand up between her legs, while keeping the other wrapped around her breasts. Then he pushed his way into her slick wetness. He was kissing the back of her neck with his warm, scratchy lips. His hot breath on her skin, and the friction of his cock moving in and out gave Katrinka a tingly thrill. She decided she was not that sleepy. She lifted her upper knee a bit, giving him a better angle, and he pushed more deeply into her. She shivered with pleasure.

110

After a few short movements, he made a half-strangled, inarticulate sound, his fingers splaying convulsively across her breasts. Then it was over, and he slipped out of her.

"Are you *done*?"

"All done."

"But I was just getting started. What about *me*?"

"You said you were sleepy. You said I could do it if I did all the work. You said—"

"But now I'm awake—"

"Baby, it's over for a while."

She laughed as he wrapped both arms back around her, kissing the nape of her neck and nibbling her ear.

She asked, "Did it feel good?"

"It was good," he replied thickly. "Damn good."

She gave a small purr of pleasure and nestled back into him. They slept.

* * *

Later, Nye knocked on the open door to Katrinka's room. He watched as Farr got up from the bedding, dressed only in shorts. The two soldiers stared tensely at one another in the dim light. He could simply order the man out or Farr could refuse him entry, and it would all go to hell very quickly.

Farr turned for his boots and trousers, and quietly took his leave.

Nye's voice was hoarse. "Thank you, Sergeant."

Katrinka sat up on the mattress. She watched him approach, her eyes raw.

"May I talk with you a moment, Trinka."

She gathered the dog in her arms as he drew near. "Get out. I *hate* you."

He flinched at her words, but he did not move.

"You grabbed Rolf... you *threw* him."

"I was wrong to do it."

Her eyes watered and she swiped them furiously. "You grabbed me and swore at me. Don't you *ever*—"

"No. I won't."

He stared down at her, but he was unable to speak. Unable to move. So he stood there, arms dangling at his sides, a stocky man with graying hair and a grieving face.

He saw the anger vanish from her eyes, replaced by tears. "Trinka. I—"

"Oh Wills, I don't know why I said that to you. It wasn't your fault Josef died. And it wasn't your fault Sofia died either. You couldn't have done anything."

He hunched down next to her then; a large man on a small bed. "I've never understood it, you know."

"I know."

He bent his head, digging his fingernails into his hairline, drawing blood. She pulled them away.

"I looked and looked. It was so cold... so damn dark. I couldn't find them." His words came in convulsed spurts. "I let her die."

"That isn't true. You did everything you could. We almost lost you as well." She rocked him in her arms as he struggled to get his breathing under control.

Eventually he sat up, wiping his eyes with the back of his hand.

She handed him a handkerchief from his shirt pocket, and he blew his nose loudly, causing Rolf to dive for the covers.

"Farr gave me hell. Was threatening to go AWOL to go and find you."

"I would not have wanted him disciplined for my actions."

"We sent out a message to a nearby SAS team. I was worried there might be retaliation against you by the Maquis."

"For Josef."

"He was a German. And he seemed to know you."

"I told you. He stopped me on the road. He was hungry, and we shared an apple."

"He was a German. These French have seen—"

Her voice tightened. "Yes, I can imagine what they have seen."

She shifted her arms, and part of the rumpled bedroll slipped from the mattress. It smelled of recent sex, and it angered him.

"I think he was hungry for something more than food. And I think you gave it to him." *Jesus*, was he really saying these things to her?

Her brows snapped together and she gave him a sharp push, apparently all sympathy gone.

"Yes, and why shouldn't he have it?" she cried. "I was his first, and now his last. Look at you. So *easy* for you to sit there and condemn. You, who've made love your whole life, and will make more love. One time. That's all he had. He knew he was going to die, he told me so. Besides, I wanted…" She stopped.

"What did you want?"

She turned away but he held her shoulders, peering into her face.

His voice was soft now. "Tell me, Trinka."

She faced him, but did not meet his eyes. "I just wanted… I wanted to make sure it was all right again. With men."

Nye drew back. He could see then that he'd failed her in the worst possible way. He should have immediately sent her to the village doctor like Farr suggested. She should have had someone to talk to, perhaps another woman. He'd made a mess of it completely.

And Josef. The boy had told her she was his first. She probably was. Now he was dead, with nothing but a letter, a small white glove, and a bedraggled animal left behind. She had seen his need, not only for the food, but for something much deeper. Yet here he was, slinging sex at her, like some soiled bed sheet.

He cupped her chin in his hand, and the hair swung back from her face. "My darling, I am so sorry. You were right. You always are, in matters of the heart. It seems I shall never learn."

She looked at him then, those startling blue eyes now warmed with love. "*Dear* Wills. You have always understood me, haven't you?"

He squeezed her hand. He'd no right to have her back, but it seems he did. He rose and walked silently from the room.

6

AFTER A FEW ROUGH WEEKS OF ASSIMILATION, Katrinka settled in as Farr's courier. Being skilled at blending in, she attracted little notice. Carrying messages hidden in the handles of her bicycle, she continued to rendezvous with the Maquis hiding in the surrounding hills. At other times she helped to find safe houses for agents and downed pilots. Her job on the road involved risks every time she faced a roadblock or was stopped for a spot check. During longer missions, she would be out until late in the evening, or occasionally for a few days, returning to wherever their camp had moved to. Sometimes, there was a real bed for her in a room in the house of a Resistance member. Other times, she curled up in the back of a farm outbuilding or under the stars in a makeshift shelter.

Valentine worked to keep their battered equipment running, and he would often send her out to pick up much-needed parts. Nye and Raphael plotted with the Maquis to make devastating blows against communication and railway lines, supply depots, and passing German troops.

There was always danger of the mobile German radio direction finder stations, tracing Farr's whereabouts, so he kept his radio operations far away from the team's camp.

An RDF could pick up a signal and track down their exact location in less than fifteen minutes. It was necessary to keep moving, and imperative to keep the messages short. Nye and his team had to be ready in an instant to take up whatever equipment they had and find a new location. Farr called it his PFFU strategy: plan for fuck-ups.

One afternoon, Farr came in with newly transcribed messages to find Nye studying a report, his brow furrowed. He glanced up and indicated Farr should sit.

"There was another incident last week, close to Trois Cloches. The Gestapo raided a safe house killing all the occupants."

Farr felt the familiar chill of apprehension. "What does it mean?"

"I don't think Bouchard was the only leak." Nye threw the report on a box. "Any ideas would be welcome."

"After we got Bouchard, things quieted down."

"Yes, well, it is beginning again. There have been rumors in Ange de Feu concerning Bouchard's son. He disappeared the night of his father's death."

"Bouchard had a son?"

"And a wife. She's disappeared as well. I don't like it, Farr. Keep your eyes open and look for anything amiss."

"Will do, sir."

* * *

The grim retaliations continued. The German soldiers, angered with French sabotage, responded with violence. Two days later, a small patrol stormed a nearby farmhouse where Nye's team had previously stayed. When the old couple refused to answer questions, the patrol set their dogs on them. Then they strung what was left of their bodies from scaffolding, and posted a sign forbidding the villagers to take them down for twenty-four hours.

Raphael and Katrinka stumbled onto this carnage when coming back from a delivery. Horrified, Katrinka scrambled from the car, fumbling for her knife.

Raphael bolted after her and grabbed her arm. "What do you think you are going to do?"

"Let me go! Don't you see… let me go! Do you think we can just let them hang there? The birds—"

He shouted over her. "Listen to me, you foolish child. Do you want another retaliation? Do you not see that, for every action, there is reprisal? How many others will die because you have not the stomach for this? We must leave, and quickly."

Driving back to camp, Raphael glanced at the girl next to him. Trembling, she kept her face averted.

He tried to make amends. "There are many terrible things. There will be many more. That is what we are fighting for. That is what we must remember."

She turned to him, her face ashen. "Please stop the car."

"What?"

"Please stop now. I'm going to be sick."

Raphael pulled to the side of the road as Katrinka clambered out, lurching for the bushes. He heard her retching and envied her ability to still feel. For him there was no more pain, just the relentless progression forward, to the end.

Presently, she came back to the car, and they drove the rest of the way in silence.

*　*　*

With reprisals escalating, the team avoided all attempts at more permanent shelter, living in the forest under makeshift canvas slung across ditches, and moving almost daily. It was a grueling existence, and their diet suffered as they scrounged whatever food they could find, to supplement the scant rations.

Most of the time, Nye sent Katrinka to the local markets for supplies. She was growing thin and dirty, and the constant hunger wore her down. She took Rolf with her, riding along in her basket. He would brace his forelegs, leaning out over the wired rim like the tiny masthead of a ship, barking at stray cats or anything else that drew his attention. During spells of inactivity, Farr taught the dog to deliver her notes, filled with very suggestive comments. He trained Rolf to perform silly tricks, which the dog delighted in. And it was Farr the dog curled up next to, on those rare occasions when he and Katrinka had a night together.

Farr had scheduled radio transmission times, and times he spent coding and decoding messages. Between these chores, boredom often set in. He was an avid reader and obtained as many ASEs as he could find.

Their rare nights together were spent making love and talking. Katrinka wanted to know about his childhood in North Dakota, his parents, and the volatile relationship he'd had with his father. He was more eager to tell her of his future plans. He would not always be a soldier.

Once, in a break between his transmissions, they shared a meal of rations with chocolate, and a bottle of wine.

"When the war ends, I want to settle down. Use that new GI Bill of Rights to go to school. Then I'll save up enough money to open an electronics repair shop." He paused, noticing her silence. "What are your plans, Trinka?"

She gave him a quick look. "Don't call me that."

"What? Call you what?"

"Trinka."

"But I've heard the major call you that. It's a nickname, right? Am I saying it right?"

"Yes, but that's *his* name for me. No one else uses it, except sometimes Papa."

Farr was incredulous, and a little hurt. But then people were strange with names. He had rules about his own as well, and had already instructed her about them. She had never called him Wolfgangus.

He shrugged and repeated the question. The intake of alcohol had made her chatty and affectionate. He was amazed at how much she could consume. Even so, he had to prod for an answer.

She was evasive. "Oh, I want to be like Emerson—an explorer."

He smiled. "Going looking for caves?"

"No. I want to find something. Someone."

"Who do you want to find?"

She hesitated. "Amelia."

"Who?"

The words tumbled out. "*Amelia.* They never found her. I *know* she's out there. She knew what she was up against. She knew the risks. I'm sure she had another plan, just in case. She wouldn't have waited till—"

Farr held up his hand. "Slow down. Who the heck is Amelia? Some relative?"

She stared at him with astonishment. "No. Amelia *Earhart.* You remember. She and her navigator disappeared right before the war."

Stunned, Farr sat back. "The aviatrix? Is that who you mean? The one who went down in the Pacific on her round-the-world flight?"

"She didn't go down. Or at least she didn't drown. She knew she was almost out of fuel. She found an island and managed a landing. It had to have been rough, but she could do it."

Farr's head was swimming.

"Don't you *see*? She's out there. She's waiting for someone to find her."

He said slowly. "So, you're going looking for Amelia Earhart."

"Exactly. I have maps. Santos gave me some extras. The United States Navy knows the approximate area where she went down. Emerson was going to help me, but..." She shook her head, sitting up straight. "Never mind about that. I'm going to hire a boat, and I'm going to go out there and search every island. I'll ask all the people who live there. Someone had to have seen something. Planes don't fall from the sky every day. She's *out* there, on one of those uninhabited islands."

She paused, taking his hand and squeezing it. "She deserves to be found, Wolfe, dead or alive. And I'm going to find her."

Farr remembered the whole story. The disappearance, the frantic search, and the gradual giving up of hope. Earhart had been a trailblazing figure back in a time when few women attempted such things. She had captured everyone's imagination with her bravery and daring. It was a damn shame when she'd gone down.

He frowned. Still, he hoped she wouldn't stick to this ambition. It could complicate matters, and his own plans for them. For the first time since meeting Katrinka, Farr realized the very tenuous clasp he had on her. It would only take a sudden shift, and she would be gone. Out into the world and never looking back. Leaving him alone and heartsick, missing her.

Later, when Farr had finished his radio transmissions, the conversation came back to his mind, worrying him. All he'd ever wanted was a home and a family. He had a fierce desire to undo the mess of his own childhood. His wife would stay home, cooking good meals, and raising good kids. They didn't have to be perfect. He'd come home from work, and dinner would be on the table. There would be no yelling and screaming, or knock-down fights. Until now, he'd never seen how unrealistic this dream was. Relationships were filled with conflicts. Kids got sick, and maybe turned out bad. He realized with a sickening jolt that she would never go for his kind of life. He'd lose her in a minute.

* * *

Farr and Katrinka were out with the radio, and sharing a small hotel room near the neighboring town of Trois Cloches. Nye had worked with Pascal's sources to get her new papers as a medical-supplies-service operative, delivering equipment to the clinics in the surrounding areas. This allowed her to stay in hotels, and Farr would meet her occasionally for a few hours at night. Using back entrances or fire escapes to creep into the window of her room, he would hook up his Jed set using the electrical mains for transmissions.

This evening, he'd prowled the area, as well as the room and fire escape, looking for escape routes. He knew that with one miscalculation, everything went to hell in a handbasket. Satisfied, he settled back on the bed, lit a cigarette, and waited for her to return from a delivery.

He smoked, staring up at the ceiling. On these nights they shared, Farr knew danger could surprise them at any moment. A desperate urgency between them continued to make every second count. His love for her had turned him into a worrier, and he didn't like it.

He finished the cigarette and sent out a few more transmissions. After several minutes of work, he glanced at his watch. He could relax. The last one did not go out for a few hours.

* * *

Katrinka came in later, smiling as Rolf bounded onto the bed and curled up next to Farr. She perched on a chair to undo her laces, telling him something her Papa Emerson had once said about the affection of dogs, and he interrupted her.

"Why do you call both men your father?" he asked.

"Because. They are."

"But one was your stepfather, or a friend of your mother's or something, and one is your true father, right?"

"No. Papa is my father, and Emerson… he was my father as well."

"That's impossible."

She paused with her undressing, giving him a baleful look. "You love to say that. You say it all the time."

"What?"

She could mimic his voice incredibly well. "Oh Katrinka, that's impossible."

"Well, so happens it is. They couldn't both be your father. Scientific fact."

"I don't care. A-mah made love to them both the night I was conceived. There was a terrible row, and my mother challenged them to show her their love. They did. The three of them made love for hours. Papa only left the bed in the morning because they had to leave port. He could barely walk. He could barely see straight. Papa Emerson needed to eat, so he crawled to the galley. He could not walk at all." She added warmly, "Otherwise, they would have made love all that day as well."

"Sometimes I think you say these things just to see my reaction."

"But it is true. You asked."

"So, you think just because your mother made love to both men at the same time, that somehow she was impregnated by them both?"

Katrinka came over and sat down on the bed, unbuttoning her skirt. "If you want to be so *particular*, of course not. Besides, Papa Emerson could not conceive. He'd had the mumps."

"He was shooting blanks."

"What?"

"Just an expression, babe."

She stared at him. Did he just call her "*babe*"?

She sat in the soft lamplight, with her dark hair hanging around her shoulders, and laughed at him. She loved the wonderful warmth and smell of his body. They were so rarely able to spend a whole night together.

He sat up, nuzzling and kissing her neck and lips. Reaching under her blouse, he traced her nipple with his finger.

She took his finger away, slowly sliding it into her mouth and quickly pulling it out again. It made a small popping sound. She could see he was growing very hard, very quickly.

"Trink?"

"Hmmm?"

"Have you ever made love to two men? At the same time?"

She was silent.

He spoke sharply. "Forget it. It doesn't matter. Stupid thing to say."

"Come here, Wolfe."

"I'm a complete asshole."

"*Come here.*"

She could see he was ready; the conversation had aroused him. He reached for her as she teased him. "Do you want to put your cock inside me?"

"Does a one-legged duck swim in circles?"

"*What?*"

"Just an expression."

"Your expressions! Oh yes, now you will shoot your blanks into me." She laughed.

Quickly he pulled her down to him, his face serious. "Baby, these aren't blanks we're messing with. Have you thought all this out? We could have a kid, you know. Doing this stuff."

Katrinka stopped laughing. She thought back to their first night of lovemaking. They'd done enough 'stuff' to have several babies that night. Later, she had insisted on protection. But all it took was one time.

As a matter of fact, she had thought a great deal about it after the rape. If the war were over, she'd return to Phyu

Thiri Kyun, her mother's island, where she had been born. She would stay there until the child was old enough to travel. Then she would take the little girl along, on her expeditions to find Amelia. Katrinka always assumed she would have a girl.

But if the war were still on, she could not return to Burma. Instead, she would go to her beloved French grandmother in Porto. Her grandmother had doted on her, spoiled her, and called her Trinkabella. Now that her grandfather had died, she was alone, living in that amber-washed house high above the Douro, where she used to sing *fado* in the taverns along the river. She would go there to have her child, and surround it with her love and that of her grandmother.

Katrinka never believed that a child would be unwelcome, or that it would inhibit her independence. Her mother had lived a nomadic life and passed the love of it on to her. She would do the same.

She brought her attention back to Wolfe, who was studying her face.

"Yes, I have thought about it. And I would want your child. It would give me something..." She stopped. She'd been about to say, "something to remember you by."

"Something what?"

"Something to care about. A child of my own."

"Our own."

"Yes. Ours together."

It occurred to her then that if she *did* conceive, he would always be a part of her life. Even if he left her, he would come back for the child. She knew he would do that. She would not have to say goodbye to him forever.

He seemed to have forgotten his recent arousal and lay on top of her, his head averted.

His chest was pressing against her face, and she twisted out of his embrace. "Wolfe?"

He cleared his throat. "Oh. Yeah?"

"You are so quiet."

He turned, and his face was as vulnerable as a child's. He passed a hand over his eyes. "Jesus, Trink, I love you so much."

She slid naked under the coverlet with him. He held her tight, but they did not make love. And after a bit, they slept.

* * *

The two Gestapo were making a final sweep of Trois Cloches. Their small squad was destined to leave in a few hours' time. They were seeking out the damning radio messages that had wreaked havoc on their communication lines during the past few weeks. Hauptmann Mühler and Unteroffizier Kraus were sitting quietly in a car near a small hotel, where earlier broadcasts had been briefly detected. Kraus wore a mobile RDF strapped under his overcoat. It had been malfunctioning for the past few days, and they were trying to pinpoint the exact location of the radio waves. They waited tensely, staring at their watches.

* * *

Farr woke a while later and sent his last communication. There were complications on the other end, and the transmission took longer than it should have. Farr began to sweat, obsessively checking his watch. When it finally ended, he donned his clothes and boots, thinking furiously. If anyone had been listening, it would take several minutes before they arrived.

He wrapped up the radio in its suitcase, looping the strap around his neck and shoulder, and woke Katrinka. Her lids flew open. One look at his face and her eyes filled with worry.

"Plan B?"

He nodded, scrambling for his knife and pistol, jamming them into his belt. With the radio strap across his chest, his hands were free. He watched as she grabbed for her clothing.

"Everything's probably OK babe, but just in case."

He was wrong about the timing. The next moment, the sound of boots filled the hall, followed by violent pounding on the door. A harsh German voice was demanding entrance. They could hear the hotel concierge shouting in the background.

Too late for them to run. He'd go over the fire escape railing with the radio.

Rolf began a frenzied barking, lunging from the bed as Katrinka called out, "*Un moment!*"

He frowned as she took her knife, thrusting it under the mattress, close to the edge.

"If there's any trouble—*any* trouble—you scream, understand?"

"They'll shoot you!"

The hidden knife worried Farr. He gripped her by the shoulders, staring into her eyes. "Goddammit, you scream."

Farr ran to the open window and climbed out onto the fire escape. Swinging himself over the railing, he hung suspended beneath its platform, gripping the webbed flooring with his fingers, the radio smacking into his side. He was going to give it five minutes, then haul himself back up into the room, his pistol blasting. God knows what she thought she was going to do with that knife.

* * *

Standing in the hallway just outside the room, Hauptmann Mühler pushed the hysterical concierge aside and drew his pistol. His tall *Unteroffizier* continued ramming the door with his shoulder. A woman's voice called out from the other side, speaking in indignant French.

"*Etes-vous fou?* Are you crazy? What is it you want? I am sleep—"

With his last thrust, Unteroffizier Kraus splintered the wood, savagely breaking the latch to the door. Mühler shoved his way into the room, knocking into a young woman standing in the entranceway. She was dressed in nothing but a sheet, a startled expression on her face. She opened her mouth to speak, but he grabbed her by the arm, pulling her close.

"Kraus, *das Fenster*," he ordered.

Kraus searched the room, stabbing the curtains with his bayonet and riddling them with bullets. Screams came from the hallway, and then the sound of doors slamming, and running feet.

The girl cried out, attempting to pull away. "What are you doing? You must leave immediately."

Hauptmann Mühler twisted her around, slapping her across the face. He spoke in precise French, so there would be no misunderstanding. "*Mademoiselle*, we will stay as long as needed."

He looked down at her dog, who was struggling to bite through his boot. He smiled, his underlip twitching. "Your little dog wishes to remove the boot, I think."

She gathered the squirming animal into her arms and tried to quiet his barking.

They both watched Kraus fling the curtains aside and lean out the window to the fire escape. He pulled himself back in, shaking his head, "*Da ist niemand, Hauptmann Mühler.*"

Mühler released the girl's arm and pressed his pistol into her side. "Show me your identification. Do not do anything stupid, or I will shoot you. And your little dog as well." He shoved his face close to hers. "Understood?"

She nodded.

Mühler pulled back, startled. For a moment, something feral—almost inhuman—passed across the girl's face. He suppressed a shiver, watching as she retrieved her papers from the bedside drawer. He studied them carefully, then returned them to her.

"Where is the radio?" he asked.

"I don't know what you refer to. I have no radio."

Kraus stepped forward, smacking her onto the bed with the back of his hand. Her dog crawled under the covers, where his muffled barks continued.

The girl sat up, putting a hand to her mouth. There was blood on her lip, and her cheeks flushed a bright red.

Mühler frowned. "As you can see, my *Unteroffizier* has a listening device strapped to his body. It is very useful. We have tracked the radio signal. It has come from this room."

She shrugged. "Then the *monsieur's* listening device is incorrect. You are in the wrong place. There is nothing here."

Kraus moved so quickly, the girl had no time to react. Grabbing her by the back of the neck he lifted her up, smashing his fist into her stomach. She gasped and crumpled onto the covers.

Kraus stood over her. "Where is the radio?"

She shook her head.

Mühler watched as Kraus yanked a handful of the girl's hair, twisting her backward as she clung to the edge of the bed. Her sheet slipped away as Kraus slammed his boot into her back.

"Where is the radio."

"There is no radio."

His kick caught the girl under her ribs, and the force of it lifted her body off the bed. She fell back onto the mattress, her breath punctuated by ragged gasps.

Kraus stepped back, undoing the buttons to his overcoat. The apparatus was becoming too cumbersome to allow him to work on the girl properly. He unstrapped the detection finder from his body, laid it on the chair, and glanced at his officer. Mühler gave him a curt nod, and Kraus turned back to the girl.

Mühler sighed and sheathed his pistol. He walked to the window and looked out onto the street. The previous interrogation had taken four hours, and the Frenchman had died at the end of it. He doubted the girl would last an hour under Kraus' efficient hands. But they had no time for this. He frowned as an apprehensive warning niggled at his brain. Something was wrong. The continued blows were powerful, but she was making no sound.

He turned back, and a glint of reflected light caught his eye. The girl had a knife. He watched in horror as she twisted her body, swinging her arm with ferocious speed, and plunged the blade straight though Kraus' chest, cracking bone. His *Unteroffizier* shrieked in anguish.

Before Mühler could react, a crash sounded behind him. He spun, grabbing for his gun, and saw a man hurl himself over the railing of the fire escape. He pulled his weapon just as the man charged through the window, knocking him to the floor. Mühler raked his fingers across his attacker's face, searching for the man's eyes, but the man dug his thumbs into his throat, pressing deep into flesh. Mühler couldn't breathe. A creeping blackness seeped into his brain. His fingers fluttered uselessly, and in a few moments they fell to his side.

* * *

Farr stood up panting, wiping the blood from his face. They had to get out.

He saw Katrinka on top of the other man, stabbing repeatedly with her knife, her cries of rage echoing in the small room.

Fucking hell. He ran to her as she pushed herself upright, retching onto the floor. Her small face was bloodied, and one eye squinted shut.

"Trink, are you all right? Can you walk?"

She nodded.

He leaned down wrapping an arm around her waist, and she cried out in pain. He flinched. "Here baby, take my hand." He watched her struggle to stand.

"I'm all right. Please, get Rolf."

"Right. Easy now, take it slow. Get your clothes; we're going back out the window."

She nodded again and struggled into her clothing.

Farr grabbed Rolf from his puddle of urine and stuffed him down the front of his jacket. He ran to the window and peered out. It was clear.

Grabbing her knapsack, Katrinka stepped over Kraus' body, his dead eyes still agape with astonishment. Farr looked away as she pressed her foot onto the man's neck and jerked out her knife. She stuck the blade in her waistband's sheath.

Farr took her hand and helped her climb out the window onto the mesh platform. He stooped for his radio, still holding Katrinka's hand, and they fled down the stairs and through the darkened streets.

Much later, from the safety of the woods, the man, dog, and girl crawled into a dense thicket of shrubs. Pressed close together, they waited for a sleep that did not come.

* * *

Katrinka had suffered a swollen lip, black eye, and broken rib. Purplish bruises covered her torso and the backs of her legs. Raphael took her to a local doctor, who gave her pills for the pain. She did not go out for the rest of the day.

Farr stayed with her until she went to sleep, then sought out the major. He found Nye sitting in his lean-to shelter.

Nye looked up from a report in his hands. "Yes, Sergeant?"

Farr didn't waste any words. "I want her out of this now, sir. She's not going on any more damn missions."

Nye stood, handing Farr the sheet of paper. Farr scanned the page. The Allies had broken out of Normandy and were now storming cross-country, headed directly for Paris.

* * *

The team's situation changed rapidly. In the next few days, another successful Allied invasion landed along the southern coast of France and funneled north, along the eastern side of the Rhône River Valley. Squeezed between the two advancing armies, the Germans retreated to the north and east in a rush to protect their borders. Others were given orders to fall back to the fortified posts near Saint-Nazaire and La Rochelle.

London sent out a call for a general uprising of all French Resistance forces in France. The remaining scattered bands of Germans retreated, viciously attacked by small groups of vengeful Maquis. Cut off from the main armies, the Germans were exhausted, starving, and vindictive. As they fled, they inflicted brutal retaliations on innocent villagers suspected of helping the Resistance.

By the end of August, Paris had been liberated, and like dominoes, other towns began falling into the hands of the Allies. Heavy fighting continued in the coastal cities and in the mountains, but by early September the Deux-Sèvres Department of France was free of German troops.

The Jeds wore their uniforms all the time now. Both Nye and Raphael went out frequently, meeting with leaders of the outlying communities, and helping to organize supplies and French troops for the new government. Pascal promised the team regular accommodation, as soon as it could be found.

The fifteenth of September was selected as the official liberation day for Trois Cloches. Katrinka was out delivering radio parts and not expected back until the next afternoon, but Farr set off with Val in the morning, each with a twenty-four-hour pass.

The town was a riot of celebration, and there were many people milling about, filling the streets with their laughter. Resistance fighters proudly wore their armbands. *Collaborateurs* were shamed, a few arrests were made, and some female *collaborateurs* were shorn of their hair. But for the most part, the tone was carefree and happy, and there was much drinking of champagne. Hidden stores were brought out and shared.

A tipsy young woman came up to Val in the street and gave him a kiss. When she received no encouragement, she gave another warm kiss and embrace to Farr, who heartily returned the favor. Smiling at them both, she continued her way down the street.

The two men visited every café and bar, rarely having to buy a drink, and by midnight both men were very drunk, their faces smeared by the red lipstick of exuberant, happy women. Stumbling into the last open café, they sank into a couple of vacant chairs, with a bottle on the table between them. Farr slumped back in his seat, grinning.

Val, who in the course of the evening had consumed considerably more than his friend, spoke first. "That was quite an encounter, yesterday."

Farr blushed deep red. He and Katrinka had been engaged in a very private celebration of their own the day before, when Val had stumbled upon them, leave passes in his hand.

"Shit. Sorry for that. She's just been so damn happy since the liberations."

Val shrugged. "I guess everyone's gone a bit crazy lately."

Farr leaned forward in his chair, thumping his elbows onto the table. "I don't know what you thought, Val, but I gotta set you straight. Tell me if I'm wrong about this, man. I know you'll tell me if I'm wrong."

"Sure, Farr. I'll tell you."

"Katrinka's great. You know how I feel about her. I *love* her."

"Serious stuff."

"You bet. About yesterday. I'd been gone a few days, and she was really happy to see me. I mean *really* happy. One thing led to another, and pretty soon she was goin' at it under the blanket. I was *crazy*. I mean, I was just *flyin'*, you know?"

"Damn, Farr." Despite his drunken state, Val felt his own organ hardening. He tried to block out the vision of Farr, with his cock rock hard, and what it had tasted like in her mouth. What it would taste like in his.

"Next thing, you're comin' along with the passes. I couldn't stop it, man. There's no way in *hell* I was gonna stop her right then. Know what I mean? I was at that *point*."

"Damn Farr, you've really got it bad."

Farr thrust himself back in the chair, grinning with satisfaction. "Yeah. That's what I know."

A while later, the men headed back to camp, both weaving unsteadily. Valentine stumbled over a branch and Farr leaned down, pulling him up, almost toppling over in the process. Val grabbed the man's face between his two hands and kissed him on the mouth.

He fell back as Farr exploded, flinging him away.

"*Christ* Val!"

"Sorry! *Fuck*, I'm sorry man. I—"

Farr wiped his mouth angrily. "Get a *grip*, Val."

"OK. Right. I'm sorry, I—"

"OK. OK. Just drop it. *Forget* it."

"Right."

Val continued to apologize as he stumbled along, trying to keep up with Farr's angry strides. When he fell again, Farr hauled him up by the back of his jacket collar. Supporting him with one shoulder, they continued on their way, Val babbling the entire time.

"You're the best frien' a man ever had, Farr," Val slurred.

"Shut up, Val."

"Right. Have to tell you Farr, you're the best frien' I ever had. You're a swell—"

"Shut the fuck up, Val."

"Right."

He succeeded in getting them both back to camp, Val in a semiconscious state and still mumbling. He dumped Val onto his cot, then went back to his own room and began unlacing a boot. It was entirely too much trouble, and he fell back onto his bedroll and slept.

* * *

Farr told Katrinka about the celebrations. Another liberated village was having a dance, and she wanted to go. There was a backlog of work, but she had not been able to participate in any of the revelries. Nye told her she could have a few hours with Farr, but he needed to be back before midnight to receive transmissions. Both of them cleaned up the best they could and set out.

The townspeople had partitioned off a portion of the main street earlier in the evening. A few older men with instruments had stationed themselves in one corner, and a long table that held many plates of food and bottles of wine stood in the other. Katrinka and Farr were hungry. They found a small table with two chairs and ate before the music resumed.

Almost immediately the men came over, asking to dance with Katrinka. Farr could not dance, and didn't want to make an ass of himself now. He nodded, and Katrinka was ushered into the throng. He sat back and lit a cigarette, watching as she was swept around in the arms of young Resistance fighters and old farmers. Her feet never missed a beat, seeming to skim over the cobblestones. Her small face was flushed, and her hair shone in the lantern light. He was sure he'd never seen anything so beautiful.

* * *

Raphael had attended the dance earlier in the evening and had made his way back to camp. It was quiet when he returned to his darkened shelter. Jack was cooing in the corner, and he fished a few grains of seed from a sack to feed him. Then he sat down, not bothering to switch on the lamp, and lit a cigarette, replaying the scenes of the last few hours in his head. The happy faces of men and women. Children running through the streets, chocolate clutched in sticky fingers. Old couples sitting side by side. The end had been so long in coming. Too long.

He sighed, grinding his cigarette into the dirt with his foot. Getting up from the cot, he fumbled for a moment in the pocket of his jacket, then returned to the bed. He looked down at the revolver in his hands, turning it over and checking the chamber. Satisfied, he reached into a drawer at his bedside and pulled out a torn and wrinkled photograph. He stared at the smiling upturned faces, until they became blurry, gray phantoms on a square of paper. Then he sat back on the bed, put the revolver to his temple, and pulled the trigger.

* * *

The song was ending, and Farr watched Katrinka drift back to the table, still doing little steps with the music. He smiled, handing her another glass of champagne. They were working on their second bottle.

"Where'd you learn to dance like that?" he asked.

"Emerson loved dancing. I wanted to learn, so he'd have me stand on his feet while he danced." She demonstrated, doing a quick turn around the table. "He would swoop me around the floor just like this, humming, with me clinging to his hands…"

To Farr's dismay, her voice cracked unexpectedly, and she began to cry. Long, ragged, drawn-out sobs. Embarrassed, he guided her away from the tables and down the path skirting the perimeter of the village until she quieted. It began to rain, so they decided to start back. Farr noticed they were taking the same route he and Val had stumbled through a few days previously. These liberations were too damn emotional. First Val, now her.

Arriving back at camp, they passed Raphael's tent. Farr was shocked to see Nye inside, crouched over an inert body. He looked up as they entered, his face a hideous white in the electric torchlight.

Raphael lay on the ground with a bullet hole through his temple. His gun was in one hand, the other clutching a photograph. The trembling fingers were finally stilled, and his face held a distorted grimace, as if his last thoughts had been too painful to bear. Katrinka drew back as Farr uttered a hoarse cry, bolting from the tent.

Farr didn't know how long he ran. It could have been for a minute; it could have been hours. The woods were damp with rain, and water from the leaves soaked into his uniform. He spied a fallen log and sank onto it, staring down at his hands, smelling the wet earth.

Sometime later, Katrinka found him sitting there.

"Wolfe?"

He didn't look up. "Go away."

He could feel her eyes on him. Then she turned and slipped back into the shadows.

Farr continued staring at his hands. After a while he slid to the ground. He shut his eyes and lay back, watching through closed lids as Raphael's face changed like a flipped photograph to the face of his father, and then back again to Raphael.

7

K ATRINKA HELPED ORGANIZE A MEMORIAL SERVICE A
few days later. Many of the townspeople came, as
well as Resistance members from as far away as the coast.
Raphael had been a quiet but strong force with the Maquis;
his knowledge of the people and villages helping to ease old
grudges and warring factions.

The rain continued. Nye's team stood under army-issue
ponchos, each with their own thoughts, listening to the
words of the priest as Raphael was laid into the ground.

Wills made a noise, and she glanced up. His face held a
kind of bleak desolation that frightened her. He turned away
not waiting for the rest, making his way back through the
rain.

For the next few days, a somber cloud of disquietude
surrounded the camp. The rain did not let up. Wolfe and Val
were immersed in fixing a broken radio, while Wills stayed
secluded in his room, working on reports. Rolf lay in the
pathway outside Raphael's tent, making others step around
him to get by.

Three days after Raphael's death, Katrinka went out
to the pigeon hutch to spend a few minutes with Jack and
give him his nightly feed. Instead, she found the little bird

lying stiff and inert on the floor of his cage. With a cry of alarm, she scooped him up in her hands. He was quite cold. Katrinka sat on the hard ground holding the small body to her breast, and wept bitterly. She was so very tired of this war.

* * *

At the end of the week, Katrinka watched as a new soldier arrived in their camp. Lieutenant Giraud was Raphael's replacement. A former Resistance fighter with the Free French, Giraud was younger than Raphael, fair haired, and high strung. He demanded to be given work immediately, meeting contacts and dealing with the various Resistance leaders. He was efficient, and assignments under his supervision went smoothly. She knew that Wills found him too abrupt and lacking in tact, but he and Nye began working together, assigning the much-needed supplies to various groups.

Things were returning to normalcy, when Nye called her to his hut one afternoon, having already briefed Farr the night before. Les Sables, a strategic port to the west, had been freed recently after very bitter hand-to-hand combat, with many casualties on both sides. Allied ships were bringing in supplies, which needed to be picked up and delivered. It would take about two days. Then he added the surprise.

"You'll recognize the vessel. *Le Flâneur*."

"Papa!"

"Just so. I suspect the entire thing is a ruse to make sure you're being properly cared for. So, any good word."

Katrinka had tried to keep the fears about her father in check. She knew of the U-boats and their lethal missions; how little protection the merchant ships had. But now he was here. For the moment he was safe, and she would see him.

The afternoon before departure, Katrinka went to the village priest in Ange de Feu to collect her mother's ashes. She would take them to her father in a small, silk-lined box. Emerson's remains would stay in the church until she could transport them. And there was something else she was taking with her. The situation in France was changing rapidly, and Katrinka wasn't sure where she would end up. Until she knew more, Rolf would be better off on the ship, and good company for her father.

That night, she gathered up his food dish and all his favorite toys, putting them in a small box to bring with her the next morning. Rolf watched, becoming more and more agitated. When she had finished, Katrinka sat on her bedroll and called to him. But he refused to come. Instead, he ran to the box and took each item out with his teeth, strewing them around the floor of her hut with short, anxious yelps. It broke her heart. She sat on the floor and pulled him close.

"Rolf, this isn't forever," she soothed. "I'll be back for you. You'll love Papa. You'll love the ship."

But he flattened his ears and wouldn't look at her.

Wolfe came in later and slipped into the bedroll with her. Then Rolf jumped in. His hairy body contained unsavory smells, and his position lodged firmly between the two of them prevented any lovemaking, but neither she nor Wolfe complained. They all managed to get some sleep.

At the last minute, Nye was able to go as well. He would be attending a meeting in Les Sables, with a colonel from London HQ. He would take a few hours to go out to the dock and see his old friend.

As Farr stepped aboard the ship, he got his first look at Katrinka's father. Remi Amparo was a tall man, lean and rough-faced, with a long nose and black mustache trimmed to the outer edges of his lip. Dark eyebrows arched over his deep-blue eyes—Katrinka's eyes. The brows gave him a slightly pensive expression. He wore his dark hair in a straight cut, which reached to the bottom of his neck, and he had thick sideburns. He smoked a pipe and wore a striped, short-sleeved shirt.

Katrinka gave her papa the small box, which he took from her wordlessly. Then they went into his office together, and Amparo shut the door.

Rightly figuring that father and daughter needed time alone, Farr walked through the cramped passageways to Katrinka's cabin. He entered her small room with some hesitation. This had been home for most of her life, and he studied the contents with curiosity.

Old photographs in brass frames perched on a railed shelf over her bunk. He picked up the closest one. A young girl was trying unsuccessfully to stuff the arms of a squirming dog into a miniature sailor suit. A young man stood over her, his face creased in laughter. With a shock, he realized it was Nye and Katrinka. He put the picture back on the shelf. Another frame held the image of a dark-skinned boy in long, white robes, standing next to a camel and examining the animal's leg. There was a gilt-framed image showing a laughing woman with fair hair, leaning over the railing of *Le Flâneur*. He supposed this was her mother. A man in a rumpled linen suit stood next to her, reading a map. Her

Papa Emerson? The last one was a photo of Katrinka as a small child, standing with her father in front of a striped tent. She was in a bathing costume, her bare knees caked in sand. She was looking away from the camera, at something in the distance.

A roughly carved Buddha with serene facial features sat cross-legged on a cane table. On either side of the wooden figure, sweet-scented joss sticks protruded from brass holders. The railed shelf above the table held a brightly painted paper mache tiger, some scattered postcards, and a jumble of books: Robert Nathan's *Portrait of Jennie*, a few works by D.H. Lawrence, and a volume of Japanese poems translated into French.

An old newspaper photograph of a slim woman with cropped, tousled hair was tacked to the wall. She wore jodhpurs, and a scarf around her neck. She looked vaguely familiar.

The large tray on a table by the porthole held a stack of maps. He picked one up and saw various islands, with notes of distances in nautical miles jotted in the margins. Someone had circled and made arcs around various coral reefs, and recorded the depth of water surrounding them. Here were Katrinka's maps of Earhart's disappearance.

He took some of them over to her bunk and sat down to study them, amazed at her attention to detail. Then Farr sat upright, his mind snapping to attention. He remembered a few articles he'd read at the London USO, just before D-Day. They'd talked about using sonobuoys equipped with sonar to detect underwater submarines. He'd been interested and wanted to find out more. Couldn't detection of this type be used in exploration? If the proper equipment were installed on a ship, if Earhart's plane had sunk near a reef or island, couldn't it work?

His eyes, once again, caught the photo on the wall. It was Amelia. Her eyes seemed to be smiling down at him with an air of encouragement. He returned the maps to their tray and put his rucksack in the corner. Then he went back out, and up to the bridge.

* * *

Back in his office, Amparo carefully placed the small box into a wall safe. Then he settled onto the battered sofa next to Katrinka, studying his daughter's face.

"So this man. He is your sergeant."

"Yes Papa."

"And you love him?"

"Very much."

"And you will marry him?"

"I… I haven't thought that far yet. Everything is so unsettled."

"Ah well, daughter, I will not advise you. I know you will do what you please, despite any warning from me."

"You would warn me?"

Her father shrugged. "Love always comes with a warning. You are young, and your life stretches out before you. You expect many adventures, and I am sure you will have them. But if you should reach old age, and you have no one who shares your memories, the end of your life will be lonely. Do not wait too long to find this person."

"But Papa, you are old and alone. Even when A-mah was alive—"

"Listen to me. I will be making only a few more runs. My job here in France is almost done. The war will continue in Europe, and in the Pacific, but I will be going home."

Astonished, she looked up. "Home?"

"Back to Coronado. I want you to know this. You will have a place to return to. You may contact me through my solicitor, Gorges—you still have the address?"

She nodded.

"Good. He will tell you where I can be reached. You can also see him for any funding you might need. You will not be stranded here."

There was more he wanted to say, but he stood up with a sigh, "And I will take your dog. Wolf—his name is Wolf as well?"

"No Papa, *Rolf*."

"Yes. He will soon get his sea legs and be good company for me." Again, he hesitated. "Just remember, there is a home for you. It will be different of course, but…"

She waited, but he did not continue.

He sighed again. "And now I go to find your young man. I believe he wishes to speak with me before Wills' arrival. Early tomorrow, we shall unload the supplies."

"Good night, Papa."

"Good night, *minha filhinha*."

Amparo waited until she left before sitting down to relight his pipe.

So, she was in love. She'd been in love many times before, but he knew the signs and she had it badly.

He remembered seeing his daughter for the first time. Holding Yujana in his arms that night, he'd asked, "Shall we call her Katrinka?"

"Why Katrinka?"

"It is my mother's name."

"Yes, of course. It is a pretty name."

Yujana had never been maternal. She was quick to strike out in anger when Katrinka misbehaved. His own mother had observed it when they were in Porto, and told him there would be trouble when Trinkabella grew up.

The trouble began sooner than that. Far from being cowed by her mother's temper and lack of affection, Katrinka grew into a wild and willful girl, exploring her sexuality quite young.

First, there had been that strong infatuation with Nye. That lasted... well, had she ever really gotten over it?

Then there had been the numerous employees working on Emerson's expeditions. The most serious had been Mshai, the eldest son of Emerson's camel veterinarian, at his cave site in southwestern Egypt. Just seventeen years old, with dark, curly hair falling to his shoulders, golden skin, and large, black eyes. Katrinka had been attracted to him immediately.

She was seen in the entranceway of his tent early one morning, half-naked and wrapped tightly in his embrace. She'd raised holy hell when both fathers stepped in. They ran away together one night, streaking out across the moonlit desert on a camel, headed for God knows where. Emerson and Mshai's father had had to track them down. She was just thirteen at the time.

And of course, before any of those, had been what both Emerson and Yujana referred to as 'the incident'.

They decided to send her to school in Switzerland, but her behavior continued to be outrageous, and she was suspended from the school. It was only through numerous donations to the board of directors that they'd managed to get her reinstated and educated. That was only a few years ago. Was it possible she had matured? Was she capable of having a relationship with this man? He sighed and rose from his seat. He'd better go and see what the young sergeant had to say about it all.

* * *

Amparo met Farr on the upper deck and studied him thoughtfully. Farr was a toughly built man of medium height, with sun-streaked hair and bruised gray eyes. He carried himself with quiet confidence, but he maintained the continual wariness of someone who had lost trust in the world.

Both settled into cane chairs, and Amparo offered him a drink, which Farr refused.

"No, sir, there is something I want to discuss with you, and it needs a clear head."

"Very well, let us sit here, where we can view the sea."

Farr got right to the point. "I thought I'd better speak to you about your daughter and me. I love her, and want to ask her to marry me as soon as the war is over."

Amparo sat back sighing. So here it was, already. "As to that, I would not recommend it." He held up a hand as Farr started to speak. "You understand, I love my daughter. But she is of the same passion, the same temperament, as was her mother. Flighty and ill-suited to one man or one home. You would not be able to hold her. You would have to accept that fact."

Amparo saw anger flare in the young man's eyes, stung by his words.

148

Farr's reply was equally blunt. "I'm not prepared to do that, sir. I don't intend to have her wandering the face of this earth, coming back to me whenever she feels like it."

Amparo drew back, astonished and a bit angered. Was this rough-spoken man criticizing his daughter? Did he really think he would be able to control her? If so, he was in for a very rude awakening. He said drily, "What you want, Sergeant, and what my daughter wants may differ. You know of her desire to find the missing aviatrix."

"Yes, sir, she's told me about that."

Amparo stared at him, frowning. Farr returned his gaze with steady eyes.

Suddenly Amparo relaxed, emitting a sharp bark of laughter. "You were referring to her mother. Yes, that was the way with Yujana. But she always came back. I knew I was the one that truly mattered. It was a question of freedom for her. She needed it like we need air to breathe."

"Yes, sir, but I believe it can be done with Katrinka and me. She loves me, and I think she wants to make it work." He added, with surprising insight, "She may not know that yet, but she's still pretty young."

"Yes, she is very young. You would have rough going at the beginning, and I doubt she would ever settle to your kind of life."

"If she's willing, I'd like to give it a try, sir."

Again, Amparo stared at the man. There was a certain surety, a fearlessness, in the way he spoke. He gave a small smile, murmuring his thoughts aloud.

Farr leaned forward. "Sorry?"

"Eh? Oh, just an old proverb my father used to say, '*Amar e saber nao pode ser.*' Love and prudence do not go together."

Amparo stared out at the water for a long time after the young man left. He remembered the pain of being young and in love. Love and prudence do not go together—thank God for that.

* * *

Hours later, Nye and Amparo were still drinking in the galley.

"So. What do you think about all this, Remi?"

"He is a good man," replied Amparo.

"And they make a good couple."

Amparo's reply was impatient, "No. No, they do not make a good couple. He is all wrong for her. You must know it."

Nye's eyebrows shot up, "What—"

Amparo snorted. "You know Katrinka would never settle down to the life this man wants her to live. He would break her heart. She would try to please him, because she loves him. But it would break her heart. And his as well."

"I think she might be willing to change for that love."

"My friend, forgive me, but I know a bit more about my daughter than you." He paused. "And she is my daughter."

Nye went crimson.

"Yes, the question of her parentage. He smiled sardonically. "We were all 'in the running,' as they say. You, me, and Emerson. I suppose it could have been any one of us. But then Emerson was sterile, and as she grew older, the resemblance, well, it simplified matters. But for a while… you remember how often we were taken for father and son. Our looks, so closely resembled."

"I remember you were more like a father to me than my own."

Amparo sat back, studying his friend. The war had taken its toll. He remembered Nye as a runaway boy. He'd asked no questions and offered him jobs doing the work no one else wanted: scrubbing the decks, cleaning the heads, and running errands. He'd been a quick learner and proved himself an excellent seaman.

He'd left the ship soon after Emerson and Yujana. Until now, neither man had ever mentioned Nye's night with her. Nye went back to his family when his mother was dying, to make amends. They'd kept in touch, and he learned that Nye had finished his schooling, gone to university, and later gotten married. But, in the fall of '33, Nye met up with him in Calcutta and resumed his job on *Le Flâneur*. He was once more running away; this time from a broken heart and a messy divorce.

Amparo continued, "Yes. Well, my friend, what I tell you now, your heart already knows. All these years Katrinka has loved you. First, as nothing more than a schoolgirl crush. It embarrassed you, and you ignored her. Rightly so. I thought this infatuation of hers would disappear, like so many others. But, as she grew older, it only grew stronger. Then, that night... that night you lost everything. She came into your cabin—"

Nye blushed again. "She wanted to comfort me. I sent her away."

"And you left ship at the next port."

"It wasn't just that, Remi. I was destroyed. I wanted nothing more to do with the sea. And then the war came."

"And you were afraid of your growing feelings for Katrinka. You saw her as a child. But she is a young woman now, with a young woman's feelings. I do not need to tell you she's had lovers in the past."

"Mshai."

"And others."

"Just what is it you are trying to tell me, Remi'?"

"This man is unsuitable in every way, but he is determined. There is love, and a very strong sexual attraction. That is not enough. There must be a sharing of goals, of life's purpose. And, with Katrinka, there must always be a flexibility and understanding. Her mother taught me that."

When Nye finally spoke, it was slowly, as if to himself. "I'm almost twenty years her senior."

"As was I, with Yujana."

Nye was silent then shook his head. "I couldn't do it to Farr. They deserve their chance. Then, if it doesn't work…"

"At that point, it could be too late."

Nye replied, his voice tinged in anguish, "It has always been too late."

Neither man saw a shadow against the passage door dissolve and fade, as Katrinka fled back up the stairwell, her thirst forgotten.

* * *

Nye stayed in port a few extra days and then began working with Giraud on his return. Messages flowed in, and supplies were arriving by plane now that the airport was open. The French groups needed more ammunition and more equipment, and the demand for new-recruit training grew daily. That afternoon, he called Farr to his tent.

"Do you remember Bouchard's son? We suspected him of continuing his father's job," said Nye.

Farr nodded. "Yes, sir. Surely this cannot matter now?"

"He was captured in Paris, tried, and jailed. We just got the news. He's escaped and headed this way."

"Why would he—"

"He's looking for the man and woman who killed his father."

Farr's head jerked up. "What?"

"He found out what happened the night of the delivery. He's evidently sworn revenge for his father's death."

"Does anyone know his whereabouts?"

"They lost sight of him outside of Chatellerault."

Farr raised his eyebrows. "That's not too far from here."

"I'm sure there is no need for concern. Just be careful, Sergeant. He probably won't get this far. Both HQ and the Jeds are looking for him. But I thought you should know. No need to spread the alarm. Katrinka…"

"Right, sir."

"Just keep your eyes open."

"Yes, sir. Will do."

* * *

Farr was troubled; everything was changing so quickly. The Allies had joined forces from the north and south, driving the remaining Germans to the borders and a few coastal pockets to the west. Marseilles and other cities to the south were free to receive shipments. Some German troops, ordered to hold out in coastal strongholds near Bordeaux and La Rochelle, found themselves trapped and unable to leave.

The mission of the Jed teams changed as well. He supposed he'd be sent back to England for more training and a different assignment. War still raged in the East. He voiced these doubts to Katrinka, who shrugged them off.

When he persisted, she replied, her voice unhappy. "Yes, Wolfe, things will change. They always do. That's why we must enjoy what we have now."

"It doesn't hurt to look ahead a little," he countered.

"But why? Everything could be different tomorrow."

Her words echoed his own fears. He averted his eyes before she could see the pain in them.

"You remember this?" She pulled the necklace with the silver medallion from her blouse, placing it in his hand. "He is Kairos, a Greek word for the special moment. See how he stands on tiptoe, running? You must grasp him by the forelock when he approaches. The back of his head is shaved and once he has passed there is nothing to hold. You must take your special moments when you see them."

He flipped the medallion back onto her breast, shaking his head. "That isn't true. Two people can share a lifetime of special moments. You say you love me."

"I do love you, Wolfe. You must know it."

"Yeah, but it's different for you. When I love somebody, I don't hurt them. I take care of them. I don't just walk away when the next adventure comes along, or the next person."

She winced. His words had hit a nerve.

He hesitated. "You love the major, too."

Katrinka replied quietly. "That is the way it is, between Wills and me."

Farr looked away. He'd known, but it was painful to hear.

She continued, "You want to be together, but you would grow tired of me and tired of the day-to-day chores that surround such a life. You would wonder what you were missing in the world."

Farr shook his head. "No, Katrinka, that's you. That's not me. I wouldn't be missing the world if I had you. You are my world."

She stared at him, mute. And after a moment, he turned and walked away from her.

Katrinka returned to her small hut, angered by the conversation. Wolfe was wrong. The world was simply too large, too beautiful, and too vast for one person to be responsible for it all. One person should not be obliged to supply the whole world to another. And as for his being hurt—well, he was suffering under the assumption that she belonged to him. She wished she had thought to tell him that.

* * *

The team had moved to another site on the far edge of farmland. Work continued, but Katrinka and Farr's relationship had become strained. Farr was using Valentine to do some of the simpler courier jobs. Nye noticed it and mentioned it to Giraud.

The man shrugged. "A lover's quarrel. He will soon be between her legs again, and all will be well."

Nye wasn't so sure. Amparo's words had haunted his consciousness for days.

One evening he was crossing the farm field, heading back to camp after a meeting in the village. It had not gone well. Nye missed Raphael, and the man's steady diplomacy.

He saw Katrinka perched by herself on the wooden steps of a small stile in the meadow. He swung himself up on a step beside her, and she gave him a warm smile.

"Can't sleep?" he inquired.

"I was just thinking."

"You've picked a good place."

"Everything is changing so fast, Wills."

"Yes, it seems we have them on the run. Farr out with the radio?"

She nodded.

"Is everything all right? Between you and Farr, I mean."

She shrugged, turning her gaze to the fields. The wind was ruffling, carrying the scent of long-bladed grasses.

He studied her face. "Does he know?"

His question surprised her. "Know what?"

"About Josef."

"Why would I tell him that? It would only hurt him. Does it matter?"

"He cares for you a great deal."

She shifted restlessly on the hard wood. "We've only just met. Maybe he likes sleeping with me."

"I think it's a bit more than that for him. Is that all it is for you?"

"What do you mean?"

"Is he just someone to sleep with."

"Why should you worry about Wolfe and me?"

He took a deep breath. "Like I've said, he's a good man. I don't want to see him hurt. You can be a bit reckless with other people's feelings."

"Feelings? Those *feelings* come with rules, Wills. Do you think I am this way to be cruel?" Her words tumbled

156

out in frustration. "Listen to yourself—so sanctimonious, so righteous. Yes, I want love. Everyone tells you how wonderful love is, but they never tell you what you must give up."

"You can explain yourself quite well. But how would you feel if Farr behaved as you do?"

"He has every right to. Don't you see? If he truly loves me like he says he does, he would come back."

"Like your mother and Amparo."

"Yes. They understood one another. If Wolfe loves me, no one could ever take my place in his heart. And if he found someone else, well, maybe he wasn't so much in love after all. Or maybe it just changed, dried up, or died. I can't explain it clearly. All I know is that your idea of love is as wrong to me as my idea is to you."

"Do you love him?"

"You know I do. But I love him, knowing that I will probably lose him. Someday, he'll give up trying to change me and leave. But I'll go on loving him until the day I die."

He spoke more sharply than he intended. "Then *act* like it, Katrinka; that's all I'm saying."

"Act like it? I don't have to *act*, Wills. It is there in my eyes for the whole world to see. It is in the way I talk to him, smile at him, and make love to him." She paused. "You are such the hypocrite. You think a woman should pledge fidelity to a man just because he sleeps with her. I don't think you were looking for fidelity when you slept with my mother!"

He recoiled. "How did you know that?"

"I didn't."

He caught his breath.

"So, it is true."

"Sweet Jesus."

"Is it *true*?"

Nye was quiet for some moments, staring out into the darkening field. A distant planet glimmered above the horizon, like a small diamond. There was the smell of rain in the air.

His thoughts shifted back to a night in Almeria. Yujana had found the letters. She and Amparo were not speaking to one another, and she was spending nights with Emerson. The drinking and arguments had started early, and by evening there had been an explosive confrontation. Weapons were drawn. Yujana stood between the two men, her arms outstretched with a knife in each hand. She shouted to them, hurling out a challenge that made both men blush. Then she'd turned and gone down into the cabin. Emerson was the first to drop his knife arm, then Amparo. Both men retreated, following her. A few nights later, she'd appeared in his cabin. She hadn't been wearing anything at all. He was a virgin then, just seventeen years old.

He looked down at Katrinka's intent face. Finally, he spoke. "Yes, it's true."

"How—"

"She was wild after the confrontation with your father. It was like the ship couldn't contain her. She came to my cabin one night. She'd always known how I felt about her. I was young. I suppose I didn't hide my feelings well. We made love. It was just that once. We never spoke of it again."

"I'm not condemning you."

"But it was different between us—"

"No!" she stormed. "I will not let you say that. You lusted after her, you wanted her, and you got her. And she wanted you."

His voice was cold. "Katrinka, I'm sorry. I don't mean to dictate to you how you should live your life. I only know how men are, right or wrongly."

"Maybe Wolfe is different. Maybe he'll accept me the way I am."

Nye's mouth turned down as he stepped away. "I shouldn't depend on it."

* * *

A few nights later, Katrinka sought Farr out. He'd just come back from the village and entered the darkened hut to see her sitting on his bedroll.

"Hi." Her smile was strained.

"Hey," he replied.

"May I speak with you?"

He stood before her, hands shoved into his pockets. "Sure. What about."

"I didn't get it right the other day."

He sat down next to her, their shoulders touching. "Didn't get what right."

"I never meant to hurt you."

"OK." He was trembling.

"I want to make it work between us. Give me time, Wolfe. That's all I'm asking. Give me time to learn how to make this all work."

He pulled her into his lap. "C'mere, baby, I'll teach you."

Katrinka pushed him away. "No, Wolfe. Stop!"

He drew back, startled. "Trink? What's wrong?"

"You don't *listen*. You're not listening to me."

He dropped his arms, speaking quietly, "OK. I'm listening now."

"You know I love you, but you want a wife who will stay home and have your children. I'm not ready for that. I—I don't know if I'll ever be ready for that. There are so many things I want to do."

His voice was rough. "Are they more important than having a home, a family together?"

She raised her head. If it had to end here, then it would end. Her heart would collapse into a pile of dust, and she would give up on men entirely. Before they broke her.

"Yes."

Farr dropped his eyes. He stared at his hands.

There was a long silence. Katrinka watched, waiting. Moonlight came through the open door, turning his hair into strands of silver. She wondered how she would ever be able to go on without him. Without his love. She should get up and walk out, while she could still move. It seemed forever before he spoke.

He raised his head, his gray eyes staring at her in the dim light. "So that's the way it is?"

She forced herself to reply. "That's the way it is. I can't lead you on with those expectations."

Farr was not an eloquent man. She could see him struggle for his next words.

"OK, you've had your say. Now listen to me. I love you, and you love me. That's enough for now. We'll enjoy what we have here, right now."

"You mean it?"

"I'll be looking ahead all right, but I won't badger you about it."

Katrinka flung her arms around his neck, pushing him back onto his bedroll. She climbed on top of him, rubbing her cheek against his rough skin, smelling his dusty sweat.

"I love you, Wolfe. I love you so much."

His voice was muffled against her shoulder. "That's all I wanted to hear, Trink."

8

I T WAS A SUNNY AUTUMN DAY THE FOLLOWING WEEK, when Farr and Katrinka were returning to camp after retrieving broken radio equipment. Farr's bike had sustained a puncture, and they were sharing hers. Katrinka perched on the crossbar in front of him, sitting sideways, inside the circle of his arms. Farr was in uniform. With the liberation of Trois Cloches and the surrounding villages, whatever Germans remained had gone into strongholds along the coast, or retreated to the battles in the north and east.

With a light heart, he peddled through the swathes of sunlight. The smell of old trees and the closeness of her, filled the man with a deep sense of happiness, making him less cautious and alert than he should have been.

"Want to just keep goin'?" His grin spread wide, crinkling the corners of his eyes.

Katrinka turned and smiled up at him, the wind lifting her hair. "Yes, please! Straight down through France and over the mountains to Spain."

He smiled again, listening to her chatter. The sunlight flashed and sparked on her hair, turning it the color of leaves.

Farr saw the flash of wire a split second before they hit it. The bike buckled and twisted, throwing Katrinka into the road. He fell off the seat, skidding along the ground. Dazed, he scrambled to his feet, grabbing for his pistol and Katrinka's hand.

"Run!" he yelled, but it was too late. The bushes exploded, and a young man blocked their way, pointing his weapon at them.

"*Arrêtez!* Drop your gun and place your hands on your head," the young man commanded.

They did as they were told. Farr eyed the boy. He was dressed in rough-looking blue trousers, and a stained shirt. He looked vaguely familiar.

"What is it you want?" Farr asked in French.

The boy approached with caution, stopping a pace or two away. "I want the one who killed my father."

"*What?*"

"You do not recognize me then? I am Paul, the son of Bouchard. The man you murdered." He turned on Katrinka. "Or perhaps it was you? It is like a woman to stab a man from behind. Or perhaps you are the *collaborateur*. One who fucks the Boche."

Flushing a deep red, Katrinka jerked out her knife, just as Farr lunged. Paul swung his rifle, hitting Farr in the face and knocking him to the ground. Farr swore, as blood spurted from his nose. The boy kicked him hard and then stood back, facing Katrinka.

"Drop the knife or he dies now."

Katrinka dropped her knife.

The boy turned back to Farr. "Get up."

Farr rose to his feet, and the boy patted him down with one hand. Finding a knife, he jammed it into his belt. He turned to Katrinka and searched her, keeping his eyes on them both.

163

A thin trickle of blood coursed down Farr's chin. He wiped it away with the back of his hand. "Paul, your father was an informant. He was killed."

The boy spat. "I know what he was."

"Then what the hell is—"

"You stupid American. You do not know what it is like to have your country taken and your parents threatened. You come here and blow up the bridges with your plastique. You send messages to direct bombs. And for every act of terror you commit, another Frenchman dies.

"The Germans came. They took my mother to a prison camp. They told my father to cooperate, or she would be tortured and killed. At first, he refused. A week later they brought photographs."

His voice was savage. "Shall I tell you what they did to her? A woman? My mother? My father asked what he should do. They said she would be safe if he cooperated."

He turned again to Katrinka. "Then you came, with your *plastique*. My father was stabbed in the back. They made me continue his job. Later, I was told my mother was dead. We were no longer needed."

There was a long silence, then Farr asked, "So, what do you intend to do?"

"I took a vow. There would come a time for revenge. It is now."

Farr's mind raced. "Think this out. If you kill us, they'll come after you."

"There is already a price on my head. I am a dead man. Enough talk."

Swinging the rifle strap over his shoulder, Paul grabbed Katrinka from behind. He pulled his knife, resting the blade under her breast. He twisted her in front of him, to face Farr. "Shall I show you what they did to my mother?"

Katrinka screamed, kicking him in the shin as Farr surged forward, slamming the boy to the ground. Paul thrust out his knife as he fell, stabbing Farr deeply in his side. Farr shouted in pain and grasped Paul's knife hand. For a few moments, it seemed as if Paul would stab again, but Farr twisted the blade around and plunged it into the man's stomach with a powerful downward thrust. The man stilled. A moment later, Farr collapsed on top of him.

"Wolfe!" Katrinka struggled to her feet, watching in horror as blood gushed from the wound in his side.

"Oh *Wolfe!*" She stumbled over to the bike, fumbling in his rucksack, and grabbed the small medical kit. Running back, she tore it open and poured sulfa onto his wound. She ripped off a strip of her under slip and wadded it tightly against his side.

His eyes clouded in pain. "You must get help," he gasped.

"No, I won't leave you."

He attempted to sit up. "Katrinka, listen to me. Get the bike—"

"No," she sobbed, clinging to him.

"Trink, you've got to go for help."

He fell back onto the ground panting. More blood was seeping through the cloth. She fumbled with it, uselessly.

"You must find help. Go. Please hurry."

She stood up. Retrieving her knife from the dead man, she ran to the bike. With a last despairing look back, she slung her knapsack over her shoulder, turned, and wheeled away.

Katrinka hadn't gone more than a kilometer down the road when she heard a roar of motors. She turned and saw a small convoy rolling toward her. Her heart pounded as she recognized the markings of the lead jeep. It was a mobile SAS patrol. Leaping from her bike, she ran into the road, waving her arms. The two soldiers in the lead jeep stopped, their expressions shocked.

Following their gaze, Katrinka looked down at herself. She was covered in blood. Farr's blood. She began to shake.

The officer questioned in passable French. "What has occurred?"

She gave a short version of what had happened, trying to control her trembling. "Please, please come. He may be dying."

The officer waved to the jeep behind. "Medic, go with this lass. She needs help."

"Yes, sir."

The officer turned to his driver. "Sergeant Roland, you'd best go with them. We'll meet up with you at the field hospital."

"Yes, sir."

Sergeant Roland and Katrinka joined the medic in the other jeep. Roland climbed into the driver's seat, slammed the gears into reverse, and pulled a sharp U-turn.

In a few minutes, she spotted Wolfe. He'd managed to drag himself to the side of the road. He was not moving. The medic and Katrinka jumped out, while Sergeant Roland went over to examine Paul's body.

Katrinka stood by as the medic frowned, sizing up the grim situation. Farr was barely conscious and bleeding heavily. He checked Farr's pulse and wound, then reached into his medical kit. A few minutes later, he'd wrapped Farr's side tightly with bandages and given him an injection.

Her mouth could barely form the words. "Will he live?"

"We have a French surgeon at the field hospital. We'll take him there," explained the medic.

They got him into the back of the jeep, and Katrinka squatted on the floor beside him. Sergeant Roland had finished his inspection of the body and took a few papers from Paul's pocket. He put them in his jacket and hauled himself into the driver's seat.

"Do you know who your attacker was?" he asked Katrinka.

"He said he was Paul, the son of Bouchard, an informant in the village of Ange de Feu."

The man nodded. "We have been on his tail for quite a while. It was lucky we came upon you." He frowned, looking down at her. "Have you anywhere to go, miss? We'll take this man to our field hospital. It's some kilometers down the road."

Katrinka gave a fleeting thought to Wills and Val back at their camp. "Please take me with you."

Sergeant Roland nodded, swinging the jeep around.

"Wait," she cried. Scrambling from her seat she ran to the bike, retrieving the radio parts from the handlebars, and jammed them into her pocket. Then she returned to the vehicle and her position on the floor, next to Wolfe.

Roland trod on the accelerator and they hurtled down the road, with Katrinka sitting in the back, cradling Wolfe's head in her arms.

* * *

After the operation, the surgeon came into the small, partitioned waiting room where Katrinka was sitting. Farr had been lucky. He'd lost quite a bit of blood. They'd stopped the bleeding, searched for any internal damage, then stitched him up. He was fortunate that the knife had missed any major organs.

Katrinka could not stop trembling. She gave her statement to the one they called Captain Burke, trying to remember everything she could. It seemed like a bad dream. Surely, she would wake from it.

Burke closed his notebook and stood up. "What about you?"

She faltered. "I'm not sure. I had a… a delivery to make. They must be wondering what has happened."

The officer nodded. You say you're with Major Nye's Team EDMOND? Over near Trois Cloches?"

She nodded.

"I'm going to send out a message to them as well as a brief of events. Spend tonight here. We can set up a cot for you, next to him. The partition will give you privacy. There is a small washroom down the hall for the nurses. You may use that. We'll take you where you need to go tomorrow."

"Thank you," Katrinka whispered.

The doctor spoke up, "If he wakes for anything, you may give him water. Nothing else. He'll need assistance to… the bedpan is under the cot."

"Of course. I will help him."

"Good girl. The nurse will bring in something for you later. We don't have much, but it will be hot."

"Thank you," Katrinka whispered again.

Burke left, and Katrinka slipped down the narrow corridor to another partitioned area, that was Farr's room.

He was lying on a hospital cot, the entire left side of his body swathed in bandages. His eyes were closed, and his pale face dotted with beads of sweat. She carried a small folding stool from the corner to his bedside and sat down, reaching for his hand. She sat for a long time, watching as the sunlight faded from the room. Presently his eyes flickered and opened, slightly out of focus. They settled on her, widening.

"Katrinka? Are you OK?" His voice was raspy.

"Yes."

"Where am I?"

"An SAS patrol found us. You are with the field hospital, and the surgeon says you are going to be all right. You are to rest. I can give you water."

"I feel all doped up."

"They've given you pain medicine. Do you need to use the bathroom?"

He shook his head, closing his eyes for several moments. Katrinka sat upright, scarcely breathing.

His eyes opened again, and he glanced at her lap. "What do you have there?"

"Oh, my knapsack. Some fruit we were going to eat, a handkerchief and a comb. My book."

"Can you read to me?" His voice was almost unrecognizable.

Forcing her shoulders to relax, she settled back, opening the book at random. The words barely disturbed the stillness of the room. It was so quiet, she thought he must have fallen asleep. She was beginning the next chapter when he interrupted, his voice agitated.

"So, where're you trying to get back to?" he asked.

"What?"

"Like in the story. Where's your home?"

"Well, it's… I guess *Le Flâneur* is my home."

"Your home's a ship. Got it."

"They said I wasn't like the rest, you know; I was born on a different tide."

"Why's that?"

"I was born on land. My mother's people always give birth at sea. But it was the time of monsoon and they were ashore. My mother gave birth to me on her island, Phyu Thiri Kyun, 'Island of the Pale Moon.'"

"Sounds beautiful Trink; tell me about it."

He wanted to hear her talk. Like a child who is afraid of the dark, asking for one last fairy story before the lights are turned out, and the monsters appear. She would tell him hers.

Katrinka put the book down and pulled her stool close. She curved an arm around his head and stroked his cheek, speaking in a low voice.

"My mother's people are the Chao Le—Burmese sea gypsies. My grandmother, Mya, fell in love with a Christian missionary. She conceived, and when my mother was born Mya and her lover were outcast. They set sail in a small *kabang*, attempting to reach the mainland. But a bad storm rose up, and the sea was rough. They struck coral, and the boat sank.

"Mya bound my mother to a plank, which managed to float back to shore. Her people considered it an omen from the sea gods, showing that all was forgiven, and so my mother was raised by Mya's family."

Farr was quiet for a long time before speaking. "Your dad, Amparo. He won't always be on *Le Flâneur*. What'll you do then?"

Katrinka reflected. "If I have to settle somewhere, it might be Coronado. We lived there when I was a small child. A-mah was back with Papa then."

"Yeah, you talked about that before. Coronado. Sounds nice; sounds peaceful…"

She looked down at his face, usually so hard and grim, now softened by morphine. His eyes were half closed, he was falling asleep. The fairy story was over. The lights were out. And she was there, her protective arms curved around him, keeping the monsters at bay. Resting her head next to his, they both slept.

* * *

A few hours later she woke, as Farr stirred restlessly in the bed. Her arm was stiff, and she stood, massaging it to get the blood flowing again.

He called out, "Katrinka, where are you?"

"I'm here, Wolfe. Right here." She sat down again.

"I need to get up, I need—"

She reached under the cot for the bedpan.

"I'm not using that."

"You most certainly are going to use that."

After a bit of maneuvering, they actually managed it. Exhausted, Farr slumped back into the pillow, his face covered in sweat. He lay still for a long time.

"Would you like me to read to you some more?"

He shook his head, wincing in pain.

"I'm going to call the nurse. Perhaps you need another injection."

She expected an argument, but he was silent. Katrinka crept down the hallway to the small desk at the far end. A night nurse looked up, and Katrinka explained.

"Yes, the doctor said another dose might be needed. Is he restless?"

Katrinka nodded. "He seems to be in pain."

"I'll be there in a minute."

Katrinka returned to Farr's side, and a few moments later the nurse appeared with a small syringe on a tray.

"This should help him sleep," said the nurse. She swabbed his arm and injected the morphine. She plumped his pillow, and after straightening the bed clothes, departed with the bedpan.

"Talk to me, Trink."

"Would you like me to sing to you? I used to sing to my *avo*, my grandmother in Porto, when she was ill in bed. When I was a small girl, she taught A-mah and me *fado*." She curved her arms around him, humming softly.

"That's nice."

"I remember A-mah singing to Papa when he was ill or tired. My mother would hold him in her arms, like now with you." She smiled down at him, speaking softly and soothingly. If only he could sleep. "A *fado* of by-gone times, sung in the cafés along the river, in Old Porto. She used to sing there, you know, to the fishermen and old men."

"What's *fado*?" he asked sleepily.

"The Portuguese have a word, '*saudade*'. I don't know the English word." She shifted her arms a bit. "It is a nostalgia or longing for home; it can be about a lost love. It is passionate and bittersweet. *Fado* is what the women would sing late at night, in the taverns, their men having gone away to sea. Wondering if they would ever return. It is about sadness and loss."

He sighed in her arms, before drifting off in uneasy sleep. "Why can't it just once, have a happy ending?" he whispered.

Farr was moved to another hospital and was to be gone several days. Valentine, who'd been slated for orders to England, stayed on, taking over Farr's job as well as his own. Katrinka worked hard to make the load easier for him.

The team had moved again, closer to Trois Cloches. They'd been given access to an unused schoolhouse that not only had electricity, but also a small kitchen, bathroom, and running water. With the Allies engaged in fierce battles in the northeastern part of France and in Belgium, the Jeds in the Deux-Sèvres area were left to themselves, in helping to organize the Resistance. Nye was frequently out at meetings with various local leaders and military officers. Giraud oversaw the training and regrouping of the Resistance into companies of the newly formed French Regiment. They were all in need of weapons and equipment.

Small pockets of Germans still held on, along the fortified cities of the west coast. The French needed to keep them contained, and prevent them from breaking out in search of food and supplies.

Valentine worked the wireless, receiving and transmitting messages, and sending them out with Katrinka to the appropriate people. They, in turn, would give her messages they needed sent back to London, which Valentine would put into code and transmit. The work was never-ending.

Sometimes, she was gone from early morning until night, and would rise at dawn the next day. Food was still scarce, and they were always hungry. The rough living conditions and exhausting schedule made her tired and cross. She was discouraged with the lack of food items for sale, and sometimes the lack of any fresh food at all. This situation brought her close to tears.

They continued to subsist on field rations and whatever else could be found. Sometimes, a villager would bring them part of their meager supplies. One brought them a roasted rabbit. Giraud swore it was a rat.

With the food supply in such a grim state of affairs, Katrinka was delighted to learn that the team had been invited to a post-wedding dinner by one of the Resistance families. Staggered by the quality and variety of food, she inquired about the supplier. The wife smiled, speaking of a '*sorce special*'.

Later, Katrinka cornered the woman, who finally gave up the information.

"But you will never be able to afford him; his prices are high. And this was only for the special occasion," explained the wife.

Katrinka had most of her papa's money left. She was determined that, in the last few weeks, she and the others would eat well.

The next day, using the directions the woman had written down, Katrinka made her way to a farm on the outskirts of Trois Cloches. An older man answered the door. He was short in stature, barely as tall as herself, and wore his belly over his belt. He had thick, dark hair, which was brushed straight back from his forehead. His deep-brown eyes flickered over her with interest.

She smiled, indicating the basket on her arm. "*Monsieur*, may I enter? I have a business I wish to discuss with you."

He nodded and led her to a small sitting room with sagging sofas. The walls were dotted with old landscapes, and framed pictures of young men and women crowded the mantelpiece. It was damp and cold, and the room smelled of stale cigar smoke.

Katrinka explained her proposition with confidence. She would pay well for the desired items. She was dismayed when he shrugged at her offer.

"*Mademoiselle*, I have many customers who are willing to part with their money."

Crestfallen and close to tears, Katrinka rose, thanking him for his time. She turned to go.

But he reached out for her arm, speaking with great diffidence, "Perhaps, *mademoiselle*, there is a way this may work. You see we are both hungry."

She looked at him curiously.

"I do not look it, yes? But I am a man who starves."

Then she saw his eyes with their naked need in them, and she understood.

"It is this way. I am a married man, a happily married man. I have been married many years now. My wife, bless her, has worked hard and raised our children with pride. But she no longer cares for the joys of the bed. For me, it is difficult. You see me. I am a strong man yet. Bursting with the desires of a man. I remember the days we had. She is a good wife. She fulfills her duty once, twice a year. These are very special occasions, but there is no joy in it for her. I know."

He paused, gazing at her body with a simple admiration. "My dear, you are young. Your flesh is soft and sweet. Would you care to exchange with me, an old man, pleasure for pleasure, to assuage our hungers?"

Katrinka drew back, studying him thoughtfully. Could she do it? Of course she could. Would she enjoy it? What would he be like in bed? She did not care to be repulsed, no matter how hungry she was.

He read her eyes. "Ah, *mademoiselle*, there is nothing to fear. I am told I was quite adequate in my day." He smiled, a smile so full of boyish bravado and charm that she decided at that moment. Katrinka missed Farr, and their shared sexual enjoyment. Sometimes her internal parts ached, which no amount of masturbation could alleviate.

"Yes, *monsieur*. I understand your meaning, and that would be quite all right." She added coolly, "If you are sure you would be up to the task."

He gurgled with laughter. "Never fear about that! Shall we set a time and a place?"

"I am often free early in the morning, which is when I go for food. There are long lines and I must wait."

"Then the *mademoiselle* must leave it all to me." He grasped her hand, pumping it vigorously.

"There is one other matter, *monsieur*."

He released her hand, "Ah."

"There must be precautions, you understand. You must have with you a… a preventative."

"Of course. *Mademoiselle* displays admirable logic. There are no worries. I will have what is needed."

Katrinka smiled. The little man seemed relieved. A *dalliance sexuelle* was one matter. A young woman appearing on his doorstep with an infant in her arms was quite another.

After Katrinka left, the man sauntered down the long hall to the kitchen where his wife was peeling a few potatoes at a large wooden table. Brushing a stray tendril back from her face, she looked up as he entered. "Did I hear someone at the door?"

He walked over to her, dropping a kiss on the top of her head. "*Oui*. Just a customer."

His wife nodded and continued peeling potatoes.

* * *

For the next few weeks, the team was able to enjoy an abundance and variety in their meals. All gave silent thanks to Katrinka's father's funding. All except Nye. He suspected the black market, and knowing the way things operated, guessed she had not been asked to use money. He was surprised he could still feel shocked at her behavior. He imagined she was not losing much sleep over it, and she certainly seemed happier.

He told Katrinka he did not want to hear about any details, and if the wife came after her with a meat cleaver, he was not going to rescue her. She just laughed.

For her part, Katrinka was quite pleased with the transaction. The Frenchman more than kept up his side of the bargain. As a matter of fact, Katrinka had a job keeping the little man in order. She was surprised by his numerous requests. He wanted her to perform fellatio on him. She said it was distasteful. She didn't like it, and she wouldn't do it. He wanted to perform cunnilingus on her. Katrinka did not care much for that either, but he did a surprisingly good job. He wanted her to masturbate while he watched, so she used a courgette from the food packet she was taking back to camp. He wanted to perform anal sex—*absolutely* not.

He then asked, a bit timidly, if he might enter her from the rear. Katrinka readily agreed. She was quite fond of that position. Being on hands and knees, it gave her the ability

177

to fondle herself, while the man operated from the rear. But in this case the little man had both areas covered, and Katrinka came to a pleasurable climax, which seemed to please him immensely. She was becoming quite charmed by this assiduous little Frenchman.

Then there were the more astonishing requests. He had a desire to urinate on her. When she refused, he asked if she would urinate on him. She waited until their next assignation, holding back her bladder, then complied, while the man masturbated beneath her in a delirium of orgasmic delight. He brought different items he wanted to insert into her, but they itched, and she refused. One day he brought her a tiny switch and asked her to strike his buttocks with it. She made a few attempts on his wriggling flesh with its sprouting black hairs. She began laughing so hard, she had to stop.

But most of all, the little man loved her breasts. Often after orgasming, he would lie on top of her, with his head burrowed into them. Katrinka liked that best. With their arms folded around one another, she would rest her chin on the top of his head. She didn't love him. She wasn't even sexually attracted. But the simple embrace soothed her aching emptiness, and she looked forward to those moments.

Katrinka wondered how his wife must have felt performing all these acts, and asked him about it one day.

His eyes bulged in disbelief. "Never! Never have we done these things!"

"Why not?"

"But, *mademoiselle*, one does not perform such acts with one's wife!"

"Why?"

For that he had no answer, except to sputter uselessly.

As for the farmer's wife, she was delighted and somewhat astonished to find her husband showering her with little gifts and added attention. She put this rare display of sentimentality down to their approaching anniversary. She wrote to her sister about the pleasant change, and received a cryptic reply:

"The old fool is up to something."

The wife put *that* down to simple envy.

* * *

Nye had a problem. On his desk lay two reports, one concerning a wounded American Army Air Corp lieutenant, and one a German prisoner. Both needed quick access out of the country. He sat back smoking his pipe, studying the summaries.

The first one was fairly straightforward and could be easily dealt with. The American pilot had been shot down near La Sansoune last spring, just before the massacre of the village. He'd been sheltering there in a safe house when the Germans attacked, seeking retaliation for Resistance sabotage. The pilot, along with a few others, had managed to escape, and another safe house on the circuit took him in until his wounds healed. Now HQ was requesting his immediate return to London, where he would name names in hopes of eventually punishing the perpetrators for war crimes.

The Germans had sent out a small unit of Waffen SS agents to hunt him down. Nye knew if these officers found the pilot, the man was dead. Valentine was bringing the pilot in tomorrow evening, and he'd spend the night here with the team.

Well, he'd send Valentine out to contact Raphael's old liaison Pascal, and Pascal would get the pilot down to Marseilles. Amparo had been working there since the Allied landings, and could take him up to Lisbon, and from there, transport to London. Lots of steps, but easy to accomplish. Problem solved.

He picked up the second report, reread it, and then threw it down on his desk. This seemed more complicated, but perhaps it would be even easier. He needed to speak with Katrinka.

Nye was pacing the small room when Katrinka came in. He gestured toward a chair. "Trinka, take a seat. I have a possible job for you. Strictly optional, but I wanted to sound you out on it. I know Farr is coming back soon."

She flushed. "Yes?"

"As you know, things have calmed down dramatically this past week. General de Gaulle has returned, and along with the Free French, will be taking control of the country. The Jeds will be sent elsewhere."

"I know, Wills. You have already told me." Her voice was tense.

"You've been asking for some time off to take Emerson's ashes down to Lascaux."

"I can go?"

He smiled at her eagerness. "Yes. But here's where the job comes in."

"At Lascaux?"

"Trinka, I'm sure you know that not everyone in the Fatherland is happy about Hitler's plans for a New World

Order. A group of student journalists in Munich calling themselves *The White Rose* were caught composing and printing pamphlets denouncing the Nazi regime. Three were guillotined, and another one was executed later. One was imprisoned, but has recently escaped. Code name: *Milou*. She's been making her way to France since her escape from the internment camp in Germany, passing from safe house to safe house."

"*She?*"

Nye nodded. "You know about the pilot Valentine is bring in tomorrow evening?"

"Yes. But what does that have to do—"

"I want you to take Milou to Marseilles where the pilot will also be waiting. Your father will take them both through to Lisbon."

"But why doesn't Milou go with Pascal and the pilot down to Marseilles?"

"Two reasons. Reason one, and it's a kicker. Last week, a Resistance member was escorting Milou to us by train, just the other side of the French border. Evidently, the man tried to seduce her. When she refused, he sold her out."

"What did she do?"

"Some German soldiers showed up at their next stop, blocking the exits and boarding the train. She stabbed one of the soldiers, as well as the man who sold her out—"

"Good for her."

"Yes. Quite." Nye smiled. "In the confusion, she managed to escape by breaking a window in one of the compartments. She made it across the border to the next safe house. But now she is refusing to get into any train, car, or vehicle."

"Can you blame her?"

"She's sworn to walk all the way to the coast if she has to. They managed to calm her down enough to have her agree to use a bicycle, with another agent as escort. She has specifically requested a woman."

"I'll do it, Wills."

"Don't you want to hear the second reason?"

"It doesn't matter."

"I think it shall." He pulled out a map and placed it on the desk between them. He leaned over, tracing the roads. "You should have no problem. Most towns and cities are now liberated as the Allies move northward. Your journey will take you here, through this town."

She looked to where his finger pointed.

"Lascaux," she breathed.

Nye sat back, smiling. "Just so."

* * *

The scrawny American pilot was brought to their school building the next afternoon. When Katrinka and Valentine reported in, the lieutenant was still there, talking to Nye. The major motioned for them to sit down in chairs by the door, while the lieutenant continued his story.

The young officer sat at the table, his back to Katrinka and Valentine, drinking coffee as he described the events of the massacre. Nye could hear the tremor in his voice, but the cigarette in his hand was steady.

The officer explained, "They were rounding up the women and children. Locked them in the town barn, and set fire to it. Shot anyone trying to crawl away. There was a

German officer, named Farber. He grabbed a small kid and threw him into an oven. I saw another nail—"

Katrinka gasped, and the pilot jerked around, spilling his coffee. Nye saw the man flush a deep red.

The lieutenant smiled apologetically. "Oh! Sorry, darlin'. Can't keep my darn mouth shut."

He paused, turning back to Nye. "So, we got the heck out of…" His voice trailed off with a quaver. His hand trembled now, as he lit another cigarette, forgetting the one already in the tray.

Katrinka crossed the floor and crouched next to him, taking his hand in hers. The man began to shake violently, his head and shoulders clenching over his rail-thin body.

Nye stood, signaling Valentine to leave with him.

"Bloody women. Always do it to us."

* * *

That night, the pilot's hoarse cries tore through the quiet building. The major heard it, hesitating over his reports, before slowly making his way up the stairs.

Lying in his bunk, Giraud heard it and finished his cigarette, flicking the stub to the floor with a heavy sigh.

Katrinka jolted awake, listening. Throwing on Farr's old shirt, she pattered down the hallway to the pilot's room. Nye stopped in the shadows as he watched her slip through the doorway. He stared for a moment, then turned and walked back downstairs.

Adjusting her eyes to the darkness, the girl felt her way over to the man's bed. He was sitting up wild-eyed, still half asleep. The smell of stale sweat hung in the air.

He swung out at her, but she caught his arm, speaking soothingly.

"Hush. You are safe." She cradled his hand in hers.

He lay back panting, his entire body bathed in sweat. "I thought—I thought…"

"It's over. You are safe now."

He finally focused on her, recognition springing to his eyes. "Darn nightmare. Don't know what's wrong with me. Haven't had one since—"

"Shhh. Do you need anything? May I get you something?"

With immense effort, he calmed himself, attempting a weak laugh. "No, sweetheart. Not unless you can rip this fool brain out of my head and give it a good wash."

She sat with him until he quieted. His eyes finally closed, and his rapid breathing slowed. Gently, she released his hand and rose to her feet, shivering. The room was chilly. His lids flew open and he grasped her wrist.

"You going?" A barely controlled terror in his voice.

Katrinka looked down at him and made up her mind. "Move over."

"What?"

"Move over, please. I'm not going to leave you, but it is cold. Move over, and I will lie down with you."

"Oh darlin', that isn't—"

She gave him a gentle shove and slipped into the small bed with him. He didn't put up much protest.

"Now get comfortable, and I will hold you. That way we can both be warm and you can sleep."

He seemed immobilized, so Katrinka turned on her side, wrapping one leg and arm around him, nestling her head onto his shoulder. He was so painfully thin.

He could sense her nakedness under the shirt. His arm stole around her shoulder, pulling her close. She could feel the beat of his heart.

"What's your name darlin'?"

"Katrinka. What's yours?"

"It's Tom. None of this Thomas business, just Tom."

"Nice to meet you, Tom."

He gave a snuffle of amusement. "Nice to meet you, Katrinka."

It was quiet for a while, and the sound of his slowed, steady breathing told her he was drifting off. Suddenly, his entire body gave a convulsive jerk. He gasped.

She raised her face, and his hollow eyes glanced down at her.

"I'm sorry, darlin', did I wake you?" He was trembling again.

She half raised herself up, leaning her elbows on his chest, and looked down at him. They both needed to sleep.

"Would you like to make love?" she suggested. "I can always sleep after making love. Maybe it is that way with you as well?"

His voice was thick in reply. "I've got a girl back home."

He was stroking her hair, and she could feel him getting hard. She felt relief—he was still operational. He would survive this war. Perhaps she would as well.

He continued, "But I don't think she'd mind. I mean, if she knew the circumstances and all. I think it would be OK with her."

Rolling over her, he leaned from the bed, his hand fumbling in his pack on the floor. "Just want to get this." He gave a small laugh. "Air Corp takes care of its own."

She pulled away, watching him peel the small packet open and roll the bit of rubber down his erection. It was as long and skinny as he was. Then she settled back, pulling him on top of her. Smoothing the hair away from his face, she reached up and softly kissed his lips. He circled her in his arms, returning the kiss.

Definitely operational.

There were no more disturbances that night. The major lay awake, staring into the darkness at nothing. Giraud, in his small bed, lit another cigarette. And back in Tom's room, a few more scars slipped out in the sweat of Katrinka's body, leaving just the remainders. The ones lying closest to her heart.

In the morning, instructions came through. A lorry would be by to pick up the pilot after breakfast. Nye put down his coffee and walked upstairs. Coughing loudly, he paused just outside the room.

Katrinka uncurled herself from Tom's arms, adjusted her shirt, and got up. She passed Nye with a defiant glance, but his eyes were averted. Neither one spoke.

* * *

All was ready. They were waiting for a sign that it was clear to begin. Nye listened intently to the afternoon BBC radio announcements for a signal concerning the German escapee. Had Milou made it to safety or been betrayed again, at the last safe house? There was no word or information coming in.

The newscaster finished his announcement and introduced the final poetry reading of the day; Thomas

Moore's "The Last Rose of Summer". As Nye listened, he relaxed and let the deep, baritone voice wash over him, filling the room with its sweet melancholy:

"Tis the last rose of summer left blooming alone
All her lovely companions are faded and gone."

Nye called Katrinka into his office. He knew she was expecting some reaction to their morning encounter, but he got straight to the point. He finished the briefing and gave her a map of where their new camp would be located, then paused, glancing up at her silence.

"And Emerson?" Her voice trembled.

Nye turned in his chair, reached into a lopsided wooden cabinet, and pulled out a small, wrapped box. "I picked them up from the priest yesterday."

She reached for the box, her eyes filling with sudden tears. "Thank you, Wills." She headed to the door.

He stood. "Trinka?"

She turned.

There were so many things he wanted to say to her. "Come back safely."

She nodded. "I'll come back, Wills."

The major sat down and flipped his pencil onto the table, his eyes drawn to the window. Outside, it was a beautiful fall afternoon. The air was heavy with the faint smell of someone's cooking. A stray breeze sent a swirl of red leaves tumbling through his open door and across the rough wooden floor. Heaving a deep sigh, the man returned to his work.

9

T HAT EVENING, KATRINKA ENTERED A DIMLY LIT café. Selecting a table, she set her knapsack on the floor and glanced around. A few rough-looking men dressed in farm-laborer clothing were drinking at the bar. A woman and her child sat at a table near the window. The child drew on a scrap of paper as the mother ate from a dish of potatoes and onions mixed with garlic. Its pungent aroma drifted through the air. The only other occupant was a pale-faced young woman sitting alone at a table near the door. She was studying the menu.

An aproned woman emerged from behind the counter to take Katrinka's order of an omelet and brown bread.

A few minutes later, the pale woman walked over to Katrinka, dabbing her eye. Leaning across the table, she spoke in French. "If you please, *mademoiselle*, have you a handkerchief?"

Startled, Katrinka looked up. The girl had spoken the code phrase, and was waiting. Her dirty, blonde hair was tied up in a scarf, and mascara lined her tired-looking eyes. Was this her contact?

The girl spoke again, a trifle strained. "If you please, have you a handkerchief? I have something in my eye, and it grows tiresome."

188

Katrinka replied hastily, "How annoying for you. I do not have a handkerchief, but here is a bit of cloth. It is clean."

The girl flounced into the seat opposite as Katrinka reached into her bag.

"*Merci.*" She took the cloth, and with an almost languid motion, made a spiral of one corner, moistening it with the tip of her tongue. Katrinka felt mildly shocked by the sensuality of such a simple act.

The girl dragged a mirror from her bag and dabbed her eye gently. "Ah, *voila*! I have it. Thank you." She returned the mirror to her bag. "May I join you? A friend has not come, and I do not wish to dine alone."

"Of course. It is always better to have company when one eats."

The girl offered her hand. "My name is Milou."

Katrinka noticed the worry lines etched around her mouth, and the suspicious look she cast at the drinking men. Her hands were small with rough-cut nails. They shook slightly as she returned the cloth.

The girl leaned forward, whispering. "This is what you must do. Soon, I will leave. You will wait and have your coffee. Later, you will come out and meet me at the village cinema. But if the men follow me out, you must go. Immediately. Do not attempt to find me. Do you understand?"

Katrinka frowned. What was this about? Did she suspect the men at the bar? She stared at the girl's face.

"*Do you understand?*" Milou repeated.

"Yes."

The girl leaned back in her chair, looking more relaxed. The waitress came again to take her order. The rest of the meal was taken up with small talk, mostly about men, and what *connards* they all were. "Assholes," she repeated. She lit a cigarette and smoked it with a sultry defiance.

Katrinka was warming to this dirty street urchin. Was it all an act? She remembered Wills' description and the horrors that had befallen her. Yet here she was, smoking and chatting away like any French schoolgirl.

After their meal, Milou leaned across the table and spoke, her voice tense. "I will leave now and wait for you at the cinema. Have your coffee, then pay the bill." She rose and leaned down, brushing Katrinka on the cheek with her lips. Then she left.

Several minutes later, Katrinka joined Milou at the cinema. The two girls linked arms as they walked down the street slowly, so as not to attract attention. Now they were out of the café, Katrinka took charge.

"There is a church in the next village. We will walk there and spend the night. There will be bicycles and packets of food. You have your papers? Good. We are cousins returning to our aunt's home in Marseilles. First, we will deliver my father's ashes to the village of Montignac. From there, we continue to Marseilles, where a ship is waiting for you."

Milou glanced at her companion's face. "Your father's ashes? I have not been told of this."

Katrinka did not reply, and they walked on in silence.

"The men at the bar, they remained?" Milou asked.

"Yes."

"I thought they would come over to us and speak."

"After you left, one did."

"*Did* he. What happened?"

"He followed me out and—"

Milou spun around.

Katrinka pulled at her elbow. "Don't worry, I was watching. He has turned around and gone back to the café."

"What did he want?"

"He asked if I wanted a cigarette and a walk along the water."

Milou laughed. "Really. What did you say?"

"That I had a boyfriend, and he was waiting for me."

"And do you?"

"Do I what?"

"Have a boyfriend waiting?"

A vision of Wolfe's pain-lined face disrupted her thoughts. She faltered and said, "I don't know."

"Oh, but that is the best kind of boyfriend. The uncertainty! The angst! Does he know you care?"

"I think he must."

"*Mais non! Never* let them know."

To change the conversation, Katrinka asked about her name. "It is very pretty. Is it a nickname?"

"Don't you know? We never give our names. You have not given me your name. You have not given any name at all." She studied Katrinka thoughtfully. "You have heard of *Tintin*, no?"

Katrinka shook her head.

"It is a famous comic here and in Belgium. The boy Tintin is a young journalist, and he gets into escapades so incredible! His dog Milou follows, protecting him, nipping at the heels of his adversaries." A shadow crossed over her face. "It was a nickname given to me."

"Who—"

"He is dead." Milou quickened her steps.

Katrinka asked no more questions.

Presently, they reached the church and entered the nave through a side door. It was a cold, dimly lit building, which smelled like wet bones. A priest emerged from the shadows. He was a tall man with sloping shoulders, his eyes disturbingly empty. He led them to a small room off the nave, where a pallet lay on the floor.

"Here is where you will sleep. It is not so comfortable, but it is dry. Down the corridor is a door to the washroom. I will leave you now and return later with food." After picking up a basket from the corner, he left the room, closing the door behind him.

Milou looked about, shivering. "It is very cold."

Katrinka nodded. She wondered if the food would be hot.

* * *

Later, the priest brought them a steaming bowl of watery broth made from potato skins and root vegetables, along with a few rolls of hard bread and cheese. He also produced a dusty, green bottle of wine.

"You will leave just before dawn. There will be bicycles. I will bring you more bread and cheese for breakfast," he explained.

They thanked him as he slipped back into the nave.

Milou's gaze followed him. "He seems troubled."

"Yes. I think it has been a bad time for his village."

The women huddled together on the pallet. Milou divided the soup into two chipped porcelain dishes painted with tiny blue flowers. Katrinka sliced the bread and cheese with her knife, and poured wine into tin mugs. Neither spoke for a while; their mouths filled with food.

After a bit Milou sat back, regarding her companion. "So. They told me nothing. Only to meet a woman who would take me to a port in the south, where a ship will be waiting. You are so young. And you are new to this? Are those really the ashes of your father in the box?"

Katrinka stopped chewing and looked down.

Milou spoke quickly, "Never mind; it does not matter."

"He was my adoptive father. He was an archeologist and was traveling to Lascaux. He was killed."

"I am sorry."

"I will bring his ashes to the cave. Others will be there who are also studying. They were expecting him, and I think they will agree to let him rest there."

"I am sure of it."

Milou topped up their mugs with more wine, and both girls settled on the pallet. The floor was quite hard and cold, but the wine had warmed them.

"They did not give you a code name. What shall I call you?" asked Milou.

"But they did. I heard them use it once: *Swallow*."

Milou stared. "Surely you jest. *L'animal*—my French guide—he joked about such a code name. The woman who gives her favors freely. There is nothing she will not do to entice the secrets from others."

Katrinka's eyes widened. "Is this true?"

"Absolutely, it is true."

Katrinka shook her head. "But the 'swallow' has another meaning. For the sailor, it is a symbol of hope and freedom. The swallow returns every year to its nest, so the sailor will return home safely from his journey, no matter how far or dangerous it may be."

Milou studied the girl's face. She wondered who had given her the name, and why they had done so.

* * *

The bottle of wine was empty, and their conversation drifted to men. It reminded Katrinka of late-night talks shared with women friends back at school. Fueled with alcohol, she became chatty.

"This boy was so upset. He tells me, 'You cannot screw around on me. It is over between us.' The way he said '*screw*'. They must choose just the right word, you know. To make it sound so ugly. So hateful. Even the *nicest* men."

Milou nodded. "Of course. When you take your pleasure with them, it is always 'making love'. But when your pleasure is with another, it is 'screwing' or 'whoring'. And when it comes to their *own* adventures, it is just a minor digression—a *passion amoureuse*."

"Exactly. Who let *them* write the rules?"

"It has always been so. For a woman, sex must not be taken lightly. When you are with a man, his needs must be *earnestly* attended to. It is not the laughing matter. I was with one such man. I was sleepy, and he was poking about with *la queue*, trying to do his business. I fell asleep. He was so offended, his manhood in tatters."

Katrinka laughed. "Before I sleep with a man, I think to myself, will he be too quick about it? How will he kiss you? Will he hold you afterward? What is the shape of his cock and how will he use it? The pleasure must drive you wild."

"Oh yes, that feeling between your legs." Milou rolled back, clutching her crotch with a theatrical moan.

Katrinka drained the last bit of wine from her mug. "It's as if I can no longer breathe. My heart is racing, as if I will pass out. Then comes this immense surge."

"Most men do not care if you get off or not."

"I don't care if I do or don't."

"Are you serious?"

"I don't think about it, I enjoy the *feeling*. His arms around me. The roughness of his skin. The groans of his pleasure. The urgency of his thrusting, like he can't wait another *moment*—"

Milou rudely interrupted. "Oh yes, of course. But then the possessiveness. Trotting about on all fours, lifting their leg, and pissing on everything within a ten-kilometer radius of you."

Katrinka looked at her in astonishment, then both girls shrieked with laughter.

Milou tried to establish order. "Hush, this is a house of God."

They laughed again, but more quietly. Much later, they fell asleep, curled together inside the blanket on the tiny pallet, still smiling.

* * *

The women settled into the routine of their journey. Getting up early, they would travel until mid-morning and then take a short break. They would push on until afternoon and combine a small lunch with a brief rest. Katrinka had been given francs for the trip, and she still had her father's money. They scrounged what they could from the village markets or small cafés, but they were always hungry.

Milou maintained a constant state of wariness. Despite the cool autumn nights, she preferred to eat and sleep in the open, not wanting to be trapped inside a building where exits could be blocked.

And there were problems. Katrinka's bike had a puncture that had to be mended. It was not easy finding the materials, and they had to search several shops. Milou complained bitterly that her *derriere* was unaccustomed to such punishment. They had to stop when it rained heavily, and then had to deal with the mud. Sometimes a dog would dart after them and give chase.

As they traveled south, rows of golden and flaming-red poplar trees lined the narrow roads. They passed other women along the way, some riding bicycles, and a few with horses and carts. The smell of moist, decaying leaves filled their nostrils.

In a few days' time, they came to the recently liberated village of Perigueux and their lodging with the local schoolmaster, Monsieur Deflout. That evening, they sat together at the kitchen table. Deflout fumbled with a pair of battered reading glasses held together with tape, and studied Katrinka's papers carefully. Katrinka tried not to stare at the left sleeve of his shirt, which was dangling empty. Its cuff was pulled halfway up and stitched closed.

He handed back her papers, smiling. "Yes, of course. We all have heard of the Lascaux Cave. It is an amazing thing. An abbot, and one or two men of science watch over it. I believe the Maquis have uses for it as well. I will write a letter, and you will take it to the abbot there. He is a friend of mine. There will be no problem."

Katrinka thanked him. Then, seeing his tired face, she impulsively leaned over to kiss his cheek. "I am happy for your village, *monsieur*."

He flushed with pleasure. "Yes, but there is much work ahead. It is not yet over. Bless you, children. And your father."

* * *

They started for the cave early the next morning, struggling with their bicycles over hills and muddy roads. Eventually, they came to the village of Montignac. A recent rain had turned the buildings a dampened-amber color, and the odor of baking bread drifted on the breeze. Rambling roses grew along the town wall, creating vivid splashes of red against the gray backdrop of sky. A river ran through the center of the town, and the cave lay in a hill just beyond. The women checked into one of the few hotels. After a brief meal, they sought out and found the abbot.

He heard Katrinka's story in dismay. "He was expected with great anticipation, your father. We waited, but he did not arrive. He is quite well known to us and to the field of archeology. There are two scientists, Monsieurs Lambeau and Gratian, who waited here expressly to talk with him. He was killed? This is a terrible thing."

Seeing Katrinka's face, he stopped. "But I am thoughtless, forgive me. I will take you there early tomorrow. There will be no problem. It is very rough and dirty. We will give you the proper clothing. What you will see will amaze you. There will be a place for your father."

* * *

Katrinka met and conversed with the scientists later that night, giving them the papers Emerson had brought along for the trip. As eager as they were to see the documents, they struggled with the news of her father's death.

Lambeau pushed himself away from the table, his voice angry and passionate. "The war has taken many things of beauty and destroyed them. It has taken the men and women who strive to keep knowledge and culture alive and crushed them. Your father was one such man. He had a deep respect for beauty and an understanding of those who came before, the ones who created such loveliness. I shall miss him." He glanced around the table at his compatriots. "We shall all miss him."

* * *

Milou did not want to go into the cave. The next morning, she opted to stay in town, while Katrinka and the abbot rode to the cave's entrance in the abbot's dog cart. It was misty with a light rain falling, but the cave was only a short distance from the hotel, nestled in the curve of a small, wooded hill.

Pieces of rounded lumber driven into the ground led to a T-shaped slit, which Katrinka realized was the entrance. Inside was an opening that had been widened for better access. The abbot held up his lamp. The hole went straight down.

"You will enter here. Please, take great care. We will go slowly."

She followed him into the dark opening, clutching her father's box. There were no steps. She slid down a rough board that someone had placed there, arriving in a heap on the floor of the cave. Lamps strung up along the crevices filled the area with a dim light. The sudden cold made her shiver, and the damp, musty smell of earth filled her nostrils. The silence was profound. Katrinka felt her ears straining for some kind of noise, anything to establish an equilibrium.

After several moments, her eyes adjusted. She followed the abbot down the narrow tunnel, stumbling over uneven ground, until it opened into a much larger area. He stopped and pointed. Looking up, she caught her breath.

"It is wonderful is it not?" he asked. "For every visitor, I see it for the first time through their eyes."

The paintings were extraordinarily lovely. Herds of horses and stags sprinted across the roof and sides of the cave. The artist had made use of the contoured walls to give shape and movement to their bodies. Most astonishing of all was the vividness of color. A little further on there were images of black bulls, one of them was immense. There was a cold draft, and she was thankful for the thick weave of her borrowed sweater.

"Your father held such a passion for *les grottes* and for the people who created this art. He had so much work for him here. He was eager to bring this to the attention of the entire world. These troubles will not last forever. Soon, our country will be whole again, and we will be able to continue your father's vision."

He pointed to a smaller passageway. "This goes further, away to the left. I will leave you now with your lamp and your father. Please, take all the time that is needed." He turned and walked away.

Then Katrinka was alone, holding the small box in her hands. The fantastical animals looked down at her from the ceiling and walls of the cave. She whispered to the shadows, "Oh, Papa Emerson. I wish you could have seen this."

Her legs gave out and she sank to the ground, wracked with an intense pain. He had always been a part of her life, and now he was gone forever. Clasping her knees to her breast, she rocked back and forth in the darkness, wretched and hiccupping in her grief. She tried to tell herself what she always did: everyone came to the same end, what else was there? You could only do the best you could.

But it didn't help.

It took a while to scatter that dark, gritty powder, feeling it sift through her fingers like sea sand. When done, she sat on a small rock, listening to the intense silence. She felt she could sit there forever, listening to that silence. Presently, she stood, gazing at the paintings one last time. "Goodbye Papa Emerson. I will never forget you."

Brushing off her clothing, she headed back up through the entrance and out into the watery sunlight.

* * *

Later that evening, the two women arrived in the small village of Treves and had a meal at the inn where they were to sleep. It was raining heavily, and to Katrinka's relief Milou had agreed to spend the night indoors. She listened as Milou chattered about the food and patrons, but she made no attempt to converse. They drank their coffee in silence.

That night, Katrinka threw back the bedcovers with a loud cry. She scrambled to her feet, her eyes wide with terror.

Milou jumped from the bed and put an arm around her, speaking quietly. "There. It is better now?"

Katrinka rubbed her forehead with a shaky sigh. "It is stupid, these frights."

"Do you remember them?"

"Yes. They come just as I am drifting off to sleep."

"Can you tell me?"

Katrinka walked to the window and looked out. "I begin to think of when I will die. Who I am, my memories, my spirit. Everything will die. And time begins to stretch out endlessly. Endlessly. I cannot fathom that. A time without ending." She turned and faced Milou. "I feel trapped."

Milou frowned, and Katrinka could see the girl was unfamiliar with such thoughts.

"I don't think we are meant to understand it. We must put our trust elsewhere. Do you believe in the Heavenly Father?" asked Milou.

"I have no beliefs."

"So, you are truly alone. You have nothing standing between you and the immensity of death."

"There is nothing."

Milou shifted uneasily on the hard floor, then tugged at her hand. "Lie back down, it is cold. We will speak of other things."

They got into bed, and Milou pulled the blankets up around them both. Leaning on one elbow, she smoothed the hair back from Katrinka's face.

"Have you ever made love to a woman?" asked Milou.

"What?"

Milou repeated her question.

Katrinka thought about it. A few experimental kisses exchanged at school, nothing more. Men had been her main interest, and she said as much to Milou.

"Then it is something you must try." Milou spoke lightly, as if suggesting a new game. "I should like to make love to you. And then you may tell your boyfriend." She laughed. "He will be so jealous. Or he may become excited. Many men have that fantasy, you know. Just themselves and two women."

She paused, then spoke again. "Well? Shall we try?"

Katrinka studied her friend's face. Was she attracted to her that way?

Milou bent down and brushed her lips against hers, slipping on top of her. Katrinka adjusted her body to fit, as Milou's hands began their exploration. Her kisses became more passionate, and Katrinka could feel herself becoming aroused. She arched her back, and her own hands began searching.

Milou whispered, "Yes, you see? This is good."

But it was not good. Milou felt soft and small, so unlike what she was used to. Katrinka pushed her away.

Milou sat up. "What is it? What is wrong?"

"I'm sorry. I thought I could. I wanted to try, but—"

"Ah, you do not like it."

"No."

"Well, there is no need for concern. There is no reproach."

"I miss my friend."

"Your lover."

"Yes."

"It happens that way sometimes, when you are in the arms of another. I myself have felt that way before. Do you want me to leave the bed?"

Katrinka smiled. "To sleep on the floor? Of course not."

They settled down together, and after a few moments, Milou spoke again. "Today in the cave, you scattered your father's ashes. There was no problem?"

"There was no problem."

"What was he like, your father?"

Katrinka shook her head, the sudden lump in her throat making words impossible.

Milou sighed. "Ah well. It is over now. We will try to sleep."

Katrinka curled into a small ball, but she could not sleep. *"What was he like, your father?"*

She remembered the first time she'd met Emerson Badeau. There was a terrible argument between A-mah and her papa, and her mother had gotten off the boat in Singapore, taking Katrinka with her.

A tall, fair-haired man met them there, and they left the next morning, taking a ship that was not her father's, bound for India. Several days later, her mother gave her flowers and a pretty dress to wear. After a brief ceremony on board ship, A-mah and this man were married. Her mother instructed her to call him 'papa', but the young girl refused. Their argument escalated until the man interceded, telling Yujana that her daughter could call him whatever she damn well pleased.

Emerson was on an expedition, and there were other men on board with him. He and A-mah spent many nights poring over maps, and making notes and beautiful diagrams in his journals. When they arrived in Bombay, Katrinka was enthralled. She had been to India on *Le Flâneur*, but she had only seen the ports.

Papa Emerson took them into cities teeming with animals and people. Coconut sellers, washerwomen, ox carts, and automobiles—all jostling for space in the narrow lanes and wide boulevards. Slow-moving camels and painted elephants lumbered under the scorching sun. There were swaying snake charmers, and women with pierced noses, clothed in brightly colored garments and golden arm bands. And always, the scent of sweet-smelling joss sticks, their musky aromas mingling with the odor of sweating animals, pungent heaps of spices, and raw human waste puddled in the gutters.

On his explorations, Emerson took them to caves, deep and cool in the mountains, away from the blazing sun. Katrinka was astonished to see paintings and carvings of men and women entwined in exciting positions. And, even further within the cool interiors, tranquil Buddhas looked down from their dusty alcoves.

Emerson was kind to her and made her laugh. He carried the most incredible things in his trunks: intricately carved beads and maps of ancient cities; a butterfly trapped in amber, and bits of shell and coral. There was even a partial skull, carried in a small bag made from the skin of a snake.

And at night, back at camp, tents glimmered with flickering lantern light, while smoky incense mingled with the smell of good food cooking in the large outdoor kitchens. But it did not last. Soon there was tension and arguments. Yujana grew tired of the dust and heat, and once again Katrinka found herself having to say goodbye to a father she had grown to love.

She sighed deeply and turned, grateful for the warmth of Milou's body next to hers. Both women slept soundly for the rest of the night.

* * *

The next morning, they left Treves early, as they wanted to be in Montec by nightfall. They were used to long days on the bikes, and were making good time now.

They stopped at a morning market, stood in another endless line for meager supplies, and then pedaled steadily until noon. They broke for lunch near some trees and spread out in the grass to eat. Drifting clouds occasionally covered the sun, darkening the air. Katrinka could smell rain. They finished their meal, and she wiped off her knife. Milou watched her sheath it.

"That is a beautiful blade. Where did you get it? I have not seen soldiers with such knives."

"It was made in Toledo. My parents gave it to me. My mother thought I should be protected."

"From what?"

Katrinka lay on her back, watching the clouds. "When I was small, we were with Papa Emerson's expedition in Spain. There was a worker who helped with the loading. One day, he took me back to his tent. He put me on his bed, pulled his penis from his pants, and began stroking it. I will never forget how it grew large in his hands. It was both terrible and wonderful at the same time."

"Did he—"

"He tried. After a few minutes, he lay down next to me and began stroking me. He lifted my dress and began stroking me inside my underthings. I didn't know why he was doing it. No one had ever touched me there.

"Then he rolled on top of me. It frightened me, he was so heavy. I felt I could not breathe."

Milou hissed, "I would have killed him."

"He was fumbling with his penis. He was trying to fit it inside of me. Of course, I did not know what was happening, but suddenly there was a very sharp pain, and I began screaming. He tried to cover my mouth, but I bit him and pulled away, screaming."

"That is horrible."

"My mother heard me and came running. She burst into the tent with her knife. She cut him and cut him, until my papa came. He grabbed her and she swung at him—"

"*Mother of God*, did she hurt your father?"

"No. She stopped then."

"Was the man—"

Katrinka shook her head. "The doctor came and bandaged him up, and he was sent away. He lost his fingers on one hand. Also, my mother had cut off—"

"No. Don't think of it."

"The next day, Papa Emerson took us to a nearby town and purchased this knife for me. They showed me how to use it and made me practice. I remember my mother telling me that if anyone ever harmed me or tried to hurt me, I was free to use it on them."

Milou's voice was crisp, "I believe I would have liked your mother."

Katrinka nodded. "I don't think she knew how to love me. But in her own way, she took care of me. She was brave how she lived. And she died a brave death."

Both women were silent, gazing up at the sky. Eventually Milou drifted off to sleep, but Katrinka could still hear her mother's words, falling like a wooden stamp on the soft clay of memory:

"It is your body. Always there will be men who try to possess it, tell you what to do with it, tell you they own it. Some will treat it poorly. It is your right to defend, and take care of it."

It was one of the few times her mother ever gave her advice, and she had not forgotten.

* * *

As the distance to Marseilles grew shorter, Milou's complaints of soreness dwindled, but Katrinka noticed tension in her movements and in her face. Despite the cold, she refused to spend their last night in a hotel room. So they camped rough, sleeping in the open at the edge of a copse of trees, facing a meadow. After eating, they curled up, lying on their jackets that they spread out across the damp grass. The night was clear, with thousands of stars sprinkled overhead.

"I am going to my mother who lives with her family in French Quebec," Milou said. "She ran away from my father before the war."

"I'm sorry. I didn't know."

"She was repulsed by his behavior and beliefs. Then I went away to university. I guess you know about that?"

"*The White Rose?*"

"Yes. We knew what was happening, you see. It was like watching a terrible accident in slow motion. These incidents; all separate, but all spelling out a dreadful foreshadowing. The book burnings, the forced incarcerations, beatings, and murders. Everyone turning a deaf ear and a blind eye. As long as their lives went on, they did not want to look ahead. We were caught, my group and I, handing out pamphlets against *der Führer*."

Katrinka looked at her. The girl was gazing upward, speaking to the sky.

"There was a trial by the Nazi *Volksgerichtshof*. It was ludicrous. They guillotined three of us, and later executed another. The rest they put into prisons. The prison was very bad. Only a little food, and every day there were tortures. Many of us died. Then there was talk of the Russians coming, so they began to destroy the camp.

"One evening, they took us out to a small cliff, with a pit at the bottom. They lined us up and ordered us into the pit. We were told to strip off our clothing, men and women. The soldiers had weapons. They sat along the rim, their legs hanging over the edge. They sat there and shot us with their guns. I remember one soldier eating a sandwich as he aimed. As the bullets struck, we toppled back into the pit. It was quiet. There was very little screaming. I was one of the last ones shot. They came over to bury us with earth."

Katrinka stared.

"They continued to shoot at anyone still moving or making sounds, so I pretended to be dead. I thought I soon would be. The woman lying next to me was groaning. They shot her, and she stopped moving.

"Later, when they were gone, I clawed my way to the surface. I climbed out of the pit and ran. I'd been shot in the leg, but did not notice it then. I was rescued by a farmer and his wife. They took care of me, and I was passed from safe house to safe house. Until I reached your people."

In the pause of conversation, the sound of a distant dog barking was the only disturbance. Sickened, Katrinka reached out to hold Milou's hand. She could think of nothing to say. Milou's eyes glistened with unshed tears. They looked like winter rain on dirty windows.

"I will be glad to leave this godforsaken place," she said.

Katrinka squeezed her hand. "But you are free now. Think only of that. You are free."

Milou gave a wan smile to her naïve friend. Free? She would never be free. In her mind there was a place that held her there, always.

* * *

The sun broke out from behind darkened clouds, just as they descended into Marseilles. The city teamed with activity. Katrinka was shocked at the sight of hundreds of uniformed soldiers, seemingly thousands of them, everywhere. Crammed into trucks and rumbling down roads in long convoys, they snaked around the limestone hills that surrounded the port town. Marching in endless rows, with weapons slung over their backs, and throwing chocolate bars to the children running along their ranks. They looked exhausted, but in good spirits.

The skeletal remains of bombed-out buildings slumped along the harbor, and anchored ships disgorged supplies along hastily constructed docks. The clamor was deafening, and a heavy smell of exhaust, mingled with that of raw fish, hung in the air. And everywhere the dust and smoke.

Amid the jumble of military craft and merchant ships, Katrinka saw her father standing on the crowded deck of *Le Flâneur*. The women found a place to park their bicycles and then struggled through the crowds to reach the small dock. It was incredibly busy, and they had to wait to board. As her father greeted them above the deafening roar, Katrinka could hear Rolf's frantic cries from below deck, sensing her presence. Her eyes teared up. She must say her goodbyes quickly.

She turned and gave Milou a fierce embrace, struggling for words. What would she do without her? Who would make her laugh?

Milou stepped back, grasping her hand. "When the war is over, you must come and visit me in Quebec. I shall leave my address with your father. You will come, yes?"

Katrinka nodded, unable to speak.

"Then I will say *au revoir*, my little swallow."

"*Au revoir*, Milou."

Santos led Milou down below decks, and Katrinka turned to her father. There were so many people jostling them and unloading cargo, it was hard to speak.

"So, Papa…"

"Dear child, come with us."

She shook her head.

He studied her face, then asked softly, "And to which one of them do you return?"

She gave him a startled look.

"I would like to tell you so many things, but there is no time. Do not make a mistake you cannot change."

She shrugged away his words. "Papa, be gentle with Milou. She appears strong, but she has seen terrible things."

"So, I believe, has the other."

"The other?"

"There is the American pilot aboard as well. He arrived yesterday evening."

"Oh, yes. I remember him." She smiled, thinking of Milou's ways. "Perhaps they will be good for each other."

Amparo laughed, "I will make sure of it."

She swallowed the hard lump in her throat. "Goodbye, Papa."

"Trinka?"

She turned, unable to meet his eyes.

"This war cannot last forever, and when it is over, there will be no place for an old man with an old boat. As I said earlier, I will go back to Coronado. There is good fishing there and a good life. And memories of happier times. I will be there, when you are done. Whatever it is you decide."

"I'll find you, Papa."

Santos thrust his head from a hatchway door, giving her a quick nod. "Captain, it's time—"

Amparo swiveled his head. "Right." He turned back to her, just as a large net of cargo swung down between them. Katrinka dodged another oncoming crate and was squeezed down the gangplank to the dock. She turned back and saw her father hurry toward the bridge. He paused at the top, scanning the crowd. Seeing her face below, he gave her a brief wave and smile. And then he was gone.

10

K ATRINKA RETURNED TO TROIS CLOCHES ON A chilly November afternoon, exactly two weeks and one day since departing from their former camp. Pascal had made good on his promise to find better accommodation for the team. With help from the map Nye had given her, she made her way out to the old, abandoned library located on the outskirts of town. Afternoon sunlight drifted across the road, turning the scattered leaves into glimmering piles of red and golden coins.

The library appeared deserted. Katrinka let herself in through the main doorway, the warped floorboards creaking beneath her feet. She glanced around. Old-fashioned maps hung from the walls amid a scattering of battered furniture. On the desk sat a Remington typewriter that had seen better days. Sunlight slanted through crooked shutters as dust motes spun through the yellowed air. Outside, trees dropped their russet-colored leaves onto a small garden, and the smell of wet earth drifted through open windows.

A slight murmuring of equipment came from upstairs, and she followed the noise. Pausing at the top of the landing, she looked into the sunlit doorway of a rectangular room. Wolfe sat at a lopsided desk, tapping out a coded message on his radio, the aerial strung out the window into an adjoining tree. She waited for him to finish and then watched as he pushed back his chair and stood, removing the headset. Stretching his arms to the ceiling, he looked out the window. There were deep creases on either side of his jaw, and in the light, his dear face looked worn and tired.

"Wolfe."

He spun around. "My God."

He was across the floor in a moment, pulling her into his arms. "You're finally here."

He pressed her close, burying his face in her hair. She folded herself around him, breathing in his familiar scent of sweat and cigarettes, feeling his heart pound against her breasts. Neither spoke for several moments.

Then she drew back, holding his face in her hands. "Are you well? Are you all right?"

He nodded. "I'm all right now, Trink."

Suddenly, he hoisted her in the air. Cupping his hands under her buttocks, he laughed as he spun her around. She had never heard him laugh.

With her legs wrapped around him, he carried her over to the bed and tossed her onto it. Trousers, shorts, and shirt were hurled to the floor as she wriggled out of her skirt and sweater. Climbing on top of her, he smothered her with kisses. She slipped the panties down her legs, flicking them away with her foot. She grabbed him from behind with both hands, as he pressed his cock into her. She wasn't quite ready, and it hurt a bit.

After a few strokes he was panting. "Wait. Ease up a little."

He pulled out and leaned back, fumbling in his pile of clothing for a condom. Katrinka peeled off the rest of her things and waited as he slipped it down his erection.

213

Then she drew him close, scratching her fingers down his stubbled cheeks.

He nuzzled her breasts, circling and flicking her nipples with his tongue. He kissed her neck and licked the inside of her ear. His hot breath tickled, and Katrinka curled her toes in delight. She pulled his mouth down over hers and wrapped her tongue around his, gently sucking and tugging.

At the same time, his hand massaged her inner thighs, working his way up to her vaginal opening. He rubbed around her clitoris with his thumb then slipped his fingers inside her, stroking and probing. She was very wet now, and he continued probing, using both his fingers and his cock until she thought she would go crazy. Then she cried out, attempting to muffle the sound against his shoulder, but bit it instead.

The muscles of his arms tensed as he shoved himself inside her, ejaculating into the contractions of her orgasm. He held himself there, straining and shuddering, until he fell back onto her body, slippery with sweat. Sealed together in each other's arms, they slept.

* * *

Katrinka woke to hear a jeep pulling up outside. Raising herself on one elbow, she watched as a cool breeze shook crimson-colored leaves from the trees. A gust blew through the open window. She shivered, and Wolfe opened his eyes.

"Are you cold?" He pulled the worn blanket around her naked shoulders.

"Just hold me close. When did you get back?"

"About a week ago now. All fine, just a scar. The nurse said it makes me look dashing, whatever that means."

"So, it was Bouchard's son."

He nodded.

"I feel sorry for him—his whole family. I'm sorry I killed his father."

"Don't think about it. There was no way of knowing."

He rolled over her body and stood up, pulling his clothes and boots back on.

"Do you have to get up? Aren't you done for the evening?"

"I need to go out and take the antenna down."

"Please, not yet."

He smiled, as she pulled him back. She put her head in his lap, and he ran his fingers through her tangled hair.

"Where is everyone, Wolfe?"

"Mostly in meetings. Giraud's working with some French groups in another village. The major's been out for a few days, talking with senior military leaders. There's been some difficulty now that the Communist Resistance and Free French Resistance are all under one government."

"It would seem they should be happy to be united."

Farr shook his head. "No, and that's the difficulty the Jeds are facing now." He frowned, switching to another topic. "How's your father?"

"Busy. I barely had time to say goodbye before leaving him. The ports are opening, and supplies and troops are pouring in. It was easier coming back, but not nearly as much fun."

"You had no trouble then."

"Not in the least." She smiled. "You Americans are everywhere now."

"And he—the German? You two got along?"

She bounced up, sitting next to him. "We traveled together quite well. Such wonderful talks!"

"That's nice."

She did not notice his tone.

"Where did you stay?" he questioned.

"On the first night, we slept on a church floor. It was very cold, but we had wine and snuggled together for warmth. Then there were inns and small hotels along the way. Several nights, we slept out in the open."

"But you managed to keep warm."

"What?"

"Sleeping together. Keeps you warm." His words were short now, biting.

Katrinka noticed and paused.

He continued, "So, you just headed south?"

"Yes. We took a small detour to Lascaux. It was so lovely, Wolfe. I wish you could have been there with me."

The silence stretched out between them. Katrinka watched as he pulled back, his face shuttered.

"Wolfe, you look so strange, is anything the matter?" She placed a hand on his arm, but he jerked away.

"You and the German. You *slept* together."

"Well, yes, of course," she replied slowly. "Our quarters were very small you know. It was a necessity. And then there was the cold. It was a great comfort—"

"You know what I mean."

"What *do* you mean?"

"Did you fuck?" The brutal words burst out, and Katrinka flushed a deep red.

Angrily, she faced him on the bed. "We actually did try it out. I thought it might be fun... something new. And it did feel good. But it wasn't you. I felt hollow and empty." She placed a hand on his arm, attempting a smile. "I missed you."

She gave a startled cry as he flung her away, leaping from the bed. He looked for a moment as if he would strike her. She could see him struggle with it. There was violence in the air.

"Wolfe—"

"Shut up!"

"*What* are you carrying on about? It was a simple thing. I'd had a night terror."

"I said shut up! I don't want to hear it."

"What is wrong with you? Surely this cannot matter. It was just something that happened."

He swung around, and this time she really thought he was going to hit her. Defensively, her hands clenched into fists, hard and tense. If he struck her, it would be over between them. Forever and irreparably broken.

But instead of the blow, he reached down, cradling her face in his hands. "How can you just sit there and *justify* this? How can you—" His voice broke. "Christ, Katrinka, I was in the hospital."

"It wasn't like that! I longed for you. I ached for you. Every breathing second. Why are you doing this? It was *nothing*."

He released her then, his anger replaced by a calm that seemed more terrible. She tried to hold him, but he moved away.

"I thought we had something together. I thought I meant something to you."

"Wolfe, please."

"I know you've had a hell of an upbringing. I've tried to understand you, tell myself you have a different way with things. Not much guidance from your parents, whoever they all were."

217

His remark struck, much worse than any blow.

She choked over her words. "You do not even know my parents. My mother…" She would not let herself cry. "You do not know me at all," she finished quietly.

"Katrinka, I can't listen to this now. I have to go. I need to go."

"No! Wait. Wolfe, please!"

But he had walked out of the room and down the stairs. She heard the backdoor slam, too stunned to move. She sank onto the bed, covering her head with the blanket, and curled into a knot. Wracked with an anguish too deep for tears, and distress so severe, she feared she would not be able to bear it.

* * *

Wolfe exploded into the street and the cool night air. Her careless words had scalded his soul. He staggered a few steps down the road. Lurching into nearby bushes, he fell to his knees in the dirt, heaving his guts out.

* * *

Later that night, Katrinka heard someone come in. She crept downstairs, but it was Wills. There were other men with him, arguing loudly. Wolfe was not there. She went back to bed but did not sleep. Wolfe did not return.

In the morning, she came down early to see Wills sitting at a small table, drinking a cup of coffee and studying some reports. He got up to greet her, then sat back down, smiling.

"I hear all went well?" he asked.

"Yes. Milou and the pilot are on their way to Lisbon."

"And Emerson? Any difficulty with his remains?"

"No, the people at the cave were very kind."

He gestured to the room. "Our last camp, I should think. New assignments going around. Things are breaking up quickly."

Her heart lurched. "You are going away?"

He shrugged. "The teams are being sent all over. Some back to England, some continuing on to Germany. As a matter of fact, a job has come up we may need you for." Nye indicated his papers. "Messages and radio parts have to be delivered to another Jed team, east of us. Might take a few days."

"Yes, of course."

"I know it's a bloody imposition. You've only just returned."

"It is not a problem."

"Did you and Farr get together? He was driving me crazy asking when you'd be back."

She nodded.

"You can spend the night there and come back tomorrow. It's a quick turnaround."

She had trouble getting the words out. "Will you still be here when I return?"

He looked up, and saw her puffy face and red eyes looking back at him. "Sweet Jesus, Trinka, what's wrong?"

"I'm fine."

He sat back in his chair, flipping his pencil onto the papers. "I wouldn't ask, but we're shorthanded at the moment. I need Valentine, and Farr left early this morning, for a meeting at HQ."

Wolfe was gone.

"It is not a problem, Wills. I can do it."

"Is there something you want to tell me? Something going on between you and Farr?"

She shook her head.

He sighed, frowning. "Right. Come back in an hour, and we'll have everything ready. And, yes, I should be here a bit longer. I would not leave without—"

She nodded and fled the room.

* * *

Katrinka was gone for a few days and returned late one afternoon. A downpour had caught her several kilometers outside of town. By the time she reached the library she was soaking wet, her clothes clinging to her body with an uncomfortable dampness. A dark, gray bowl of sky loomed above her, filled with rumbles of thunder. Lightning flashed in the distance.

Giraud was working with a small group of French recruits in the main room, and he waved to her as she passed. She could hear Valentine upstairs on the radio. She did not see Wills. Wolfe's room looked strangely bare, and his rucksack was gone.

Katrinka washed in the small bathroom. She pulled on a long shirt, a castoff of Wolfe's. It was much too large, but it smelled of him. She hung her undergarments to dry in a corner of her room, too tired to do anything more. She would meet with Wills in the morning and ask about Wolfe.

She had just settled on her small bed when Nye appeared in the doorway, holding a bowl of something hot and a small plate of bread.

"You're back." The smile of greeting he offered did not meet his eyes.

"Yes, I arrived just before dark." She rose from the bed and they both sat down at a splintered wooden table by the window.

"I returned a short time ago and heard you in the bath. Thought you might want something to eat."

"Wills, where is—"

"Any trouble with your delivery?"

"None at all."

"Got some messages concerning supplies. Big disagreements. Trying to form a coalition between the damn Communist French and Free French is like—"

"Wills."

He stopped.

"Where is Wolfe?"

"Look, you're tired. Get some sleep. Tomorrow we can talk." She pushed back the chair.

"Wait. Where are you going?"

"If you won't tell me, I'm asking someone who will. Val will know."

Nye held out his hand. "Trinka, come here and sit down. I'll tell you."

She sat down.

"As you know, many of the SAS and Jed teams are being sent back to England for training, or given new assignments. Our job here is pretty much done."

Her fingers were shredding the bread into tiny pieces. She forced herself to stop. "Yes, you've said as much."

"I think I'd mentioned the colonel's meeting a few days ago. He was looking for volunteers."

"Yes." Her fingers were at the bread again. The smell of the soup was making her sick.

"They need experienced radio operators to go to the Far East, and Malaya."

Nye was close, but she could barely make out his face. Black dots swarmed in front of her eyes and a ringing in her ears made his voice unnaturally distant. She felt clammy.

"Farr mentioned wanting a change. He decided… he's volunteered, you see."

Katrinka fainted.

For a man who took charge in the worst possible scenarios, Nye was hopelessly inept in this one. He tried ineffectually to revive her. When this failed, he bellowed for help. Valentine sprinted in and surveyed the scene. He carried Katrinka to her bed, put her down, and elevated her feet with a rolled blanket.

"Sir, some cold towels I think?"

The major ran to get them.

Valentine looked down at her face. He guessed she'd been told.

"Dammit all to hell," he swore viciously, to no one in particular.

* * *

Katrinka awoke. The room was steeped in gray light, and a figure sat quietly in the corner, not moving. She sat up.

"Wolfe?"

Nye jerked awake and stumbled across the room to kneel at her bed. "Sweetheart, I had no idea you'd go over like that. I am so sorry. I put it all the wrong way."

He was going to talk about it. The pressure in her head came back.

"He is truly gone."

"Yes."

"Where?"

"A small convoy drove up to Paris yesterday. He'll be put on a waiting list for transport to England for more training, and orders for his next assignment."

She looked away. Outside the window, it was growing dark. The rain had stopped, and the damp smell of wet leaves filled the room. Down below, a small bird hopped through the brown grass, looking for worms. It meant nothing to her. He was gone. He would never again be just a few footsteps across her room, into the hall, and through his sunlit doorway.

"Trinka, what happened?"

She was silent.

"Farr looked like hell before he left. He wouldn't say anything."

She got up from the bed and went to sit at the table. Nye followed, sitting opposite her.

Slowly, as if each word might implode, she spoke. "Milou and I made love. Or at least we tried. It came out later, when Wolfe and I were talking in bed. He went crazy. He wouldn't listen to me."

"You and Milou? Made love?"

"Yes. It was the day with Emerson's ashes and the cave. I had a night terror, and she was in bed with me. She said we should make love. I wasn't sure I'd like it, but I said yes."

"Did you?"

"Did I what?"

"Did you like it?"

223

"We tried, but I had to stop. It... it made me miss Wolfe even more. You may have the pleasure, but it is an entirely different thing."

Nye frowned. "Trinka?"

"Yes."

"Did Farr know Milou was a woman?"

"Yes, of..." Katrinka thought of the brief conversation. The rapidly accelerating emotions, careening out of control.

"He was so angry, he didn't listen. I did not mention she was a woman. Would it have mattered?"

"For a man, it would matter a great deal."

"Well, it shouldn't. A man or a woman, it is the same thing. A little fun, a little comfort."

"It's not the same thing at all, as you just said yourself."

She caught her breath. He was right. She would never have spoken like she did, had Milou been a man. She would not have spoken of it at all. Her words came back to her with a sickening clarity. How could he have thought her so cruel as to say them?

Her anger continued to ferment, and she encouraged it. So much better than anguish. Suddenly, she missed Milou. She would have something snappy to say. She would not let this crush her.

Well. It was over now. All the weeks of keyed up emotions, danger and risk. Suddenly deflated like one of those carnival balloons, flying out in random directions. Everyone scattering. What would she do? Go back to Porto, or her mother's people in the Andaman Sea? Papa had taken them there a few times over the years. But the war was on. There were her mother's ashes. She could return them to Coronado.

"So. It is over now. Time to move on?"

Nye fumbled for words. "I don't know… Farr might—"

"No. No, I mean our jobs. They are finished?"

Nye was silent for a long while, and Katrinka saw the dismay in his eyes.

He reached for her hand. "Trinka, would you like to go back to Porto? I could try to find you transport."

She let out a small gasp, drawing away. "Now? Leave here? Leave you?"

"Sweetheart, we'll all be leaving soon. I should be getting orders in the next few weeks. Giraud will be moving up to Paris, and Valentine is being sent back to England."

The time had come. Everyone was going. Katrinka felt she could shatter at any moment, scattering into irreparable fragments. She forced herself to think. She still had her father. And *Le Flâneur*.

"I want to find my father. He spoke of leaving as well, returning to California. He said this was all a young man's game."

"He's been through two wars, Trinka. I should think he would be ready to go."

She rubbed her eyes and thought. To be on the deck of *Le Flâneur* again, headed to Coronado with a good wind at her back. The striped tents were long gone, as well as the old horse Paycheck. But the little town drowsing in its sunlit bay, would be waiting for her.

"You've got a proper passport, haven't you? Proper papers? I know it was easy going on *Le Flâneur*. Your father had his ways."

"Yes, that's why A-mah and Papa Emerson married. It meant nothing to her, but she wanted me to have birthright citizenship. They gave me a visa to attend school in Switzerland, and I was issued papers by Emerson's business contacts to get me to Lascaux."

Nye seemed relieved. "I could arrange your transport to England aboard a troop ship, but once there, you would need a job while waiting. Some authorization. Then from England—"

"I can get in contact with Papa in London, through his solicitor," she said with sudden eagerness. "He spoke of leaving from Liverpool Docks."

"That's settled then. But what can we have you do? We'd better move fast, as my contacts are shifting. We can get you papers and a working visa. Secretary? Nanny? Clerk?"

She shrugged.

"I have a friend who works for a small news agency in London. He is always in need of office help, especially now with the rocket attacks. It would give you a legitimate reason to be there, while waiting for your father. He should be almost to Lisbon now, with Milou and the pilot."

Katrinka forced all thoughts of Wolfe from her head. She would deal with that pain later. "Yes, Wills, please."

"Leave it to me. I will arrange for your documents immediately. We can get you in a convoy up to Paris late next week. From there, with your papers, it will be easy to get a transport to Dieppe and across the channel to England. I'll give you the directions to the London office."

Katrinka nodded, feeling very tired. Wills had on his take-charge expression. She was a problem, and he was going to solve it with his usual efficiency.

"How are you set for money? You were never on the payroll you know, just what we could give for your transactions."

"Papa gave me money, and I have what's left from the last trip. I'm to contact his solicitor for any funding."

"Your father has done very well for himself over the years."

"Yes, I suppose he has."

"Nonetheless, I will leave you something before you go. We have a general fund for our expenses."

"So, I was just an expense?"

The take-charge look vanished.

His voice shook. "You know what you are to me, Katrinka."

She looked at him, and for the briefest moment, his eyes were open windows.

He stood up, clearing his throat. "I'm off early tomorrow for a meeting near Faucher, then another one to the east after that." He pulled a slip of paper from his pocket and scrawled something down. "This is my sister's address in Bristol. She forwards my mail to me wherever I am. I would ask for yours, but…"

"Let me give you the address of Papa's solicitor. Gorges handles Papa's papers and communication. He will know where to find me."

She tore the sheet in half, writing the information down.

Nye pocketed it. "Right. Well."

They stood awkwardly, facing one another.

"Do you need help with the pack up?"

She shook her head. "Will you be back before I leave?"

"There may be a possible space between meetings, but I shouldn't count on it."

"So, I will see you when the war is over?"

"I shall look forward to that, sweetheart."

Nye seemed to hesitate. The next moment he was pulling her close, clasping her head between his hands, and kissing her with a hungry ferocity. Katrinka drew away, startled, and he hastily released her, stumbling back with apologies.

She reached out for him, "No, Wills, please…"

But he hurried from the room, leaving her too stunned to do anything but stare after him, drawing tremulous fingers across her scratched lips.

* * *

Farr was not sleeping well. The disastrous encounter with Katrinka had loosened a barrage of emotions he'd always kept under tight control.

Christ, he'd come close to hitting her. He could still feel the rage in his fists, the desire to strike out and hurt her like her words had hurt him. He was no better than his old man. But he wasn't going to be like his old man. He'd not turned into a drunk, and by God, he wasn't turning into a woman-beater.

Their last conversation replayed endlessly in his mind, and the whole thing seemed off. She may have dealt with sexual matters differently, but she'd never been cruel. What had been missing? Something he should have heard before storming off. Volunteering for this mission halfway around the world, that he was already regretting. The answer came a few days later, when two messages arrived at the Rue de Aalis HQ.

Val's message was cryptic: "*You need to write to her. Sort it out.*" There were a few more sentences, but the censor had blacked them out.

Nye's message had been less circumspect: *"The escapee was a woman. Clear this up."*

Farr stared at the papers in his hand. Snatches of their last conversation came back to him now, along with a painful understanding. The brutal carelessness of Katrinka's replies suddenly made sense. *"I thought it might be fun… something new. It felt hollow and empty… I missed you."* The wonderful traveling companion had been a woman.

The enormity of his mistake left him feeling sick. It was so like her, something she would try out. He'd goaded her by his angry questioning, into the last flippant confession. And it had blown up in their faces. He did not ask himself why a woman lover made a difference.

She'd told him to give her time. She'd never been confronted with someone like him or the kind of demands he made. Her unconventional upbringing had not given her the guidance or role models. She'd sensed the difficulties to overcome, while he'd turned a blind eye.

All their talks had centered on his hopes and plans. Hadn't she mentioned something once? Her search for that aviatrix. He remembered the excitement he'd felt when he saw her maps and diagrams. His idea of using sonar in an underwater search. Could he be content following her, and working with the electronics of the ship? Was this all too late?

* * *

After the meeting, a few officers invited Nye out for a meal in Faucher. Nye suspected there would be little food but plenty of wine. God only knew where the French kept all their bottles. But he declined, telling them he would return in the morning for transport to Poitiers.

Hurrying to the motor pool, he inquired about a car. There were none to be found, so he requisitioned a bicycle and wobbled out of the city, heading west. It was twenty kilometers to Trois Cloches and a few more to the library.

Surely there could be nothing difficult about riding a bike, but he was tired and thirsty by the time he got to the outskirts of the village. The sun dipped below the horizon just as he toiled up the last small hill to the fields and the library beyond. Thick grass and vines had overtaken the path, impeding his progress.

He caught sight of Katrinka drowsing in an old farm cart, her skin glowing in the pearl-colored light. Crickets were serenading, and an evening wind rippled across the fields, bringing with it the delicate scent of wild thyme. He stopped a few feet away, gazing down at her face. The scarf in her hair had come undone, and dark locks tumbled about her face. The man shivered. He experienced an ineffable sense of elation, as if stepping weightless out into a great void.

* * *

Katrinka heard a cough and started awake. She smiled, seeing Wills before her. She regarded him with sleepy eyes.

"You've come back."

"We ended early. I've got to return tomorrow. What are you doing here, Trinka? Asleep like the king's daughter in the straw."

"I knew if you came back, you would have to cross this field. I was waiting for you."

He was standing with the bike between his legs, leaning on the handlebars and smiling down at her. Desire for the man rolled over her in a wave so thick, she swallowed, thinking she would taste him on her tongue.

She reached out with her arms, "Make love to me, Wills, here in the straw and soft light. Before you go away."

His smile faded. Slowly, he dismounted from the bicycle, laying it in the grass. He stood contemplating her, with an almost thoughtful expression. The next moment, he was sitting next to her in the cart. He was warm where the sun had touched his skin. He leaned down, brushing her mouth with a kiss, and then pulled back, searching her face. He seemed to be haloed in the fading light. Katrinka licked his saltiness from her lips. Her entire body reverberated with the taste of it.

She undid his buttons. He unfastened her skirt, and pulled off her jumper and blouse. There was nothing underneath. She helped him out of his clothing, and they were naked. His cock was hard and pointing upward. She saw him hesitate.

"I have a… do you want—" he began.

"No. I want you without any—"

He interrupted her. "Trinka, if you had our child, do you think I could ever let either of you go?"

The pain in his voice cut her to the quick. She spoke without caution, and straight from her unpractical heart. "I love you, Wills. And I'll take everything that might come with it."

He nodded, but his fingers trembled slightly as he flattened his tunic on the bed of the cart. "Lie down on this, sweetheart, a bit more comfortable, I think."

She slid back, looking up at him. A scattering of dark, curly hair crossed his chest; his shoulders were ropy with muscles. There were tan lines at his wrists where white arms met browned hands. Strong hands that she'd seen perform so many tasks. His sexual presence heavied the air around her, making her shaky. She trailed her fingers down either side of his neck and along his arms, feeling the hard muscles ripple. "Kiss me again, Wills."

* * *

A while later, Nye woke, needing to relieve himself. Afterwards, he came back to the cart and lay down next to Katrinka's slumbering body, propping himself up on one elbow. Her hair was damp with sweat and clung to her shoulders. Her head rested in the curve of an arm. He leaned over her and cupped one soft breast in his hands, kissing it tenderly, smelling the woodsy scent of her skin. He stroked the hair back from her face, feeling its damp warmth. He would never let her go.

Under his touch, she half-opened her eyes and smiled. Nye rolled onto his back, pulling her on top of him. She leaned down to give him a lazy kiss, sealing her lips over his and licking the inside of his mouth. Placing a hand on his shoulder, she raised herself up onto her knees. She grasped his penis and began massaging the shaft, while stroking herself with its head, letting it slip in and around the moist opening to her vagina.

He was making hissing noises between gritted teeth. He pushed himself into her, holding her waist with both hands. She squealed with pleasure. Leaning over him, she used her knees to raise herself up and down on his cock.

He moved slowly at first, then faster, with deepening strokes. A few moments later, unbelievably, Nye felt himself growing soft. He pumped harder, but it was useless. Dammit, what the *hell* was going on?

"Wills."

Frantically, he continued pumping. His penis began to slip out of her.

"Wills!"

He looked up, mortified.

She sat back and laughed. "*Dear* Wills, we need to stop. We're finished for a while."

His voice was distraught. "I don't know what happened. You felt so good, I…"

She smoothed back his sweating hair. "How far did you ride your bike tonight?"

"Not too far, around twenty kilometers, but—"

"And you must ride it back tomorrow." She peered at his watch. "Rather, in a few hours."

"Is it after midnight?"

"It's two in the morning."

"Sweetheart, just give me a minute. I'll be fine."

"You will not be fine in a minute. You are going to sleep right now. Do you want to go up to the library for a proper rest?"

"No."

She rolled off him. "Then lie down, I'll hold you in my arms. Yes, like that; get comfortable. You're exhausted. Have you had anything to eat?"

"There wasn't time."

"Of course not, you had to go rushing off on your bicycle. There will be other times, when we don't have to use the back of a haycart."

"I can't imagine any place I'd rather be right now."

"No more talking; try to get some rest."

He turned over with his backside pressing against her, and she curled herself around him.

He was asleep in moments.

* * *

Later, Nye roused himself, feeling stiff and sore. It was cooler now, and the sky was lightening. An early morning mist hung over the fields. He should be heading back.

He sat up and stretched, dangling his long legs over the end of the cart. He wished for his pipe. He glanced back as Katrinka stirred, rubbing her eyes.

"You are leaving?"

He nodded.

She sat up and leaned against him, sliding both her arms around his waist. They sat together in the gray light.

She sighed. "Oh Wills."

He wrapped an arm around her shoulders. "Yes. Quite."

II

FOR THE NEXT FEW DAYS, KATRINKA TRIED TO KEEP busy. The library had a small garden at the back of the building, and after finding tools, she began some weeding and pruning. The feel of moist earth tumbling between her fingers soothed her nerves, and she loved its loamy smell.

One afternoon, a small, bulky package came by courier, addressed to her. She opened it, and found her visa documents and working papers. Wills had also purchased her a suit of warm, green wool to replace her schoolgirl clothing. There was a personal note, which Katrinka read and then tucked into her pocket. He would not be returning before she left.

There was nothing more to do but pack her few possessions and wait for next week's transport to Paris, and from there to the port of Dieppe. In the packet, she also found directions to the news agency's office, where she would meet the editor.

* * *

Early the next morning, Valentine came in before his departure, grinning down at her in his jaunty way. "I hear you're headed to London."

"Yes, the major found me a placement. I will work there until my father is ready to go back to California."

He nodded.

"And you? Where are you off to after Paris, Val?"

"I'll be sent back to England for training. After that— who knows. When the war is over, I'll go back to England. There is nothing for me here."

"Any special person waiting for you in Paris? Any hearts to break?"

He blushed. "A good friend is on leave there now, just in from North Africa. I hope we'll meet up."

Katrinka gave him a long look. "He must be pretty special."

Val started, and then blushed again.

She spoke gently, "It must be very difficult for you."

He shrugged. "Oh, it's the war, you know. Puts people in these intense situations one would never normally have to deal with."

Her eyes watered.

He peered down at her. "Look here, is there somewhere we can talk? I have a few hours. Come down to the café with me, and we'll have a last meal together."

They took the old Norton into town, Katrinka clinging to the back, as Val drove in his normal hair-raising manner. Sitting at a table in the rear of the café, they placed their order, and made small talk until the food arrived.

After the meal Val reached over, taking her hand. "Kat, I don't mean to interfere, but you must speak to Farr. You have to clear up this thing between you. The man was a mess."

She looked away.

"You need to fix it," he urged.

She shrugged, "How?"

"He was in Paris to collect his orders and papers from HQ. I sent him a message. He might still be there, waiting for transport. I won't have much time, but I'll try to look him up. If he's still there, where can he contact you? Where can you be reached?"

"I'm often out running errands, but I should be here until next week. Then I'll be going up to Paris and on to London."

Val frowned. "Look, this is no good."

They were both silent.

Suddenly he exclaimed, "Come to Paris with me now! You're finished here, aren't you? The major's gone. Come with me. I'm riding with Giraud in a supply truck this morning. There would be room for you. Have you everything? Your papers? Money?"

She nodded, her face flushed.

"Then come with me. If he's still there, we'll find him."

She struggled with a surge of pleasure. "He won't want—"

"Of course he will. We leave in an hour. Can you be ready?"

She grinned, her heart slamming in her chest. "Yes, *please*, Val. Let's go back now. I'll get my knapsack and say goodbye."

Val stood up, glancing at his watch. "Right. Get your things together and meet me out the front of the library as soon as you can." He smiled down at her, "We'll find him, Kat."

Thirty minutes later, Katrinka had changed into her French schoolgirl skirt and sweater. She packed her knapsack with her book, identification papers, and the new wool suit. She stowed away her knife as well. Standing in the doorway of her small room, she took one last look around. Her throat was dry, and she had to keep swallowing.

She turned and ran down the stairs to the waiting truck. Val tossed her knapsack into the back and boosted her up, before jumping in next to her in the front seat, and then they were off.

* * *

They got to Paris late that evening. It was early November, and a cold drizzle fell over the city. Despite the gray weather, the streets were crowded with men in uniforms, their arms wrapped around laughing young women, while people spilled out from the cafés and cinema. Times were hard, food was rationed, and fuel in short supply, but after almost three months since its liberation, Paris was still *en fête*. The smell of pipe tobacco drifted in the air, its acrid odor reminding her of Wills.

After Giraud dropped them off, Val checked in at the transit barracks, then helped her to find a room at a small hotel nearby. Leaving her there, he went out to see what he could find.

Katrinka sank into the bed and fell asleep immediately. Later, she was awakened by a knock, and stumbled to the door. Val stood there with another man. He was slender and had a wide mouth with a lopsided grin. Both swayed slightly, and Val's eyes were bloodshot. The strong smell of alcohol permeated the room.

"Val. Come in."

"Can't stay, we're off to meet friends." He indicated the young man. "This is Andrew. Andrew, Katrinka."

238

The tall boy drawled, "How d'you do?"

Val shoved a piece of paper into her hands. "He's still here. One of the Jeds knew his whereabouts. He has a room over at the Hotel Chaillot near the Rue de Aalis, which is not too far away. Can you find it all right? Shall we go with you?"

In his present condition, she doubted Val would be able to find anything. She shook her head. "I can find it."

He and Andrew were already out the door, weaving down the hallway. At the stairwell, he turned unexpectedly, giving her a radiant smile. "I hope it all goes well for you, Kat."

"And you," she called softly.

Then they were gone.

She sat on the bed, studying the paper and its roughly drawn map. It did not look too difficult. She could always ask someone. Her throat was dry, and she was having trouble swallowing again. Grabbing her sweater, she set off.

The streets were thronged with people, and the jumbled aromas of food cooking, stale urine, and cigarette smoke filled her nostrils. The air was cold and wet.

Presently she found the hotel, a small, run-down building tucked away on a backstreet. She looked up at the windows, their broken shutters hanging from rusted fastenings. Katrinka entered the building and despite the cold, broke into a clammy sweat. The concierge sat in a little alcove darning a sock, a cigarette drooping from her lips.

She gave her request to the woman.

The concierge stopped her darning and squinted up at her. "This man you are looking for, he has fair hair, does he not? Broad-shouldered, with unhappy eyes, I think."

Katrinka nodded.

239

"His room is up the stairs, number four. I do not know if he is in. I was gone to the market earlier. His key is not here."

Her heart pounding, Katrinka thanked her and headed for the stairs. What if he didn't want to see her? What if he slammed the door in her face? What if he was there with another... She shook her head.

She stopped at his door. Dizzy and feeling slightly sick, she leaned over the balustrade, with her head down. After a minute she turned to the door, raised her hand, and knocked loudly. Nothing. Just a long silence. She raised her hand to knock again, when the door next to her flew open, and a young couple tumbled out. A woman with very blonde hair and slash of red lipstick clung to a man in uniform.

She spoke in rapid French. "Is it the American soldier you look for?"

"Yes, has he gone out?"

"*Oui*, he has gone out."

"Do you know when he might return?"

The girl laughed, exposing bad teeth. "But no! You see, we celebrate. There are many parties. That one will not be back tonight."

Seeing Katrinka's face, she made amends. "But you are here now. Assuredly, he will return soon." She smiled and continued down the stairs with the soldier, leaving a trail of cheap scent.

Katrinka stared down the dark, empty hallway with its dirty walls and peeling paper. A fetid odor came from a small door at the end of the corridor, as well as a cold draft. She settled onto the floor to wait.

* * *

Much later, she woke with a start from her curled position. She stood, stretching her stiff limbs. Through an open window, she could hear laughter and voices drifting up from the street. The small hotel seemed entirely empty. Rummaging in her knapsack, she retrieved a pen and a slip of paper. After scrawling a brief message, she went downstairs to find the concierge still sitting behind the little desk. She showed no surprise at seeing Katrinka. Perhaps these things happened often.

"*Madam*, I leave you this note. Please tell the *monsieur* he can contact me when he returns, no matter what the hour."

The woman nodded, taking her note.

Katrinka walked out, pulling her sweater more tightly around her. As she rounded a corner, the nutty, sweet aroma of roasting potatoes drifted through the air.

Following the smell to a small side street, she saw a street vendor behind his cart, wrapping potatoes into cones made from bits of paper. A large dog lay next to the cart, sleeping. She waited her turn, observing the young couple in front of her. The man had his arm wrapped around the woman's waist and was whispering something in her ear. She leaned into his side to listen, then smiled. When Katrinka's turn came, she gave the man a few francs and then walked away, holding the potato between her hands, its warmth seeping into her fingers.

The vendor's dog followed, staring at the food with alert eyes, his tail motionless in the air. Katrinka stooped down, pulled off a bit of potato, and placed it in the flat of her palm. His tongue was warm and rough as he lapped it off, immediately begging for more. She broke off another piece, which disappeared as quickly as the first. That seemed to

241

satisfy him, and he ambled to the other side of the street, to investigate a lamppost.

She turned the corner and picked up her pace, watching the shimmer of lights on the dark river. She wondered where Farr was, and what he was doing at this moment.

* * *

The two young women pressed their services upon him, and in his inebriated state, Farr agreed. But on arriving at their squalid, airless, little room, he found he could not perform. Disappointed, but determined to show him a good time, the women began their lovemaking without him, on the other bed. Farr lay on the sagging mattress smoking a cigarette, watching their exaggerated movements. He could not help but think that Katrinka and Milou's lovemaking had probably involved less expertise, but a great deal more tenderness.

The women finished in a united climax. Farr stood up and paid them their money. Stepping from the building into the dark street, a strong breeze struck his face. His head felt heavy from drink and too many cigarettes. Transport to the boat would be mid-morning. He turned back to the hotel.

The streets were quiet now. Everyone had found a place for the night or gone back to their rooms. He turned down a darkened lane, empty except for a lone street vendor and a girl at the far end. The girl squatted down, feeding a dog. The dog strolled away, and the girl continued down the cobblestoned street, turning a corner. Farr stood for a moment, something tugging at the back of his drink-fogged brain. He watched the street vendor pack up his cart and leave. He continued his walk, and in a few minutes arrived back at the hotel.

The concierge looked up as he entered. "*Monsieur*, there has been a visitor."

Farr realized then, how desperate he was to talk to someone. Maybe Val had arrived. "Did he leave his name?"

"No, *monsieur*. It was a young woman. She waited a long time for your return. She has just left a short time ago."

His body jolted into violent movement, his voice harsh. "Where was she headed? Did she give her name?"

"Yes, *monsieur*, an unusual one. *Swallow?* A nickname, I think."

Farr whirled and was out the door.

She called after him, "*Monsieur*, she has left a note—" but he was gone.

Farr sprinted down the pavement, cursing himself. Why hadn't he realized? The young woman in the street. She'd had Katrinka's posture. Katrinka's walk. What was she doing here? Was it possible?

In a few minutes, he rounded the corner. Of course it was empty. He ran down the lane, turning into another. Then another, and another. She had to be here. He stood for a few moments on the curb, his heart slamming. She had vanished. Paris and its maze of alleyways and lanes had simply swallowed her up.

In angry desperation, he cupped his hands to his mouth, calling out her name, his voice echoing and bouncing off the old buildings and paving stones. He continued searching and calling until he was hoarse and exhausted. Stopping by a park bench along the river, he slumped over, holding his head in his hands.

* * *

Katrinka hurried back through the streets to her room. Perhaps he had returned to his hotel. Perhaps at this moment he was reading her note and coming to find her.

She was so tired. If she could just sleep tonight, waking up in Wolfe's arms. It seemed she could almost hear him calling her name. His voice echoing through the darkened and empty streets of Paris like some defiant Rochester, demanding the return of his recalcitrant Jane.

* * *

Farr woke from his cramped position on the park bench. The sun was just coming up over the river. His joints were stiff, and he needed a hot drink.

He found a small café, but could not face the food. He drank the bad coffee, then made his way back to the hotel. He'd just enough time to wash from the basin and grab his rucksack, before a large truck sounded its horn in the street below. After giving a swift glance around the room, he ran down the stairs. He'd already settled his account when checking in. The concierge was not about, so he left his key on the desk.

After throwing his rucksack into the back of the truck, he pulled himself up. There were a few other soldiers, and a Jed member he recognized from his training days. Most looked in the final stages of a bad hangover, and there was not much conversation. He slept the rest of the way to the port.

* * *

Katrinka spent a wretched night listening for the knock on her door, but he did not come. As the minutes and hours dragged by in the bleak, unfamiliar room, her loneliness became intolerable. She shivered, seized with irrational panic. What was she doing here? Wills was gone. Her father gone, and her parents dead. Wolfe was never coming back. He would never forgive her. Her entire body throbbed like an exposed nerve.

She got up, stumbling in the dark, to her knapsack. Deep in the back of an interior pocket, she found what she was looking for. She gazed down at the glass vial nestled in her hand. The tablet seemed to glow in the darkness. Unscrewing the top, she shook the pill into her sweating palm, staring at it. Then with a sharp cry, she flung it to the floor, stomping and smashing it into tiny bits.

Katrinka returned to her bed and crawled under the thin covering, doubling herself into a tight knot. She was going to be alone forever, and would just have to cope with it. She sank into a dreamless sleep.

* * *

Katrinka checked out of her room in the late afternoon, dressed in the green woolen skirt and jacket. It felt heavy but warm, in the chilled air. With her identification papers, she was able to arrange a lorry transport to take her to Dieppe. As she struggled to climb into the back, helping arms reached out to pull her up. She found a place to sit along the wooden bench; she was the only female. The soldiers looked a bit worse for wear, and after a few minutes of casual chatter, most of them fell asleep. It took over five hours of sitting on that hard bench, stiff with cold, before they reached the port.

Checking in with the dock clerk, she found that no boat or ship would be leaving for Newhaven until after midnight. She took a tram to the cinema, and later stopped at a café for a hot meal, and read a magazine. When she got back to the port, she handed her papers to the dock master and was allowed to board the vessel.

They would be traveling in a small convoy of ships, and they had to wait for them all to be loaded and ready. They did not leave until two in the morning, and it was a rough crossing. Unable to sleep, Katrinka went up top, staring at the black water and fog-streaked sky as the coastline of France receded into darkness. She would never return.

12

London, 1944

T HE SHIP AND ITS PASSENGERS REACHED NEWHAVEN
early the next morning. Katrinka followed the
directions, going up to London by train, her clothing still
damp from the moist air of the sea crossing. The sun was
shining, but it was a hard, bright light, and held no warmth.
Arriving at King's Cross Station, she disembarked and
walked out into the city.

The destruction shocked her. Entire neighborhoods had
been bombed into rubble. Rows of skeletal houses leaned
into each other, their masonry crumbling. She passed a few
houses that had somehow remained intact, but with windows
blown out or entire walls missing. Several streets were torn
up and closed off.

This was another side of the war, one she had not seen in
France. Although heavily oppressed with threats of violence,
the countryside had remained relatively free of destruction.
But here, war had left its mark everywhere.

Even with the devastation, Katrinka thrilled to the
immediate sense of energy. There was a determined vibrancy
amid the grit and dirt, and its raw excitement lifted her

spirits. Crowds of people went about their daily business, and cafés buzzed with activity. Despite the bombings, cinemas and some theaters remained open, and were decorated with colorful playbills.

She eventually found her way to the news building and stopped just outside the entrance, searching her bag to make sure all her papers were in order. Her hands were shaking. She'd better get this over with.

Nigel Brockley met her inside the large newsroom, and led her through the maze of desks to his office. With its clacking typewriters and voices shouting into phones, the newsroom was a cacophony of noise. The air was multilayered with tobacco smoke, and it stung her eyes.

Katrinka settled into an old leather chair by the door, its springs digging uncomfortably into her thighs. Mr. Brockley was a wiry, middle-aged man with thick-framed glasses and a round snubbed nose. She watched as he called for his secretary to bring tea and buns. After studying the papers she gave him, he asked her a series of questions. She could not take dictation and had no typing skills. He noted her obvious inexperience, but nonetheless remained professional and courteous. He told her he was short of staff, and she could run errands and answer the phones.

After tea, he directed her to a woman's boarding house near the Batavia Mews, where a room and meals could be had for a small charge. Then he stood up, shook her hand, and told her to report for work on Monday morning. Before she left, he'd scribbled down the directions to the nearest bomb shelter, which she had pocketed in shocked silence.

* * *

Except for her old schoolgirl clothing, Katrinka had nothing to unpack. She stood in the middle of the tiny room at the Batavia Mews Boarding House and looked around. There was a chipped water basin in the corner with a yellowed mirror hanging above it. She tried the taps, and cold water trickled out. The bath was down the hall. A small window overlooked an abandoned rubbish heap below. She closed the window, shivering. There was no coal fire, but the hearth contained a coin-operated gas log. She could not imagine living here very long.

She took off her jacket and hung it on a battered coatrack in a corner of the room. Then she sat down to write a brief letter to her father's solicitor, telling him she had arrived and where she was living. She left it on the table to post the next day, and went downstairs to dinner.

The helpings were sparse, but the food was tasty and warm, and her spirits lifted. Katrinka hoped never to see another field ration. She glanced shyly around the table. There were four or five young women like herself, and a few of them gave her a smile.

After finishing her meal, and being unwilling to return to the room, Katrinka took her cup of tea into the tiny parlor. She sat in one of the two chairs pulled close to the gas fire, letting the warmth seep into her exhausted body.

A few minutes later, a raw-boned young woman walked in with her tea. She wore a dress of blue wool, which was bunched at the hem. She had applied some dark coloring to her legs that carried a fusty odor. Her rough-chapped hands were constantly in motion, tugging at the belt around her waist or patting the dark hair back from her face. She greeted Katrinka and asked if she could sit in the chair opposite. Katrinka nodded, smiled, and introduced herself.

After settling into her chair, the young woman introduced herself as Beryl. She mentioned the weather. She mentioned her current state of health and that of her fellow boarders. With these civilities accomplished, Beryl launched into a barrage of information, skillfully diminishing any chance reply from her companion.

"You new 'ere?" asked Beryl.

Katrinka nodded.

"Got a job yet? There's plenty to be found, what with bombs going off every day. Cause quite a ruckus, they do. There's some folk that are gettin' out. They told us it was gas explosions, but it weren't that at all. Them Boche got this new kind of bomb. Gives you no warning, just a loud bang, sudden like."

Katrinka had heard Raphael talk about the rocket attacks. It was an entirely different matter to hear about them now, with the locality painfully close.

Beryl continued, "My auntie up north tells me to come stay with 'er, the man gone and all, but I says, 'And what would I do up there, with no picture shows or places to go dancin', and not even enough food to feed the pigs with?' I'll take my chances 'ere, thank you very much. It's an excitin' place now, what with all them American blokes on leave. Plenty of chocolate, they've got, and they know how to show a girl a good time, too."

She paused for breath, looking at Katrinka curiously. "You got a boyfriend?"

Katrinka shook her head. To her dismay, tears filled her eyes. She blinked rapidly, but Beryl saw it.

"Now, none of that; it's no matter. We'll have a good time, just you see. Tomorrow's Saturday and I've got shoppin' to do. We'll go up to Woolies, 'ave tea, and later we'll go out to the pictures."

* * *

So, the next day at noon, after spending her first sleepless night in a bomb shelter tube station, Katrinka and Beryl boarded a tram and headed to the Woolworths department store. Beryl chatted excitedly. They would do some shopping, as there was a sale on. Then maybe they'd find a warm place to have their tea.

But at the first stop, Katrinka realized she'd forgotten her coin purse. After promising to rejoin Beryl in front of Woolworths, she jumped down and hurried away, as the tram lumbered on.

A sudden, violent explosion shattered the air. This was followed a split second later by a blinding flash, which illuminated the entire area with an eerie blue light. Katrinka's body was flung out onto the road, and the breath sucked from her lungs. She attempted to stand, but her knees collapsed. Her ears shrilled as shards of metal, glass, and rock, rained down. She tried to scream but could not get any air. The ringing in her ears terrified her, and she clutched her head with both hands, screwing her eyes shut. If it continued much longer, she knew she would go mad.

It stopped finally, and she pushed herself upright, gazing about in disbelief. All was dust and pandemonium. Her eyes were gritty, and she smelled fire. She turned to see a huge column of black smoke rising from a jagged crater that had once been the Woolworths store. Down the street, she saw the tram. She stood up and began limping toward it.

Bodies and fragments of bodies lay scattered everywhere, some with their clothing torn away. The smell of scorched flesh filled her nostrils, making her gag. The twisted wreckage of cars lay scattered across the road. She came to the tram and peered in through the smoke, coughing and gasping Beryl's name. One look told her all the occupants were dead, some decapitated bodies still sitting upright in their seats. A few mangled body parts protruded from Beryl's seat. Katrinka did not look further.

The screams of trapped victims came from the street. She turned back, scrabbling over the wooden boards and sharp wires. She could hear the wail of ambulances in the distance. Dense dust and smoke was everywhere. Her eyes burned.

"*Please…*" came a voice, and an arm reached out. She was shocked to see a face looking up at her, half buried in the rubble. She bent over, heaving away shattered cement blocks and twisted metal, as a woman's body began to appear. Katrinka crouched over her.

"Are you all right? Can you move?"

With help, the woman sat up and grasped Katrinka's arm. She seemed dazed. Blood was trickling from her ear.

"What happened?" she asked.

"I'm not sure. I think the building has been bombed." She scanned the woman frantically for signs of injury. "Your ear is bleeding, do you have any pain?"

The woman seemed bewildered and licked her lips. They were caked with dust. "I think… my ankle may be broken."

The sirens were quite close now; the alarms pierced the air, mingling with the cries for help. Katrinka pulled a handkerchief from her bag and gave it to the woman. "You must wait here. I will bring help." She scrambled to her feet and hurried over to an ambulance that had just pulled into the side of the road. Many more were arriving. She spotted a man unloading equipment, and ran up to him.

"Sir. There is someone injured—"

He looked up from his crouched position, his face set in grim lines. "Bloody hell, lass. We've massive injuries here. Get to work and help us out. There's a good girl."

"But there is a woman. She is—"

"Make them comfortable. Do what you can. Someone will be around soon to see to the injured."

She whispered, "Yes, of course."

She stumbled back to the woman, who was sitting motionless, still in a daze.

"They say they will be coming soon. Is there anything I can do for you?" Katrinka asked.

"No, thank you, dear. I believe it is just my ankle. I will wait here until…" Suddenly, the woman toppled backward into the dust.

Katrinka cried out and leaned over her. She took the woman's wrist, but there was no pulse. There was nothing. The woman's eyes stared vacantly into hers, the mouth open and her lips still caked with dust.

A spasm rose in her throat, and Katrinka lurched behind a semi-collapsed wall. After a few terrible minutes, she returned to the woman and covered her with a piece of cloth.

She spent the rest of the afternoon helping the rescue workers and the other volunteers. Once, she passed a heavyset man sitting in the dirt, drawing circles with a bent twig. He sang in a plaintive, high-pitched voice and seemed unaware of his surroundings.

Back and forth she went, helping with the wounded, digging and clawing through the rubble, at times having to step over scattered body parts. Her brain blocked out much of the horror. It was beyond all comprehension.

The sun was going down when she heard a feeble cry coming from a large pile of wreckage. Tearing away the bricks and glass shards, she came upon a child clasping a small kitten. The little girl was barely conscious, her ginger-colored hair matted in blood. She wore a yellow dress with tiny elephants embroidered on the smocking. The kitten's breath was a raspy, rattling sound. Fearing to move them, she crouched, wrapping her arms about them both. She whispered soothing words, violently wishing for help to come.

The kitten died first, and a few minutes later the child, still clutching the small animal in her arms. She continued holding them until rescue workers arrived. Then she stood up and backed away. There was no feeling at all in her arms. She must have gone back to the searching, but she did not remember much of anything after that.

Eventually Katrinka became aware of a dull, throbbing sensation, and saw that her hands were torn and bleeding. She stopped at an ambulance to pick up a few bandages, then made her way down the streets to her boarding house.

Most of the women were back. Spying Katrinka, they rushed out to greet her, their concerned faces making her cry. They'd heard news of the attack, and Katrinka had to tell them about Beryl. There was a great deal more crying after that.

They took her to the parlor, and one of the boarders brought her a cup of tea. Another gave her a soft, clean cloth to wrap around her hands, and helped her to her room.

Katrinka took her towel to the bathroom. The water was barely warm, and her injured fingers made it difficult to wash, but she removed the grime and blood the best she could. Once back in her room, she changed into her schoolgirl skirt and sweater, the only other clothing she had. She would try to find a place that would clean her suit.

She wrapped a few thin bandages around her fingers and sat on her bed, staring at the wall for what seemed a very long time. Eventually, her eyes fell on the letter she'd written the night before. She picked it up in her trembling hands, ripped it in half, and threw it into the dustbin. Then she sat down to write another, struggling to hold the pen between her damaged fingers.

"Tell Papa that, as soon as he is ready to leave, I will come with him. I will meet him anywhere."

She would mail it the next morning, along with a letter to Will's sister.

* * *

That night, one of Katrinka's housemates took her to a different tube station bomb shelter. Cynthia told her she did not need to bring blankets, as they were provided. Entering the shelter, Katrinka was astounded to find many rows of beds, but surprisingly, the place was only half full. Apparently, many Londoners, hardened from the years of sporadic bombing, chose to stay in their homes at night. Cynthia took her to an air-raid-shelter warden, who directed her to where she could sleep, and the location of the toilets. She also handed Katrinka a gas mask and showed her how to use it.

Soft conversation and murmuring drifted around her until very late. Then, a vast silence settled on the station, unbroken except for the occasional snore. Her fingers ached horribly, and she was cold. She heard skittering across the floor and wondered about rats. She got very little sleep.

* * *

On Monday morning, Katrinka reported for work at the news office. There were dark circles under her eyes, and two of her fingers had become infected. She informed Mr. Brockley that she would try to find a physician during her lunch break. She apologized, since the newsroom seemed frantic with activity.

The man grimaced when he saw her hands. They were swollen and raw, and in some places the skin was torn away. Katrinka explained what had happened, and he offered to take her to a doctor that he knew. She accepted gratefully. The pain was becoming unbearable.

The doctor saw her right away, while Mr. Brockley waited in the outer office. The doctor washed her hands in a soothing solution, then applied a salve mixture of sulfonamides. He assured her it would bring down the swelling and infection, but she was to come back in two days' time, so he could check on the progress of the healing. After the appointment, Mr. Brockley took her to a local chemist shop to pick up the prescription and sticking plasters.

They returned to the newsroom in the late afternoon. Mr. Brockley led her into his office and called for tea. Weak sunlight filtered through the crooked blinds behind his chair.

Katrinka was sleepy and sat back with the warm cup in her hands, hypnotized by the swirling dust motes. His office smelled like the old wood in her grandmother's attic.

"I'd like to do a news article about your experience," Mr. Brockley was saying. "A firsthand account of your impressions. With the censorship, we can't publish anything about it now, but the paper could use it later."

Dragging her eyes away from the dust motes, she turned to him, surprised. "About the bombing?"

"Exactly." He explained that he wanted to interview her about the rocket attack, for it had been a rocket attack— one of the newer, more frightening versions of the V-1 the Germans had been using previously.

Katrinka had no desire to revisit those thoughts, but after some hesitation she agreed. Under his gentle questioning, the terrifying images spilled out. Beryl's tram, with its dead occupants still upright in their seats. The man sitting amid scattered body parts, singing gibberish and drawing circles in the dust. The embroidered elephants on the little girl's dress, and the dying kitten.

* * *

For the next few weeks, Katrinka became his reporter. She would go out in the morning looking for news. "Human-interest stories," Mr. Brockley called them. She would come back in the late afternoon, and dictate to him what she had seen and heard in her walks through the city.

When her fingers healed, she could type her own news articles and submit them before leaving each day. It seemed everyone had a story to tell her: hospital nurses and patients, bomb shelter wardens, shop keepers, and regular people on the street.

The deadly rocket attacks continued. Because of their incredible speed, there was no defense for them. There was nothing to warn of their approach before they struck. The results were indiscriminate and lethal.

Katrinka did a story on the social activities supplied in the London tube bomb shelters. Tea and other items were offered for sale, some even had small bands for dancing, and there were always improvised singing groups. One night, a woman brought in a portable record player and several records. She was besieged with requests to play certain songs. Another night, she passed a group of children learning arithmetic from an elderly man, who had set up an easel and portable chalkboard.

Katrinka became a fast and accurate typist, often staying after hours to finish a story. Life settled into a routine, and she formed friendships with some of the women at the boarding house. But, for the most part, she remained aloof. She stood back, reporting the events and people as a distant bystander, with nothing really touching her.

Each night, she would pocket a few belongings and join the others deep underground. She had no nightmares. She had no dreams. For Katrinka, it was a time of waiting, but she did not know what it was she waited for.

* * *

December arrived, and London celebrated the Christmas season in a muted fashion. Because the bombings were now indiscriminate, there was no need for a blackout. For the first time in four years, churches were able to light their stained-glass windows. However, it was one of the coldest winters on record, and there was very little fuel for heating. The earlier belief that war would be over before Christmas was now just a bleak memory. Fierce battles were being fought in the Ardennes, and German troops had surrounded the town of Bastogne. There were several rocket attacks throughout the month, and over thirty attacks in England on Christmas Eve, but the British would simply not give in.

Katrinka wrote an article about the women in her boarding house. They had elaborate beauty methods they used before heading out on dates with young soldiers. There were no stockings to be had, so they applied gravy browning as a leg tint and used eyebrow pencil to draw the seam up the back of the leg. Burned cork was used for mascara, and sometimes beetroot juice for lipstick. They felt it their duty to help boost the morale of the men and tried to keep as well turned out as possible.

Katrinka stayed busy, but the short, dark days depressed her. One night, she woke to find herself sitting up in bed and searching the covers for Wolfe's warm body. She could not believe it possible to miss anyone the way she missed him. Like a bad toothache, his absence became a physical pain that never went away, wearing her down. She wondered where he was and if he was still alive.

The holidays came and went. There was no word from her father.

* * *

At the end of her second month in London, a letter came to her at the Batavia Mews, postmarked from Switzerland. It was from Gorges, her father's solicitor. She tore it open and read it:

My dear Katrinka,

I am glad to hear you have found a place and are working in London. I have received a wire from your father. I am to inform you of his planned departure to California, on Saturday next, from Liverpool Docks. I regret the short notice, but evidently there is an illness at home, and he hastens to be there.

If you wish to follow, be at the Liverpool Docks Master Station on or before that date, and you will be taken to your father's ship. If not, your father wishes to assure you he will understand, and he looks forward to seeing you, whenever that may be.

I will also be sending you certain papers when you have made a decision as to your living arrangements. You stepfather, Emerson Badeau, left you—in trust—a large sum of money to be given to you when you are age twenty-one. He desired that you be able to pursue your search for Amelia, should anything ever happen to him. I will go into more detail in our next communication. You may send a reply to me, via paid message return.

Fond regards,
A. Gorges.

Katrinka sat on the bed and reread the letter several times, bewildered by its contents.

The sudden departure of her father to California. What home was he referring to? And who was ill? His only relative left living was his mother in Porto.

Her eyes burned with tears when she read of Emerson's generosity and forethought. He had always taken her dream seriously. For many years, she had looked forward to the time when they could begin the search together. She would have to find Amelia now. She owed it to both of them.

She sat on the bed for a long while, holding the letter. Then she looked around the room, as if seeing it for the first time. It seemed impossible to her that she had ever lived here.

She loved the excitement of the city, the courage of the people, and their carelessly contrived attitude to facing death. But it was a cold, gritty place, and there were no familiar, friendly faces. She longed for the warmer air and sunshine that she'd grown up with. Now she would be headed back. Would it be home? And if not, where did she belong?

13

F ATHER AND DAUGHTER LEFT TOGETHER FROM Liverpool Docks in late January. After boarding the ship, Katrinka did not see much of him, as he and the crew were absorbed in getting out of the North Atlantic U-boat territory as quickly as possible. The times they were together, her papa was unusually nervous and restless. He seemed distracted, speaking to her in disjointed sentences, and sometimes walking away in the middle of a conversation.

Amparo and his crew fully intended to reach San Diego by early spring, a journey that would stretch over seven thousand nautical miles. He would avoid the coasts and sail for open sea as soon as possible. They would stop in the Azores to pick up cargo intended for the naval bases in San Diego, before heading to the Caribbean islands and transiting the heavily defended Panama Canal. In truth, the man was more worried about storms than an attack. Crossing the Atlantic mid-January was serious business.

The weather at sea was extremely cold. For the first week, Katrinka seldom ventured out onto the decks, preferring to stay curled up in her cabin, studying maps and reading, with

Rolf lying close. The little dog had been delighted to see her again, running in circles with wild yelps and bumping her with his wet nose. For the first few days he'd walked just in front of her, looking anxiously over his shoulder to make sure she was there.

Despite the poor weather and fear of U-boats, Katrinka felt intense relief and gratitude. *Le Flâneur* was her home, wherever it took her. Once again, she felt the subtle shifting of her bodily fluids as she adjusted to the movement of the sea. This was where she belonged.

* * *

She woke one night, seized with a restlessness and longing to be out on deck. She glanced at the small clock on the bureau; it was just past two in the morning. Kneeling, she opened a small chest at the foot of her bunk, and pulled out a thick sweater and coat. She put these on, as well as a heavy woolen hat, and slipped outside onto the deck.

The blast of frigid wind took her breath away. She leaned into it, letting it pierce through her body, cleansing and purifying. Thousands of stars glittered overhead, their reflections twinkling like scattered diamonds across the black-velvet cloth of the ocean.

Rounding a corner of the deck, she gasped with delight. A full moon was just rising over the dark water. It was majestic and immense, unfurling its light as if inviting her to step onto its silvery bridge and run out across the waves. She leaned against the railing, mesmerized by the sight. She would sail like this forever, never setting foot on land again.

Amparo's concerns were well founded. A vicious winter storm caught them halfway to Ponta Delgada. They tried heading south to avoid it, but even the outer winds were raising ten-meter waves. The wind and rain started in the afternoon, with the sea becoming rougher as dark descended. It was perilous to be moving about without support.

Dressing in warmer clothing before dinner, Katrinka was standing by her bunk when a violent wave propelled her into the bureau across the cabin. She caught sight of her startled face in the mirror as she hurtled toward it and thrust out her hands to brace for impact.

The rough seas continued all night, but the blow that struck at four in the morning bounced Katrinka from her bunk onto the floor. It felt like an earthquake. A few moments later, the jarring blare of the ship's warning system shrieked. Scrambling up to the bridge with her life jacket and a terrified Rolf in her arms, she found the world had become pitch back.

"Papa?"

Her father and the Chief mate crouched over the instruments in the dim light.

"Katrinka?" He looked up and moved swiftly toward her.

"Papa, what—"

"It is all right. A false alarm. Seaman Salazar saw water coming into the engine room and sounded the bell."

"What was the crash?"

"A wave hit us against the strong current. All is well." His face looked strained in the dim lighting of the bridge. "All is well," he repeated. "Go back to bed."

Katrinka returned to her cabin, but she could not sleep. Although a seasoned sailor, she was nonetheless feeling queasy. The boat surged up the face of each wave, teetered on the crest as if suspended in the air, then dropped back down again into the churning trough with a sickening plunge. These surges and plunges were interspersed by the violent slamming of waves against the sides of the boat. She wondered if they would lose any of the containers lashed to the deck. Rolf retired to a corner of her bunk, his eyes miserable.

She could not just sit there. Clinging to the railings, she climbed down the inside passageway stairs to the galley, where Hipolito made her a cup of ginger tea. Despite the severe listing, he and Gil were attempting breakfast. She took her tea back to the day room, braced herself against a chair, and drew back the blackout curtains. Huge waves crashed outside the large portholes. The sky lightened with the coming of dawn, but she could see only rain and dark gray all the way down to the horizon. Amazingly she was hungry, and after a while, managed to make it back down to the galley for breakfast.

* * *

As they neared their destination, Katrinka noted her father's increasing restlessness. One evening after dinner, he found her sitting in a chair on the upper deck, with Rolf stretched out at her feet. An orange sun glinted off the water, catching thousands of flying fish midair, turning them into miniature silver disks.

She watched, surprised, as he placed a wooden chair next to her. Then, he pulled two mugs and a bottle from his pockets, and poured them drinks. The port was an old one—a special treat they did not have often. He sank into the chair with his pipe, squinting up at the sky. Katrinka noticed with a pang, the deepening wrinkles and large crow's feet around his eyes. It saddened her to think of him getting old.

He sighed deeply, glancing at her. "Trinka, there are things we need to discuss."

She settled back, sipping the sweet liquid. Maybe he would tell her what had been on his mind. "Yes, Papa?"

"You will remember when we last gathered in Porto, when my father died. Before Emerson's trip to Lascaux."

She nodded. It seemed like another lifetime, but the pain had not lessened.

"Before he died, my father gave me unexpected news." He remained quiet for some minutes, staring out at the sea.

Katrinka controlled her impatience. "Yes, Papai?"

"He told me that the daughter of… an old acquaintance of mine had contacted him. Her father had recently died, and Gabriella—that's the daughter's name—had been trying to reach me."

"Who is—"

"That night you came for the plastique, you asked me why I never married your mother."

Katrinka nodded, slightly bewildered. "I remember."

"We had a discussion, your mother, Emerson, and I. We decided it best for you to have American citizenship. I have retained my Portuguese citizenship, and had a working visa for the United States, but there was another reason."

"Yes, Papa?"

"I never married your mother because I was already married."

She had never suspected this. "*What?*"

"It was many years ago. As you know, I came to the United States as a young man and worked as a commercial fisherman, as well as with the tuna fleet in San Diego. It was a hard job, but a good life and good money. In the summer, I would stay in Coronado in the small city of tents, near the Hotel Del. You will remember it."

"Where you took A-mah and me. Yes, of course I remember."

"It was a wonderful place, and on those warm summer evenings there would be music and dancing at the large pavilion.

"One night there was a singer. She was so beautiful; dark-haired with large, black eyes. I asked my friends, 'Who is this dark-haired woman?' Her name was Maria. I found out she was married to another fisherman and had a young daughter, Gabriella. But a few years previously, he had been lost at sea, and there had been no word of him. I fell in love with Maria, as only a young man far from home can do. She sang the *fado*. Her voice was so pure, so clear; heavy with *saudade*. She'd learned it growing up in Porto, before immigrating with her husband."

"A-mah sang *fado*."

"Yes." He shrugged. "Perhaps I was trying to recreate the past with your mother. When at last the church declared her husband legally dead, we married. Gabriella was young and barely remembered her own father; she accepted me easily. We had five wonderful years together before—"

Katrinka interrupted. "My book! Gabriella was the child with the book. The one who left it behind when she went away."

"Yes."

Katrinka sat back trying to absorb it all. "Papa, were there... did you have children?"

"Two years after we were married, Maria gave birth to a boy. There were complications, and he died. She was unable to conceive after that."

Katrinka reached out and took her father's hand. How that must have hurt him. He had always wanted a son.

"Then came the war. The merchant ships had very little protection. There were never enough ships, never enough supplies getting through. I kept busy. It was dangerous work. After the war, I returned to Coronado. She was gone."

His words were stark, but she felt the anguish in them.

He continued, "They told me her husband had returned, and they had moved back to San Pedro. I was enraged, like a man who is crazy. I refused to believe it. I went up there to confront her."

"What happened?"

"Her husband, Renato, had been working in a town up the coast, where he'd been found drifting alone in a small dinghy. He had no memory of the shipwreck and recalled very little about himself. The doctors said it was a rare form of amnesia. He lived that way for many years, until one day it all came back to him.

"He began his search for Maria and eventually found her. The courts reinstated the marriage. Ours of course, was declared void, both in the eyes of the law and of the church."

He turned to Katrinka, his face twisted in grief. "But never, *never* for one moment, did I accept it. Maria... she could not deny him. It was painful for her. Gabriella did not handle it well. When she was fifteen, she ran away."

Katrinka squeezed her father's hand. "How terrible for you all."

"I turned my back on my previous life, on everything I had loved. I returned to Portugal, rebuilt *Le Flâneur,* and then set out for the Far East. I knew some people working the rubber trade, and later pearls. There was good work there, for a fast boat and small crew. Later, I met your mother. It was when she found Maria's letters that we had our serious row."

Katrinka sat back, trying to fit the puzzle pieces together. She thought of her mother and that final time in Porto, preparing for the last adventure. What had she known? It seemed to her now that there had been a forced gaiety, a hard set to her mother's eyes.

"Papa, when we left for Lascaux, did A-mah know? Had you spoken to her about it?"

"Yes. I told her what I knew and that I would be going back after the war, to see if anything remained. I felt I had to tell her in case she needed to make any decisions about her own life. I always loved your mother, but she was not the kind to be settled with one man."

"She never mentioned it."

"Your mother was private about many things."

"And you as well," she reproached. "Oh, Papa, you never spoke of it. You never told me."

"No, I thought it was over. There was no need."

"So, you are going back?"

"Yes. Maria is widowed now and recuperating from an illness. Don't you see? I have to try."

They were quiet for some time, both with their own thoughts.

"Papa?"

He answered absently, "Yes, *filhinha*?"

"Do Maria and Gabriella know about me?"

"No. Maria and I have not been in communication since the Great War."

"Then will there be difficulty with—"

"Of course not. Please do not worry; everything will be fine."

Katrinka gazed out across the water, watching the setting sun turn the skies a brilliant pink. It was heartbreakingly beautiful. Why couldn't she just stay on *Le Flâneur* and keep sailing into that sunset forever?

* * *

Although overjoyed to have Remi back, Maria was not so happy to find he now had a daughter of his own. And Maria was allergic to dogs. She could not abide the hair. She pointed this out to Katrinka a few days after her tearful reunion with Remi. Katrinka, Rolf, and her father had come to visit them in their bungalow on Elm Street.

"He cannot stay here. You will put him outside." Maria looked as though she wanted to put Katrinka out as well.

Katrinka had never heard of such a thing and was not sympathetic. Also, she was shocked to meet Gabriella. She had envisioned a young woman of about her age, but Gabriella was in her late thirties and tall, with pale skin and warm, brown eyes. They sparkled when she laughed, and she laughed frequently. She had long, thick hair that she wore woven into a braid that wrapped around her head, and there were touches of gray at her temples.

She rolled her eyes at her mother and gave Katrinka a smile, saying, "Come. We will take the despised animal for a walk."

* * *

Remi stood in the screened doorway, watching the two women as they turned down the lane, Rolf running in tight circles around them. Taking Maria's elbow, he guided her to the sofa in the front room.

She saw the expression on his face. "What is it, Remi?"

"We have spoken of this the other night. You know that I love you and I want to marry you. I am prepared to be a good husband, one who stays. I am prepared to give up my ship. Gabriella will be a daughter to me. But there is one thing you will do, to make this work."

She seemed anxious now. "Yes, Remi?"

"My daughter, Katrinka."

Maria's eyes hardened.

Remi pulled her around, bringing his face close to hers. "I love her, make no mistake. I would lay down my life for that child. I do not need to tell you of her upbringing, what she has endured in her short life. But I will tell you this. You will learn to love her, or you will damn well *act* like you love her, or it is over between us. It is over between us now."

Maria gasped. "*Minha querida*—"

"You will love her. Her own mother did not know how. I will not deal with this another time."

"What do you tell me?" she demanded. "A mother does not know how to love her child? What kind of a woman—"

"And I loved her mother. We will not talk of this again."

271

Maria fell silent. When she finally replied, she seemed to be weighing each word carefully. "Remi, my love, the two wars have hardened you, but your heart remains loyal. When I turned you away, you found another. You loved this woman, and she bore your child. Well, she is dead now, may God rest her soul, and you have suffered as much as I. You are right. It is better to let it go."

Amparo would not have admitted it to anyone, but it was pleasant to be back with a woman who knew when to agree and hold her tongue.

* * *

Gabriella and Katrinka strolled together along the beach in the warm sunshine. Like colorful flowers, splashes of brightly colored umbrellas dotted the sand. A small troop of Girl Scouts were hiking along the shoreline, and the aroma of roasting sausages drifted up from a family's birthday celebration.

After making a short detour to the sausage roast and getting shooed away, Rolf ran off to attack the waves, only to be knocked down by the first surge. Astonished, he bobbed to the surface. He scrambled back up the sand to shake his fur, which now stood out in small spikes all over his body. Keeping his eye out for the women seated on a bench, he launched another assault into the waves.

Gabriella was telling Katrinka about her daughter. "Marissa was only seven when she died. She contracted diphtheria. She would have been about your age now, I think. I had her very young."

"And the father?" asked Katrinka.

"He was a musician, and he traveled. I never saw him again after our few months together. There was no way to search for him. I was on my own then. I had no money and nowhere to go. I had run away from home a few years earlier."

"Why did you do that?"

"There were many reasons. I missed Papa—your papa—so much when he left."

Katrinka hadn't thought of that. "Did you call him 'Papa'?"

"Yes, but it must be different now. I will use another name if you like."

Katrinka remembered looking dismayed when Gabriella had addressed her father by that term, and wondered if the woman had noticed.

"It was not so easy when my own father came back," Gabriella said.

"He must have seemed a complete stranger to you."

"That is it exactly! I didn't even remember him. When your father went away to war, I thought it was something I'd done. Then my own father returned. I was expected to love him—a newcomer and an intruder. I believe my mother felt the same. Sometimes, when my father was at work, she would shut herself up in her room. I could hear her crying."

Katrinka was stricken. "I am so sorry."

Gabriella sighed. "It was a very long time ago. Things will be better now." She smiled. "Enough of this. Tell me about yourself. You lived with the gypsies? What was it like to live on a boat? I cannot imagine—"

Katrinka interrupted, taking the woman's hand. "He is your father too. You must call him Papa. I insist you call him Papa. He will have two daughters now. It will please him, and he will feel cherished. We will be sisters. I have always dreamed of having a sister."

Gabriella's eyes filled with tears as she gave Katrinka's hand a squeeze. "And I as well."

Turning to the ocean, they watched Rolf's frantic paddling efforts to keep afloat. Gabriella laughed. "Do you think we could teach your Rolf to surf?"

* * *

It was late evening when they made their way back to the bungalow; Katrinka carrying the exhausted dog. She'd tried to clean him up as best she could. His damp fur had a sour odor, and the women sat in rocking chairs on the veranda until it dried. Gabriella brought out a small bowl of water for Rolf, and a pitcher of cold water and bowl of oranges for them.

Sipping the cool liquid, Katrinka sat back, surveying the scene with deep satisfaction. If she should ever have a home, it would have a small veranda just like this, decorated with seashells, glass fishing floats, and rocking chairs. Maria had painted the lattice and wooden planks a dusky-cream color. Brightly braided hemp rugs were scattered across the deck, and scarlet geraniums sat in pots on the steps. She closed her eyes, listening to the distant thrum of waves and smelling the tangy scent of orange peel in her lap.

Conversation dwindled. Rolf was dry, and the pitcher emptied. The two women rose and went inside. The front room was dark, and the bedroom door was closed. Sounds of muted laughter came from within. Gabriella smiled, and

Katrinka did too. It had been such a long time since she'd heard her papa laugh.

* * *

The next day, Katrinka and her father settled into rooms at the Cherokee Roses Boarding House with Rolf. Many military wives and their children were living on the island now, and they were lucky to find vacancies.

There was an edgy truce between Maria and Katrinka that lasted the entire first week. On Saturday night, Katrinka was invited to a dinner with her father, Gabriella, and Maria. They had been too busy all week to have any kind of a schedule, but on Wednesday, Maria firmly announced that she was, 'preparing a dinner'. Katrinka was to come. She could leave Rolf in the hallway if he behaved and kept his hairs to himself.

Katrinka arrived early to help set up. Gabriella and her father were in the front room, looking at pictures in an old photo album. She found Maria in the kitchen, leaning over a large pot, her hair tied back, and a blue-checked apron spread across her large breasts. The kitchen was full of spicy smells and was warm from the oven. Impulsively, Katrinka skipped over, giving the woman an affectionate hug.

"It smells good in here, Maria."

Maria hid a smile, and pushed her toward the table and a cutting board. She poured Katrinka a glass of port. "Your father tells me we both share a love of good Porto wine. I always cook better with a glass. Drink this, and you can be of help."

Katrinka picked up the knife and began chopping vegetables, while Maria watched critically.

"No, it is better to slice like this, watch me." She took the knife from Katrinka's fingers, then sucked in her breath. "What happened to your hands?"

Startled, Katrinka looked down. She had forgotten the red marks and jagged, pink lines. The infection was gone, but the scarring had yet to fade. She hastily put them in her lap. "It was while I was at college. We were having a campfire, and I fumbled with the cooking dish."

She could see that Maria did not believe her, but the woman said nothing. Instead, she demonstrated with the knife, quickly making a pile of wafer-thin carrots. "My own daughter does not care for cooking. Is it a wonder there is no man?"

Maria turned back to the stove, lifting lids to release delicate aromas, and explaining the ingredients and preparation for each. Katrinka came over to observe, hovering at her elbow.

Maria gave her a sharp look. "You are much too thin. I will make you my *Feijoada Transmontana*, and then you will see what Portuguese food is."

Katrinka returned to the table to chop potatoes. "We had two cooks on the ship; Hipolito and Gil. They prepared our meals."

Maria turned from her pots and folded both arms across her breasts. She nodded at Katrinka. "You will come here in the evenings, and I will show you how to prepare real dinners. We have our Victory gardens. If you are patient and wait in the lines, you can get what you need at the market, with ration cards. You will soon fatten up."

From then on, Katrinka was in Maria's kitchen most evenings, listening to her endless instruction and advice, as well as the history behind each dish. Maria supervised, showing her exactly the way to grind seasoning, releasing its flavor into the sauce, and how to make a broth from bones, using every bit of their rationed meat, for her *Cozido* à *Portuguesa*. Gabriella would offer help, but mostly she would sit at the table, chatting about her day at work, and what she had seen.

During these times, Remi was banished from the kitchen. Rolf was now allowed access to the front room, so he and the dog would retreat there. Remi liked to listen to the *Burns and Allen Radio Show*, and his laughter drifted back into the kitchen. On hearing his laughter, the three women who loved him would share a smile.

* * *

Gabriella might not have been handy in the kitchen, but she was a great planner. She planned breakfasts and dining out. She planned picnics to the park and bicycling trips around the bay. It was as though she were in a desperate race to make up for all the lost years. Katrinka and her father let themselves be caught up in it. Katrinka marveled at the change in her papa. He was like a young man: laughing, telling them funny stories of the past, and teasing Maria.

One afternoon, Gabriella brought out brochures for Big Bear Mountain and the walking trails. "I thought we could go camping in the fall, when the leaves change color. We could go hiking, and perhaps do some horseback riding. Do you ride?" she asked.

"Yes, I enjoy it. We had riding classes at school in Switzerland."

"Then we must all go at Thanksgiving. I will arrange it."

Katrinka was doubtful. "I don't know if we can plan that far ahead. We might be gone by then, or—"

"Gone?" Gabriella's eyes widened. "But wherever would you go? What do you mean '*gone*'?"

Katrinka stared, as the realization hit. This was journey's end. There would be no more voyages, no more running away to Emerson in far-flung ports. Her father was already talking of selling *Le Flâneur.*

She did not reply. She turned and stumbled out the doorway.

Gabriella's eyes followed her, with a troubled gaze.

* * *

As the days became warmer, Katrinka's sense of restlessness grew. Then, in early May, came the announcement of VE Day in Europe. But Coronado was quiet. There were many family members still fighting in the Pacific, and several more declared missing in action or held captive in prison camps. Instead of celebrations, churches held quiet services marking the date, and remembering those who were never coming back.

Even with the ending of the European war, goods were still scarce, and the need for ration books continued. But the War Production Board rescinded the Coronado brownout order and almost immediately, the city began planning recreational events. The Yacht Club held a gala opening with a special sailing race. A new outside cinema called 'Movies Under the Stars' opened. Patrons would come to sit on the long, wooden benches with popcorn and sodas, and watch films.

Katrinka and Gabriella went to see *The Clock* one evening, starring Judy Garland and Robert Walker. Katrinka loved movies, but seeing them had been rare events in her life. As the picture began, she and Gabriella settled on the bench with their popcorn. Rolf lay at their feet, catching any stray kernels that chanced to fall.

It was a war movie of course, set in New York City. Garland and Walker meet while he is on a forty-eight-hour leave. During their tour of the city together, they fall in love. But they are separated in a subway station crowd, and lose one another. Walker realizes he doesn't even know her last name, or where she lives.

Katrinka began crying. She was crying so hard that she had to get up and leave, with Rolf tripping under her feet, expressing whiffles of concern. She found a park bench on the outskirts of the viewing area and sat down, struggling to regain control.

Wolfe would never find her. She'd told him once about Coronado, but he'd been so sedated, he probably didn't remember. She scooped Rolf into her arms and he licked away the salty tears, his tail wagging furiously.

Why hadn't she appreciated what she had? Always searching for new excitement, never having enough. Never realizing that the man with steady grey eyes, had always been enough.

* * *

Summer came to the island, and the restlessness that had begun as a seed was now a full-fledged ache in her heart.

Coronado was lovely, and Katrinka was happy to see her father so settled and at peace. But things were different from what she remembered. Tent City was gone, of course. Most of the tuna fleet had been overhauled into Liberty Ships and were out in the Pacific where the last remnants of war raged on with the Japanese. And somewhere out there, was Wolfe.

It seemed wherever she went, couples strolled by, linked arm in arm. Despite her lack of cooking skills, Gabriella now had a man friend who worked with the Navy, and they were often together. Even Rolf had deserted her for the pretty terrier next door to the boarding house.

Her papa came over one evening, just at twilight, when the air was heavy with the scent of night-blooming jasmine. They'd received permission from the owner of the boarding house, and together they took the silken box of Yujana's ashes out into the garden and scattered them among the roses. Later they sat on the veranda, watching the moon drift through the treetops. Two of her parents were at rest. They were the only ones left now.

Her father took her hand. His own was trembling. "I loved your mother so."

"I know, Papa."

"She didn't know how to raise you. Her freedom was everything to her. I let her drag you along, with her headstrong ways. I should have prevented it."

Katrinka's throat constricted, barely managing the words, "I didn't mind, Papa."

"I don't know why she was so restless. I don't know what she was looking for. But she loved us both. She was a strong, defiant, courageous woman. And she loved us both."

He was crying now, very softly. She wrapped her arms around him, tears streaming down her own cheeks. Why had she never told her mother that she loved her?

They sat together on the veranda gazing at the roses, long after the moon had gone down.

* * *

One morning, a few months after VE Day, Katrinka headed to the library, stopping off at the post office on the way. Her papa had given his solicitor their new mailing address and he was expecting documentation for his American citizenship papers. He and Maria intended to get remarried as soon as possible, and there were many forms to be completed.

His papers had not come, but there was a letter from Milou, whose real name appeared to be Sasha. It contained surprising news—although, knowing the young woman, perhaps not so surprising after all. She'd fallen in love with Tom the pilot, who was now working with the Canadian Royal Air Force. When the war was over, they planned to get married at her mother's house in Quebec. She wanted Katrinka to come to the wedding.

Katrinka grinned. Poor Tom ('*not* Thomas'). He hadn't stood a chance.

She was also delighted to see a letter from Wills. Even with the censorship blackouts, it managed to be newsy. He'd gotten her letter. He hoped she'd had safe passage to California, and heaven help any German U-boats they might have run into. He was with—but here his location and job had been heavily blacked out.

He missed her and hoped she was well. He hoped she was working on her California suntan, and would be his tour guide when he came to visit. She could write to him at the San Francisco Post Office Box he gave her, which would forward his mail to the base. He ended with a bit of wry humor, followed by a completely inexplicable remark: *"It's stinking hot, and the damn bugs are driving me crazy. Wish you were here."*

And then came: *"Dakota found, with the flying fishes."*

She stared at the words, her fingers gripping the page. 'Dakota' was Wolfe's code name. She repeated the sentence aloud, willing it to make sense. 'Flying fishes'? Was this his new team? Where had she heard that phrase? It was tugging at the back of her memory. Was it from a poem? Or the fragment of a song?

Folding the letter, she carefully replaced it in the envelope, telling herself it did not matter. It would not change anything. But he was alive. Wills had found him, and he was alive. Was Wills in the Far East as well? That last part of the letter sounded a bit forlorn and unlike him. He must have been very worn out when he wrote it.

The library was set back from the main street, its lovely Grecian columns drowsing in the dappled sunlight, amid pungent smelling eucalyptus trees. A welcoming coolness washed over her as she entered the building. It was very quiet, cut off from the noise of the road.

Her eyes roamed over the bookshelves while running ideas through her mind. She would get a job, maybe with the Hotel Del. She would pursue archeology classes at the college. She wanted to be prepared for any opportunity to begin her explorations for Amelia.

On her way out, she glanced at the bulletin board covered with public notices and items for sale. She would need to purchase a bicycle and...

Her eye was caught by a small notice, half torn from the pin that held it.

Wanted, immediate replacement. Local USO entertainment group, in conjunction with the Los Angeles Hollywood Victory Committee, desires the talents of a singer/dancer. Will need inoculations, passport, and a notarized copy of your last will and testament. Must be prepared for imminent departure to the Pacific Islands, Okinawa, and Burma. See Mr. Withers at his office in the high school, for auditions.

Burma.

The fragment of a long-forgotten Kipling poem her papa used to recite, drifted through her memory like sea sand drifts through coral:

"...On the road to Mandalay,
where the flyin'-fishes play..."

Wolfe was in Burma.

* * *

Mr. Withers regarded her from over the rim of his glasses, indicating a chair for her to sit in. "Are you here for the opening?"

"Yes." Her heart was pounding. Could he hear it?

He nodded, pushing his glasses further up the bridge of his nose. "We can't pay you much. We're a small troupe—twelve entertainers in all. You'll just be part of the backup group and chorus line on our Pacific Tour. Have any practice? Any shows you've been in?"

"I studied theater at college, as well as music and languages. My mother was a singer." She doubted he'd have time to check on her embellished curriculum.

"You have an accent. From around these parts?"

"My father worked the tuna fleet in San Diego. I've spent time abroad and was studying in Switzerland. I've just come back."

He nodded, then said abruptly. "Let's see your legs."

Katrinka was shocked, then amused. Placing her knapsack on the chair, she hoisted her skirt clear to the top of her thighs, giving a provocative little twirl and thrust with her hips.

"Well, what do you think?" she asked.

Mr. Withers' face lost all coloring. "Those are very acceptable legs. They will be—"

"Would you like to view anything else?" Her hand hovered over the buttons of her blouse.

"No! I mean…"

Flustered, he handed her a sheet of music and walked her out into the auditorium. Katrinka noticed a man sitting quietly beside a large piano in the corner of the stage. He had been observing the interview. He gave her a wink.

Mr. Withers continued, "We have two other girls coming in shortly and you will audition with them. You may study the song." He went over to speak to the piano man.

She sat down in the first row of seats and glanced at the music sheet. It seemed like a carefree ditty that made no sense whatsoever. Presently, a young woman came in and sat down next to her. She had dark hair, which was cut short and set in little pin curls around her earnest, freckled face.

"My name's Cricket."

Katrinka smiled, introducing herself.

"Are you here for the audition?" Cricket asked.

"Yes."

"Me too. I'm so excited! I've never traveled outside of California even."

"It all seems rather sudden."

"That's 'cause one of the girls dropped out. There were a couple of us here to audition on Monday, but they said the position was filled and to go home. Then the call back came yesterday. The girl they hired didn't work out, or something like that."

Another young woman came in and joined them. She had startling blonde hair, tightly crimped and swept up on both sides of her face in a Victory roll. She did not look at either Cricket or Katrinka, but sat a few seats away, furiously smoking a cigarette.

"That's May-Day Flowers," Cricket whispered. "Her stage name. She's really steamed up with Scooter, her sailor boyfriend. He came stomping in here the other day during auditions. They were *screaming* at each other. He practically dragged her out of here! I guess she's back to give it another try."

She leaned around Katrinka and called out, "Hi there, May-Day."

The girl looked at them and blinked.

After a few minutes Mr. Withers came back, sat at the far end of the front row, and called for Miss Flowers. Was Katrinka just imagining his furtive backward glance to the entrance doors?

May-Day got up, dropped her cigarette on the floor, and ground it out. Climbing the few stairs to the stage, she gave the piano man a nod, threw back her head, and belted out the song.

Katrinka's mouth dropped open. It was nothing more than a screech. Tuneless. But what she lacked in tonality, May-Day made up with a lot of gusto. Katrinka noticed that her bosom, confined in its tight sweater, was of ample proportions.

After the song ended, Mr. Withers graciously thanked her, and signaled for Cricket. Cricket knew the song and had a pleasant, melodious voice. It filled the auditorium, ending with a theatrical little trill.

Katrinka was last and walked quickly up the short stairs to the stage. Giving the piano man a tentative smile, she launched into the song. She had a natural pitch and followed the tune well, but her voice came out rather weak. Well, she could work on that. She saw Mr. Withers steal a peek at her legs before scribbling more notes in his little book.

He stood up, clearing his throat. "Thank you, ladies. That will be all. You will hear—"

Suddenly the auditorium door slammed back, and a gangly young man in a baseball cap trotted down the aisle, heavily tattooed arms swinging at his sides.

Mr. Withers paled. Scooter had returned.

Everyone stared as Scooter pulled May-Day aside, his hiss echoing admirably in the acoustics of the theater.

"Dammit, Maybelline, I *told* you. You're not gonna trail your bee-hind all over the Pacific, paradin' around in front of a bunch of horny GIs who probably—"

May-Day pushed him away. "Get over it, Scooter. You can't stop me."

The young man backed up a few paces, standing very straight. His face was flushed, and he swallowed compulsively. "I can, if I make you my wife."

May-Day squeaked. "Your *wife?*"

Everyone else pricked up their ears; *his wife?*

He was stammering. "If that's the only way I can stop you from makin' a damn fool of yourself… well, I guess that's gotta be it."

"Scoot! *Yes.* Yes, I accept!"

Turning to Mr. Withers, the boy spoke with relief. "She ain't goin', and that's final. Don't want to hear no more about it."

With a nod to Katrinka and Cricket, Scooter linked arms with his wife-to-be and exited the auditorium.

There was a slight adjustment in the atmosphere. Mr. Withers cleared his throat and turned to Cricket. "Ahem, Miss Cricket, we will be glad to have your services if you can get yourself ready in time. We depart for Los Angeles this Friday."

Cricket clapped her hands. "Oh *yes,* please!"

"You'll need to report to the clinic for your inoculations and kit bag. Don't take anything you'd want to lose. Make sure you leave the notarized documents of what you want done with your… well, if you should not come back, your nearest relative should know what is to be done."

"*Thank you,* Mr. Withers. You're a dear, dear man. I've already gotten everything ready. I only have a few items to pack."

With a nod and wave to Katrinka, she ran out.

Mr. Withers turned to her. "Miss, ah, Miss—"

"It's Katrinka." Her heart sank. What had she been thinking? It had all been too good to be true.

"Ah, yes, Miss Katrinka. Thank you for coming. You have a cheering voice, but Cricket has had more practice with this and—"

Again, the man was interrupted. This time by a thin woman with cold, close-set eyes, buried in the wrinkles of a pallid face. She was moving at a fast pace down the aisle, her hand around Cricket's arm like a vise. She spoke as she walked, and had to pant a little with the combined effort of it all. The effect was disturbing.

"You deliberately disobeyed me. I told you explicitly not to come here. Thankfully Mrs. Benson saw you leaving, or I wouldn't have even known."

She confronted Mr. Withers with a grim smile. "I apologize, Mr. Withers. Evidently, my daughter crept out when I was at the shops. She was forbidden to come."

She turned back, leaning into Cricket's flushed face. She spoke softly, but Katrinka heard every word. "When you get home, I'm going to give you such a tanning, you won't be able to sit for a week." Still gripping her arm, they swept back up the aisle and out the door in silence.

Giving a hasty nod to Mr. Withers, Katrinka darted after them.

When they got outside the woman turned on her daughter. "Just what do you think you were doing?"

"Mom, I wanted—" Cricket began.

The woman slapped her in the face. "Don't talk back to me. Get in the car."

Katrinka lunged forward. "Get away from her!"

Surprised, the woman turned. "Excuse me?"

"Leave her alone. She has a right to be here."

"Katrinka don't," Cricket said. "It's all right, Mom. I'm coming, OK? Let's go."

Without a backward glance, Cricket got into the car. Her mother, still staring at Katrinka, got in the driver's side, and they drove away.

Katrinka returned to the auditorium, shaken by what

she had seen. Cricket seemed to have lost all spirit when confronted with that hard-eyed, gray-haired woman.

The auditorium was very quiet. The piano man was still sitting, hands in his lap. Katrinka marveled at his serenity.

Mr. Withers watched her approach. "Well, Miss… Miss?"

"Katrinka," she supplied.

"Yes, Miss Katrinka. It seems there is an opening. You have the job if you want it."

"Yes. I want it."

The piano man smiled.

* * *

It was a whirlwind few days, getting all her papers in order, having to bid a tearful farewell to Maria and Gabriella, and promising to return before Christmas. She gave them the address the USO had given her.

The women's bewildered reactions to the sudden turn of events hurt, but saying goodbye to her father was much more painful. The old man just nodded and sighed, his eyes filling with tears. If it were not for Maria and Gabriella, Katrinka wondered if she could ever have left him. He was not going to the airport with her, and they shared a final embrace on the pier of the ferry station platform. There was a shuttle waiting on the other side of the bay to take her to the Air Transport Command Airport in Burbank.

The ferry arrived, and with one last round of hugs and kisses, she boarded the boat. Climbing up to the top deck, she leaned over the railing and waved farewell to the small figures on the dock. She continued waving until the boat turned, making its sweep across the San Diego Bay.

A few hours later, Katrinka found herself in the heavily camouflaged Lockheed Air Terminal with Mr. Withers and Dave, the piano man. Without his piano, Dave was now the guitar, drums, and banjo man.

A small troupe of entertainers sat in the waiting area, all talking and laughing together. Mr. Withers barely had time for introductions before they were hustled out onto the pavement to board the plane.

It was a C-54 Skymaster, outfitted to take passengers, and it had been stripped down for the long haul to Honolulu. Katrinka found a seat, carefully placing her knapsack in the storage area above, and her large shopping bag next to her, on the floor. Maria had prepared a parcel of food for her, and she nibbled on a small portion of it, watching the vehicles ferrying the rest of the luggage and supplies into the plane's large cargo doors.

Katrinka had never flown in a plane. Despite reading the many articles and books about Amelia, she was quite nervous, especially when the C-54 hurtled down the runway at last, pressing her back into the seat. Scenery tilted at a crazy angle outside the window as they lifted from the ground.

Below her, farm fields and little houses appeared through the clouds. She felt queasy and hoped she would not be sick. Dragging her eyes from the window, she tried focusing on a point in the interior of the cabin. Several seats up, a young woman stood and ran for the small bathroom door.

A few minutes later, as the plane leveled off and headed out across the Pacific, a loud pounding from the rear cargo door startled everyone. Heads swiveled as they watched the steward approach cautiously.

"Who is there? What do you want?" demanded the steward.

There was more thumping, accompanied by a forlorn plea. "Please, let me out!"

The steward pulled back the door, and to everyone's surprise, Cricket tumbled out into the stunned silence. Katrinka noted the girl's blackened eye.

Mr. Withers unfastened his harness and stood, his eyes bulging. "What in heaven's name are you *doing* here? How did you get in?" He glanced apprehensively around the cabin. "Where is your mother?"

The other women scrambled out of their safety harnesses and seats. Dave the guitar man remained where he was, his face composed.

"Oh, Mr. Withers, I *know* I shouldn't have come, but I can do a good job! You said yourself, you were spread too thin, that there weren't enough entertainers," pleaded Cricket.

"But we have no funding for another person, no—"

"She can split my salary," Katrinka said.

You could have heard a pin drop.

Katrinka continued doggedly, "She can share wherever I sleep, and my food. She won't be a problem. I hardly eat anything at all. I'm on a diet anyway. Honestly."

Mr. Withers considered the situation. After a few moments, he announced to everyone he would deal with it all in Hawaii. He shot a suspicious look around. "Well, is there anything else anyone needs to tell me? Any other stowaways?"

Tired of being confined to the blanket in Katrinka's shopping bag, Rolf popped his head up, barking, announcing his presence in the grand scheme of things.

Mr. Withers gawked.

Katrinka blurted out, "I had to bring him. My stepmom is allergic. He has all of his papers and shots."

Before Mr. Withers could reply to this latest unexpected turn, Annabel emerged from her third visit to the small latrine. With a tearful face, she announced to the group at large. "I want to go home."

Her best friend, Bunny, rose to stand beside her, glaring at Mr. Withers with defiance. "She's been sick like this for a month. I *told* her not to come. I *told* her she was pregnant."

At this point, all hell broke loose. Mr. Withers collapsed into his seat, pulling a silver flask from his small travel bag. Unscrewing the top, he called for the steward to bring him a glass. The young women turned from Cricket and rushed forward to comfort Annabel, offering advice.

Dave the guitar man rose to the occasion. Pushing his way through the excited babble, he escorted Annabel to her seat, giving her a few air sickness bags and packet of tissues, instructing Bunny to take care of her. Annabel, he said, would be sent home from Hawaii as discreetly as possible.

He rounded up Cricket and told her she was now replacing Annabel in the review and would be assured her own salary, meals, and bed.

As for the dog, he turned to her and smiled. Rolf would be their mascot. He'd read about a British entertainment group using a clown and a trick dog. The troops went crazy over it. Maybe Rolf knew some tricks. If not, she could teach him some. She could make costumes for him. Evidently, Rolf had all his needed papers and inoculations. He could board at the *Dogs for Defense* kennels on Hawaii and Guam between tours.

Calm was restored. Mr. Withers had his drink, followed by several others, and lapsed into a deep slumber. Everyone returned to their seats. Bunny came back, giving Cricket's shoulder a squeeze. "Honey, we'll all help you out. You've got grit and spunk, and we're darn glad to have you with us."

She returned to her seat, and Katrinka moved over for Cricket to sit next to her.

Cricket clasped Katrinka's arm, gazing up at her, "I will *never* forget this. We will be kindred spirits forever!"

Katrinka guessed that *Anne of Green Gables* had been one of Cricket's favorite books.

14

The Pacific, 1945

OVER THE NEXT FEW WEEKS, A STRONG BOND formed between the two women. Cricket admired Katrinka's independence, and the exciting childhood she'd had on board her father's ship. But Katrinka did not talk about her time in France. Wills had warned her never to speak of it to anyone. Cricket taught her the ropes of the entertainment world, and with a natural flair for music, Katrinka caught on quickly.

On the smaller Pacific Islands, the troupe put on shows in very primitive settings. Privacy was scarce and bathing accommodation limited, with little or no water. They performed in makeshift amphitheaters or on hastily constructed stages with large tarps for roofing. Supply boxes and old oil drums supported the wooden-plank stages. The performers ducked behind vehicles or trucks for costume changes. Sometimes, canvas tents were available for their use. There was little protection from the rain or bugs.

The bathrooms were the same as for the troops— rudimentary outhouses with a hole in the ground and bits of hanging cloth to give them privacy. Their skin turned yellow from the malaria tablets. And there was always the mud, the grime, and mosquitoes.

But the troops were a wonderful audience, no matter what the entertainers sang or danced. They were lonely, homesick men and women, and the sight of anything from the States was welcome.

As Dave predicted, Rolf (stage name 'Ralph', since in Dave's opinion, Rolf was too Teutonic) was a hit with the young patients in hospital wards. With his silly face and valiant attempts at tricks, Rolf reduced the battle-scarred soldiers to helpless laughter. His visits to their bedside were always followed up by reminisces of "the old boy back home"—Butch, or Sparky, or Buddy. Tattered photographs were brought forth for the two women to admire.

Katrinka still had Amelia in her thoughts. Now she was in the islands and had direct contact with military personnel, she took every chance to make inquiries and future contacts. It was on one of these smaller Pacific Islands that two very important things happened. First came the news of the Hiroshima and Nagasaki bombings. A few weeks later, Japan surrendered.

Then, while performing on Tinian, she met a Navy lieutenant who invited her for a drink after the show. During their talk that evening, she was astonished to find out that Lieutenant Rigby had served on the *USS Lexington* before the war. *Lady Lex* had helped in the frantic search for Amelia and her navigator, after radio contact was lost.

Rigby took a napkin, and began to draw lines and circles on it with a pencil. "We think she might have flown off course as far as the Phoenix Islands. It is such a wide area, too wide for any detailed exploration. Eventually, we had to stop the search."

"I have maps of possible landfalls," Katrinka responded eagerly. "I calculated the amount of fuel she had left, and where she might have tried to come down. I don't think she waited too long."

Rigby tapped his pencil on a small circle he'd drawn on the napkin. "Howland's such a little island, just a speck in the blue. The men and I, we all became a bit obsessed with the search. Felt we had to do right by her. The lady had guts, if you pardon my expression."

They walked back to her barracks tent later, along the sandy beach. Palm trees etched their silhouettes against the black, star-scattered sky. The soft sand made velvety scuffling noises under their shoes, and the waves lapped along the tideline with a gentle swooshing sound.

They exchanged addresses in front of the women's tent. She promised to contact him when he got back to the States. The man nodded and pocketed the slip of paper. Then bending down, he rested his hands on her shoulders and gave her a quick kiss.

Startled she pulled back, shaking her head. "I have a boyfriend."

He released her, apologizing, "I'm *so* sorry. I crossed the line on that one. It just seemed…"

Katrinka placed a hand on his arm. "No, it's fine. These are strange times."

"Hey, no need to explain; just my luck. He should be headed home soon? Now the war is over."

Katrinka did not reply.

He studied her face. "Well, thanks for your address. If we don't run into each other before you leave, have a safe trip onward. We're going to find her, you know."

Katrinka waved to him and went into the tent. Most of the women were asleep, and within a few minutes, all lights flickered out. She lay on her cot in the darkness for a long while, thinking about the kiss. Was this the way it was going to be? The lieutenant had been kind, and they both shared the same keen interest. Why had she clamped down on that exciting sexual arousal? It was her body, wasn't it? The way she'd understood it, no one had a claim on you unless you were married. Did it end sooner than that? She shuddered, recalling the look in Wolfe's eyes; it seemed there was an uncharted sensitivity zone. Even if she were right, she had hurt him terribly, and the memory of it pierced through her like shattered glass. Heaving a shaky sigh, she settled onto her hard cot and eventually went to sleep.

* * *

In late September, the show landed in Guam for supplies, rest, and medical treatment. This would be their home base for jaunts to Okinawa and Burma. The war was over, but thousands of troops were still at their posts. Katrinka wondered if Farr was still in Burma, and what he would do now the war was finished.

One afternoon, she and Cricket were visiting patients in the large dispensary before their evening show. As they approached a long row of cots, Rolf froze, his tail pointed skyward in a quivering vertical line. A moment later, he hurtled rocket-like down the aisle, his victim, a pale-faced man sitting up in bed, quietly reading a book. The dog landed on his chest with all fours, and the patient jerked back.

"Bloody hell!" the patient exclaimed.

Katrinka stared. "*Wills?*"

A nurse appeared, admonishing them to be quiet. Nodding, she and Cricket hurried down the aisle as other patients leaned out of their cots, gaping at the dog wriggling in the officer's lap.

Pushing Rolf aside, Katrinka flung her arms around the man, avoiding his bandaged leg. It was really him. Hiding her tears, she buried her face in his neck. He smelled like antiseptic. He didn't smell like Wills.

"Sweetheart, what the hell are you doing here?"

She drew back, brushing a hand across her cheeks. He seemed dazed and glanced at Cricket, who was smiling down at him.

"Wills, what happened? Are you all right? Are you badly hurt?"

He grimaced. "Caught some shrapnel out on one of the islands. The damn Japanese don't seem to know the war is over. Not a big deal, but it became infected, so here I am. Just a few more days I'm told, then I'll be good as new."

He took her hand, clasping it warmly. "Trinka, what is this all about? When Rolf landed on me, I thought the medication was giving me hallucinations."

"Just a minute. I'll be right back."

She stood up, pulling Cricket aside. "Will you finish the rounds with Rolf? My friend—"

Cricket reassured her, "Don't worry, I'll take care of it. But you have to *promise* to explain later; I want to hear everything. That man's a *dreamboat!*"

Cricket gathered up Rolf and continued the bedside visits, while Katrinka pulled a small stool next to Wills' bed. They both sat, grinning at each other.

Nye repeated his question. "Darling, what is this all about?"

So she told him.

* * *

At the end of the week, she and Wills had dinner together to celebrate him getting out of the bandages. He would do a few days of physical therapy, and then begin his job in Personnel. Katrinka's troupe had four more shows on Guam before heading to Okinawa.

After settling in their seats at the Officers Club and ordering food, he told her about his job. He'd left France soon after her departure and gone back to England for jungle training. Later, he'd received orders for Singapore. But before he could finish training, his orders were changed to the Philippines. After his injury, a new set of orders was being processed for him to remain in Guam, working in the Base Personnel Office to finish up his commission.

He sat back with his pipe and lit it. "So, what are you really doing over here, Trinka?"

She told him about her ongoing inquiries for Amelia, and her recent meeting with the Navy lieutenant.

He nodded, and Katrinka blushed. If he hadn't known her so well, she might have convinced him her search for Amelia was the sole reason for coming halfway around the world. Turning away from his probing gaze, she poked at the remains of spam on her plate.

"It's just that I never got to tell him what I really meant. I hurt him," she explained.

"He knows."

Her voice was sharp. "Why do you say that?"

"I sent him a message. When he was in Paris."

"He *knew*? In Paris?"

"Yes."

"But he never came to see me. He—"

"What do you mean?"

She told him of her hasty trip with Valentine. How she'd gone to his hotel and left a note.

Nye was silent, and Katrinka could see him struggle with this new information.

"Maybe—"

She held up her hand. "No, Wills, stop. It's over. It really is, I just haven't let go yet. Let's talk of something else. How much longer will you be here?"

Nye frowned, relighting his pipe, and they talked of other things until the club was almost empty.

Katrinka glanced at a clock on the wall. "I suppose I better return to the barracks."

"Where have they put you?"

"The nurses' Quonset. It's cramped, but there's a roof over our heads *and* water for bathing."

He nodded. "Listen, if I can requisition a vehicle, would you like to go out tomorrow night, after your show? There's a rather nice view from the cliffs outside of town. Called Puntan Dos Amantes or something romantic like that."

"Yes, please! I haven't seen much of the island."

Wills walked her back to the Quonset. It started to rain, so after setting up a time to meet, she ran inside, and Nye sprinted back to his quarters.

* * *

The next night, Wills showed up at the Quonset in a dusty-looking jeep, and they drove out along the cliffs overlooking the bay. After parking the vehicle, they followed the short trail up to the Point. He placed his uniform jacket on the short scrub, and they sat down on it.

"I wanted to show you this. Nice, don't you think?" he said.

She gazed around, her eyes adjusting to the darkness. A crescent moon hung in the sky, sending its crinkled ribbon of silver across the black water. Thin rows of bioluminescent waves raked the briny-scented shoreline.

"It's beautiful, Wills."

They sat for a long time in comfortable silence, watching the constellations wheeling above them and looking out to sea. Katrinka felt the lovely ballet within her body, as her fluids synched with the ocean's steady rhythm.

Wills spoke quietly in the darkness. "Would you like to hear the legend about these cliffs, and the two young lovers?"

Nodding, she moved closer, wrapping her arms around his waist and shifting to avoid the sharp pebbles. He draped his arm about her shoulders.

He began, "Long ago, when Spain ruled this island, there was an aristocratic family that possessed much wealth and land. They had a beautiful daughter, and as she grew older, the parents negotiated her engagement to a Spanish captain. But the girl had fallen in love with a young Chamorro warrior. The family forbade them to see one another. The two lovers met in secret, and one night before her wedding, they ran away together."

Katrinka was intrigued, remembering her own impetuous camel ride across the desert with her young lover Mshai, years earlier. "Did they escape? Did they get away?"

"Her father's men pursued them. Cornered them here, at the edge of this precipice. The warrior took his long, black hair and tied it into a knot with hers. When it was secure, they held each other tightly and plunged over the cliff to the waves below."

"Oh!" Katrinka's disappointment was sharp. She looked out over the ledge, watching the tide crash against rocks. She wondered if she would have allowed Mshai to entwine her hair with his. To take her with him, tumbling over the cliff into that dark and restless ocean.

They sat again for a long while, listening to the waves. Wills reached down, running his fingers through her hair. "We have some unfinished business, you and I."

The man's sexual desire settled over Katrinka like a thick, warm mist.

He leaned down, softly kissing her lips. They were as salty and moist as the sea air. He probed her mouth with his tongue while sliding a hand under her blouse, gently pushing it up over her breasts. His fingers were warm against her skin. He eased her down and bent over her, kissing her nipples.

As she arched back, he brought his other hand down between her legs, caressing and fondling. Katrinka was aching for him to be inside her. She reached up, unbuttoning his shirt.

He shook his head, taking her hands. "It's too unprotected. Just sit up… yes, like that."

She straddled his lap facing him, feeling his rigidness pressing between her legs.

"Wait. Let me get a—"

She was breathing fast. "*No.*"

To her dismay he stopped, drawing her face close. "Trinka. You don't want this."

302

"I *do*."

"You don't want a child now. Wait until you're sure."

"I *am* sure."

"There's Farr…"

Katrinka drew back, staring at him. He knew her better than she knew herself. "Yes, then. Please, Wills."

He was quick, and she was back in his lap in a few moments. She raised herself up, undid the buttons of his fly, and helped him with the condom. Then she eased down onto him, and the man's entire body shuddered. The intense pleasure of him inside her made Katrinka feel faint, and she closed her eyes, wrapping her arms tightly around his chest.

He pulled out as she raised back up on her knees. "Easy, don't move yet."

She waited, suspended for a few moments, until he pulled her back onto him. She rocked slowly while his hands slid down her buttocks, separating them with a probing a finger, pushing more deeply into her. She clung to him, hyperventilating.

Suddenly, there was a startling blast of siren and their bodies were pinned in a garish blaze of light. Momentarily blinded, they recoiled, gasping. Their gasp was echoed by an even louder one, and the sound of a flashlight clattering to the ground. After a frantic scrabbling, the flashlight was retrieved.

A strained, disembodied voice came from the darkness. "*Sir*. I'm *sorry*, sir. Corporal Savino here. I was on my patrol. This area is off limits, you know… curfew and all."

Nye was cursing, fumbling with his trousers. Katrinka scrambled off his lap, pulling her blouse down and readjusting her skirt. Both stood. The flashlight pointed discreetly to an area about two meters away.

"Understood, Corporal. Just showing the young woman…
that is, we were looking—we are leaving immediately."

Nye grabbed Katrinka's hand, and pulled her over the
rocks and bramble, back to the vehicle. Switching on the
ignition, he spun the wheel in his hand, and they roared off
down the road, the sound of muffled laughter trailing behind
them. He got out onto the main track, and they gaped at one
another.

Katrinka burst out laughing. "Oh Wills, you looked so
shocked!"

"Dammit, I *was* shocked. Not quite the… *Bloody hell!*
There's something for the young man to remember."

* * *

They drove back to the nurses' barracks in silence. Nye
stopped the jeep and switched off the ignition. It was very
dark. Somewhere, a dog barked. They both stared straight
ahead, neither talking.

Katrinka whispered, "I want you."

"Yes, that unfinished business is becoming rather—"

"I want you now." She put a hand in his lap, her fingers
searching.

Nye was painfully erect. Good God, he couldn't take her
right here. Was she asking that he have her right here? "Is
there somewhere—"

Bending down she parted his thighs, pressing her face
into his lap. Gently, she mouthed and nibbled his erection
through the canvas of his trousers, exhaling in hot breaths.
Nye made a guttural sound deep in his throat. She released
him, sitting back up.

"Do you know where our show is performed? The stage they've made from oil drums and boards?" she asked.

He nodded, unable to form any words.

"They've fashioned a bit of dressing room for the women's costume changes. I have the key."

"Any sentries patrol the area?"

She smiled. "Not the women's dressing room. Shall we try?"

* * *

Later, amid props and set designs of the backstage, both were able to finish their date in a most satisfying manner. Reluctant to leave one another, Katrinka cuddled next to him, his jacket giving them the barest protection against the rough wood floor. There were mosquitoes, and she got a splinter in her arm, but neither complained.

Katrinka found herself talking about her father. "You should see him, Wills. He just stays around the house, working in the garden. Sometimes he goes down to *Le Flâneur* and cleans her out."

He smiled. "That doesn't sound so bad."

"You would like such a life?"

He hesitated. "Yes, I would. When I get back home, I hope to have a small cottage in a quiet village near the sea, with a bit of garden."

"That is what you want?"

He shrugged. "I've battered around this old earth for quite a while now. I think it's time to head for home." He added lightly, "Of course, none of that sounds appealing to a young woman like yourself. Her whole life ahead of her."

"That's not true. It is a *very* appealing idea."

"As anchorage?" He shook his head. "I think you'll always be searching for your Amelias, Trinka."

"Would you have a veranda? With rocking chairs?"

He smiled. "Absolutely, there would be rocking chairs."

"And you would have a chair just for me? For when I came to visit?"

He sobered. "It will be there for you, sweetheart. With warm arms waiting."

She twined herself around him, stroking his face, "I love you so much, Wills. We have no secrets, you and I."

* * *

For the remainder of her time in Guam, they spent every night together, wrapped tightly in each other's arms in the little makeshift dressing room of boards and canvas. Nye had a few days' medical leave before beginning his job in Personnel. He sent in paperwork for a short pass and chartered himself a seat on the transport taking the troupe to Okinawa, their next stop.

It was typhoon season, and the previous month a large storm had battered the island. As the troupe prepared for departure, there was a strange stillness to the air. By the time the sun came up they were airborne, heading west out across the ocean. Their first inkling of trouble came when a sudden pocket of turbulence caused a galley shelf to dislodge, sending dozens of dishes tumbling down.

The ride became progressively rougher. Some of the girls were sick. Katrinka tried to sleep while Cricket chattered away at her side.

"It seems so *bumpy*. Look at Mr. Withers. He's turning green!" exclaimed Cricket.

Katrinka vowed if she ever got out of this machine, she would swim home before boarding another.

The hours went by with periods of quiet, followed by a series of more turbulence.

The steward came back with reports from the cockpit. They were trying to go south of the storm, but it was too big, and they could not waste any more fuel. Hopefully, they would just skirt its outer bands.

Later, he came back again and told them they would be descending into Okinawa shortly. A collective sigh of relief came from the young women. As they began their descent, a violent gust of air bucketed the plane into a downward plunge. The steward flew into the ceiling, striking his head. He staggered to a seat, bleeding. Another steward rushed for the first aid kit.

One of the women screamed as the plane tilted, slipping sideways across the sky. A steep lurch was followed by a shrill blast from the cockpit's loudspeakers, warning everyone to assume the crash position. The plane's right wing pitched severely, and Katrinka gathered Rolf into her arms, bending her body over his. He squirmed frantically and scratched her cheek. Cricket was silent, gripping Katrinka's arm. Nye hurried down the aisle, clinging to the seat backs, and buckled himself into a position next to them. Katrinka gave him a shaky smile.

She looked out the window, shocked to see the water only meters away. She screamed, and they hit the waves with a sickening jolt, slamming along with a series of stomach-churning skids, until finally coming to rest. The bloodied steward struggled to his feet, and he and Dave managed to pull open one of the cargo-bay doors. He turned, shouting above the roaring wind, for everyone to abandon the plane. Nye helped them drag out the emergency rafts and throw them into the sea. The rest of the passengers scrambled out of their seats and to the open door. Katrinka had Rolf in one arm and grabbed Cricket with the other. Together, they stumbled down the aisle to the open door.

"I can't!" screamed Cricket.

Katrinka grasped her tightly, hauling her into the doorway. The wind whipped across the waves, drenching them. Nye came up from behind. He jumped, pulling both women out the door with him, Rolf clinging to Katrinka's neck. All three hit the water hard, and she was ripped from Wills' grasp. There was a terrifying amount of noise. The plane dipped over onto its side, beginning its slide into the waves as the last of the passengers leaped from the doors.

Katrinka struggled to keep her head above the surging water, holding Rolf tightly in one arm. She could see Wills several meters away, pushing Cricket onto one of the rafts. Now he was turning, fighting over the towering swells to get to her. She struggled to swim toward him, but her wet clothes were dragging her down.

A monstrous gust whirled her body out of the water, slamming her against an oncoming wave, and Rolf was ripped from her arms. She cried out in horror, choking on the saturated wind. She couldn't breathe. Thrashing wildly, she kicked her legs in a futile effort to propel herself forward. Rolf drifted further away, nothing visible but his small, spiked head. His ears were flat, and his eyes rolled back in terror. She sobbed, crying out his name, but her voice was drowned out by the howling wind.

Dragging wet hair away from her eyes, she saw Wills fighting his way toward her, hurtling his body through each mountain of surf. In the distance, a cresting wave tossed a life raft, and the faint voices of passengers called to her. A moment later, a man leaped from the raft with a life preserver, swimming in their direction.

Something came spinning across the waves, heavy and dark, and struck her head. And then there was nothing at all.

15

Burma, 1945

Shouting over the ricochet of bullets, Captain Stoddard waved his team ahead. "Scatter yourselves!"

The men sprinted into the village, darting between thatched huts for cover and picking off the remaining Japanese soldiers.

Rounding a corner, Farr spied a Karen villager crawling in the dirt. His arm was raised in a futile defense as a soldier stood over him, stabbing downward with his bayonet.

Farr pointed his rifle and pulled the trigger, but he was out of ammo, and the soldier turned on him. Jerking his knife from its sheath, Farr dodged the blade and grabbed the rifle's handguard. He dragged the soldier into him, raising his knife. Before he knew it, Farr was thrown over the man's hip, his back slamming onto the ground. The soldier raised his bayonet. The sharp crack of a rifle sounded, as Stoddard cut the man down.

Farr sat up, his voice unsteady. "Good shot, sir."

Farr crouched over the Karen, who was bleeding from the mouth. As he leaned in, the man vomited a final gush of blood and then lay still. He felt for a pulse and found none. Farr sat back on his heels, still holding the man's wrist.

Stoddard came over. "Let's go, Sergeant."

Farr sat, motionless.

"Sergeant!"

Farr blinked and looked up. "Yes, sir."

Dropping the man's wrist, he looked around. It was obscene to leave the Karen like this, his wounds gaping in the sun. He found a dirty tarp that had blown off one of the huts and used that, wrapping it around the dead man's body.

Stoddard's voice urged again. "Let's go."

There was nothing more to be done. After searching for remaining villagers, the team headed back to their camp.

* * *

An explosive clap of thunder shook the thatched hut, and Farr's eyes flew open. Hoisting himself up from the straw mat, he fumbled in the darkness for the half-smoked cheroot he'd left on top of his kit. He lit it with shaking hands. No more cigarettes here. No more anything.

He'd spent the past several months working with Special Forces in the Karenni hill country of Eastern Burma, fighting alongside the Karens. Besides being couriers for the British Army, the Karen levies were ruthless fighters, proficient in guerrilla warfare, and extremely loyal to the British. They had been working with Farr's team since his drop in mid-April.

He stood in the doorway, watching rain pound the thatched roofs. A warning spasm from his stomach sent him hunching down the steps to an area of dense brush. Scraping a hole, he squatted down, as his bowels expelled the bits of rice and rations he'd consumed earlier.

A rustling in the twigs announced the dung beetle's predatory attack. Farr swore loudly, fending it off while trying to complete his business. He was shocked to hear laughter coming from a nearby bush. Apparently, Corporal Summerfield was out on the same reconnaissance.

He called out to Farr above the crashing thunder. "A man can't even shit in peace. I signed up to kill Japanese, not do battle with these damn bugs."

Farr mumbled a reply. He wasn't in the mood for small talk.

Summerfield popped a loud bubble with his chewing gum. "Hear about Benson? Goes out on attacks with a square cut out of the rear of his khakis, so he can keep fighting. The smell probably kills more Japs than his bullets ever do."

Summerfield was hauling himself up, popping another bubble. "Well, back to the Ritz. Don't take too long down here."

Farr shifted his weight. Another beetle struggled through the twigs, and he squished it with his hands. With his bowels finally empty, Farr pulled himself up, thinking of Summerfield's last remark. So far, he'd managed to keep his ass intact. Not that there was much of his uniform left.

He headed back to the stairs, soaking wet. They were setting an ambush in the morning, and he needed to get some sleep.

* * *

Farr wiped his brow, glancing at Summerfield, who sat several feet away, nervously chewing gum. The team had been sitting for hours in the hot sun with their rifles and grenades, hiding in cover on both sides of the main road. Rangoon had been freed a few months previous, and they heard of Germany's surrender soon after. But here in the jungle, the war raged on with hundreds of Japanese troops fleeing to the Siamese border. They left trails of destruction behind them, wiping out entire communities and burning them to the ground. Those Karen inhabitants unable or too old to flee, were brutally attacked and killed. In one village, an old man had been crucified, and the Japanese had left his body hanging from a wall. What was left of it, anyway.

The angry buzzing of insects swelled around them. Farr checked his weapon again, sweat running down his face in grimy rivulets. Then he heard a low whistle; the Karen levies announcing an oncoming squadron. He signaled Summerfield, and both men crouched down in position, their rifles leveled.

The first truck came lumbering up the road, flanked by Japanese, carrying bayonets. The soldiers were emaciated, their uniforms hanging in tatters, and their eyes staring straight ahead.

Stoddard tossed a grenade, and the lead truck exploded. Then Summerfield stood, tossing a grenade at the last truck in line. The explosions ripped through the vehicles, hurling shrapnel into the air.

As soldiers fled the burning vehicles, Farr's team picked them off, shooting anything that moved. It was a grim, ugly business, and seemed to go on forever, but the entire fight lasted only a few minutes.

Cautiously, the team crept down the hill to the road, inspecting the bodies for any signs of life. Suddenly a Japanese soldier sat up, pointed his pistol, and fired. Summerfield recoiled and hit the ground, blood spurting from the hole in his chest.

"*Medic!*" Farr screamed. He pointed his rifle and unloaded it into the Japanese until the man's body was no longer recognizable as human.

A young soldier scrambled down the hill with his kit as Farr knelt in the dust. Summerfield's flailing hands grasped Farr's arm, squeezing with ferocious strength.

Farr clenched his teeth. "Hang on, buddy."

The medic squatted down, grabbed a small bag from his kit, and ripped it open, sprinkling powder onto the man's wound. As he reached back into his kit, Summerfield made a gagging sound and dropped Farr's hand. And then he was gone.

Stoddard shouted orders, but the words seemed to come from a long distance away, so Farr paid no attention to them. He sat in the road of dead men and scattered body parts, staring into Summerfield's astonished eyes.

The medic stood and prodded him with his boot. "C'mon, Farr. We gotta go."

Farr got up, and the team climbed up the hill and headed back to camp.

Later, Farr and the medic returned, carrying a stretcher for Summerfield. They took him back to camp and buried him in the evening, after a brief ceremony. You couldn't let bodies stay out too long in that heat.

Farr sat by the gravesite until early morning. When the sky began to lighten, he stood up, laying his last stick of gum on top of the newly dug soil. Then he turned and went back to his hut.

* * *

Fucking prick.

Sitting astride an elephant, Farr watched the Karen levy lash the mule's back with his dagger-like stick. The animal let out a hoarse braying sound. This had been going on for several days. There were cuts on the mule's back and legs where the weapon had slashed. The Karen guides used gentle persuasion to lead the beasts, encouraging them through the hilly terrain and jungle paths. This man's behavior surprised Farr.

Traveling in a small convoy of elephants and mules, his team neared the end of a four-day trek to Major Braithwaite's camp to deliver munitions and supplies. It was now late summer, and they were in monsoon season. The team, along with a few Karen levies and Burmese sappers, were forced to travel in single file as they followed narrow trails through the jungle.

Farr watched a shudder ripple through the mule's body as Thet Maung again brought the weapon up to strike, the beast apparently not moving fast enough.

Another bleat of pain from the animal, and Farr was off his elephant, dropping to the ground with a hard jolt. He strode over and jerked Maung by the arm. The man shouted as he twisted around, the sharp weapon still in his hand.

The sudden activity caught Captain Stoddard's eye and he turned, astonished to see Farr and the guide grappling on the path. Farr grabbed the weapon from the man's hand and threw it down.

"Get the hell out of here," growled Farr. "I'll take care of the damn animal myself or find someone else to do it."

Maung waved his arms, speaking loudly in Burmese, but Farr shouted him down. "Get out. Your job here is finished."

Turning to quiet the agitated animal, Farr heard Stoddard's warning cry. At the same time, he saw Maung retrieve the stick. He ducked just as Maung swung, bringing the pointed tool down with incredible force, ripping through Farr's shirt. The momentum threw Maung into the side of the elephant. The startled animal rocked back, knocking Maung down, and in a moment, his head was caught under its shifting feet and crushed.

Farr drew back in horror as the other Karen levies came running, using their hooks and ropes to subdue the frightened elephant, and led it to a quiet, level area of the trail.

Stoddard hurried over, staring at the grisly scene and then at Farr.

"Are you…" Stoddard paused, uttering a sharp cry, "Christ! Your shirt."

Farr looked down. Blood seeped through the worn cloth of his jungle khaki, spreading a stain of bright red; dripping down his canvas shorts and legs. He peeled his shirt open and saw a long scratch where the sharp point had sliced through his skin. More blood was coming out. Shit.

Stoddard examined the wound. "You'd best get this taken care of immediately. It will turn septic in this climate."

Farr pulled a ratty handkerchief from his pocket, thought better of it, and stuffed it back. "Yes, sir."

Stoddard squinted. "I don't think it needs stitches. Ask the guide to find you a bandage in the rucksacks. I think I saw a medical supply box in one of them. When we get to Braithwaite's camp, get some sulfa tablets from the medic, grind them into powder, and apply it to the cut." He nodded to the levies. "And tell them to bring Maung's body back. We'll have it taken care of." He shook his head. "The filthy blighter had it coming to him. The levies have been complaining. I should have spoken to him myself."

* * *

Arriving at camp that afternoon, Farr helped the men unload and distribute the supplies to the Karen levies of the village. Later, he sat down to clean his rifle while he smoked a cheroot. He heard Stoddard's voice and looked up to see the captain exiting Major Braithwaite's quarters and walking in his direction.

Farr stood, attempting to adjust what passed for his uniform. The months in Burma had wasted his body away. Like most jungle soldiers, his uniform was in shreds. When sleeping or in camp, he dressed in whatever was available. Today, he'd changed into a dirty longyi, wrapped around his middle. He was shirtless, his chest partially bandaged in an attempt to cover the long cut. A bit of twisted tree vine tied back his hair, revealing a gaunt chin and a thick growth of beard. None of them had shaved in weeks. Since running out of malaria tablets, his yellowed skin had developed an unhealthy pallor. Sores covered most of his body. The captain looked just as bad.

As Stoddard came over, Farr straightened up, omitting the tell-tale salute. "Sir?"

"Sergeant, the major wishes to have a word."

"Yes, sir."

He'd expected this. If there was going to be military action against him, it had been worth it. The mule was now in care of the other guides, his cuts being seen to.

He entered the small mission house that served as the camp HQ. Major Braithwaite was inside, studying papers. Farr waited respectfully.

The major stood, motioning Farr to take a seat on one of the ammo boxes, then returned to his folding chair. He began abruptly, "The man who was killed today, Thet Maung. He had a wife."

Farr winced. "Are there any—"

Braithwaite shook his head. "No children. And according to the Karens here in the village, there will be no love lost. Seems the man abused her as well. Still, amends should be made. Her husband's parents will be coming from another village in a few weeks' time. Until then, see what you can do to help out."

"Yes, sir. We might be gone occasionally—"

"I've briefed Stoddard but let me catch you up on events. The BBC has reported some new kind of bombs being dropped on mainland Japan. Large ones. Destroyed entire cities."

"What—"

"Rumors of a Japanese surrender have reached us, and Rangoon has just confirmed those reports."

Farr could not take it in. "The war? It's over?"

The major nodded. "It's going to take a while for news to trickle down. The Japanese, for all practical purposes, are done, but there will still be skirmishes and small squads of them coming through, as they head for the border. We've been ordered to cease fire, unless directly attacked. Very little ammo left anyway. They should not be much trouble. Nonetheless, take care. No one wants to be killed now, when it's all over."

"Right. Will do, sir."

"Meanwhile, make yourself useful. Radio parts have arrived with supply. It's fairly flat here, so you shouldn't have any trouble sending messages. I'll see if we can get you some proper medication for that cut, but…" He shrugged.

"Yes, sir." Farr rose, but the major waved him back down.

"One more matter, Sergeant. It shall take time, and will go according to draft dates, but we'll all be sent back and demobbed, or given orders for new assignments. You've come to us from the OSS, and worked with the Jeds in France. Being an American, it will be a bit different for you. Of course, we can get you as far as Rangoon. But from there, you'll head east, I presume? Across the Pacific, rather than through the Suez?"

"I would like that, sir; get me home a bit quicker."

Braithwaite smiled. "Understood. Where is home, Sergeant?"

The memory of North Dakota wheat fields drifted through Farr's mind, dissipating as quickly as it had arrived. "California sir, down San Diego way."

Braithwaite nodded. "Nice place. Been there a few times myself. Well, I'll make sure to notify the proper personnel in Rangoon. No problem with your orders."

"Thank you, sir."

"Lodge where you can. See if you can square up with Sergeants Lewis and Wilkie for a place to sleep. Report each morning for radio transmissions. Stoddard and I will be moving out in the next few days, going back to Rangoon. We've been given orders, and will be catching the boat to Colombo soon."

Farr was dazed. "Yes, sir."

Braithwaite gave him directions to Maung's, then Farr exited the hut.

Walking back to the clearing, he picked up his rifle and cheroot, and sat down. It was over. Just like that. It seemed he'd been here a lifetime, an eternity.

After relocation leave and training, Farr had left from Liverpool Docks in late January. The trip had taken over a month by ship, stopping in various ports along the way. Then there had been a brief stint of jungle training in Horana and Colombo, where he joined with Major Braithwaite and Captain Stoddard to form Team STARFISH .

They were dropped from a Dakota in mid-April and met by the colonel in charge of the jungle operation. After several briefings, they were taken by elephant to meet other teams already established under Special Forces. Then Farr and his team had moved on, farther east toward the Siam border, to stake out their own camp from which they would operate.

Their job had been to get in and out quickly, before the monsoon season. Due to the hilly terrain, there had not been much radio work. Farr had overseen the training of levies, worked with his team to transport ammunition and supplies, and prevented the retreating Japanese from passing across the border into Siam. Now it was over. They would all be going home.

Home. During the long, sleepless nights, Farr had made plans. They were simple. He'd go to Coronado and find a room for rent. He'd ask questions. He'd check all the ships coming into the harbor. He'd find her and apologize for being an incredible ass. If only he could hold her in his arms again, everything else would fall into place. Nothing else mattered. Nothing.

His rifle cleaned, Farr stood, carefully extinguishing the tip of his cheroot. Hitching his rucksack and slinging the rifle over his back, he went off to find Lewis.

He found Wilkie instead, in one of the bamboo huts propped up on stilts, next to the mission houses. The man sat on straw matting, eating his rations and some rice. Wilkie was from Chicago, and he and Farr got along well.

He looked up as Farr entered. "Welcome back. You look like shit."

Farr squatted next to him on the mat and grabbed a rations packet.

Wilkie glanced at his face. "I heard about Maung. Don't lose any sleep over it. He was a sneaky little bastard."

Farr shrugged. "No man deserves to die like that. It wouldn't have happened if I hadn't blown up."

"Yeah, he'd still be walking around torturing animals and beating women."

Farr changed the subject. "Did Braithwaite tell you the news?"

"Damn right. We've suspected for a few days. Figured we'd wait till you got back instead of sending a runner. Nothing to be done right now anyway. We're all playing the waiting game."

Farr looked around. "This our new sleeping quarters?"

Wilkie grinned. "Yeah. Lewis and I got the small platform over there. Guess you get the corner."

The wooden platform was prime real estate, offering some escape from the wet and the bugs that crawled through cracks in the flooring. Not much, but some. He stared at the small cleared area between bales of cargo and wooden crates. At least it appeared dry. He finished his food and got up, staking out his territory by dumping his things onto the mat. He looked over his shoulder at Wilkie. "Going out to find Maung's wife. See what I can do."

Willkie grunted, and continued eating.

Farr walked along the path to the outskirts of the village where Maung's hut lay. The late afternoon sun intermingled with dark clouds, and the air was sticky with heat. Absently scratching an open sore, he looked down at his skin. It had turned yellow with the constant use of mepacrine anti-malaria tablets, but when they'd run out, some of them had come down with it. Farr had been out a week with a high fever.

Maung's hut was about a ten-minute walk outside the village, on the other side of a fallow rice field. It stood on stilts and was all beat to hell. Some roofing had been torn off in the last storm, and parts of the thatched walls were shredded. Maung hadn't been much of a handyman.

The cloying smell of rotting mangoes filled the air, and he was careful not to step in any of the decayed pulp that lay scattered around the hut. He stopped at the bottom of the steps. There'd been no interpreter to accompany him, but Stoddard said she'd gone to the mission school as a kid where she'd picked up some English. They'd told her the news already. She hadn't shed any tears over it.

He climbed the rickety ladder to the entrance and hesitated, peering in. Shafts of late afternoon sunlight pierced through the thatch, and he squinted. Everything—the walls, the floor, even the air—seemed to shimmer with golden dust. In one corner of the tiny room, a young woman squatted on thin matting, rolling rice into small, green leaves. She was golden-toned as well, with dark eyes and long, black hair woven in two braids down her back. Seeing him enter, she rose and bowed, speaking a few words in English.

He motioned to himself, saying his name, and she did the same. It sounded something like Aung Nan. After the struggle of polite introductions, the man faltered. What do you say to a woman whose husband you've just killed? It seemed, nothing. By her gestures, he understood that she was asking him to sit and eat.

Sitting cross-legged on the floor, Farr looked around the room as she arranged the food on a large, green leaf between them. A few colorful cloths were folded across a raised platform in one corner, and some pans hung suspended from looped twine along the walls. Several clay jugs and woven baskets stood in the other corner, and items of clothing hung from the wall. There was very little else. The interior walls had some ragged holes, as well as the roof. After their meal, he conducted a brief inspection. She followed him, watching intently as he examined everything.

He turned back to her and, with a series of gestures and words, indicated that he would return later to help repair the torn thatch. She nodded, then surprised him by taking his hand and leading him over to a small, wooden box. She lifted the lid, showing him the few tools inside. He barely saw them, his hand still tingling from her warm touch. Christ, how long had it been?

He said his goodbye, which she repeated. Bowing again, she followed him to the doorway and watched as he climbed back down the stairs. He made his way along the path and through the fields, feeling her dark eyes on him, until he turned past the last bend before the village.

* * *

For the next few days, Farr spent the mornings working the radio, cleaning weapons, and doing practice drills with the visiting levies. But every afternoon he made his way to Aung Nan's, to repair the thatch.

She showed him how it was all done, and he was able to hoist the materials up to the roof after finding out it supported his weight. They would work though the afternoon, and in the evenings, she would prepare him a meal. He taught her a few words of English, and she taught him some of her Karen dialect, but he could never remember them later.

One afternoon, she met him at the door with a clean longyi, indicating for him to give her his ragged clothing. Farr turned beet red and retreated down the stairs to change, away from her laughing eyes.

Together they went to the river, and while he stretched out on a rock in the sunlight, she pounded his clothing onto the river rocks, water droplets splashing in sparkles on her golden skin. Farr was shocked to feel himself growing hard. He was glad when she finished the wash and they returned to her hut.

That evening they had rice wine with the vegetables. Unaccustomed to the alcohol, Farr felt his muscles relaxing and his eyelids growing heavy. The next thing he knew, he was lying on the platform of quilts, with Aung Nan kneeling next to him on the floor, lightly patting his arm. He reached out and held her hand. He held it for a long time, before eventually excusing himself and heading back to camp.

* * *

He could hear Aung Nan's screams coming from inside the little hut. He bounded up the stairs, pistol in his hand, and faced two Japanese soldiers. One had the woman in his grasp. He had torn her longyi away and was making a long incision down the middle of her breasts.

Farr shouted out to the soldiers, firing his pistol, but it was jammed. The other man turned, and in horror, Farr saw Thet Maung's half crushed face, his eyes staring wildly from their sockets.

Farr shouted again and jerked awake, finding himself lying in a puddle of sweat on his rice mat. *Jesus*. He sat up, glancing over at Wilkie and Lewis. They were sleeping. Apparently, he hadn't made a noise.

He got up and looked out the doorway into the clear nighttime sky, still trembling. Suddenly, there was a brilliant streak of light as a shooting star arced over the silhouette of distant trees. The sheer unexpected beauty of it took his breath away.

He climbed down the stairs and began walking out along the village path. A silence settled over the camp like a velvet cloak, muffling all noise and calming his nerves. He'd walked quite a distance before finding himself standing near Aung Nan's hut. There was a light inside, and he slowly climbed to the top of the stairs. No soldiers, no ghosts. Aung Nan was awake, sitting on her pallet of woven rice matting.

As he stood in the doorway, she removed her longyi and raised her arms. Farr stared at her warm, curved body and dark tumble of hair. He uttered a sharp cry, and stumbled over to her. She took him, folding him into her arms.

She spoke little English, and he knew less Karen, but there was no language needed for what they did with each other that night, in the small thatched hut east of the Irrawaddy, deep in the Burma jungle.

16

Okinawa, 1945

NYE WAS PULLING RANK, PULLING STRINGS, MOVING heaven and earth to remain on island. He finally got a colonel he'd worked with previously in North Africa to put in an amendment on his orders back to Guam. The officer in charge of Personnel on Okinawa had just been demobilized, and Nye would take over the job. His own discharge was imminent, and it was a waste of time to move again. He could just as easily out-process from here. Many troops were arriving daily from the outlying islands, for demobilization and transport back home. Nye sighed with relief. He was cleared to remain on island for a while longer.

That done, he checked in with his new post and then headed to the chow hall for some food. He was amazed at how quickly the troops had reassembled the base after the typhoon's destruction. Most Quonsets had been flattened like pancakes, and temporary structures had blown away. They would have been in trouble, but supplies for the previous month's typhoon were already coming in. Within a week, food, water, medical supplies, and most shelters had been restored.

Grabbing a tray, he scanned the hot Quonset for some spare seats. Since the storm, the mess hall had not yet been segregated for officers and enlisted, but the officers tended to clump together. He spied a small table by the door with an emaciated enlisted man sitting at the end of it, smoking. He didn't give a damn who he ate with. He brought his tray over to sit down, and almost dropped it when he realized who the man was.

Farr was equally surprised. "Sir!" He hastily rose to his feet.

"What the hell, Farr! Good to see you."

They grinned furiously, shaking hands, then took their seats.

"What—?" Both men spoke at once.

Nye laughed and nodded. "Go ahead."

Farr briefly related his experiences in Burma and what had brought him to Okinawa.

Nye sat back, listening, studying the man's face. He'd not had an easy time of it over there, he could see that. The man had dropped at least two stone, and he'd never been bulky to begin with. A sudden realization hit him like a blow.

"How long have you been here?" he asked.

"About two weeks. They had me over in intensive care. Had some infections. The fever needed to be brought down."

"Have you caught up on current events?"

"The war's over. Not much else matters. The big news was the last typhoon. Crazy stuff. Like one of those tornados back home. The men in my squadron rode it out in one of the caves along the river. How about you, sir?"

"Unfortunately, we arrived just as the typhoon hit. We were caught out in it, you see."

Farr stared. "On one of the ships?"

"It was a transport plane, coming in from Guam. We got—"

"You mean that C-54? The one that went down with all those civilians?"

Nye nodded. He could see where this was headed, and didn't want to deal with it here.

Farr continued slowly. "They say there was a major on board. Did a pretty decent job of rescuing passengers. Made sure everyone got on the rafts OK. That was some good work, sir."

"Everyone pitched in. The pilot did one hell of a job landing that crate in the lagoon."

"There were some serious injuries. Some are right here in the hospital."

Nye nodded again. He seemed to have lost his voice.

Farr squinted at his face, as if puzzled by his silence.

Nye stood abruptly, his food barely touched. "Are you finished here? Have you any plans for the afternoon?"

Farr looked up surprised, "No, sir. I'm still on medical leave. My number's pretty low, so I'll be here for a while before being processed out. I guess they'll be putting me to work over in Communications next week, on the radios."

"Do you have time for a walk? There's someone I want you to see."

Farr nodded. "Sure. Let me take a quick trip to the..." He grimaced. "Still got some of that damn Burma Belly."

Nye waited outside, and Farr emerged a while later, his face pallid. He followed Nye over to the hospital. It was quiet and cool in the long corridors of the Quonset; the nurses moving efficiently alongside the beds, murmuring to the patients. They'd done a good job getting everything put back together.

They entered a tiny partitioned area, its sole occupant a young woman. She lay on the small cot, her dark hair strewn across the pillow. Her eyes were closed.

Farr gasped.

Nye gripped his shoulder. "Easy man. She's unconscious. She was knocked out when the plane crashed and has been in a coma ever since."

Farr had gone so pale Nye was afraid he would pass out. After guiding him out into the small waiting area, he sat him down, went to a table that held glasses and a pitcher, and poured him a drink.

Farr had regained a bit of color. "What the *hell* is she doing here?"

"She was with the road show, working as one of the chorus girls. They were on the plane."

"She joined a road show? For the Far East?"

"Don't be an ass, Farr. She said she was staying on after, to explore the islands in her search for Earhart, but you and I both know why she's out here. They were headed to Burma before the crash."

Farr's pale face flushed a deep red.

Nye forced himself to continue. "The damnable thing is, I'm heading back to Guam. My leave is almost up. I'd like to continue keeping an eye on her, but…"

Farr jolted out of his thoughts. "Absolutely, sir. I'll be here for a while. What is her prognosis? When's she going to wake up?"

Nye did not want to get into the prognosis with Farr. "The doctor can fill you in on all the details. I don't understand half of it myself."

Farr nodded, his expression disorientated.

Nye urged the man to his feet. "Come with me. Rolf is over in the kennels."

When they reached Rolf's cage, the dog took one look at Farr and began running in tight circles, yelping and crying with delight, and urinating on the pavement.

Nye left Farr there and walked back to the barracks, hands jammed deep into his pockets. Well, this was it. It had to happen eventually. Just not here. Not now. He'd have to make up some excuse to the colonel who'd gotten the job for him, and get back to Guam. He hoped to hell he'd be able to get his other job back. That way, if she woke…

He paused, mentally correcting himself. *When* she woke, he wouldn't have to say goodbye. It was a cowardly retreat on his part, he knew it. But he couldn't bear to say goodbye.

* * *

Farr sat quietly by Katrinka's bedside. The doctor and nurse were talking in the hallway, and their voices drifted in.

He comes in every day with the little dog, and just sits there by her bed. Is there any chance of her regaining consciousness?" asked the nurse.

The doctor frowned. "There is always a chance in these cases. All we can do is to monitor her progress. I would recommend evacuating, but she's doing satisfactorily, and I'd rather wait until better transport becomes available. It will be a tricky journey to get her back to Guam."

"Have any relatives been notified?"

"Her father lives in California. Major Nye cabled him. There are no other known relatives."

The doctor left after consulting his charts, and the nurse departed a few minutes later.

Farr sat motionless at Katrinka's bedside. This girl lying before him with her pale and unresponsive face, was all he had in the world. It was unthinkable that she might die. He fumbled in his pocket for a cigarette, then reminded himself he was trying to quit. He recalled a time they'd been in bed together, and he'd lit one up. She'd surprised him by taking it from his fingers and putting it to her lips.

"I didn't know you smoked."

"I did for a while, back at college. Would you like to see what I learned while there?" She'd never talked about that part of her life.

"Sure."

She'd flopped on her back next to him, the cigarette in her hand. "They had a contest in my dormitory one evening to see who could blow the most smoke rings. I blew thirty-two in one breath." She'd smiled in a satisfied way. "Of course, I won."

"That's impossible."

"But it is true. I may not be able to blow quite so many now, as I am out of practice. Would you like to see?"

"Yeah, give it a try."

He'd watched as she took a long pull on the cigarette, fascinated and aroused by the perfectly round 'o' her lips made. And one after another, in short little huffs, she'd proceeded to blow twenty-seven smoke rings. Sure, the last few were a little wobbly around the edges, but they were definitely smoke rings.

"Well, what do you think?"

"I'm thinking something disgusting and very male, that I'm not gonna share with you."

She'd pounced on him. "*Tell* me."

"I'd like to see what else you can blow with those delightful lips."

So she'd showed him.

Farr stuffed the cigarette packet back into his pocket. A nurse walked down the hallway, making checkmarks on her clipboard. She glanced at Farr and nodded, then continued down the corridor. He felt something trickle down his cheek and surreptitiously brushed it away.

* * *

For the next few weeks, Farr established a routine. He was working now, and could only come in during mealtimes and after his shift, when he would bring Rolf along. The little dog would jump onto the cot and lie with his muzzle close to Katrinka's face, his exhalations blowing softly on her skin.

During visits when he was alone, he would carry on long conversations with the sleeping girl. Reminiscing about the times they'd shared, the things they'd talked about. He reminded her of her father, and *Le Flâneur*, and Rolf.

He ran into Nye a few times, who told him he was having some trouble getting off island. There was a holdup on his orders or some problem with his job back in Guam. Sometimes, he would visit as well. Both men would sit quietly, neither one speaking much.

Other times one of the performers, a young woman called Cricket, would come. She chattered on and on to Farr in a soft voice. After she left, he could never remember anything she'd said.

One day when Farr sat alone with Katrinka, the major came in with something in his hands. It was Katrinka's knapsack.

"I wanted to give this to you before leaving. It was strapped to her back, and one of the nurses took the liberty of taking the items out. She opened the book and dried the pages before they became stuck together. It took her quite a while."

Surprised, Farr stood and took the bag. "You're headed out, sir?"

Nye nodded. "Hope to be going back in the next week or two. From Guam, I'll await transport for Rangoon and on to India. Then a troop ship through the Suez to England."

Farr studied the man's face. "Well, that's great news, sir. If you have time, come around before—"

"Yes. Absolutely."

Farr nodded, looking down at the knapsack. He fingered its weathered straps, remembering the first time he'd ever seen it. He glanced up to thank Nye, but the man was gone.

* * *

The next evening Farr returned, bringing the knapsack with him. He sat down and pulled out the book, which was even more battered now than it had been when he'd first seen it. He turned the pages carefully. They were warped and crinkled, but still intact. He skimmed over the first few lines. Glancing at Katrinka, he settled back and began reading aloud in the quiet alcove, his words barely ruffling the silence.

He read for almost an hour, then sat watching her sleep until the room got dark. Then he stood and stretched, putting the knapsack on the chair. As he did so, something fell to the floor with a silky whisper, and he picked it up. It was her necklace. The medallion was missing, but the silver vial was attached, still stoppered tight. Incredible how it had survived the crash.

He knew Katrinka never used the oil, there was too little of it, and it was too precious. But there were times, especially when she was under great stress, he'd seen her opening the vial and smelling it for a few brief seconds.

He looked thoughtfully at the small chain draped loosely around his fingers, then at the girl's pale face on the pillow. He sat back down.

"Babe, I have to apologize. I know this stuff is really special to you. Even opening it without your permission's going to get me into a hell of a lot of trouble. But I'm taking a chance here. For you and me."

With great care, he pulled the tiny plug. "Remember this? Your Papa Emerson gave it to you, the one who used to take you and your mother on those expeditions of his. It's jasmine. He gave your mother one too, because of her fair hair."

He passed the vial under her nose, but there was no response.

"Remember when you showed me this, Katrinka? We'd slept together the night before—the whole night, we held each other tight. And the next morning you came in, and you showed me this. I was so in love with you, I could barely talk."

He passed the vial under her nose again. Was there the faintest flicker of her lashes? The slightest blush of color in those pale cheeks?

He sealed the vial, putting it into the knapsack, then hesitated. Moving closer to the bed, he pushed Rolf aside and rested the book on her hands.

"Here's something else you showed me. Guess it was a favorite of yours. We talked about this too, remember?" He was pleading with her now, the ache in his throat painful, making it difficult for him to speak.

"You told me about this young girl and her dog. She'd lost her way in a storm and was trying to find her way back home. Try to remember. *Please* remember."

There came the thinnest noise. A bit like a sigh, or maybe just a slight exhalation of breath that held sound. He waited, but there was nothing else.

* * *

The next afternoon he arrived to find the nurse at her station, in a high state of excitement.

"She woke last night, briefly. The night nurse thought she heard crying, and came running to check her out. She was unresponsive, but there were tears on her cheeks."

Farr's voice was harsh. "Did she say anything? Will it happen again?"

The nurse shook her head. "We don't know. But I would say it's a positive move forward. Anything is better than this."

Farr returned to Katrinka's room and pulled the chair close. It seemed to him there was more color in her face today, her breathing stronger.

He began reading in a low voice. He'd read for about a half hour when he heard a small sound. His fingers froze on the page. He waited several minutes, scarcely breathing, before continuing. He stopped at the end of the next chapter. His vision was blurry, and he could no longer see the print.

Before leaving he leaned over to give her a kiss, and a tear slipped from the corner of his eye, a tiny trail of liquid fire, falling onto her cheek. Had they both come so far, to have it all end like this?

He rose to leave, turning at the curtain to call to Rolf. But the dog was frozen, staring intently into Katrinka's face.

There was a whisper, so small it wasn't really sound at all. He stared. Her eyes were open, and they were looking at him. They seemed cloudy, as if she were seeing him from a long distance, through murky waters.

Her lips moved and she whispered again. "Wolfe."

He crept back across the floor and knelt by her bed, her eyes still watching him, becoming more focused. He reached out, taking her hand.

"Katrinka."

"Where are we?" Are we together now?"

"Yes. We're together now."

Farr never cried. Not when they buried his mother or when he found his father lying dead, and not as a witness to all the horrors of war. Not even that time in Paris, when he thought he'd lost her for good. Now, pressing his face against the thin blanket, he wept. Tearing, ragged sobs, that ripped through his emaciated body.

She ran her fingers through his hair. "Oh please don't cry, Wolfe. Please don't cry."

But he continued, with Rolf wriggling under his face, licking away the tears.

* * *

The next day, Cricket was at her bedside, chattering away. "It was your officer boyfriend who saved you. He saved both of us, and Rolf too. He wouldn't let go, even though he was half-drowning and delirious."

"He was delirious?"

"Well, he seemed to be. He kept calling you Sofia, or Billie, or something like that. He… he was crying a bit, but don't tell him I told you that."

Katrinka was still struggling with everything. "You mean he's still here?"

"Yes, although I haven't seen him around since he brought in your knapsack. He gave it to that sergeant."

Wills had brought her knapsack.

"Where is he now? The major?"

"Would you like me to go find him for you?" asked Cricket.

Katrinka smiled. She knew Cricket much preferred the *dreamboat* major to Wolfe's scrawny appearance. "Yes. Please do."

Cricket left, and Katrinka absently patted Rolf's warm head. He'd not left her bed since she woke, except to do his dog duties, always returning immediately. She tried to put together pieces of memory. The terrifying crash, the shrieking wind whipping the breath from her mouth. Seeing Wills struggling across the waves to reach her, and Rolf's dark head bobbing in the water. She was drowning, and there was nothing she could do to save him. Then something struck her in the darkness, and that was all she remembered.

* * *

It was after hours. Nye stood outside the small Recreation Center Quonset with Farr, watching a spontaneous game of basketball. It was early evening, and a welcoming breeze blew in from the sea, carrying with it the smell of ship fuel.

Farr's friend Bennie had just made a basket, by shooting a free throw from the foul line. A heated argument broke out about whether Bennie had stepped over the line in the toss. It was obvious the ref had not seen it, so he called for another throw, much to the chagrin of Bennie's team. Bennie took the shot and missed.

Farr lit a cigarette and leaned back against the wall, watching Nye out of the corner of his eye.

"Went over to Personnel today for my orders and paperwork. Things were backed up. Had to wait awhile. Evidently, some major was supposed to fill a vacancy. Fought like hell to get the damn position, then changed his mind. He's going back to Guam."

Nye turned, and the men locked eyes for several moments. A player made a basket, and a wild cheer went up from the few spectators. They turned their attention back to the game.

Afterwards, the men walked back to the barracks in the dark.

Nye faced the sergeant, holding out his hand. "Well, I'm on my way. Might not see you again before leaving. All the best to you, Farr."

Farr took his hand, shaking it warmly. "And to you, Major."

Nye turned to leave.

"Sir?"

Nye stopped.

"Katrinka's told me— I mean we've both talked about it. How it is with you and her, and all." Farr took a deep breath. "Anyway, sir, it's fine with me. And if I'd had to… well, even before our talk, I just wanted to let you know. It wouldn't have been a problem. It never has been."

Nye nodded and left abruptly. Walking back to his quarters, he reminded himself to breathe, taking deep gulps of sea air. Bloody hell, it was time to end his commission. He'd almost lost composure in front of another soldier.

17

Home, 1945

WOLFE MET KATRINKA AFTER WORK ON FRIDAY. "A radio's broken at a small encampment of Marines up by Hedo Point. Needs to be repaired. I'm taking parts, and you could come along. It's a great ride along the coast. Most of Route One goes all the way up, now."

"Yes! Where is it?"

"Tip of the island. Sacred place. Beautiful cliffs, and a great view. Thought we could take our time heading up the coast. There's a road, but it's rough in some places. Camp out at the Point, and head back in time for work the next day."

"I'd like that, Wolfe. It sounds lovely."

But Katrinka wanted to take Rolf with them. Farr rejected the idea, saying there was nowhere for him on the motorcycle. It was an Army Harley Davidson WLA with barely enough room for them both on the seat. She might end up having to sit on the luggage platform in the back, so there would be no room for Rolf. Katrinka said she could hold him in her lap. Farr objected again, saying he would get hot and restless.

Finally, Katrinka gave in, and left explicit instructions with Cricket, who was delighted to have the dog. She would take him over to the hospital for a visit with the patients.

The troupe would be heading out the following week, skipping Burma and taking a troop ship back to the States. Some of the dancers still suffered from injuries sustained in the crash, and everyone just wanted to go home. So as not to disappoint the troops, a British ENSA troupe would be diverting their show to include Burma.

Cricket was going to stay on in Guam, to see if she could get a job with the USO. She'd made a couple of friends with the Navy nurses and had no desire to return to California. She told Katrinka that she could come see her, and use the island as a home base in her exploration for Amelia.

Katrinka was thrilled. It would give her expedition a center of operations. A place to regroup and make plans. With so many military on Guam, she hoped to find a referral for a good commercial vessel with a reliable captain. Since this was going to be at least a year away, she would think carefully before broaching the subject with Wolfe. So much depended on his answer. And how she would react to it.

* * *

Nye woke early the next morning, wanting to see Katrinka one last time. His orders had come through and he was leaving early Monday morning. They had already shared a private and very emotional farewell. The nurses' Quonset door was open, and he saw her just inside, sitting on her barracks bed.

342

"Morning, sweetheart," he called in.

She looked up, seeing him standing in the sunlit doorway.

"You're up early," she smiled.

"Thought I'd better see you safely off."

He watched as she dumped the contents of her knapsack into her locker, refilling it with her camera, a toothbrush and few other items, including some fruit. She finished packing, and he walked over to Farr's barracks with her.

The sun was out and the air humid. Farr stood in the shade of a banyan tree, just outside the Quonset.

The two men shook hands, and Katrinka climbed onto the back of the bike, slinging the knapsack over her shoulder. Farr started the cycle with a roar, and they both turned, their arms raised in farewell. Nye watched them go until they were nothing but a small black dot in the distance. He stood watching, even after the dot disappeared completely, melding into sea air.

* * *

They headed north along the west coast. It was a beautiful day, with fat cumulus clouds resting over the Nago Mountains. Frothy waves crashed out along the reef, but the opalescent lagoon was calm. A large white bird stood with folded wings at his side, amid the jumble of sea rock.

Katrinka could see bowed figures out in the tide pools, carrying large baskets and plucking things from the rocks. Much better to keep focused on the sea than the battered and flattened villages. On this beautiful day, it was easy to forget the horror the island and its people had experienced as pawns of the Japanese troops.

They passed diminutive women walking with baskets on their heads, and babies slung over their backs. Young boys carried long stalks of sugar cane, and old men shuffled along, burdened down with sacks of rice or potatoes. Occasionally, an army jeep rumbled past them, but the traffic thinned as they sped north.

They stopped at a roadside shack where an old woman squatted on a bamboo mat, rolling balls of rice. Farr gave her some money, and she offered the rice on a palm leaf, with some greens and raw fish.

* * *

That evening they camped out somewhere north of Ogimi, and later they perched along the cliff edge to watch the fishing boats silhouetted against the purpling islands. A large, pale sun sank into orange-flamed clouds, and the close roar of the tide filled their ears and noses with spray. They sat for a long while, neither speaking.

When it grew dark, Farr took her hand, his eyes troubled.

"Katrinka. There's something I've wanted to tell you."

"What is it?"

"When I was in Burma, I caused a man's death."

"Can you tell me about it?"

Farr shook his head. "It was an accident. But I went to see his wife, to explain to her what happened. I helped fix her hut, and she cooked me food. I was missing you so damn bad—"

She stopped him. "You don't need to tell me these things."

"But all along, I've held you accountable. For doing the same thing."

Katrinka looked at his face, still marked with bites and infection, and thought of the terrible things he'd seen, the things he'd had to do.

"I am glad there were arms to hold you," she said softly.

"But I needed your arms. I wanted your arms."

She wrapped herself around him. "They're here now, Wolfe."

* * *

After dinner, they made love. Both were still weak from their recent illnesses, and it was a gentle lovemaking, interwoven with the muted sound of waves and the smell of salt spray in the warm nighttime air. Later, they lay back, watching the moon come up over the horizon. It was big and red, throwing its shimmering, jagged light across the water. The tideline glowed with luminescence, and the air blew soft on their faces.

Katrinka turned to trace a finger down his cheek, loving its sandpapery feel. "It might take a few years to get my expedition for Amelia organized and ready."

He rolled over, studying her face. "In a few years I could get my schooling done, my electronics certificate. Then we'd be ready to go. We could go together."

"I'd like that, Wolfe."

"So would I."

* * *

They got to the Marine encampment early next morning. Farr examined their broken radio, took it apart, and reassembled it with the new components. When it was in working order, they headed back.

The sun was already warm with a strong breeze blowing white cloud shadows across the water. High above them, a sea bird dipped and circled, shadowing the bike as it sped down the winding road from Hedo Point. Stretching its wings out over the rice terraces, it appeared and disappeared around the bends of the road, always following the sea.

Katrinka perched on the back, holding Farr in the circle of her arms. Swooping and diving with the bike, she leaned into the curves, seeing the endless blue sea to their right and the dusty road before them. And as she held him in her arms, she felt the last scars fly off her body, dissolving like mist in the wind behind her.

Farr accelerated. The warm sun on his face, and the closeness of her, filled the man with a deep sense of happiness.

Katrinka rested her chin on his shoulder and laughed, as the wind lifted her hair.

"Let's just keep going, Wolfe. Straight down to the beach and across the ocean to California. We'll be home in time for dinner. Papa will be so surprised!"

Farr saw the flash of metal a split second before they hit it. Suddenly, there was a loud explosion, and the startled sea bird swerved. A thick column of smoke rose above the road, and the bird passed over it before heading once more out to sea, its wings outstretched, circling above the sea foam of waves.

* * *

Later, Nye went back to her barracks.

He had chosen not to be there when the bodies were brought in. A cable sent to Amparo confirmed her final wishes. Her body was to be cremated and scattered into the nearest sea. They had all at one time or another, been her home.

There were no relatives or final wishes for Farr, so Nye did what he thought the man would have wanted, by keeping him with Katrinka.

He looked around the barracks room with a sense of helplessness. What could he have done? Surely, surely, she would be returning soon. Laughing and hungry, with Rolf leaping up to greet them. Rolf. He was curled up on Katrinka's pillow, refusing to look at anyone.

Nye sat on the small bed, the contents of her locker spilled into his lap. Her book she'd always carried. The small white glove, still smelling faintly of scent, with the mud-spattered letter rolled and tucked inside. He pulled it out now and stared at the blurred address. She was going to return it after the war. To meet Josef's mother in Germany, and tell her about his last moments. He brushed a hand over his eyes. Here was something he could do for her. He could at least do this.

He pocketed the items. Picking up Rolf, he left the room. He did not look back.

* * *

The door opened, and a pleasant-looking woman in her mid-thirties with deep-green eyes looked up at him—a tall, barrel-chested man with sad-looking eyes. He was standing in the snow. He held a leash, which had a dilapidated sack of fur and bones at the end it.

"Frau Bischoff? Silke Bischoff?" he asked.

"*Ja.*" Pushing back a sweep of blonde hair from her forehead, she watched as Rolf began shaking, making small whining noises. The woman gasped, placing a hand over her heart, and slipped silently to the floor.

Nye was better prepared this time around. Carrying her into a room, he placed her on the bed. A tea towel was found, and he moistened it with cold water from the pump at the sink. He gently wiped her forehead until she opened her eyes.

"*Der Hund,*" she said.

Rolf had wormed his way onto the bed and was lying next to the woman's side. She indicated a carved box on the bureau. Nye retrieved it and brought it back to her bed. She sat up, pulling out a much-creased letter. At the bottom of the page was a penciled sketch. It was of a sunny day, and a small dog with a freckled muzzle and bent ear. He sat on his hind legs, begging for a bit of apple from a young woman with laughing eyes and dark hair.

Katrinka's words came back to him. *"He was a boy I met on the road. We shared an apple."*

"It was the last letter I received from him." She pressed the letter to her breast, and wept.

* * *

Later, they sat in the small kitchen near a large, green-tiled ceramic stove. Nye reached into his case, and withdrew the letter and glove, placing them on the table.

"He had these in his pocket," he explained.

She fingered the glove and smiled. "I thought I'd lost it."

Then she picked up the letter. Her hands trembled, but her voice was steady. "He was so young. His father was killed early, in Saarland. Later, they were conscripting the children. Josef had just finished his schooling, he wanted to study art. He was not meant for war." She hesitated. "Were you there when he died?"

"Yes."

"Was it… did it end quickly?"

"Yes." Nye paused, wondering how much to say. "There was a young woman who knew him. She held him in her arms. He did not die alone."

"Thank you for that. It makes it easier, knowing. And the dog, Rolf? How do you come to have him now?"

It was uncanny how Rolf had responded to the woman, wriggling and whining in her lap. He'd read once that dogs could recognize family members by their scent, even if they'd never laid eyes on them before.

"Your son had taken him from the streets after a shelling."

"He had a kind heart, that way."

"After he died, the woman… Katrinka…" It was difficult for him to say her name. "She took the dog."

"She is here?"

"She died as well."

"I am sorry."

"So, I took Rolf. I wanted to find you. To return these things to you, as she had planned to do."

They talked for a long time. She told him about her life before the war. She had been a school instructor, teaching languages and art.

349

Nye told her a bit about his growing up in Bristol, and his life on board *Le Flâneur*. Under her sympathetic gaze, he found the words pouring out of him. He told her about Katrinka, and then the tears came.

She listened, letting him cry.

The lamp was burning low when Nye finally stopped, his voice hoarse. A great sense of peace washed through him, leaving him very tired.

Silke rose and relit the lamp, then brought over a woven basket. "There is little fruit, but I have my trees. We will share an apple."

Nye looked on, as she sliced into the sweet flesh of the fruit. Then he sat back, glancing around the kitchen, with its checked curtains and polished dishes in a wooden cabinet. He felt the warmth of the stove and inhaled the lingering scent of food cooking. He watched Silke's face in the flickering light. Rolf was asleep now, curled up at her feet, snoring slightly. The man could not shake the feeling that in some obscure way, he had come home.

* * *

Nye rocked on his veranda, gazing out at the water, an unread newspaper on his knee. He sat in the fading light, enjoying the last rays of the summer sun, and watched Rolf dig yet another hole in the garden. Silke finished the dishes and came out with their baby, to join him. He glanced over, smiling.

It had been Katrinka's final and ultimate gift of love, this gentle woman sitting next to him rocking in the chair, the baby in her arms. She had given him so many things in her short life. Through loving the young boy, she had guided his way to this.

A fine mist was blowing in from the Bristol Channel and across the green fields. It set the jasmine blossoms drifting in his garden, and the empty chair next to them rocking slightly. It could have been the breeze, but Nye, enveloped in the soft-scented warmth, chose to believe otherwise.

18

Okinawa, 1983

MICHAEL AND HIS WIFE KATRINKA SAT IN THE rental car, pulled over at this small, scenic spot along the coastal road. Okinawan music played on the radio, intermingling with the sounds of waves crashing on sea rock below.

"I guess this means a lot to the old man," Michael remarked quietly. He hoped Kat would explain to him more clearly why her father had asked them to come along on this sudden trip, halfway around the world. But Katrinka was silent.

Michael sighed, and got out of the car to stretch. A few moments later another car pulled up, and a young couple with a toddler got out. They began taking pictures, but the toddler bolted, and ran screeching toward the guard railing and a sea gull. The mother ran after her.

The man strolled over to Michael, smiling. "Beautiful spot," he said, indicating the expanse of water. "You visiting, or are you stationed here?"

"No, just visiting," Michael replied.

"From the States?"

"We've flown over from London."

The man raised his eyebrows. "Helluva long way from home. What brings you to the island?"

Michael laughed. "Ask my wife." He pointed to the woman sitting in the car. "We're on a bit of a pilgrimage, I guess you could call it. My wife, Katrinka, is here with her dad."

"A war veteran? So many are coming back these days. My dad fought here with the Marines. Never thought I'd be following in his footsteps."

"Her father was a veteran, but didn't fight here," Michael replied. "He was on medical leave. Came here right after the war."

The men sat on a small cement bench, looking out at the water.

Michael offered him a cigarette. "My name's Michael."

The man waved off the cigarette. "Pete. No thanks. The wife wants me to quit. Having a kid and all…"

Both men sat, watching the toddler. The mother had given the child a cracker, and they were breaking bits off, feeding it to the seagull.

"So, what's the pilgrimage about?" Pete asked. "Did a buddy of his die here?"

"Two, actually. A man and a woman."

"I'm sorry. Must be tough for him."

Michael tried to explain. "You see, this whole trip was quite a surprise. A few weeks ago, her father was cleaning out his house. He's moving in with us. He found an old book in the attic that used to belong to this young woman he knew, Katrinka. The one my wife is named after.

"Katrinka and her lover were killed here, just after the war, in a motorcycling accident. Later, my wife's dad built

353

a small memorial, a roadside shrine, like they do when someone dies nearby. He's brought the book here, to leave at the shrine. Said it was where it belonged."

"Wow," Pete gave a low whistle. "There's gotta be a story behind that."

"Yes. I wish I knew it."

Pete's wife came over with the toddler struggling in her arms. "Are you ready, honey? Sarah's getting fussy."

Pete stood, reaching down to shake hands. "Better head out. Good luck with everything."

"Thanks." Michael got up watching them go, then walked back to the car. Kat had gotten out and was leaning against the door, smoking. He put an arm around her waist. Both of them gazed out at the water.

Kat finally spoke. "You know, I can feel her here. I can see her on that bike, holding her lover in her arms. The wind blowing in her hair. Laughing."

"So, who was she, Kat?"

"Don't you see? I wish I *knew*." She tossed her cigarette over the railing and faced him. "She was someone my father loved, before he met my mother. And she was with my half-brother Josef, when he died. My father never told me much about my brother's death, except it was during the war. And he never talks about the war.

"When I was a little girl, I used to dream about her. Holding my brother in her arms as he lay dying. She's been this mystery all my life, just knowing the odd bits and pieces. Mom never explained, not even before she died. She told me it was up to Dad. But one fact stands out. It was Katrinka's love that brought my mother and father together."

354

Michael nodded. Another sad war story. Just one of the hundreds of war stories that soldiers brought back with them. Keeping them locked tight in their hearts. He wondered what secrets the young Katrinka had kept locked in her heart.

He turned and looked up to the Nago Mountains behind him, now sprinkled with cherry blossom trees. It was a damn beautiful island. Evidently the entire place had been flattened in the war. Some called it the '*Typhoon of Steel*'. Hundreds of Okinawans had committed suicide, leaping from cliffs just to the north of them. They said that on nights of a full moon, you could see their upturned faces in the waves.

He shivered. All of that was over now. Apartment buildings sprouting up along the coastal roads, traffic jams down in Naha. But there was still something left of the old island ways. He'd seen it in the people's faces, and in these northern hills, with their tea houses and tinkling wind chimes. He'd heard it in the plaintive notes of the stringed sanshin.

He stood watching the sea with Kat, wondering about his father-in-law and what all this meant to him.

* * *

The old man walked along a rocky path and came to the small shrine with two stone cairns set side by side. He stood in front of it, the sun's rays warming his bones, as memories came drifting back.

The last time he'd seen her, she had been sitting on back of the motorcycle, her arms wrapped tightly around the young man's waist, holding him as if she would never let him go.

Other memories came to him. The dark head, bobbing just out of reach in the storm-tossed waves. Holding her body close in the tiny dressing room, where they'd sorted out their love for each other. A young woman's sleepy eyes, gazing at him from the back of a haycart. A kiss on the lips, a slap on the cheek, a silver necklace slipping around a small white neck. Seeing her battered face looking up at him that morning, in the sun-dappled forest. And the young girl, creeping into his cabin one night, her eyes so full of concern. Both of them waiting for her to grow up. Forgetting that the other, would also grow old.

He pulled a tattered book from his coat pocket and placed it on the small platform of the shrine. Barely discernible figures waved in the breeze from the page. A young girl and her dog, linking arms with a motley crew of friends. All facing the open road.

Perhaps she and Farr would have made a success of it after all. She had always been wiser than he, in matters of the heart.

He turned, and made his way back to the waiting car.

Acknowledgements

THERE ARE SO MANY PEOPLE I WANT TO THANK FOR their help in the creation of this book.

First and foremost to my dear mother; my first editor, who always knew that I would find my way home again.

I wish to express my deepest gratitude to Leslie Lutz. Not only an excellent editor, but an excellent teacher; a rare and happy combination. She taught me so much about writing, and my book is better on so many levels because of her guidance and wisdom.

I would also like to express my warm appreciation to the supportive staff at Matador Publishing. Through their skill and dedication, they turned this conglomeration of words floating in cyber space, into a beautiful book.

I am deeply grateful to Bobbie Lyons; mentor, traveling companion, and dear friend. I don't know what I would have done without her feedback, support, and analytical eye, that always went straight to the heart of the matter.

I also want to recognize Vickie Stone, and her wonderful team at the Coronado Historical Association, who came up with much needed last minute information. And to Virginia Jones, who knows everything there is to know about the Cherokee Lodge.

I want to express a very warm thanks to my staunch supporters and dear friends. Without their belief in me, I don't know if I could have survived the discouraging year of rejection slips. To Christina, who was always there to make me laugh and cheer me on. To Maria, Heather and Donna, whose confidence in me kept me going. And to Maryann, who really wanted to read it all. And also to Brenda, the original restless woman. A very grateful thanks to DeeAnna and Peter, who invited me to Germany, and helped me find a place to begin my book—and fed me the most delicious waffles! A very sincere thank you to Kim, who guided me through the intricacies of publishing with much needed advice. And to George Galdorisi. An author in his own right, who took the time to help a fledgling writer, and who was my first reader. And also my debt of gratitude to Marni, whose words of encouragement got me over those brick walls.

I would like to acknowledge my debt and thanks to the following works: *My War in SOE: Behind Enemy Lines in France and Burma with the Special Operations Executive* by Harry Verlander; *The Jedburghs: The Secret History of the Allied Special Forces, France, 1944* by Lt. Col. (Ret.) Will Irwin; *Phantom At War: The British Army's Secret Intelligence and Communication Regiment of WWII* by Andy and Sue Parlour; *Churchill's Angels: How Britain's Women Secret Agents Changed the Course of the Second World War* by Bernard O'Connor; *The Spy Who Loved: The Secrets and Lives of Christine Granville* by Clare Mulley; and *Coronado: the Enchanted Island* by Katherine Eitzen Carlin and Ray Brandes.

I wish to acknowledge my use of an excerpt from Rudyard Kipling's poem, "Mandalay" (1890), and an excerpt from Thomas Moore's poem, "The Last Rose of Summer" (1805).

Reading Group Questions

- The main characters in this book all carry scars. Do you carry scars? How have you managed them?
- How do you feel about Katrinka's interlude with Josef?
- War can place humans into almost impossible situations. If you had been in Bouchard's place, would you have cooperated?
- If you had been Lucienne and your son was in danger, would you have remained silent?
- Was Bouchard's son Paul justified in seeking revenge? Why or why not?
- Were you shocked by Raphael's reaction to the liberation of France? Explain.
- There are many types of hunger. How do you feel about Katrinka's business transaction with the little Frenchman?
- Describe Yujana. Do you agree with the advice she gave Katrinka?
- What was Katrinka's reason for joining the entertainment troupe? Would she have stayed settled otherwise?
- Do you agree with Katrinka's final choice? Who would you have chosen? Explain.

- In one of the last scenes, Nye is on his veranda and feels Katrinka's presence. Has she come to say hello, or is she leaving on another journey, and come to say goodbye?
- Do you think Farr and Katrinka would have made a success of it? Why or why not.